What others are saying about
BRITFIELD & THE RISE OF THE LION

A Combination of C.S. Lewis & Dan Brown!
"A smart, adventurous young adult series for the modern reader."

An Absolute Masterpiece!
"The *Britfield* book series is a historical marvel."

A Unique and Original Series!
"Doesn't remind me of any books I've ever read."

I Absolutely Loved the Sequel!
"Great, fast paced adventure for all!"

This Book was Fantastic!
"A must read for anyone in your life."

Thrilling, Entertaining, and Hilarious.
"I highly recommend it to children and adults alike."

Non-Stop Suspense!
"As a teacher and parent, I strongly recommend these books."

C. R. Stewart

Copyright © 2024, 2021 by C. R. Stewart

All rights are reserved. No part of this publication may be reproduced, stored in a retrieval system or transmitted in any form or by any means, electronic, mechanical, photocopying, recording or otherwise, without the written permission of the writer.

Devonfield Publishing
"A Home for Exceptional Writers"
DevonfieldPublishing.com

ISBN: 978-1-7329612-6-5

Cover Design by Silvertoons.com / Art by Tiffanie Mang

Make sure to experience
The World of Britfield
Britfield.com

BRITFIELD

&
THE RISE OF THE LION
BOOK II

C. R. Stewart

Continue the Story!

Devonfield Publishing
"A Home for Exceptional Writers"
DevonfieldPublishing.com

C. R. Stewart

This book is dedicated to
Dawn Michelle Dingwell
Primus amor. Sine fine mihi love

Arte et marte
By skill and valor

Consilio et animis
By wisdom and courage

Fide et Amore
By Faith and Love

PROLOGUE
BRITFIELD & THE LOST CROWN
BOOK I

Escaping from Weatherly Orphanage, a place where learning is suppressed and children are treated as free labor, best friends Tom and Sarah outsmart the nasty owners, Mr. and Mrs. Grievous; the seedy caretaker, Mr. Speckle; and even the legendary watchdog, Wind. Shortly before running away, Tom discovers that his parents might be alive, a revelation that haunts him. Relentlessly chased by the illustrious Detective Gowerstone, an expert in apprehending lost children, Tom and Sarah narrowly evade capture by commandeering a hot air balloon and flying over central England.

Crashing at Oxford University, they met Oliver Horningbrook, a kind student, and receive the sympathy of Dr. Hainsworth, an esteemed professor, who decides to help them safely get to London. As the facts unravel, Tom learns that he was believed to have been kidnapped and killed as an infant and discovers that he might be the last surviving Britfield and the true heir to the British throne. Forced to land the balloon at Windsor Castle, Hainsworth seeks the patronage of a former student and head butler, Philip, only to learn that Philip is a conspirator involved in Tom's kidnapping.

With the help of Professor Hainsworth, Dr. Beagleswick, and the Archbishop of Canterbury, the facts come together in a compelling chase through St. Paul's Cathedral and the London Underground, with Detective Gowerstone in hot pursuit. As the story concludes, it is revealed that Gowerstone has been trying to help protect Tom, the kidnapped child he was assigned to locate ten years earlier. The despicable caretaker, Speckle, is actually an undercover agent working for Gowerstone, who is investigating the corruption of Weatherly and a ring of dishonest orphanages across England. And finally, the prime minister, Gowerstone's closest friend, is revealed to be part of the plot to eliminate Tom to protect the British crown.

After receiving vital information from Alexander, the Archbishop of Canterbury, who is a close friend of the Britfields, Tom, Sarah, and Professor Hainsworth board a ferry from Dover, England, to Calais, France, in search of the truth and the last surviving Britfields, hoping to confirm Tom's true identify. Their destination is Castle Chambord in the Loire River Valley, where the Britfields are presumably hiding. However, on the way across the English Channel, the ferry capsizes and sinks

CONTENTS

ONE
Engulfed by the Sea · 1

TWO
A Miraculous Escape · 17

THREE
City of Lights · 41

FOUR
A Welcomed Friend · 63

FIVE
A Sinister Group · 87

SIX
Confrontation · 107

SEVEN
The Hidden Codex · 127

EIGHT
A Woman of Wisdom · 149

NINE
An Uncle of Valor · 175

TEN
The Unexpected Guests · 207

ELEVEN
Resistance · 239

TWELVE
A Veiled Secret · 263

THIRTEEN
A Renaissance Masterpiece · 291

FOURTEEN
Kidnapped · 313

FIFTEEN
The Rise of the Lion · 337

SIXTEEN
The Wolves' Den · 369

SEVENTEEN
An Old Ally · 403

EIGHTEEN
Divine Intervention · 429

NINETEEN
A Revelation · 453

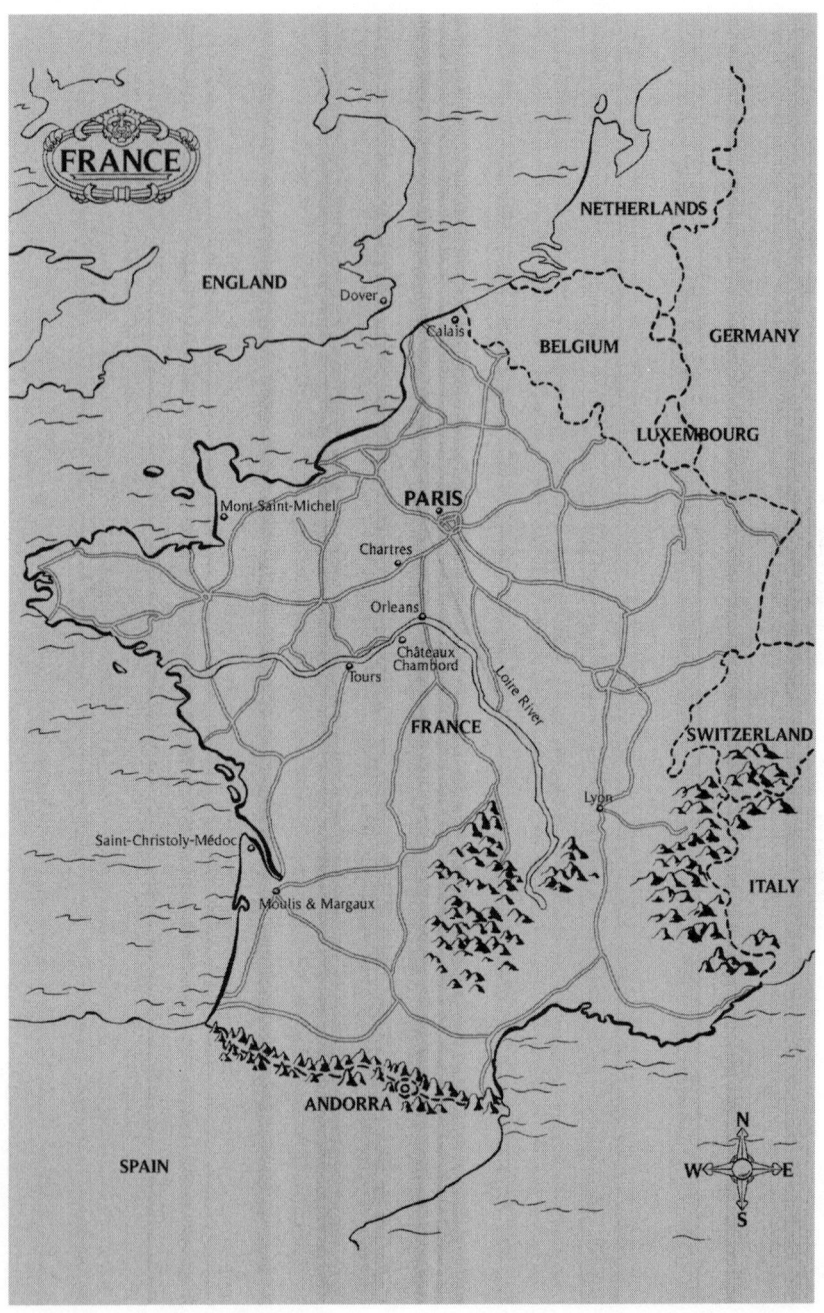

Britfield & the Rise of the Lion

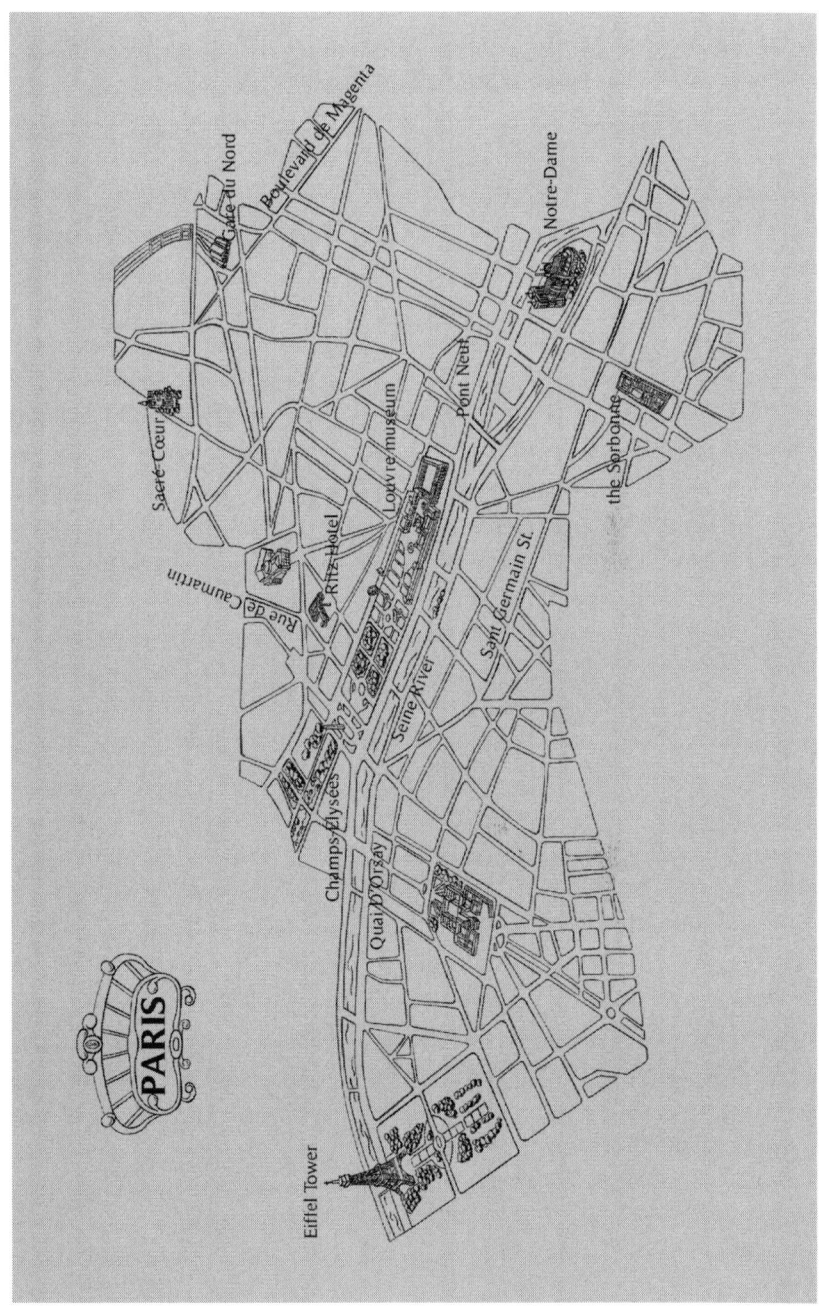

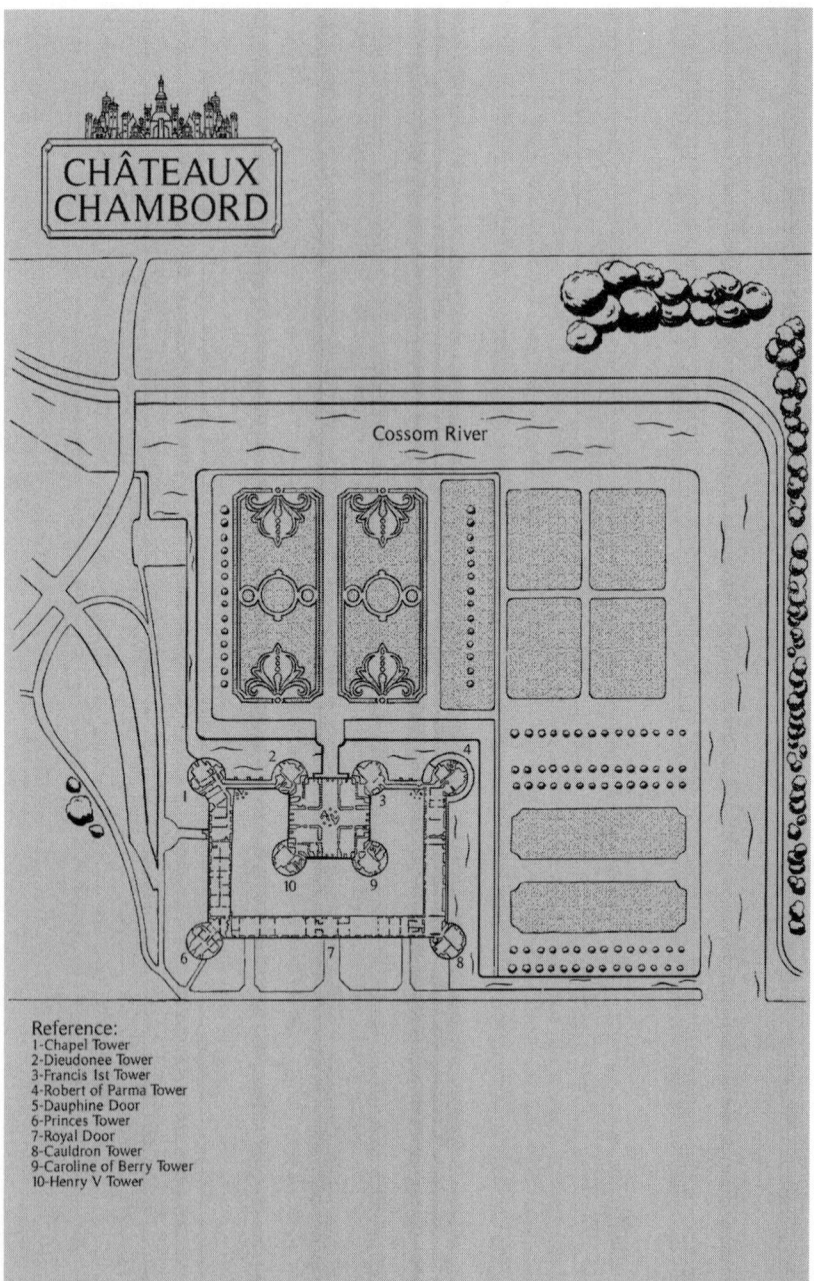

1
ENGULFED BY THE SEA

When the ferry from Dover, England, to Calais, France, sunk in the English Channel, Tom and Sarah, who had become separated from Professor Hainsworth, vigorously rowed a lifeboat toward the French shoreline, its lights barely visible through a thick fog. Enduring days of turbulent weather, they drifted two hundred and fifty miles south until they landed on the shores of Mont-Saint-Michel.

Masked in mist, engulfed by the sea, and soaring above the glistening sands, the island outcrop was about one mile off France's northwestern coast. Linked to the mainland by a causeway, Mont-Saint-Michel had a massive tenth-century Norman monastery perched on top. Below the structure were winding cobblestone streets and a medieval village. The monastery was nicknamed "St. Michael in peril of the sea" by traveling pilgrims because the changing tides posed a constant threat to anyone walking across the wet sand. Founded in AD 529, the Order of Saint Benedict was a strict religious organization of communities that observed the Rules of Saint Benedict: obedience, work, prayer, and charity.

Freezing and half-conscious, Tom and Sarah were found by Brother Gabriel, an elderly, benevolent monk who brought them to the Benedictine Order. After discovering they were orphans, the other monks decided to raise the children as their own. Not sure where to house a female, the monks moved Sarah to a secluded section on the opposite side of the monastery and tasked her with organizing their enormous library. Although she was told only to categorize the ancient texts, she spent hours reading by candlelight. She discovered all kinds of interesting facts and secrets, including essential clues about the Britfield Dynasty.

* * * * *

"Brother Thomas, make sure you thoroughly clean the Refectory tonight. I found crumbs under Brother Michael's chair this morning, and you forgot to scrub the cupboards after lunch."

"Yes, Brother Joseph. I'll be more careful," Tom replied in a downtrodden tone.

"Don't be more careful, be more thorough," the monk scolded with a trace of displeasure.

Brother Joseph, about sixty years old, stern, with red curly hair, gave Tom a solemn gaze and left the room.

Tom, age thirteen, a wiry yet strong boy, stood motionless, his brown hair disheveled and blue eyes glistening. Dressed as he always was in a light brown robe and wearing leather sandals, Tom had heard these words every morning, afternoon, and night. No matter how hard he cleaned, swept, dusted, or mopped, he could not please these Benedictine monks.

* * * * *

An hour later, Tom finished his grueling chores and headed toward his tiny dorm room, more a prison cell than a cozy boudoir.

Candle in hand, he ascended an inner staircase toward the Cloister Dormitory, then quietly crept down a back flight of steps to Saint Martin's Quarters, two floors below.

He tiptoed over the pitted cobblestone floor, through an arched hallway, and lightly tapped on an oak-paneled door.

"Sarah, you in there?" he asked softly.

"Where else would I be?" she replied sharply from the other side of the door.

"Well, you don't have to answer like that," Tom countered. "I took a big risk coming down here."

"Sorry, I just hate this place, and I'm all out of candles."

"I have an extra one. I grabbed a few from the workshop when no one was looking."

Tom removed a candle from under his robe and slid it beneath the door.

"Thank you. Now I can see," Sarah said. "Not much to look at, but I don't like the dark."

"Me neither," Tom agreed with a shudder. "This place reminds me of Weatherly: cold, harsh, and depressing. How long do you think we've been here?"

"Over six months," Sarah answered. "I've kept track with a calendar I found in the library."

"It seems like years," Tom remarked, wondering if they would ever escape this miserable imprisonment.

"Speaking of years," Sarah hinted, her tone shifting.

"My thirteenth birthday is in three days, on Monday, July eighth."

"I know. You have told me ten times."

"Just reminding you," she added nonchalantly. Sarah continued in a distressed voice. "I'm worried about Professor Hainsworth. I hope he made it safely to the French shore."

"Me too," Tom sighed, disheartened. "He was such a good friend."

"He was—" Sarah stopped in mid-sentence and quickly corrected herself. "He *is* the best of friends. There must be some way to find out if he survived."

"The only way to do that is to get out of here," Tom whispered guardedly, glancing over his shoulder, always wondering who might be listening.

"Agreed," she said eagerly. "Any ideas?"

"Not yet, but I'm working on it."

"Well, work harder," Sarah pleaded, a sense of desperation in her voice. "I can't imagine staying here another day."

Tom edged closer to the door. "Have you discovered anything else in the library?"

"Lots of interesting things," Sarah replied, her voice rising. "I've found all kinds of ancient manuscripts written in Old English, Latin, and French."

"You read French?"

"Of course," she replied. "Remember, I attended the best girl's prep school in Scotland."

"Yes, you've told me many times."

"But I'm having a problem with the Latin."

"Have you read anything more about the Britfields?"

"Their name is mentioned in some of the older books, but those manuscripts are kept in a private room, and I'm not allowed in there."

A door creaked open, followed by swift footsteps.

"Someone's coming," Tom warned her as he backed away from her door.

"Who's down here?" someone bellowed in a bloodcurdling tone.

Tom cringed, instantly recognizing the voice. "It's just me, Brother Jasper."

Brother Jasper came closer, revealing his ghastly face etched with pockmarks and a scar across his left cheek.

Tall, slender, and pale, Brother Jasper had devoted his life to the Benedictine Brotherhood and its tyrannical Code of Ethics, and he held the second highest position next to Abbot Chevalier. He always wore a dark brown robe and a silver cross around his neck.

"Brother Thomas, you don't belong down here—especially on this side of the monastery."

"I . . . I got lost again coming up the back way."

"Sure you did. Now go to your room," he ordered, his eyes fierce and his lower lip quivering.

"Yes, Brother Jasper," Tom replied obediently and turned to the door. "Good night, Sister Sarah."

"Good night, Brother Thomas."

Defeated, Tom marched back to his room and collapsed on his thin mattress. The confining space reeked of old wood and damp stone. A chill ran through his body from the nighttime air and the lack of heating. All the doors were always locked at eight o'clock, making any nocturnal escape impossible.

As Tom blew out his candle, he was consumed by the same stillness that overtook the monastery each night. Drifting off to sleep, he remembered the horrible incident that had brought them to Mont-Saint-Michel.

It happened after midnight over six months ago, when the ferry from Dover to Calais was chugging across the English Channel on Christmas. Tom and Sarah stood by the back rail watching the lights of the British coast fade into darkness. Professor Hainsworth sat nearby, pondering their journey ahead.

When the ferry was about halfway to Calais, an enormous explosion rocked the boat. Tom and Sarah were slammed against the railing and fell to the wooden deck. Black smoke poured from the center of the ship. The passengers panicked, running about and screaming wildly. The ocean pounded the vessel, freezing seawater shooting into the sky and crashing down on the terrified passengers. The ferry swayed from side to side, tossing people across the deck, pitching others overboard into the icy water.

Rushing to Tom and Sarah, Hainsworth guided them to a small lifeboat. As Tom and Sarah climbed in, the ferry shifted, throwing Hainsworth to the deck. Tom reached out his hand, calling to the professor. Hainsworth crawled over and grabbed Tom's arm, but the ferry lurched again, rapidly filling with water. Hainsworth lost his grip as the lifeboat broke free and crashed into the fog-covered ocean. That was the last time they saw Professor Hainsworth.

Breathing hard and covered in sweat, Tom jerked awake. This nightmare had haunted him for months. While he longed to see the professor again, Tom knew that Hainsworth would want him to escape from the monastery, get to Castle Chambord, and find the Britfields.

* * * * *

At six the next morning, the monks were finishing their sparse breakfast of fresh bread and raw vegetables in the Refectory, a vaulted room with rows of smoke-streaked granite columns. Colored light from stained glass windows brightened the grim space.

Sarah, her long, sandy blond hair tucked under a bonnet and wearing a light blue robe, sat alone in a corner.

Born into an affluent family, Sarah Wallace had led a privileged life in Edinburgh, Scotland, before her parents died in a suspicious automobile accident five years ago. She eventually ended up at Weatherly Orphanage and had become best friends with Tom. Smart and athletic, Sarah had hypnotic hazel eyes and an infectious laugh.

Tom also sat by himself, punishment for a long list of infractions that included talking, missing choir, and coming late to prayer.

Tom glanced at Sarah and gave her a nod. They both rose from the wooden benches and slipped into a dimly lit corridor, trying to steal a private moment.

As they began to whisper, Brother Gabriel approached from the far end. "Good morning, Brother Thomas and Sister Sarah," he said cheerfully.

"Brother Gabriel, where have you been?" Tom asked, shocked to see their rescuer, whom they hadn't laid eyes on since the day they had come to the monastery. "No one would tell us anything."

"I've been in solitude."

"For over six months?"

"Yes, it was ordered by Abbot Chevalier," Gabriel replied evenly.

"Why?" Sarah inquired, perplexed.

"The abbot wanted to remind me of our rules."

"Which ones?" Tom murmured under his breath.

"I wasn't supposed to leave the monastery the morning I found you on the shores of Mont-Saint-Michel."

"You saved our lives, Brother Gabriel," Sarah acknowledged tenderly. "We're grateful."

"So am I, and it was worth it." Gabriel smiled. Noticing their distraught faces, he asked, "What's troubling you?"

"We hate it here. Why won't they let us leave?" Tom asked bitterly.

"I don't know," Gabriel replied. "I thought you would've been on your way by now."

"We would like to go," Tom continued. "I need to find my family, or at least I hope they're my family."

"You know where they are?"

"Yes, but I'm not supposed to talk about it."

"Then don't. I'll speak with Abbot Chevalier today and see what I can do," Gabriel promised. "For now, you better get to your chores."

Brother Gabriel gave them a comforting smile and walked into the Refectory.

"We need to figure out what to do," Tom whispered, his determination renewed. "Let's meet tonight when everyone else is at evening prayer."

"It's too risky," Sarah cautioned him. "They're watching our every move."

"Since when have you been afraid of risk?"

Sarah paused, reflecting on his comment. "Where do you have in mind?"

"The Knights' Tomb."

"The Knights' Tomb," Sarah repeated, uneasy.

"It's the safest place to meet," Tom assured her. "No one goes down there."

"And for good reason—all those bodies."

"They're in marble caskets. I don't think they'll be bothering anyone."

The image gave her a chill. Nevertheless, Tom was right—it was safe.

"Fine," she agreed hesitantly. "I'll see what else I can uncover about the Britfields and meet you later."

As Sarah headed to the library, Tom hurried to the workshop where he helped make candles and leather sandals the monks sold in coastal towns and villages.

* * * * *

Shortly after Tom and Sarah left Dover, England, Detective Gowerstone had gathered a police force and headed to Weatherly orphanage, in Yorkshire, Northern England. He arrested the owners, Mr. and Mrs. Grievous, who were sentenced to thirty years in prison for fraud, abuse, and other sinister activities. Although they showed little remorse, their despicable enterprise was shut down forever. Afterward, Gowerstone worked relentlessly to find each child a safe home and a loving family. The orphans were indebted to Tom and Sarah, knowing that after their escape, they had helped the authorities bring an end to Weatherly.

For months Gowerstone was hailed as a national hero, besieged with awards and interviews, but he wasn't interested in the attention or the accolades. The detective knew that he had only scratched the surface of a corruption that went far deeper: it involved the prime minister of Great Britain, members of the British Parliament, and a clandestine organization that was behind many nefarious activities hidden from the public.

Although Gowerstone was determined to expose the truth, *he* was also exposed—with his ongoing investigation, he had become a threat to the secret organization he wanted to destroy. They knew who he was and wanted him eliminated.

*****

Three hours later, Sarah was still busy in the monastery library, a stone labyrinth of interconnecting rooms housing centuries of ancient documents.

After dusting and organizing the main sitting area, she snuck into a private room crammed with old manuscripts. Reading by candlelight, she became engrossed in a nineteenth-century English text written on vellum. Folded between the delicate pages was a royal decree signed by Queen Victoria of England—it was a revelation. While Sarah was reading, she heard a sound in the adjoining room.

She swiftly stuffed the royal decree into her robe and stood. The chamber door swung open so hard it slammed against the wall.

"What are you doing in here?" Brother Jasper demanded, the candlelight revealing his face, contorted with anger.

"I, um, was organizing the books," Sarah stammered.

"This area is forbidden."

"Is it? I just thought—"

"You thought wrong."

Jasper aggressively approached Sarah, backing her against the shelves. "I don't like you snooping around in here," he stated, eyeing her suspiciously.

He grabbed her arm and yanked her forward, tossing her toward the doorway. Stunned and shaken, Sarah scurried into the other room, closely followed by Jasper, who locked the door behind him.

"Don't ever let me catch you in there again," he thundered with an undercurrent of malicious intentions.

* * * * *

Later that night, Tom and Sarah met in the Knights' Tomb, a medieval crypt crammed with burial vaults of noble families and the Knights Templar. Rows of alabaster columns supported a domed ceiling painted with biblical frescoes showing the great flood and Noah's ark. The colorful images shimmered in the candlelight.

Sarah stood by one of the pillars, shivering in the damp.

"Did you discover anything else about the Britfields?" Tom asked, eager for more information.

"I did," Sarah responded enthusiastically. "Everything Professor Hainsworth and Dr. Beagleswick told us about the Britfields is in the manuscripts I've read. There's information about the Britfields' true claim to the British throne, documents indicating their property was stolen and that they were murdered."

"So it's written down somewhere, which means that not all the evidence was destroyed," Tom realized.

"Exactly," Sarah said, her eyes aglow.

"Somebody has worked very hard to keep all this hidden."

"I don't think it's just one person or even a royal family," Sarah said, not sure where to begin. "I've discovered clues about an organization, a secret group that seems to control everything: royal dynasties, governments, even world events—"

"That's crazy," Tom dismissed. "No one has that kind of influence."

"They do when they have money," Sarah countered. "They can buy anything or anyone."

"Why? What do they want?"

"From what I can gather, power."

"What does this have to do with the Britfields?"

Sarah lowered her voice. "It's why they were

murdered. They couldn't be bought or bribed, so they were eliminated."

"You don't just mean physically, but from history altogether?"

"Yes," she replied, pulling the document from her robe. "I found a royal decree to execute the Britfields, signed by Queen Victoria."

"Really?" Tom questioned, then looked around nervously. "You shouldn't have taken that from the library."

"I'm just borrowing it," she said defensively. "Anyway, if you're the last Britfield, technically it belongs to you."

"I suppose there's a certain logic to that," he agreed. "What's it doing in France?"

"I think the Britfields shipped some of their documents to Europe to protect them," Sarah speculated, pondering the question. "I doubt if anyone knows they're here."

"What does the decree say?"

"It's mostly in Latin."

"And you don't read Latin."

"Not really," she admitted grudgingly. "But there are sections that list specific names and dates."

Holding it next to a candle, Tom examined the decree.

"If it's real, this is actual proof," he concluded, realizing just how important this piece of paper was.

Tom gave it back to Sarah and paced around the crypt, wondering what to do next. "We must get to Castle Chambord and find the Britfields," he stated with resolve.

"Agreed, but what's the plan?"

Tom removed a small business card from his robe and examined it.

"You have a pocket inside your robe?" Sarah asked, intrigued by the secret compartment.

"I stitched it there so I could hide things."

"Clever," she said, impressed by his ingenuity.

Tom showed Sarah the card. "Detective Gowerstone told us to call Inspector Rousseau if we needed help."

"How do we contact her?"

"I don't know, but she's our only hope."

* * * * *

When Tom and Sarah failed to arrive at the port of Calais over six months earlier, French inspector Fontaine Rousseau was frantic. She had promised Detective Gowerstone that she would protect the children and get them to Chambord, but she didn't know where they were.

The youngest inspector at Interpol, Fontaine had to work twice as hard to earn the respect of her elders. Born in Nice, France, Fontaine had three older brothers, all in prominent corporate positions across Europe. She excelled in school, graduating early from the Sorbonne and earning a master's degree in criminal psychology from Cambridge University.

An exceptional investigator, Fontaine had a warm heart but a tough exterior, the result of once being in love with a man who had put his work before their relationship. In her mid-thirties, she was a natural beauty with shoulder-length auburn hair, green eyes, and a petite figure from years of classical ballet as a child. She trained in martial arts, enjoyed playing the piano, and ate only organic food.

Learning that the ferry from Dover had sunk, Fontaine and her partner, Agent Gustave Devereux, spent months scouring the shoreline from Dunkirk to Brittany, hoping to find Tom and Sarah. They had searched neighboring villages, questioned local authorities, and monitored police radios. Not knowing if Tom and Sarah were alive, Fontaine continued to search for any news of their whereabouts.

* * * * *

Conflicted about what to do, Brother Gabriel humbly stood before Abbot Chevalier in his private quarters. The abbot was an imposing figure who towered over the other monks. Stern and arrogant, late sixties, he had a deep, menacing voice.

"Sir, may I speak with you?"

"Of course, Brother Gabriel," Chevalier responded. "What's on your mind?"

"It's about Tom and Sarah," Gabriel initiated. "They'd like to leave the monastery."

The abbot let out a throaty chuckle with a trace of agitation. "They're orphans," he said dismissingly. "Their desire will pass."

"I understand, but if we could find them a family or a more suitable place to live ... This is no place for children to grow up. They need to have a normal childhood."

"No, they don't. The children belong to us."

Gabriel was taken aback by the abbot's statement. "How long do you plan to keep them?" Gabriel inquired, deeply concerned.

"We'll raise Tom as one of our own and send Sarah to a convent."

"Abbot Chevalier, with all due respect, we're here because of our own commitment. Tom and Sarah deserve to have that same choice."

"The world is a harsh place, Brother Gabriel, filled with wickedness and deceit. They are much safer in our care."

"You mean locked behind our walls."

"That's enough," the abbot declared, angered. "Didn't you learn anything from your time in solitude? Why are you arguing with me?"

"Because someone needs to look out for their future."

"And we're not? We took them in, clothed them, fed them, and gave them a place to live."

"That's charity, which is what we're called to do," Gabriel retorted. "But to dictate the rest of their lives—"

"That's my final answer," the abbot stated decisively. "Tom will become a monk, and this Friday we will relocate Sarah to the Eglise Convent in Strasbourg."

2
A MIRACULOUS ESCAPE

The next morning as Tom and Sarah finished their meager breakfast, Brother Gabriel entered the refectory and motioned them to a back stairwell. They followed, unnoticed by the other monks.

"I spoke with Abbot Chevalier," Gabriel began, his voice distraught.

"W-what did he say?" Tom inquired anxiously.

Gabriel paused, trying to gather his words. "He's not going to let you leave the monastery."

Tom's eyes opened wide. "Ever?"

"I'm afraid not," Gabriel sighed deeply. "It seems the Brotherhood has its own plans for your future."

"What plans?" Tom griped, flustered.

"They want to raise you as one of their own and send Sarah to a convent."

"Raised as a monk?" Tom exclaimed.

"A convent?" Sarah questioned, bewildered. "I'm not going to be a nun."

"What can we do, Brother Gabriel?" Tom asked urgently, their future hanging in the balance.

"We must act fast," Gabriel replied with conviction. "It's not good for either of you to stay here any longer."

"What do you suggest?" Tom asked, intrigued.

"At exactly eight thirty tonight, I will help you escape."

* * * * *

That evening Brother Gabriel snuck a rope from the workshop and unlocked Tom's and Sarah's doors. He promptly handed them donated clothing and shoes from a local thrift shop.

After quickly changing, Tom grabbed the documents Archbishop Alexander had given him at Canterbury, a map of France he had "borrowed" from the library, and the locket Sarah had given him at Weatherly.

Sarah hastily dressed, then wrapped the royal decree in plastic she found in the kitchen, tucked it under her shirt, and tied her hair in a ponytail.

"We must be quiet," Gabriel whispered as he escorted them down a shadowy hallway and around a corner.

They both nodded as they tiptoed through a maze of corridors and down a spiral staircase that ended at a large iron gate. Gabriel removed a set of keys attached to his robe and unlocked it.

"We can't use the monastery entrance," Gabriel cautioned them. "It's watched too closely."

Stealthily guiding them to the monastery wall, Gabriel fastened the rope around an ancient cannon and tossed it over the side. Thirty feet below was the quaint village of Mont-Saint-Michel, its terra-cotta rooftops glistening in the moonlight, smoke curling upward from the chimneys.

"You'll need to climb down and head to the west gate," Gabriel instructed, gesturing toward the village entrance. "It leads to the only road off the island."

"We don't know how to thank you," Sarah whispered, her heart warmed by his kindness.

"It's an honor to serve," Gabriel stated with a slight bow, then handed Tom a one-hundred-euro note. "This will help you on your journey. With a little blessing, it will get you to where you need to be."

Tom was stunned by his generosity. "Thank you—for everything."

"What will happen to you?" Sarah wondered aloud, mindful of the grave risk he was taking.

"Don't worry. You have enough to deal with," Gabriel replied evenly. "But you must hurry. Once you're safely on the mainland, head north about four miles until you reach the town of Avranches. It's Tuesday, so the trains stop running at 1:00 a.m."

"We'll get to the train station," Tom assured him.

"And remember," his voice rose, "the tide is coming in. Make sure you stay on the causeway until you reach the other side. We've lost many visitors who were swept out to the sea by the rising tides."

Taking a deep breath, Sarah trembled at the thought.

"We understand—stay on the road," Tom acknowledged, mentally preparing for the task ahead.

They both hugged him and walked toward the wall.

"God bless you, Sarah," Gabriel said tenderly. "May the Lord protect you and keep you safe."

Sarah smiled, comforted by his kind words.

"And you too, Lord Britfield," Gabriel added reverently. "Godspeed to Chambord."

Sarah and Tom froze, looking at each other. When they turned, Gabriel was gone.

"Did he just say what I think he said?" Tom mumbled under his breath.

"I think so."

"How did he—?"

"Know about Britfield?" Sarah inquired, a blank expression on her face.

"Yeah."

"And Chambord?"

"Yep."

"No idea," she replied. "Perhaps someone is looking out for us."

They both glanced toward the sky.

"Maybe so," Tom shrugged, encouraged by the notion. He grabbed the coarse rope and prepared himself. "You ready?"

Sarah peered at the village below. Although it was a daunting task, climbing around rooftops and scaling obstacles were essential skills they had mastered at Weatherly Orphanage.

"I'm ready," she said confidently.

Tom mounted the stone wall, its rough surface chafing his skin as he eased over the edge. Sarah waited for a moment and followed behind.

Dangling from the medieval structure, they skillfully scaled down hand under hand as they tried to find footing along the wall. The wind was brisk, throwing them off balance.

While Sarah advanced, her feet kept knocking into Tom's head. "Do you mind?" he grumbled, glancing up with a frown.

"You're moving too slow," she whispered loudly.

"We can switch."

"It's too late," Sarah said dismissingly. "Just move faster."

"Easier said than done."

They swung from side to side, taking each step with caution until they finally reached the bottom, their hands and arms aching.

Tom caught his breath and scanned the area. The town was relatively quiet, just a few locals wandering the streets: a nearby pub echoed with laughter, and a restaurant bustled with activity as the waiters glided back and forth serving their patrons. The summer breeze carried the scent of the ocean.

Tom unfolded his map and pointed to a dot. "We're right here on this tiny island. Once we get across the causeway, we'll walk along this main road until we reach Avranches."

"And from there we'll take a train to the Loire Valley and find Chambord," Sarah added, using her finger to skim the map's surface to their destination.

"That's if we can find the town and the train station."

"One thing at a time," Sarah advised. "Let's get off this island first."

Tom folded his map, and they hurried toward the village entrance, periodically asking locals for directions. Hastening along the cobblestone streets, they worked their way through the sleepy village and finally reached the main gate.

The waves pounded the fortified walls as the tide rose rapidly. The sea air smelled like freedom.

"We should hurry. The water seems to be rising," Tom urged.

"How far across?" Sarah wondered, her heart pounding.

"It looks like about a mile to the mainland."

Sarah stood motionless, glaring at the untamed ocean smashing against the causeway. She was petrified, recalling her recent experience.

"You okay?" Tom asked, noticing her anguish.

"Y-yep," she muttered, feeling rather timid.

"We should get moving."

Sarah nodded, accepting the inevitable. She closed her eyes, calmed her breathing, and focused on getting to the other side.

They edged onto the sandy causeway and headed for the mainland, its distant lights scarcely visible as fog draped across the damp surface. Marching forward, their feet sloshed through the seawater lapping the sides.

"Brother Gabriel wasn't kidding about the tide," Tom said, unnerved, the frigid water squishing inside his sodden shoes.

"I can barely see," Sarah murmured.

"Here, grab hold." Tom clasped her hand as he led the way, each step becoming more difficult.

Waves rolled in, crashing against the rocks and spraying icy saltwater into the air. Within seconds, they were drenched.

"So much for staying dry," Tom complained, his hair dripping.

"And w-warm," Sarah stammered, her teeth chattering and hands shaking.

Sarah stopped and stared hard at Tom, her eyes wide with terror. "I can't swim," she reminded him.

"Trust me, I remember," Tom mumbled to himself.

"What do you mean by that?"

"Hyde Park, London . . . the balloon crashing into the lake . . . desperately trying to find you."

"As I recall," she countered, her hands now on her waist, "you were the one steering the balloon."

"Details," he scoffed, dismissing the comment.

"Really?"

"All right. Point taken," Tom conceded with a grumble.

Sarah nodded, taking a firm hold of his hand again. "Now let's get to dry land."

Quickening their pace, they soon became disoriented in the fog. The thundering waves added to the confusion as water flooded their path, making it difficult to navigate.

"I can't see a bloody thing," Tom griped, searching back and forth.

"Me neither," Sarah added tensely.

"Just hold on to me."

"I am."

"But not quite so tight."

"Sorry, I'm just nervous."

"I know, it's all right," Tom reassured her. "I think we're at least halfway across."

They glanced back. Displayed in a kaleidoscope of lights, Mont-Saint-Michel looked like a Christmas tree floating on the ocean. It was beautiful, yet surreal.

Unable to see the road, they kept drifting toward the shoulder, slipping by the edge before veering back toward the middle.

"Let's try to stay in the center of the road," Tom

suggested, whipping his head from side to side. "That's if we can find the center."

They traveled another fifty yards, shifting from the right to the left until they walked too close to the edge. In one swift flash, their footing gave way and they skated down the side, sinking into the freezing Atlantic.

Caught by surprise, they frantically attempted to climb toward the road, but the tide rushed in and snatched Sarah, ripping her from Tom's grip and carrying her away. She was now at the mercy of the sea.

"Tom, help me," Sarah screamed, right before she slipped under the waves.

* * * * *

Thirty minutes after he returned to the monastery, Brother Gabriel was summoned from his room and taken to Abbot Chevalier's quarters. Jasper stood by, seething with fury.

"Why aren't Tom and Sarah in their rooms?" Chevalier asked, suspicious.

Gabriel remained silent, concerned his voice would betray him.

"What have you done?" the abbot continued, his calm demeanor shifting into contempt.

"What is right and just," Gabriel responded.

The abbot motioned to Brother Jasper. "Notify the local police that two children have escaped from our monastery."

"Yes, Abbot Chevalier."

Jasper glared at Gabriel as he left the room.

"I'm very disappointed in your actions tonight," the abbot fumed.

"You have no right to hold two children against their will," Gabriel said bravely.

"I'm the abbot of this monastery. I have every right."

"And separating them, sending Sarah away to a convent, it's just cruel."

"These are my decisions, not yours."

"I'm only looking out for their futures," Gabriel asserted.

"Your actions tonight are deplorable," the abbot continued, shaking his head furiously.

"I'm sorry to disappoint you."

"You've done more than that," he said, taking a document from his desk. "You've given me no choice but to remove you from Mont-Saint-Michel and the Brotherhood. We can no longer trust you."

This comment wounded Gabriel, now distressed that his character was being brought into question. "Where will you send me?"

"The Abbey at St-Jean in Lyon."

"But that's where I began forty-three years ago," Gabriel stressed, saddened.

"And that's where you'll start again."

* * * * *

Now engulfed by the Atlantic Ocean, Tom and Sarah were fighting for their lives. Pushed up and down by the turbulent swells, they were helpless against this powerful adversary.

Desperately trying to save Sarah, Tom grappled for her arms, straining for a grip. He'd get within a finger's length, only to be knocked back by a wave and forced under the water. It was a tug-of-war between his determination and the relentless ocean wanting to claim another victim.

Sarah thrashed hopelessly as she tried to keep her head above water. She would catch the tip of a rock beneath her foot and balance for a second before being pulled away again. Why her parents never taught her to swim was beyond her comprehension, but now was not the time to think about it.

Tom swam after her, struggling against the undercurrent and gagging on seawater.

"Tom!" she hollered.

"I'm here!" he shouted back.

"Where?"

"Over here!" he called, waving his arms.

"I-I can't get to you," she gasped, feeling her last bits of strength slip away, thinking this might be the end and not wanting to die.

Tom dove under the freezing water and swam blindly toward her, fighting against the swirling current. After coming up twice for air, he finally surfaced next to her and grabbed her arm.

"Take hold," he yelled, stabilizing himself on a rock below.

Sarah clamped on to his shoulders and balanced next to him, disoriented and desperate to catch her breath.

"T-thank you," she wheezed.

"Let's get back to the road."

Sarah nodded, her cheeks white and her eyes stinging from the saltwater.

Using the submerged rocks as leverage, they carefully maneuvered back to the causeway and climbed up the side.

Sarah plopped down, shivering. Tom knelt beside her, frozen and exhausted.

"Are you all right?" he asked, his hand resting lightly on her shoulder.

"J-just give me minute," she coughed, struggling to breathe.

"This whole thing's going to be underwater soon," Tom warned. "We should hurry."

"Okay," she sighed heavily, trying to slow her panicked breathing. Sarah looked at him affectionately. "Thank you for saving me."

"Of course, although I had no choice."

"W-why's that?" she wondered.

"I don't speak French."

Sarah rolled her eyes as Tom grinned. "I knew there was a reason," she half chuckled.

Tom gently lifted her up and they continued to trek across the causeway. The wind roared violently as the tide kept rising. It was all they could do to remain upright and stay on course.

"We're almost there," Tom encouraged her, pointing at the brightening lights on the distant shore.

After a grueling march over the last hundred yards, they reached the mainland and collapsed on the soft sand, their clothing soaked and their teeth chattering uncontrollably.

"I thought we'd never make it," Sarah admitted.

"I was beginning to wonder myself."

"You were scared?"

"A little," he confessed reluctantly. "I've never wrestled against the ocean before."

Sarah leaned back and tried to relax, her heart racing and hands still trembling. She then delicately pulled out the plastic-wrapped royal decree.

"It's still dry," she uttered, astonished.

"That's good—that document may come in handy."

Sarah tucked it away, then lifted her head, suddenly hearing voices. The entire coast was lit by flashing red and blue lights.

"The police," Sarah motioned, grabbing his shoulder.

"They know we escaped," Tom exclaimed. "I thought we'd have more time."

They jumped to their feet and ran toward an area camouflaged by shrubbery. Flashlights danced across the sand as officers searched the beach.

"We definitely can't take the main road," Sarah reckoned, peering out from the bushes.

Contemplating a strategy, Tom tried to read his drenched map by the hazy moonlight.

"Avranches is north of us," he began, developing his thoughts. "If we hike along the shore, maybe we can make our way up the coast."

"That'll take longer. We might miss our train."

"I know, but it's our only choice."

* * * * *

After hours of scurrying along the coast and avoiding the local authorities, Tom and Sarah found Avranches.

Its ancient streets were lined with half-timbered buildings and quaint shops, offering a variety of goods: a cheese shop, grocer, fishmonger, shoe cobbler, hardware store, a few cafés, and a bar, mostly deserted.

They wandered the town in search of the train station. The summer air had slightly dried their clothing, but they still felt damp and sticky with salt.

"Where is everyone?" Sarah asked, an uneasy feeling in her stomach.

"I guess they're in bed," Tom speculated.

"We need to find the train station."

Looking around, Sarah noticed an elderly woman walking her poodle on the opposite side of the street and briskly approached. "*Bonsoir, madame,*" Sarah said, her accent perfect.

"*Bonsoir.*"

"*Où est la gare situé?*"

"*C'est plus par le palais de justice, à environ trois rues.*"

The woman indicated a large classical structure composed of ashen stone and rose-colored brick.

"*Merci beaucoup.*" Sarah waved as the woman passed by.

Tom walked over, somewhat intimidated. "You need to translate for me when you do that," he reminded her.

"Right, I forgot." She laughed. "I asked her where the train station is."

"And?"

"About three blocks from here, over by the courthouse."

"Gotcha," he responded. "You know, it's going to be handy having you in France."

"Then it was a good idea that you saved me."

"We'll see," he jested with a playful smirk.

As they continued along Rue du Dr Gilbert Street, a local police car crept around the corner, its spotlight skimming the storefronts.

Tom and Sarah immediately ducked into an alley and dove behind a hodgepodge of trash cans and empty boxes.

"I don't think they saw us," Tom whispered, his breathing rapid.

Their hearts pounded as the vehicle drove into the alley and stopped. The bright spotlight glided across the brick walls until it landed directly on their surprised faces.

"Stay right there. Don't move," one of the officers yelled from his open window.

Tom and Sarah sprang from behind the cans and sprinted toward the train station, the police car racing after them.

In the distance, a long silver train began pulling away from the terminal. Even though they were unaware of its destination, Tom and Sarah ran alongside and leaped on the back platform, yanking themselves up by the exterior guard rail.

The police car screeched to stop. Two officers jumped out and rushed toward the train, but it was too late. The train had picked up speed and hastened into the countryside.

"That was close," Tom gasped, sweat glistening on his forehead.

"Do you think they'll follow us?" Sarah asked nervously.

"Hopefully they have better things to do," he replied. "Although they could radio ahead."

"And have the police waiting for us at the next stop?"

"It's possible. We might have to jump off before we get there."

"At fifty miles an hour?" Sarah exclaimed, giving him frown. "I don't think so."

"The train will slow down as it approaches the next destination."

"Then you can go first, and I'll follow."

"Let's worry about it when we get there." Tom sighed, stretching out his arms and yawning. "I'm too tired to think, and my body aches."

He plopped down on the cold steel decking and stared at the passing countryside, its images streaming by.

"Where do you think we're headed?" he wondered.

"Could be anywhere," Sarah replied, watching Avranches disappear into the darkness.

"I feel all soggy and sticky from the ocean."

"The warm breeze should dry our clothes."

Sarah held out her hands to feel the wind glide between her fingers. It felt good to be free, at least for now. She curled up next to Tom and closed her eyes.

"I'm just glad to be out of the monastery," she said. "That place was creepy."

"It's certainly an odd way to spend your life."

"Like I wanted to live in a convent."

"And raising me as a monk," Tom sneered, shaking his head defiantly. "No way."

"At least you learned how to make leather sandals," Sarah teased. "That'll be useful if you ever want to be a cobbler."

"Yes, it's my life's ambition," he chuckled.

They laughed quietly as the train accelerated, its smooth rhythm offering a brief moment of tranquility.

The train wove its way across the French countryside, moonlight blanketing the lush farmlands and green meadows. The fragrant summer breeze was mixed with the scent of wildflowers and lavender. On the left side was the Atlantic Ocean with its windswept cliffs and beaches. On the right were cedar orchards and rows of blossoming dogwoods.

"It's beautiful," Sarah whispered, mesmerized by the scenery.

"After over six months at the monastery, anything's beautiful."

"I just wish I could have taken some of those books," she thought aloud. "It was a treasure trove of information."

Tom leaned forward. "Tell me about what else you found."

"It's all there," Sarah started. "Centuries of history kept from the world. I've spent months reading about things I've never even heard before."

"Why do the monks have all those books?"

"And the private rooms where they're hidden?"

"Yeah," Tom contemplated.

"I don't know, but they certainly didn't want me in there."

A male voice inside the cabin interrupted their conversation. "*Les billets, les billets s'il vous plait,*" the man called.

"What's he saying?" Tom inquired, his voice dropping to a whisper.

"He's asking for tickets," Sarah answered quietly, peeking in the back window.

"*Prochain arrêt, Rouen, Pontoise et Paris,*" the man continued.

"Paris?" Tom exclaimed, his eyes bulging. "I understood that."

"I've always wanted to see Paris," Sarah said wistfully, her eyes lighting up.

"Now?"

"I'm just saying..."

Tom frantically pulled out his map and searched for their location. "That means we're traveling east, not south—nowhere near the Loire Valley."

"Let me see."

As she grabbed the map, the wind whipped it from her hand and carried it into the night.

"Thanks," Tom grumbled, watching it disappear.

"Sorry."

"That's the least of our worries."

"Meaning?"

"What are we going to do in Paris?"

"Have fun, see the monuments, go to the museums, eat fabulous food."

"I'm serious," Tom continued, troubled. "We have no place to stay."

Sarah leaned on the guardrail and pondered their dilemma. "Remember when we were speaking with Alexander at Canterbury Cathedral?"

"Sure, I still have the information he gave us," Tom said, double-checking his pockets.

"Alexander said that if we ever needed help, we should contact Archbishop Filberte at Notre-Dame."

"So?"

"Notre-Dame is in Paris," she informed him, rolling her eyes.

"Right, but what if the archbishop's not there?"

"Then it's going to be a long night."

* * * * *

Two hours later, the trained pulled into Paris Nord Station, a historic structure modernized with steel and glass. A large four-sided, cast-iron clock hung from the ceiling, displaying 12:43. Although it was late, the station was bustling with people—a synthesis of locals, foreigners, and tourists.

Avoiding detection, Sarah and Tom skillfully jumped from the back platform as the train eased to a stop. They hastened toward the exit when Tom saw a nearby vendor and bought a map of Paris.

"How much do I owe you?" he asked.

"*Ce sera sept euros,*" she replied in a crisp, rude tone.

"What?"

"That'll be seven euros," she repeated snappishly.

"Oh, okay," Tom agreed, handing her the damp hundred-euro note.

"Don't you have anything smaller?" she asked, agitated.

"Nope."

"Foreigners," she huffed, then grudgingly gave him his change.

Sarah snatched the map from Tom's hand and studied it, her spirits lifting. "Okay, we're here at Paris Nord Train Station," she began, pointing at a spot on the map, "and Notre-Dame is right there, in the center of Paris. It shouldn't be more than a couple of miles."

"Right now that sounds far."

"We can take the metro, if it's still running."

"I'm tired of trains," Tom protested.

"Then stop complaining and start walking," Sarah goaded in a lighthearted manner.

"I'm also starving," he moaned, rubbing his stomach.

"You're always hungry."

"I can't help it."

"Well, there's nothing we can do about that right now." Sarah folded the map, turned on the spot, and marched away.

"Hey, wait up," Tom clamored, exasperated. "You know I don't speak French."

They left the station and wandered onto Boulevard de Magenta, a sprawling avenue packed with luxury shops and high-rise apartments, their greenish-copper rooftops and spiral chimneys towering overhead. A passing shower had transformed the pavement into a glimmer of colors.

Tom stopped in his tracks, gawking at all the sights. "Wow," he gasped. "This place is amazing."

"Welcome to Paris," Sarah announced. "Come on, let's explore."

She grabbed his hand and yanked him forward, her enthusiasm contagious.

Strolling along the boulevard they passed an array of chic clothing shops, posh cafés, funky art galleries, and trendy coffeehouses. The sidewalks were crammed with small marble tables and wicker chairs, a variety of yellow and blue umbrellas hovering above.

In the distance was Pompidou Center, an avant-garde monstrosity designed with metal pipes, steel cables, and air ducts displayed on the exterior.

"Look at that thing." Tom pointed, aghast.

"That style of architecture is called postmodernism."

"I don't care what it is—it's hideous."

Sarah shook her head. "If only you could appreciate art."

"If that's art, I don't want to appreciate it."

"It's simply a style of art, a type of expression," she tried to explain.

"It's expressing something, that's for sure."

"You need to learn about the finer things in life."

"I do know about plenty of finer things," he argued, annoyed by her preoccupation with art. "Which is why we should find something to eat."

Tom searched the area and noticed a cheese shop across the street, its front light still on. "There's hope," he declared as he ran over.

Sarah reluctantly followed.

Tom tapped on the window, impatiently gazing inside. An interior light from a back room flickered on. A figure moved toward the glass. The door eased opened.

"*Oui, qu'est-ce que vous voulez?*" the man inquired, perturbed.

Tom glanced at Sarah.

"*Nous voudrions acheter du fromage,*" she replied, motioning to enter.

"I speak English, but we're closed. Everything is closed."

"Please, sir, we're starving," Tom pleaded, trying to make his eyes convey innocence.

"You're British," the man perceived.

"Yes, sir."

"Figures," he sighed, hesitating.

"We haven't eaten all day," Tom persisted.

"That's not my fault."

"But we're desperate."

"Watch the *we*," Sarah interjected.

The shopkeeper relented, shaking his head. "Fine, come in, but make it quick," the man told them.

As they walked into this paradise of Parisian delicacies, their senses were overwhelmed by aromas. With hundreds of choices, it was like a candy store, except it was full of cheese: Brie, Cheddar, Gouda, Pipo Crème, Bleu de Bresse, Stilton, raclette, vacherin, and Roquefort. They tasted a bouquet of samples, and both favored the Brie.

The man gave them a hardy selection, including a loaf of bread and two bottles of sparkling water. Tom happily paid the thirty euros, and they sat outside, enjoying their provisions.

"Maybe I was a bit hungry," Sarah admitted, devouring the delicious treats.

"So it's not just me?"

"No, it's not just you," she agreed.

After the nourishing meal, Tom and Sarah continued toward Norte Dame until they reached Quai de Gesvres, a parkway next to the Seine River, its majestic reflections sparkling with lights.

Now in the heart of Paris, they stood in wonderment. The city was a flurry of sounds and movement: the hum of traffic, flashes of colors, and the lingering fragrance of smoky wood and damp leaves. The vibrant metropolis radiated a sense of excitement and sophistication.

Looking up the Right Bank (north side) and down the Left Bank (south side), they marveled at all the activity: couples walking along, cars rushing by, and boats illuminated with colorful lights cruising the Seine. The poplar-lined avenues were filled with Parisian cafés, bourgeois townhouses, and historic monuments. Modern structures merged with French Renaissance and Baroque architecture. The Eiffel Tower glowed in the distance, dominating the skyline.

"It's like nothing I've ever seen before," Tom admitted, astonished by the carnival of lights.

"It's another world," Sarah declared, her eyes gazing in bewilderment. "I always longed to see Paris, and now I'm standing in the center of it."

"We should find that church," Tom reminded her.

"You mean Notre-Dame? It's a bit more than just a church," Sarah clarified.

They crossed over Pont au Change to Ile de la Cité, a small boat-shaped island. Behind them was the Conciergerie, a sinister-looking building.

In front of them was Notre-Dame, a marvel of medieval engineering and craftsmanship. Started in 1160 by Bishop de Sully, the extraordinary cathedral soared over two hundred feet into the heavens.

Tom stared at the enormous stone structure, its three gigantic arched entryways decorated with biblical figures, life-sized statues supporting an upper rim, and a massive rose window. Flying buttresses reached for the walls, the steep-pitched greenish rooftop pierced the sky, and grotesque gargoyles stared down.

The wind whipped around the courtyard, rattling the stained glass windows and howling through two Gothic towers overhead.

"Maybe this isn't such a good idea." Tom's body tensed.

"We've come this far," Sarah reasoned. "Just knock on one of the doors and see if anyone's there."

Tom timidly approached the massive entryway and hesitantly knocked. No answer. "Well, at least we tried," Tom said feebly.

"Try again," Sarah persisted, motioning him back.

Tom knocked harder. The door vibrated, making a thunderous sound.

After a moment of silence, they heard noises coming from inside.

3
CITY OF LIGHTS

A moment later, they heard footsteps echoing off the interior walls. The gigantic wooden door was unlatched and creaked open. A figure appeared out of the blackness, the exterior light catching his elderly face.

"Can I help you?" the man questioned.

"Archbishop Filberte?" Tom inquired timidly.

"Yes, what can I do for you?"

"We were told that if we got into trouble, we should contact you."

"And we're in real trouble," Sarah added.

"Who told you to contact me?" Filberte asked skeptically, examining their faces.

"Archbishop Alexander from Canterbury," Tom replied, hoping the name stirred his memory.

"You're Tom and Sarah," Filberte said ecstatically, his eyes brightening.

"You know us?" Sarah asked, delighted.

"I've been waiting over six months for you two," Filberte expressed with relief, gently motioning them through the doorway. "Thank God you've made it safely. Please, come in."

Relieved, Tom and Sarah entered the nave aisle while the archbishop quickly locked the door with various bolts and latches.

"You're wet. You must be freezing," Filberte observed,

wondering where they had been. "Come in the other room and warm yourselves by the fire."

Now standing in the light, Tom and Sarah could clearly see the archbishop: a short, stout man in his mid-sixties, with a whitish beard and a balding head. He was wearing a black velvet robe, and a golden cross hung around his neck.

All three walked along the black-and-white checkered floor, passing rows of decorated pillars stretching upward. Candlelight fell on a cluster of pews and flickered off the walls. Medieval chandeliers dangled from long brass chains.

Standing in the transept, Tom stared up at the awe-inspiring ceiling vividly adorned in magnificent colors and supported by projecting ribs of stone. Separated by pencil-like columns, the stained glass windows glowed in a kaleidoscope of purples, reds, and blues.

The archbishop escorted them to his private quarters where they stood by a lively fireplace. The heat felt soothing against their chilled bodies.

"You'll be safe here," Filberte assured them. "You can stay as long as you need."

"Thank you, sir," Sarah said, relieved by his generous offer. "It's been a long night."

"I'm sure it has," Filberte asserted.

"We've just escaped from Mont-Saint-Michel," Tom blurted out, unable to contain their secret.

"Tom," Sarah scolded him, followed by a frown.

"It's okay, I understand," Filberte said to reassure them.

"We're a bit overwhelmed," Sarah confessed, her expression revealing the hardships they'd endured.

"I'm sure you are," Filberte said delicately as he considered their comments. "But for now, let me get you some dry clothes and show you to your rooms. Once you've changed, we can share a meal and talk more."

* * * * *

An hour later, Tom and Sarah sat in the refectory, enjoying a late supper. Sarah wore a modest light blue dress that fit loosely, and Tom had on a pair of brown corduroy pants and a white flannel shirt.

"Another bowl of hot soup?" Filberte offered, grabbing their bowls.

"Yes, please," they mumbled in unison, mouths full.

The archbishop moved to a bulky stove and ladled out two more servings of bouillabaisse, a hardy fish stew.

"I'm supposed to contact this woman." Tom handed Filberte the card with Inspector Rousseau's information.

"I've been in contact with Ms. Rousseau," the archbishop informed him. "She's a very determined inspector. She seems thoughtful and trustworthy."

"That's good to hear," Sarah acknowledged, hoping for any encouraging news.

"She'll be relieved to know you're safe and unharmed. I'll notify her first thing in the morning," Filberte promised, then looked at his watch, "or later this morning, given the hour."

"Have you heard from Professor Hainsworth?" Sarah asked with a trace of optimism.

"No, I haven't," Filberte sighed.

Tom and Sarah shared a glance, their hopes dashed.

"But you know who he is?" Tom asked.

"I'm aware of your situation," Filberte replied discreetly, his eyes widening and tone serious. "Along with the inspector, I've spoken with the Archbishop of Canterbury."

"Alexander?"

"Yes," Filberte replied with a smile. "After hearing that the ferry had sunk, he was extremely concerned. He's checked back at least three dozen times since you left Dover. I look forward to sharing the wonderful news of your safety with him."

"How do you know Alexander?" Tom inquired, looking for the connection.

"We've been friends for over forty years," Filberte reflected fondly.

"What did he tell you?" Sarah asked, wondering how much had been revealed.

"Alexander told me about your escape from Weatherly Orphanage, the chase through England, how Detective Gowerstone helped you, and why you're in France."

"Basically everything."

"Only what I needed to know."

"We couldn't contact anybody while we were at the monastery," Tom interjected, feeling a bit guilty. "We weren't allowed to leave."

"You don't owe anyone an explanation or an apology," Filberte said gently. "Mont-Saint-Michel has always been shrouded in mystery. The Brotherhood has isolated itself from the outside world and operates by their own rules."

"You're not connected with them, are you?" Tom asked hesitantly.

"No, not at all," Filberte assured him.

"They're a bit controlling, aren't they?" Sarah questioned, a hint of bitterness in her voice.

"Yes, they are," Filberte confirmed.

The archbishop sat down next to them and began eating the soup and day-old bread. "What was your experience like?" Filberte asked.

"Most of the monks were nice, but we didn't really talk much," Tom replied.

"It's part of their oath and rigorous discipline," Filberte explained. "They tend to keep to themselves."

"It's hard not talking," Tom confessed.

"You don't seem to have a problem," Sarah teased.

Tom gave her an icy stare. Sarah chuckled under her breath, staring back at him.

"Tell me more about your time at Mont-Saint-Michel," Filberte continued, intrigued.

"We were both very sick when we arrived, after washing up on the island," Sarah began. "We spent about three months in the infirmary."

"I spent most of my time resting and eating awful food," Tom remembered, shaking his head.

Sarah laughed. "It was bad, wasn't it?"

"Yes, the Benedictine monks have a strict diet, along with their other authoritarian rules," Filberte added in a tone of condemnation.

"I recovered first, and they immediately put me to work in the library, buried on the bottom floor," Sarah continued. "But it was like they didn't want me at the monastery. I never sat or spoke with anyone."

"I hardly ever saw Sarah," Tom recalled, frustrated. "They didn't let us sit together or talk."

"The entire island is run by the abbot. He definitely has a distinct way of doing things," Filberte stated disapprovingly.

"What else did Alexander tell you?" Tom asked, hoping to learn more.

"He informed me that you need to get to the Loire Valley but didn't go into detail. Alexander encouraged me to help you if you found your way here." Filberte paused and leaned in closer. "He also told me to be extremely careful and not to discuss this with anyone other than Detective Gowerstone and Inspector Rousseau."

"We're not supposed to talk about it, either," Tom whispered.

"After speaking with the inspector, I've gathered what's going on," Filberte informed them. "I understand the seriousness of your dilemma."

They finished their meal and relaxed, feeling a sense of safety they hadn't felt in a long time.

"I'm sure you're tired, but would you like to see Paris from the rooftop?" Filberte asked with a contagious grin.

Their spirits lifted as they nodded, anticipating the spectacular sights.

"Then follow me," Filberte initiated, slowly getting up from the table.

All three walked down a long corridor to a granite staircase and began to climb the 422 narrow steps up to the famous Bell Tower.

"No elevator?" Tom wondered, his legs tightening.

"Tom," Sarah remarked, giving him a shove.

"I was just asking."

"I'm afraid not," Filberte answered as he struggled with each step. "I'm not too sure where we would put one."

Ten minutes later, they reached a flat section of the rooftop. The wind was vigorous as they gripped the parapet wall.

Gazing at a golden sea of twinkling lights, Tom and Sarah stood in awe, breathless at the amazing view. The boulevards crisscrossed the city like flowing rivers of color. The dome of Sacré-Cœur Basilica shimmered from its hilltop, and the Eiffel Tower dominated the skyline. It was a long way from Mont-Saint-Michel and Weatherly.

Glancing to his left and right, Tom noticed the life-sized gargoyles ready to swoop down and devour intruders.

"These things don't come alive, do they?"

"Not that I've seen, but you never know." Filberte laughed.

Sarah marveled at the views. "It's wonderful."

Tom watched her hair ruffling in the breeze and glistening in the moonlight. He gently leaned over and whispered softly, "Happy birthday, Sarah."

"You remembered." She smiled warmly.

"Of course I did."

"Thank you, Tom. What a perfect birthday present."

* * * * *

More than six months earlier, when the ferry from Dover to Calais began to sink, Professor Hainsworth had fallen overboard into the freezing water. He managed to grab a piece of wreckage, staying afloat and hanging on for his life. After hours of desperation, Hainsworth was eventually rescued by a local fisherman and taken to Boulogne-sur-Mer, a small northern community full of seafaring men who spent their days mending nets, scraping barnacles off boats, and telling heroic tales of their maritime adventures.

Weakened by his ordeal, Hainsworth was deathly sick and bedridden for months. He slipped in and out of consciousness, mumbling words and phrases, often calling out for Tom and Sarah. A few times the villagers thought they had lost him as Hainsworth sunk into a deep slumber, but he would always revive, though feverishly tossing and turning in bed.

Without any identification or a way to find out who he was, the villagers kept quiet about their guest, helping him however they could and hoping he would recover soon. Once again unconscious, they eagerly awaited his awakening.

* * * * *

Early the next morning, Detective Gowerstone drove to 10 Downing Street, Westminster, London. This address had been the official residence of the British prime minister since 1732. Adjacent to St James's Park, Number 10 was near Buckingham Palace, a residence of the British monarch, and the Palace of Westminster, where both houses of Parliament, the House of Lords and the House of Commons, met.

Gowerstone parked his cobalt Mercedes GLS 550 by the legendary black door and entered.

Although the detective had not spoken to the prime minister for months, he had been summoned to meet him. Through his ongoing investigation, Gowerstone knew the prime minister was involved with a clandestine group that controlled and manipulated the British government. Nevertheless, Gowerstone needed to play along with the game until he could gather enough evidence to expose and arrest everyone.

Gowerstone walked into the prime minister's office, their eyes locking. "You called for me?" Gowerstone inquired evenly, his manner cool.

"We've hardly spoken since your successful closures of eight corrupt orphanages," the prime minister remarked.

"No, we haven't," Gowerstone replied nonchalantly.

"Even though you were previously suspended and asked to leave the case," he continued, his voice rising.

Gowerstone stepped closer to the prime minister. "I did what was needed," he declared, defiant.

"Yes—and you disobeyed a direct order," the prime minister fumed. "I could have had you arrested."

"When I joined Scotland Yard, I swore an oath to protect the public and condemn the unjust."

"And I haven't done that?" the prime minister retorted, incensed.

Gowerstone remained quiet, choosing to ignore the question.

"You're supposed to follow my instructions and never question my decisions," the prime minister continued, standing behind his desk.

"It was a complicated case that required unwavering commitment. I couldn't just hand it off to someone else."

The prime minister sat back down, his mouth tight, his eyes cold.

"You've put me in an uncomfortable position. Your popularity is overwhelming, but the royals want you terminated." The prime minister paused, correcting himself. "I mean removed from your position."

"Why would they want that?"

"Because you're reckless."

"And because I didn't follow orders," Gowerstone surmised, "even if it meant bringing criminals to justice and helping hundreds of orphans find homes."

"You challenged my authority and made me look incompetent," the prime minister lashed out, exasperated.

"Yet the whole country admires what I've done."

"Don't put too much faith in the public," the prime minister cautioned. "They're fickle and will be on to something new next month."

"I doubt it," Gowerstone disagreed. "They have a great capacity to want to know the truth."

There was a long pause as both men waited for the other to yield, divulge a clue, or expose a secret. It was a sophisticated fencing match of wits, a complex game of cat-and-mouse.

"And those two orphans, what were their names?" the prime minister asked, pretending not to know.

"Tom and Sarah."

"Yes, whatever happened to them?"

"I told you in my official report. When I arrived at

Canterbury Cathedral, they had disappeared," Gowerstone responded, concealing the truth. "They could be anywhere in England. For all we know, they're dead."

"That's not what I've heard."

"Then you were misinformed," Gowerstone said, desperate to hide their true location.

"I was told they had boarded a ferry for Calais."

"Are you speaking about the ferry that sank?"

"Yes," the prime minister answered.

"It's my understanding that a bomb blew a hole in it. That it was sabotaged."

"That's just speculation," the prime minister said dismissively. "It was the rough seas that capsized the boat."

"That's your position?"

"That's the narrative we're committed to—all of us," the prime minister emphasized in a stern voice.

"I see," Gowerstone said.

"I hope so, for your sake."

The prime minister leaned back in his chair and stared at Gowerstone, wondering how much he knew. "And now what?" he asked directly.

"I'm continuing my investigation," Gowerstone replied, his tone firm.

"I know you are," the prime minister said, his tone conveying his displeasure. "You've been digging into areas you shouldn't."

"What's that supposed to mean?"

"Stop your meddling and stick to your job," the prime minister advised. "You're entering an area beyond your depth or understanding."

"Is that a threat?"

"It's a warning," the prime minister stated firmly. "And it's your final one. If you weren't so admired, you would have been dealt with already."

"Not everyone can be bought or intimidated," Gowerstone declared.

"What are you implying?" the prime minister asked pointedly.

"That there are things more important than money and position."

"You're willing to risk your entire career just to be right?"

"To be honorable," Gowerstone avowed.

"You just won't learn, will you?"

"I'll take my chances."

"You're on thin ice, and you've been warned. Now get out of my office," the prime minister thundered, his face contorted with rage.

* * * * *

Exhausted from their journey, Tom and Sarah slept soundly until nine the next morning.

They got dressed and went down to the refectory, where Filberte was preparing breakfast. Sitting at a long wooden table, they nibbled on their meal and discussed the next steps they would need to take.

"I've phoned Inspector Fontaine and told her what happened," Filberte updated them. "She'll be here shortly."

"What did she say?" Tom asked, impatient for information.

"She's ecstatic that you're safe but warned that you must be extremely cautious. You cannot leave Notre-Dame until she arrives."

"So she'll help us?"

"Yes, of course," Filberte answered cheerfully. "I also notified Detective Gowerstone as well. He was thrilled and will contact you shortly."

"Thank you. That's good news," Tom acknowledged.

"Yet still nothing about Professor Hainsworth?" Sarah asked, her eyes saddened.

"No, I'm sorry," Filberte replied tenderly.

Tom and Sarah slumped in their seats, wondering what had happened to their lost friend.

"Be of good cheer and always have faith. Never give up hope," Filberte encouraged them.

"We'll try," Tom murmured halfheartedly.

Filberte poured three cups of hot tea and placed them on the table.

"Sarah, earlier Tom was sharing about his life growing up in the different British orphanages and how he never knew his parents. I'd like to hear more about your background."

"There's not much to tell," Sarah said.

"Sure there is," Tom insisted. "For one thing, Sarah's really smart. I think the proper term is gifted."

Stunned by the unexpected compliment, she blushed. "I didn't think you noticed."

"Hard not to," Tom admitted.

"Sarah, where are you originally from?" Filberte asked.

"I grew up in Edinburgh, Scotland. My family had a house on the edge of town," she replied, fondly remembering her home.

"It was a mansion and even had servants," Tom interjected. "They also owned ancestral estates throughout the country."

"That must have been nice," Filberte remarked.

"My father inherited it," Sarah explained. "His grandfather was in the wool trade. He started with a small company and built a prominent business."

"An empire that stretched across Europe, right?" Tom clarified.

"It was quite large." Sarah laughed, remembering a time long forgotten. "My dad loved the business, and he was good at it."

"What about your mother?" Filberte continued, eager to learn more.

"She was a concert pianist and toured Europe, playing classical music. That's how I got to travel to different countries, when I wasn't in school."

"Do you have any brothers or sisters?"

"No, I was an only child."

"Tell him about your family roots," Tom nudged. "Their last name is Wallace, as in Sir William Wallace, the famous Scottish knight."

"It's no big deal," Sarah said modestly. "Our family line traces back seven hundred years."

Filberte sat down by Sarah, fascinated by her history.

"I'm familiar with the family name and legacy," Filberte affirmed. "This means you have heroic genes in your bloodline."

"I guess." Sarah chuckled, not sure how to react.

"If you don't mind me asking, what happened?" Filberte inquired delicately.

Sarah became quiet, her expression melancholy.

"You don't need to answer." Filberte gently retreated. "I was just wondering."

"That's all right," Sarah replied somberly, her eyes drifting. "It's been a while since I've talked about it."

Sitting by her side, Filberte offered a comforting presence.

"About five years ago," Sarah began, clearing her throat, "my mother and father were killed in an automobile accident. I was supposed to be with them but had stayed at my prep school that weekend to study for an exam."

"It must have been extremely difficult for you," Filberte said empathetically.

"I was devastated," Sarah recalled, heartbroken. "I miss them and think about them all the time."

Everyone was quiet for a moment, reflecting on her loss.

"Do you know how it happened?" Filberte wondered.

"I never learned all the details, but there was something very odd about it," Sarah remembered, the images vivid in her mind.

"In what way?"

"They were run off the road and into a ravine, but there were no other vehicles or witnesses. Even the police acted suspiciously, rushing through the investigation and quickly concluding it was an accident."

"Strange," Filberte agreed. "How did you end up in an orphanage?"

"It's interesting about family and relatives," Sarah answered candidly. "They're there when things are good but seem to vanish when they're not."

"She was left with a cruel uncle," Tom interceded.

"He couldn't care less about me," Sarah added coldly. "He just kept me around long enough to steal everything we had, and then he got rid of me."

"That's terrible," Filberte stated.

"And that's how I eventually ended up at an orphanage, where I met Tom."

"I apologize for bringing up sad memories."

"It's okay," Sarah sighed. "It is what it is, and it's the past."

"Which is why we're so focused on the future," Tom added with vigor.

"Exactly," Sarah agreed, her spirits lifting. "Regardless how hard it's been, escaping from Weatherly Orphanage was one of the best things that ever happened to me. I owe Tom for that. He rescued me."

* * * * *

Rushing into the main Paris office of Interpol, Inspector Fontaine went straight to her desk. She was wearing jeans, a black silk turtleneck, and a beige Burberry coat. Her auburn hair was tied back.

"Get your gear together. We need to move fast," she informed Gustave.

"What is it?" he asked, sitting upright in his chair. He had on a grayish plaid suit and a dark blue tie.

"We've found Tom and Sarah."

"Where?" Gustave asked.

"Notre-Dame. They're staying with Archbishop Filberte."

"Notre-Dame," Gustave repeated, surprised. "How long have they been there?"

"Less than twenty-four hours."

"Are they okay?"

"As far as I know, but we must hurry."

Inspector Fontaine removed her Glock 34 9mm from the bottom drawer and nodded to Gustave to grab his Smith & Wesson.

"Any idea where they've been for over six months?" Gustave inquired as he holstered his weapon.

"Something about Mont-Saint-Michel, but that's all I was told."

"Does anyone else know?"

"Just the chief, and let's keep it that way," Fontaine said as she made her way toward the exit.

"Understood," Gustave agreed, following behind her with a bag of equipment.

Gustave Devereux was a fifteen-year veteran at Interpol. Tall and handsome, he had a sharp wit and an analytical mind. Like Detective Gowerstone, he was cleaver, smart, and determined to win. Gustave came from a prominent family and was well connected throughout Europe. He made a strong ally and a good partner. Although this was his first assignment with Fontaine, she was already very fond of him.

*****

Thirty minutes later, there was a knock at one of the cathedral doors.

"That must be Inspector Fontaine," Filberte announced. "You two wait here. I'll bring her back to see you."

"Whatever you think is best," Tom agreed, eager to meet the inspector and make their way to Castle Chambord.

Filberte left the room and approached the main entryway. As he opened the door, a man probably in his early thirties, blond hair and well-built, stood by the entrance.

"My name is Marcel. I'm here for Tom and Sarah," the man stated in a German accent.

"Where's Inspector Fontaine?" Filberte questioned, confused.

"She's been detained. She sent me ahead."

"I see," Filberte said, suspicious.

"May I see the children?"

"I'd prefer to wait for the inspector, if you don't mind."

"She instructed me to take care of the situation."

"That doesn't sound like Fontaine. Perhaps I should call her."

"I'm in a hurry," Marcel demanded, his eyes becoming cold.

"It has been over six months; you can wait until she arrives."

"I don't have time." Marcel shoved his way in, knocking Filberte to the ground. "Where are they?" he demanded, now enraged.

Dismayed, the archbishop tried to stand, but Marcel pushed him back down.

"I'll ask you one more time," Marcel threatened as he removed a Ruger 10mm from his leather jacket. "Where are Tom and Sarah?"

"You're going to shoot me for not betraying my friends?" Filberte asked bluntly, staring at the weapon.

"I'll do whatever I have to," Marcel warned, a dangerous tone in his voice.

Tom and Sarah had been listening from the refectory. Hearing all the commotion, they walked into the nave aisle.

As Marcel glanced over, Filberte grabbed a candelabrum from a nearby table and struck Marcel's right knee.

"*Auch,*" Marcel cursed in German, whacking Filberte across the head with his Ruger. "You stupid old man!"

The archbishop fell to the floor, his body completely limp.

Shocked, Tom and Sarah wanted to help the archbishop but were afraid for their lives. They sprinted toward the rear of the cathedral, searching for an exit. They rushed down a hallway and reached the cathedral apse, a rounded termination point, with paneling and stained glass windows.

"It's a dead end," Tom exclaimed, panicked.

"There's got to be another way out," Sarah cried, desperate to escape.

The two frantically searched the area, tapping on wooden panels and looking behind the heavy drapery. They could hear Marcel stumbling toward them, the loud thump of his right foot hitting the tile floor.

"Over there, in the corner," Sarah motioned, noticing traces of light emitting from a hidden door.

Tom fumbled around with the panel and found a concealed latch. "It's an exit. Let's go," he whispered loudly, waiting for Sarah.

They pushed their way outside and then blinked, briefly blinded by the morning sun.

Marcel was close behind, sputtering with rage.

Dashing through the cathedral courtyard, Tom and Sarah swiftly crossed Pont Neuf, a bridge leading to the Left Bank. Crammed with antique shops and trendy cafes, the bohemian neighborhood was packed with tourists.

Tom and Sarah darted in and out of vendor stalls and through a maze of cobbled streets. Pushing his way through the crowd, Tom collided with a fruit stand, scattering apples everywhere.

"Hey, come back here and pay for that," a merchant shouted, shaking his fist.

"Sorry!" Sarah hollered back.

Marcel limped after them, his swollen knee slowing him down.

Entering a market square, Tom and Sarah headed for the public gardens where locals strolled along pea gravel pathways, an array of Parisian culture on display: foreign students reading on benches; Eastern Europeans engaged in animated conversations; an Asian businessman on his phone; a young French couple lying on a blanket; parents chasing their child through a flower garden; friends walking their dogs.

Turning a corner and ducking into a passageway, they stopped to catch their breath. Their faces glistened with sweat.

"He's still coming," Sarah gasped, glancing behind at the stalking figure.

"Should we find a policeman?" Tom asked anxiously.

"We don't have time."

"Maybe we could hide in one of the shops."

"And be trapped inside?"

"Then we keep going and outrun him."

Sarah nodded, grabbing one last breath.

The two continued up Saint Germain Street and onto Quai D'Orsay, a busy avenue parallel to the Seine River. People strolled along the water's edge, where artists sketched portraits and painted the city scenery.

"Now which way? Right or left?" Sarah asked.

"I don't know," Tom replied, confused. "It seems like we're going in circles."

Searching the boulevard, Tom noticed people boarding a sightseeing bus. "Let's join the tour," he suggested. "We should be safe with all those people."

"Good idea," Sarah agreed. "We'll just try to blend in."

They ran over and waited in line while a man stood at the door, collecting money.

"Two tickets, please," Tom said impatiently.

"That's twenty euros each."

"Fine," he said, thrusting the money into the man's hand.

They entered the bus and sat by the front, peering out the window and exchanging nervous looks. As the last passengers boarded, the vehicle took off.

Leaning back with a sigh of relief, Tom noticed Marcel in the distance—and for a second their eyes met.

"He just saw me," Tom gasped, sliding down in his seat.

Sarah edged closer to the window and watched Marcel hobble into a vehicle. "He's getting into a cab," she whispered.

"Which means he's going to follow us."

As the bus motored along Quai d'Orsay Avenue, a tour guide stood at the front speaking into a microphone: "To our right is the Musée du Louvre, one of the world's most popular museums. It was once Europe's largest royal palace until King Louis the XIV moved his court to Versailles, twenty minutes southwest of Paris."

"He's gaining," Tom stammered, watching the cab zip through the traffic.

"To our left is Musée d'Orsay," the guide continued. "This converted railroad station now houses an extraordinary collection of Impressionist art."

Tom arose from his seat. "Can't you go any faster?" he asked tensely.

"This is a tour, not a train," the guide snapped. "Now sit back down or you'll have to get off the bus."

4
A WELCOMED FRIEND

Fontaine and Gustave arrived at Notre-Dame fifteen minutes after Sarah and Tom had fled. Noticing the main door slightly ajar, they approached cautiously.

Fontaine pulled her Glock, holding it at shoulder height and easing the door open.

"Archbishop?" she called out, scanning the room for movement.

Gustave removed his Smith & Wesson 45mm and covered the opposite direction.

"Archbishop Filberte, are you here?" Fontaine continued, an uneasy feeling in her stomach.

"Look!" Gustave noticed, gesturing to an unconscious body sprawled across the floor.

Fontaine hurried over and knelt by Filberte's side. She held a vial of smelling salts under his nose, gently examining the bloody gash on his forehead as he regained consciousness.

"Are you okay?" she asked tenderly, helping him sit up.

"I . . . I don't know," Filberte mumbled, disoriented.

"Call for an ambulance and backup," Fontaine instructed. "Then search the entire cathedral. Hopefully Tom and Sarah are still here."

Gustave nodded, rapidly dialing his cell phone as he left.

"What happened? Who did this to you?" Fontaine asked, switching to interrogation mode.

"A man came to the front door," Filberte whispered, slightly cognizant, his breathing shallow.

"Go on," she encouraged him.

"He said his name was Marcel and he demanded to see Tom and Sarah—said he knew you."

"Knew me?" Fontaine questioned. "Did you recognize him?"

"No, I've never seen him before."

"What did he look like?" she probed, removing a notepad and pen from her coat pocket.

"He was stocky, blond hair, blue eyes, medium height," Filberte began, trying to recall the man's physical characteristics, "late twenties, maybe early thirties, a leather jacket, and he had a gun."

"That's helpful," Fontaine conveyed, scribbling down the details. "Can you remember any distinguishing features, like a scar or tattoo, anything at all?"

"No, I don't."

"Any security cameras placed inside or outside that may have caught a glimpse of him?"

"No, the congregation doesn't allow it, believes it's an invasion of privacy."

"Understood."

"Wait, there's something else," Filberte interjected, trying to muster strength. "His voice, it wasn't French. He had a German accent."

"Interesting," Fontaine said, reflecting on the comment. "Where are Tom and Sarah?"

"They were in the refectory."

Fontaine analyzed the situation, impatiently waiting for Gustave to return.

"I'm sorry for failing you and the children," Filberte apologized, grief-stricken.

"You did nothing of the sort," Fontaine assured him. "You nearly lost your life protecting them."

Gustave hurried back, a worried expression etched on his face.

"I didn't find anyone," Gustave informed her. "Interpol is sending a team, along with an ambulance."

"All right." Fontaine handed him a piece of paper. "Call in this description. Put out a citywide APB. This man is armed and dangerous. Interpol can search its databases for a possible match and monitor the street cameras."

"Right." Gustave nodded as he grabbed his cell phone.

Fontaine turned back to the archbishop. "Can you provide us with an accurate description of Tom and Sarah, what they're wearing and anything else you can remember?"

"I'll do my best," Filberte replied, distraught.

* * * * *

The tour bus parked at Champ de Mars, a grassy field enclosed by lofty elms and gardens bursting with vibrant flowers.

"Last stop, ladies and gentlemen, the Eiffel Tower," the guide announced proudly. "Erected in 1889 for the World's Fair, the Eiffel Tower is 1,063 feet high. Named after its engineer, Gustave Eiffel, this iron lattice structure is divided into three separate levels as it tapers upward to the top observatory platform at 915 feet."

The guide finished and prepared to get off the bus. "If you have time, you can join me for a separate tour to the top of our famous monument."

"You don't go any farther?" Tom asked.

"Not unless you want to repeat the tour in an hour."

"No, thank you."

"Please file out," the guide requested. "I'll meet everybody in front of the main elevator tower."

"Now what?" Sarah wondered, glancing out the window.

"We can't stay on the bus. Maybe we could tell somebody."

Sarah nodded, nudging him toward the guide.

"Sir, could you help us?" Tom pleaded. "There's a man chasing—"

"Everyone off the bus."

"But, sir, we need your—"

"Everyone includes you," the guide snapped. "I'm getting tired of your disruptions. Now, off the bus."

The guide abruptly climbed down the bus steps, walked to the sidewalk, and began chatting with some of the tourists.

"So much for French hospitality," Tom sighed dismally.

"Let's at least stay with the group," Sarah said as she stood from her seat.

With their heads bent, they merged with the crowd as it advanced toward the Eiffel Tower.

A yellow cab parked nearby, and Marcel exited. Observing the tourists leaving the bus, he marched in their direction.

Seeing a group waiting in line for the elevator, Marcel scanned the crowd, and spotting Tom and Sarah, made eye contact with the girl.

"He saw me," Sarah exclaimed, then grabbed Tom's hand and pulled him toward a tower stairwell. They tried to push through the turnstile, but it was locked in place.

"You need tickets!" a female attendant yelled.

"Pardon?" Sarah asked sharply.

"To go up the stairs. It's eleven and a half euros each."

"Just to walk to the top?" Sarah questioned, offended by the price.

"Sarah," Tom intervened. "I'll pay it."

He swiftly surrendered the last of his money. They shoved through the turnstile and ran toward the metal stairs.

Marcel quickly followed.

* * * * *

Once the ambulance arrived at Notre-Dame, Fontaine and Gustave left Filberte with the medics and ran outside. The inspector was pensive as Gustave finished a conversation on his cell phone.

"Anything?" Fontaine asked, searching for answers.

"I got a call from the Latin Quarter. Two children just ran through there, causing chaos and disruption."

"That's them—I know it," she said intuitively, then looked at Gustave, who seemed preoccupied. "Is there something else?"

"No, that's all I have."

"I know this is our first assignment together. You don't mind working under my supervision?"

"No, it's an honor to partner with you," Gustave assured her. "I'm just curious who that German was and how he knew where to find them."

"So am I, but right now we need to act quickly, before Tom and Sarah get too far," Fontaine said urgently. "They could be anywhere."

"That's what I'm afraid of," Gustave admitted, worried.

"We'll split up and search the Latin Quarter," Fontaine began, focusing her thoughts. "Question everyone in the vicinity—shopkeepers, tourists, residents. We need some clue to where they're headed."

"I'll take the west side, and you can take the east side."

"Good, we'll touch base in thirty minutes."

Gustave had volunteered to partner with Fontaine, and she was fortunate to have him. A highly gifted agent, he had a way of discerning the truth and distinguishing fact from fiction. If anyone could locate Tom and Sarah, Fontaine was sure she and Gustave were the best for the task.

* * * * *

Their legs burning, Sarah and Tom had climbed 362 stairs to the first platform level. They could still hear the relentless clatter of footsteps behind them.

"He's coming," Sarah warned, seeing a figure approaching two flights below.

"What does he want?" Tom asked, scared and frustrated.

"I don't know, but you saw what he did to the archbishop," Sarah said, looking around for a way to escape. "Let's try the elevator."

They moved to the center and pushed a button.

The footsteps grew louder.

The bell dinged, and the elevator door opened.

Tom and Sarah scurried into the jam-packed interior, a fusion of international tourists. As the door shut, a hand clasped the edge, preventing it from closing all the way.

The steel doors reopened. Marcel stepped into the elevator. Sweaty and panting, he glared down at Tom and Sarah. The door shut and the elevator progressed upward.

Marcel tried to get closer but was pressed to one side by the crowd of tourists. Sarah's heart raced as the man stared at her, his sinister eyes conveying malicious intentions. Tom's mouth felt parched as he tried to swallow, his body trembling.

The elevator stopped at the top, and the doors slid open.

Shoving through the crowd, Tom and Sarah hastily exited. As they reached the spiral staircase to the summit, Marcel blocked their path.

Distracted by the panoramic views, the other tourists remained oblivious to what was happening right in front of them.

Twenty feet away, Marcel slowly herded Tom and Sarah toward an isolated corner and reached for his gun, methodically attaching a silencer to the end. Sarah's eyes widened as she stared at the weapon.

Trapped in the corner, Tom motioned Sarah to climb over the safety railing and onto the towering structure.

"Are you out of your mind?" she whispered, taking in the long drop.

"There's nowhere else to go," Tom reasoned.

Eyes wide open, she gulped and looked down again, her heart thumping. Out of options, she nodded in agreement.

They warily crawled over the guardrail and down onto the exterior girders. Paris sprawled almost a thousand feet below.

Marcel proceeded to the railing and watched them disappear into the edifice, scurrying in and out of the girders.

Grasping the iron beams, Tom and Sarah scaled the massive structure, swaying in the wind and holding on for their life. The wind was vigorous, shifting directions and howling through the rafters.

Sarah's hair flicked back and forth, her dress flapping like a sail. Her body was tense, her mind a flurry of frantic thoughts.

"This is the dumbest thing I've ever done," she admitted, petrified and trying not to glance down.

"Me too," Tom confessed, rethinking his decision.

"You know I'm not crazy about heights."

"I know," he said nervously. "Just move around the outside until we find a different stairwell."

Marcel slithered along the interior guardrail, searching for an angle to shoot them.

Tom and Sarah inched forward, navigating the

intricate metalwork that crisscrossed in every direction. As they ducked under one girder and crawled over another, they felt the steel edges cold and sharp under their hands.

Reaching up for an overhead beam, Tom's hand slipped, and he started to fall backward. Sarah grabbed his arm to steady him but lost her balance, slipping to one side.

Tom reached out and clasped her hand, holding on to a girder with his other hand. Sarah was now in midair, her feet dangling over Paris. People looked like moving dots, the cars like toys, and the trees like sticks.

"Don't let go!" she panted, her entire body numbed with fright.

"I won't," he replied, his eyes filled with terror. The tension in Tom's arms and hands was tremendous, straining to maintain his grip as it began to loosen.

"I'm slipping," Sarah cried out, staring at him.

"I've got you! I'm not letting go!"

Suddenly, with heroic determination, Tom heaved with all his strength and swung her toward one of the girders.

Sarah reached out, grabbed hold, and pulled herself upright.

"Yikes, that was close," Tom wheezed, taking a deep breath.

Looking down, Sarah tried to recover, her heart beating rapidly. "T-thanks," she gasped.

Tom nodded, making a silent vow never to climb large objects again.

"Are you two nuts?" a serviceman shouted, walking to the interior edge. "You can't be out there!"

"Someone is after us," Tom yelled back.

"I don't care who's after you," the serviceman griped. "Get back in here, or I'll call the authorities and have you arrested!"

Tom and Sarah hesitated, their eyes searching for Marcel. He had vanished.

"Now," the man yelled.

While Tom and Sarah carefully crawled back to the platform, the serviceman shook his head in disbelief.

"Get to the stairs and either go up or down," he ordered, shocked by their audacity. "And stay off the girders!"

"Yes, sir," Tom said obediently. "But can you help us . . ."

The serviceman marched away, mumbling under his breath. "These stupid, crazy tourists—unbelievable."

Shaken and tense, Tom and Sarah stood for a moment, watching for Marcel.

"Where do you think he went?" Sarah wondered, her head darting back and forth.

"I don't know, but I'm sure he's close."

"Should we go up or down?"

"Let's head down before he . . ."

Tom's voice trailed off as Marcel reappeared, strategically blocking the stairwell exit.

"I think we should head up," Tom concluded, grabbing Sarah's hand.

They raced up the spiral staircase to the top observatory, where people were taking pictures of the spectacular view. It was a chaotic cluster of tourists, young couples, and children scampering around with their parents. The constant chatter of voices and howling wind made it impossible to talk without shouting.

Tom and Sarah looked around frantically for a policeman, then imbedded themselves in a group of people. The sightseers were admiring Paris, a dramatic jigsaw of tiny buildings and intersecting streets. Directly below, the Seine was filled with glass-top boats and commercial barges, navigating the turquoise river. A canopy of white puffy clouds blanketed the sky, and the views continued for miles: the city, the suburbs, and the distant countryside.

Seeing the children confined to the observatory platform, Marcel crept up behind Tom and Sarah.

Startled, Sarah angrily lashed out, "I'll scream."

"It doesn't matter," Marcel sneered and reached for his gun. "It won't save your life, since I'm going to push you over the side anyway."

Marcel moved closer, backing them toward the railing's edge.

Searching for an escape, Tom closed his eyes and said a silent prayer. When he opened them, he noticed a familiar friend standing with a young woman.

"Over there," Tom motioned to Sarah. "It looks like—"

"Who?" Sarah asked frantically.

"Oliver?" Tom yelled in desperation, hoping indeed it was their friend from Oxford.

The young man turned, his face bursting with surprise. "Well, I'll be . . . ," Oliver blurted, immediately walking over to greet them.

Stylishly dressed, wearing blue slacks, a white polo, and a dark coat, Oliver Horningbrook, with blue eyes and sandy blond hair, was a tall, gangly university student whose athletic pursuits often interfered with his academic studies. Kind- hearted and well-liked, Oliver longed for adventure and to escape from his father's domineering control.

Tom and Sarah lovingly embraced him.

"It's been months," Oliver marveled, stunned at the sight of them. "Whatever happened? When I came back from my Oxford rowing match, you both were gone."

"Oliver—we need your help," Tom interrupted, his voice unsteady. "T-there's a man following us . . ."

They turned, but Marcel had melted into the crowd.

"Where?" Oliver asked, ready to defend his friends, his fists tightening.

"That man in the leather jacket," Sarah replied, turning to point out the man but realizing he was gone. "But he was right there."

"We were chased from Notre-Dame, up the stairs, onto the girders, and finally to the top platform," Tom explained with frantic gestures.

"By whom?" Oliver questioned.

"We have no idea," Tom responded, shaking his head in bewilderment.

"But I think he wants to hurt us—permanently," Sarah added.

Oliver once again surveyed the crowd. "Whoever he is, he's gone."

Tom and Sarah exhaled, trying to relax.

"I can't tell you how glad we are to see you," Sarah said, comforted by his presence and friendly face.

"Me too," Oliver agreed, grinning. "Ever since you left my flat, I've always wondered if you safely made it to London."

"We have a lot to tell you," Tom asserted with an undercurrent of gravity.

"I'm sure you do," Oliver acknowledged, anxious to hear everything. "Oh, by the way, this is my friend Clarissa."

"Girlfriend," Clarissa stated, glaring at Tom and Sarah.

"Right, girlfriend," Oliver repeated clumsily.

Clarissa was petite yet well proportioned, her black hair pulled tight in a bun, her brown eyes hidden by sunglasses. She wore a Vanessa Bruno dress, Tiffany jewelry, and a purple scarf around her neck. A privileged debutante from an aristocratic family, Clarissa had little compassion for others.

"It's nice to meet you," Tom and Sarah said, shaking her frosty hand.

"Charmed," Clarissa replied coldly, forcing a smile while avoiding eye contact.

"Let's get out of here," Oliver suggested. "You guys hungry?"

"I'm always hungry," Tom replied.

"I've got just the place in mind," Oliver declared, inspired by the moment. "I want to hear every detail."

Tom and Sarah scanned the observatory once again and then closely followed Oliver and Clarissa to the elevator. They rode down and got into a cab parked curbside.

Twenty minutes later, all four arrived at the Hotel Ritz. One of the most prestigious hotels in the world, this four-story, eighteenth-century palatial mansion had been turned into a hotel in 1898 by Swiss hotelier Cesar Ritz. The taupe sandstone exterior had arched entryways, elongated windows separated by Doric columns, and a Mansard rooftop with a row of small, rounded dormers. Prominently displayed above the entrance was a massive blue, white, and red striped flag flapping in the breeze. A line of black Town Cars was parked in front when the taxi pulled up.

They entered the luxurious lobby with pink marble pillars, golden chandeliers, French antiques, Louis XV chairs wrapped in cobalt silk, and oriental rugs masking the marble floors. Everyone trailed behind Oliver, who was clearly a regular.

"Hi, Alexandrine, nice to see you again." Oliver waved, greeting the receptionist.

"Welcome back, Mr. Horningbrook," she said pleasantly.

"Oliver, is that you?" a distinguished man asked, sipping champagne at a nearby table.

"Dr. Jacquan, it's been a while," Oliver said cordially. "How's your romantic novel coming?"

"Slow and tedious."

"Oliver, you mad Brit," a Frenchman shouted from across the room. "Where were you last night?"

"Hello, François," Oliver acknowledged tactfully. "Sorry I couldn't make it. I was having dinner with Clarissa at Le Meurice."

"You missed the best party in Paris," François said, stumbling off.

They continued through an opulent hallway, down a

set of carpeted stairs, and emerged at the Bar Hemingway, named for the famous writer Ernest Hemingway, who frequented the hotel in the 1930s and '40s.

* * * * *

An hour passed as they indulged in a gourmet feast, including mushroom crêpes and wine-poached salmon with black truffles. Neither Tom nor Sarah knew what they were eating, but it tasted heavenly. The meal was followed by tarte Alsacienne and chocolate mousse for dessert. During their blissful meal, Tom and Sarah shared everything that had happened since they'd left Oliver's Oxford flat, including a few details about the Britfields.

Oliver was completely engrossed in the conversation while Clarissa was annoyed by these intruders who were stealing his attention.

"So after you left Canterbury and went to Dover, what happened on the ferry?" Oliver inquired, captivated.

"The weather was rough. We were halfway across the channel when we heard a loud explosion," Tom expressed dramatically.

"An explosion? Like a bomb?" Oliver asked.

"Yeah, exactly. The boat began to sink. It was complete chaos, with people running everywhere," Tom conveyed with intensity. "After Professor Hainsworth helped us into a lifeboat, we got separated as the raft crashed into the water."

"It was freezing cold and really dark," Sarah remembered vividly. "All we could see was the foggy ocean and a glimpse of the French coastline, so we rowed toward the shore."

"Or at least what we thought was the shore," Tom added. "Then I guess we drifted for a couple of days. The lifeboat had blankets, water, and a few provisions, but at some point we must have passed out."

"Finally, this wonderful monk, Brother Gabriel, found us on the shore of Mont-Saint-Michel and took us in," Sarah reminisced fondly. "We were extremely sick and stayed in the infirmary for months."

"Once we were released, the Benedictine Brotherhood taught us all their rules and rituals," Tom explained. "They put me to work in their shop, and Sarah was sent to the library to organize all their books."

"The problem was, they were never going to let us leave," Sarah emphasized. "So, with the help of Brother Gabriel, we escaped at night and caught a train to Paris."

"That's when we met Archbishop Filberte at Notre-Dame. He was going to help us, until a strange man came to the door and chased us all over Paris," Tom concluded, breathless.

"Unbelievable," Oliver proclaimed, impressed by their courageous journey.

"That's a cute story." Clarissa rolled her eyes.

"Cute?" Sarah snapped, her fiery Scottish temper flaring. "What's cute about it? We were almost shot."

Noticing the growing tension, Oliver swiftly interceded. "Where are you headed now?" he asked.

Tom surveyed the room and whispered, "The Loire River Valley. We believe my parents are staying at one of the châteaux—or at least I hope they are my parents."

"That's fantastic news," Oliver conveyed.

"We're hopeful," Sarah said, half-smiling. "For now, we'd like to check on the archbishop and call Inspector Fontaine, who was on her way to Notre-Dame. She's supposed to help us."

"I'm sure once the inspector arrived, she took care of the archbishop," Oliver responded. "But let's give her a call right now."

Tom handed Oliver the card with the inspector's contact information on it, and he dialed the number. After a few minutes, he hung up.

"It went straight to voice mail and her mailbox was full," Oliver informed them. "We can try again at my apartment."

"Great," Tom acknowledged, keen for his help.

"Anything I can do, just let me know," Oliver offered, excited to be reunited with his long-lost friends.

Clarissa gave him a frosty glance, disapproving of his charitable gesture and impatient to leave.

"Oliver, what are you doing in Paris?" Sarah wondered.

"I have a summer internship at the Louvre," he replied halfheartedly. "My father set it up, thought it would be good for my education. He's a rabid art collector and owns several paintings worth millions, so I'm told."

"How did he acquire them?" Sarah questioned.

"I'm not sure, but he got me interested in art. We used to spend hours studying each painting, and he'd tell me all about their history," Oliver elaborated.

"I thought you didn't get along with your father," Tom recalled from their previous conversations at Oxford.

"I don't," Oliver admitted. "But this is one area in which we share an interest."

"It was Oliver's father who introduced us," Clarissa interrupted. "It's the perfect match between our families."

"Ah, yeah, sure," Oliver mumbled, uncomfortable with the topic. "Anyway, my father flew over at the beginning of June and set up the internship, an apartment, and introductions to society."

"High society," Clarissa was quick to articulate.

"Whatever," Oliver said dismissingly. "I'm not really into any of that. I'm just doing my duty."

"You should be more interested," Clarissa reproached him. "It's an important part of your future."

"If I decide on that future."

Oliver glanced at Tom's and Sarah's odd clothing.

"Now that you're in Paris, we should get you some nice clothes," Oliver said as he got up from the table. "Are you interested? My treat?"

"You bet," Tom replied.

"Sarah, what do you think?"

"Absolutely," she answered eagerly, her eyes beaming.

* * * * *

After diligently questioning bystanders and local merchants, Fontaine and Gustave learned that Tom and Sarah had gotten on a tour bus. Carefully retracing their steps, the two agents arrived at the Champ de Mars.

Fontaine and Gustave stood by the Eiffel Tower interviewing the tour guide and a few attendants.

Fontaine had shown them a picture of both children, which she had retrieved from her files.

"Could you say that again?" Fontaine asked a woman employee.

"I remember seeing these two children leave with a young man and woman. I think he was British."

"What makes you say that?" Fontaine questioned.

"The accent," the woman replied snobbishly.

"Were the children being taken against their will?"

"What do you mean?"

"Did it look like they were being kidnapped," Fontaine clarified.

"No, it seemed like they knew the young man."

Fontaine glanced at Gustave, puzzled.

"What did he look like, this young man?" Gustave inquired, feverishly writing down notes.

"I didn't really pay attention. He was tall, blond hair, that's all I remember."

"How old was he?" Gustave probed.

"Maybe late teens or early twenties," the woman speculated. "He was well dressed and sort of looked like a university student."

"Well dressed?"

"Like he had money, nice clothes."

"What about the young woman?" Gustave continued.

"Black hair, cute."

"I see," Gustave pondered, more confused than ever. "Anything else?"

"No," the woman answered sharply, anxious to leave.

"Okay, thank you for your time."

As the woman walked away, the serviceman from the Tower platform marched over, eager to assist.

"I saw another man," he blurted out.

"Go on," Fontaine encouraged him.

"This man seemed to be following the children," he recalled. "I didn't think much of it at the time. I just thought the kids were horsing around—we get a lot of that here."

"Anything suspicious about the man?" Fontaine asked directly.

"He was an odd fellow, lurking about the top platforms and watching the two children," the serviceman replied. "I don't think he realized I saw him. I was going to notify the authorities, but he disappeared."

"What did he look like?"

"Husky, well-built, leather jacket," the serviceman replied. "There was something weird about him. I can't explain it, but he was creepy."

"That's helpful," Fontaine told him. "We'll let you know if we have any more questions."

Fontaine pulled Gustave aside.

"A man with a gun somehow locates Tom and Sarah, then follows them all the way up the Eiffel Tower," Fontaine recapped, distressed. "It sounds like a professional hit."

"For two children?"

"You know their history. They're no ordinary children, especially Tom."

"You may be right," Gustave agreed. "But who is this assassin, and who sent him?"

"All I know is that we need to find Tom and Sarah before he does."

* * * * *

Tom and Sarah accompanied Oliver and Clarissa to Champs-Élysées, one of the finest boulevards in Europe. The posh avenue was lined with flowering chestnut trees and luxury shops: Chanel, Hermès, Louis Vuitton, Max Mara, Yves Saint Laurent. Sarah's eyes were glowing.

As they went from one boutique to another, Clarissa kept glancing at her watch, perturbed that her day was being wasted. She was oblivious to how important it was for Oliver to help his friends.

Several hours later, Sarah was wearing Max Mara khaki pants, a white blouse, Kate Spade shoes, and a cashmere sweater and carrying a Louis Vuitton purse. Tom wore stylish jeans, a light blue buttoned shirt, a suede jacket, and leather shoes. They both looked like young fashion models from a glamour magazine.

Sarah twirled in a shop window, admiring her reflection as she adjusted her blouse.

"It's the nicest outfit I've ever worn," Sarah marveled, delighted. "I don't know how to thank you."

"You're welcome," Oliver said gallantly, delighted to assist.

"Yeah, better than anything I've ever had," Tom admitted, fiddling with his shirt and rubbing his hand across the smooth suede. "How can you afford all this?"

"My father provides a generous allowance," Oliver replied offhandedly.

"It's a trust fund," Clarissa interrupted. "That's typical of the upper class."

"Meaning?" Tom asked with furrowed brow.

"It's money put aside for me," Oliver explained nonchalantly. "I can use it at my own discretion."

"Oliver, we've wasted three hours," Clarissa huffed. "We need to leave."

"Sure, no problem," Oliver agreed, hailing a passing cab.

A few minutes later, they pulled up to Rue de Caumartin, a fashionable street three blocks from the Seine and close to the Louvre.

Exiting the cab, they walked toward a grand building. The pale limestone exterior had a neoclassical façade and intricate Art Nouveau ironwork around the windows and balconies. A sharply dressed doorman stood by the private entrance.

"You guys can stay with me for as long as you want," Oliver offered.

"Really?" Tom said, excited by the prospect.

"Oliver," Clarissa exclaimed, displeased. "We have tickets for tonight's performance of Wagner at the Opera House."

"Oh, that's right," Oliver remembered. "Perhaps we can go another time."

"Tonight is the only performance," Clarissa reminded him. "You bought the tickets two weeks ago."

"I can't just leave Tom and Sarah. They need my help," Oliver argued, struggling with what to do.

"Can we talk for a moment, alone?" Clarissa insisted, tugging on Oliver's arm, her erratic mood turning ugly. "Look, I appreciate you helping these two kids, but they're not my problem and they're not going to ruin my evening," Clarissa protested indignantly.

"That's a bit insensitive, don't you think?" Oliver tried to reason with her. "Tom and Sarah have been through a great deal, and they need me right now."

"That's not my concern or responsibility."

Oliver sighed, stunned by her callousness.

"I'll make this simple for you," Clarissa declared. "It's either me or them. Is that clear?"

"Crystal clear."

"Well?" Clarissa demanded impatiently, her hands on her waist.

"I'm sorry, but goodbye, Clarissa," Oliver said decisively.

"What!" she huffed, stunned by his reply.

"You heard me."

"If that's the way you want it."

"That's my answer," Oliver stated firmly.

"You're making the biggest mistake of your life!"

"Maybe, but I doubt it."

Clarissa gave him a withering look and got into a cab.

5
A SINISTER GROUP

Hidden outside of Paris, among acres of forest, was an ostentatious sixteenth-century Gothic castle known as Ravencliff. This structure was comprised of elaborate stonework, Corinthian columns, and a steep slate roof with turrets encircling the outer rim. The entire fortress was surrounded by a pentagon-shaped moat and life-sized marble creatures that guarded the courtyard.

Deep in the underground vaults was a chamber lit by torches and thirty-three candles arranged in a circle. In the center, around an ancient round table, sat a group of thirteen older men cloaked in black robes, their faces scarcely visible beneath their hoods.

Marcel stood in front of them, head slightly bowed. Behind him in the shadows stood a macabre creature known as Strauss. Unnaturally proportioned, this seven-foot-tall giant had olive skin and black, piercing eyes. He remained silent but observed everything.

"We're extremely disappointed," an Italian man stated venomously. "We gave you a simple assignment: exterminate those two children."

"Yes, sir," Marcel murmured reverently, a slight tremble in his voice.

"I can't believe we're still discussing this issue," an Egyptian man vented in a high-pitched squeal, slamming his hand on the table. "How are they still alive?"

"When the ferry left Dover in late December," Marcel began, "I planted the bomb as requested, set the timer, and swam back to shore."

"We were led to believe that your mission was successful, that the children had drowned and that this ordeal was *finished*," the Italian summarized. "Yet we come to find out that Tom and Sarah are still alive."

Marcel swallowed deeply, knowing his future was grim. "How they escaped from the ferry and got to the shore is beyond my—"

"It doesn't matter," the Italian's voice rose, echoing in the chamber.

"Yes, sir," Marcel stammered.

"And today you had them in your grasp," the Egyptian stressed. "We don't invest billions of dollars in surveillance technology and intercept countless phone calls only to waste this valuable information. You have all the resources you need."

"They escaped out the back door of Notre-Dame," Marcel tried to explain.

"And the Eiffel Tower?"

"They were in a crowd."

"Then you eliminate the crowd," a British voice thundered, showing no empathy.

"I would have, but there was a complication," Marcel revealed, hesitant. "There was a young man with them."

"That's not our concern," the Italian dismissed, his tone cold.

"The young man is Oliver Horningbrook."

Surprised by the disclosure, the thirteen men began to whisper among themselves.

"This is unfortunate," the Italian continued, contemplating their next move. "What is Oliver Horningbrook doing with them?"

"I don't know," Marcel murmured. "It appears that he knows them."

"Find out where he's staying in Paris. You will personally accompany an assault team to extract the children."

"As you command." Marcel bowed.

"Once you've secured the children, you will quickly eliminate them, along with any evidence," the Italian instructed.

"There's another problem," Marcel added reluctantly.

"What is it?" the Italian asked in a sharp tone, his temper erupting.

"Inspector Fontaine, from Interpol," he answered timidly. "She's getting too close."

"Use our assets to phase her out."

"And if she continues?"

"Then remove her permanently," the Italian ordered.

* * * * *

Immersed in discussion, Tom and Sarah sat inside Oliver's lush two-bedroom townhouse, which had ten-foot-high ceilings, gilded paneling, and arched windows that opened onto a balcony. The place was furnished with a comfy couch with a woolen blanket on top, two leather chairs, and had thick Berber carpet.

"We're sorry about your girlfriend," Tom offered, noticing Oliver's melancholy.

"I'm not," Sarah stated firmly, never a person to hide her opinions. "She wasn't very nice. You deserve a thousand times better."

"Sarah!" Tom interjected.

"She's right," Oliver agreed in a mournful groan. "It wasn't a very good match, was it?"

"Clarissa didn't seem to like us very much," Tom reflected.

"I was only with her because of my father. He was hoping to merge our families," Oliver explained. "He's always meddling without asking. I learned to put up with her, but it was exhausting."

Tom leaned back and admired the lavish surroundings. "Thanks again for letting us stay."

"As far as I'm concerned, we're family," Oliver said with an infectious grin. "And family sticks together."

This comment meant a lot to Tom and Sarah. After years of being on their own, they finally felt like they belonged.

"So, you have no idea who was chasing you?" Oliver asked, returning to the problem at hand.

"No," Tom replied, wishing he could offer more.

"I guess the real question is, why?" Oliver pondered.

"And who told him where we were?" Sarah questioned, wondering who had betrayed them.

"That's a good point." Oliver got up and began to pace the room, his mind reviewing everything he had been told so far. "Might this involve what you had shared with me at lunch, what Professor Hainsworth told you about the Britfields?" he continued.

"It might," Tom considered with a leaden heart. "I guess we hoped all of that was behind us."

"It's obviously not," Sarah interjected. "After all these months, how did that man know we were at Notre-Dame? It had been less than twelve hours since we arrived in Paris."

Oliver sat down, absorbed in thought. He turned to Tom and Sarah.

"Tell me more about the Britfields," Oliver prompted, curious. "I've studied history, but I've never heard of that name before."

"Supposedly no one has," Tom disclosed, somewhat cryptically.

"They're one of the oldest families in England and the rightful heirs to the British throne," Sarah explained.

"The *real* bloodline," Tom emphasized proudly.

"But over the centuries, other dynasties seized control and murdered the Britfields," Sarah continued. "Little by little, they erased the Britfield name from history, burning documents and killing anyone who spoke of it."

"Unbelievable," Oliver said, feeling out of his depth. "And Tom may somehow be connected to this?"

"What we learned from Dr. Beagleswick at Kings College, and from the Archbishop of Canterbury, is that the last Britfield heir was kidnapped as a baby over twelve years ago," Sarah articulated.

"And Tom was that child?" Oliver asked, quickly deducing the connection.

"It's what we believe."

"That's amazing," Oliver murmured, astounded by the implications. "I might be sitting next to real royalty."

"Please . . . ," Tom mumbled, waving it off.

"Although if everything was destroyed, it's nearly impossible to prove," Oliver reasoned, comprehending their dilemma.

"Exactly," Tom confirmed. "But Sarah was doing research at the monastery and came across some interesting information. Tell him what you found."

"When I was organizing the monks' library, I stumbled across these ancient manuscripts, centuries old," Sarah revealed. "It was the first time I actually saw the name Britfield in print, right there in the documents."

"She even found a royal decree to execute the Britfields, signed by Queen Victoria," Tom interjected.

"Really?" Oliver questioned, a bit skeptical.

"Take a look," Sarah said, removing the document from her purse and handing it to him.

Oliver intently studied it, reading what he could and closely examining the writing style and type of paper.

"This definitely seems original," Oliver speculated, impressed. "How did you get it?"

"I, ah, borrowed it from the monastery," Sarah replied awkwardly.

"But there's more," Tom exclaimed. "Tell him."

Sarah took a deep breath and continued. "It's not just the royal dynasties that took power. Not the historical families we've read about."

"What do you mean?" Oliver asked.

"I kept coming across other names, secret organizations that reappeared in the different texts," Sarah recalled. "Groups like the Black Nobility, the Club of Rome, the Thirteen, Knights of Malta, the Roundtable, and something called the Committee."

Oliver was unnerved. He sat very still, rubbing his forehead.

"Does this sound familiar?" Sarah asked, noticing his reaction.

"I've heard a few of these names before, in conversations at Christ Church, Oxford," Oliver said cautiously. "Aristocratic students boasted about these groups at their private clubs and secret societies. I just thought it was nonsense."

"You're not a member, are you?" Tom wondered, suspicious.

"No, I just attended a few of their meetings at some group called the Lords of Saxony," Oliver replied.

"Well, it isn't nonsense, although that's exactly what they want you to think," Sarah stated, adamant. "I've read about it in the manuscripts."

"What you're saying is that these groups really exist, but only a few privileged people know about them?" Oliver tried to clarify.

"Yes, but I've only scratched the surface," Sarah confessed. "We need proof."

"We're not going back to the monastery," Tom asserted, shuddering at the thought.

"You might not have to," Oliver interjected with a hint of mischief. "We have some of these manuscripts at the Louvre. There's a restricted vault, deep underground, that houses ancient documents. I've been there once."

"I bet they'd have all kinds of information." Sarah

envisioned the vault, her mind stirred. "Do you think we could see some of them?"

"It's private and relatively impossible to access," Oliver answered.

"This is really important and would be a huge help," Sarah stressed.

"It'll be difficult and risky," Oliver warned them.

"How were you able to get into it before?" Sarah inquired.

"My father," Oliver replied, a bit hesitant. "As I said, he's very well connected. Right after I arrived in Paris, he flew over and took me to all these different places."

"What about getting to the Loire Valley and seeing if the Britfields are still at Chambord?" Tom reminded them. "That's why we came to France."

"We will," Sarah promised. "But aren't you interested in finding out more about the Britfields—actual proof?"

"Sure, of course."

"It does sound intriguing," Oliver admitted, already devising a strategy.

"Can you get us into that secret vault?" Sarah asked.

"Let's go tomorrow, and I'll see what I can do," Oliver agreed, then looked at his watch. "Perhaps we should try to call Inspector Fontaine again, let her know you're both safe and see how the archbishop is doing."

"That's a good idea," Tom said, handing him Fontaine's card.

Oliver pulled out his phone and dialed the number. After trying a few more times, he slowly hung up.

"That's odd," Oliver sighed, disturbed.

"What is it?" Tom inquired.
"The number has been disconnected."

*****

After leaving the prime minister's office, Detective Gowerstone was fuming. Although he tried to play it cool, he had lost his temper. The simple fact was he didn't like being threatened or bullied. Gowerstone understood the façade was gone, that both men were aware of the other's plans: Gowerstone knew the prime minister was corrupt and involved in fraudulent activities; the prime minister knew Gowerstone had discovered the truth and was planning to expose him. It was a race against time.

Over the last six months, the detective had gathered critical information through his research: classified files, secret documents, and interviews from people involved in illegal activities. However, it wasn't enough.

This clandestine organization and its malevolent groups were good at covering their tracks: anything they did, they quickly destroyed the evidence. Although they controlled practically everything, these puppet masters hid in the shadows. They bribed politicians, used phony corporations, and had others do their dirty work. They also manipulated the mainstream media, so that whatever story the public saw was the propaganda or disinformation they dictated. If people weren't bought or blackmailed, they were fired from their jobs, arrested on false charges, or terminated.

Gowerstone felt alone. He had limited resources

and didn't know who to trust. His only hope was to find enough evidence and present it to the world, but how? What method could he use? How could he get this information to the public?

There was one person he'd been talking with who might be able to help: Kate Watson. She was a social media guru who ran her own alternative news website. The elite hated her, but the public loved her. Kate's global website, blog posts, and social media platforms received millions of views each day. Working under an alias and using an untraceable IP address, she reported the truth behind the events.

After explaining his situation to Kate on untraceable satellite phones, Gowerstone planned to meet her at the seaport town of Ipswich in northeast England. During his drive north, he tried to reach Fontaine to check on Tom and Sarah, but her phone had been disconnected. He found it disconcerting and was worried. He would try to contact Fontaine later and see if Tom and Sarah were safe.

Arriving early at a local pub, the detective sat at a small table sipping a pint of Speckled Hen. He was wearing a blue trench coat and a Scottish cap that concealed part of his face.

Kate cautiously approached.

In her mid-twenties and plainly dressed, Kate had short brown hair covered by a hat, and she wore black-rimmed glasses. She was intelligent, vigilant, and determined to expose the truth.

"Detective?" she asked in a whisper.

"Kate, thank you for meeting me," Gowerstone said amiably, standing to shake her hand. "I hope this hasn't put you in jeopardy."

"It's all right," she assured him. "It's a pleasure to meet a national hero."

"I don't buy into all of that."

"I know." She smiled and sat down at the table. "That's why I trust you. You're one of the last true gentlemen."

"I'm just doing my job," he remarked, sitting back down.

"The difference is, you're succeeding."

"You've done well yourself," Gowerstone complimented her. "I've read some of your posts. Through your website, you've exposed quite a bit of corruption."

"I think we're all entitled to read the truth," Kate emphasized. "Not the propaganda we're spoon-fed by the mainstream media. They've tried to shut me down several times, which is why I'm so careful. If they ever found me . . ."

"I understand," Gowerstone consoled her, trying to ease her nerves.

"What information do you have?"

Gowerstone lowered his voice. "I'm gathering enough evidence to bring down the current government."

Kate's eyes lit up. "I'm listening," she said, leaning across the table.

"I don't have all the evidence I need, but when I do, I must get it out to the public," Gowerstone insisted.

"That's where I can help you," Kate vowed, hoping to win his trust.

Gowerstone paused, not sure how to articulate his comments. "The people I'm dealing with are extremely dangerous," he warned her. "You might be risking your life."

"I take that risk every day I publish the truth," Kate stressed. "My life is always in danger."

Gowerstone smiled, impressed by her courage.

"Can I ask what you have so far?" she inquired, searching.

"I'd rather wait," Gowerstone cautioned. "What's the best way to contact you in the future?"

"Email me at this address," Kate replied, handing him a coded number. "When I receive your message, I'll call you."

Gowerstone nodded. "Until then, be safe, and watch your back."

"You too," she said gravely. "I've a sense you're a walking target."

Kate rose from her chair and walked out the backdoor. Gowerstone waited a few minutes before he left through the front entrance.

* * * * *

Oliver studied Fontaine's card and redialed. "Nothing—the line's dead," he said, perplexed.

"But that's the number the archbishop called this morning," Tom said, alarmed.

Sarah and Tom exchanged panicked looks.

"Don't worry about it," Oliver comforted them, attempting to lift their spirits. "We'll find out where Interpol is located and go there in the morning."

"Okay," Tom agreed, slightly relieved.

"Wait," Sarah cautioned, her mind already two steps ahead. "That might not be a good idea."

"Why?" Oliver asked.

"If these groups I've read about are so powerful, then they can influence anyone, right?"

"You mean Interpol?"

"Think about it. A phoneline disconnected to our only ally in Paris, less than a day after we arrived," Sarah pointed out.

"And a stranger showing up at Notre-Dame when only Detective Gowerstone and Inspector Fontaine were contacted," Tom added, now following her logic.

"You don't think she's involved, do you? That she's part of it?" Oliver wondered aloud.

"No, I don't," Sarah replied decisively. "Gowerstone trusts her, and I trust Gowerstone."

"Me too," Tom agreed, his faith in Gowerstone unwavering.

"Okay." Oliver took a deep breath. "A bomb on the ferry, corrupt officials, and attempts on your life—this really goes deep."

"It seems that way, doesn't it," Sarah said in a sigh.

Oliver walked to a window and gazed at the street below, wondering who was watching them right now.

"What's wrong?" Sarah asked, concerned.

"It wasn't just at Oxford that I heard about these groups," Oliver mentioned, suddenly uneasy. "My father has spoken of them too."

"Your father?" Sarah questioned. "How does he know about them?"

"In his position, he's familiar with things like this."

"What does he do?"

"I'm not really supposed to discuss it," Oliver answered guardedly. "But I know I can trust the both of you."

Oliver walked back and looked at them.

"My father is the prime minister of Great Britain and has been for over twelve years."

Tom and Sarah sat in silence, their mouths and eyes wide open.

"What?" Oliver asked, noticing their stunned faces.

The mood in the room changed. A stone cold look came over Tom and Sarah as they stared at each other, trying to think of what to say to Oliver.

"Um," Sarah began, not sure how to approach the subject. "When we were outside of Canterbury Cathedral, Professor Hainsworth told us something."

"Told you what?"

"That the British prime minister is involved in all of this."

* * * * *

Fontaine and Gustave finished questioning a group of bystanders and hurried back to their vehicle. They stood outside and discussed the case.

"This is quite a story we're weaving together," Gustave said.

"None of this makes sense, but we must locate that young man," Fontaine stressed. "We'll use Interpol's database to review all British passports that have gone through French Customs in the last year."

"That's a good place to start," Gustave agreed.

"Log in what we know: males between the ages of eighteen to twenty-five; five feet, nine inches and above; blond hair; possible university student," she summarized. "Look at college exchange programs, semesters abroad, and internships in Paris."

"That could take some time."

"We'll split the list," Fontaine proposed. "I'll take *A* through *L* and you take *M* through *Z*."

"Good, that'll be faster."

"Also, check on Archbishop Filberte at the hospital. Find out if he remembers anything else and where he thinks Tom and Sarah might go next. And make sure there's someone guarding his room."

While Gustave finished taking notes, Fontaine grabbed her cell phone, eager to check her messages. She dialed, but nothing happened. "That's strange. My phone doesn't work."

"The battery?" Gustave guessed.

"No, the service has been shut off."

"Here, use mine," he offered, handing over his phone.

Fontaine dialed her number, then slowly lowered the phone, her eyes glazed over.

"Now what?" Gustave asked.

"The number has been disconnected."

"Your Interpol number?"

"Yeah," she answered, her mind racing.

"I'm sure it's just a glitch."

"Perhaps it's not."

"What do you mean?"

"Maybe someone turned it off," Fontaine suggested,

then looked at Gustave. "Tom and Sarah have no way to reach me."

Suddenly aware of the magnitude of the situation, Fontaine understood she was no longer tracking a suspect; she was the one being tracked. She systematically scanned the area, taking in every person, object, and detail.

She saw a dark van parked curbside: no visible markings, tinted windows, and two figures in the front seat. It meant only one thing: surveillance.

"What are you staring at?" Gustave asked, giving her a strange look.

"Follow me," Fontaine said.

She positioned her hand over her firearm and briskly marched toward the vehicle. Gustave followed.

As she got close to the van, it quickly pulled away and whipped around the corner, speeding out of sight.

"Did you get the plate?" Fontaine asked, her senses alert.

"I got it," Gustave responded, writing down the numbers and letters.

"Why are we being watched?" she questioned.

"I don't know." Gustave shrugged. "It might be nothing."

"You don't think that's suspicious?"

"We're in Paris—everything's suspicious," he said frankly. "Maybe we should ask the chief what's going on."

"I know what's going on," Fontaine hinted, not quite ready to share her worst fears.

"You want to tell me?"

She hesitated, unwilling to reveal more. "Not yet, but I've noticed some irregularities lately."

"You're beginning to worry me."

"Just trust me, I'll explain later."

"Fine," Gustave relented, puzzled by her behavior. "I'll start on the list and see what I come up with."

"One more thing," she said. "Could you give me your Interpol passcode? I have a feeling that mine has been shut off."

* * * * *

"What are you talking about?" Oliver exclaimed, trying to grasp their insinuation. "You don't even know my father."

"Detective Gowerstone does, and he acted the same way when he heard the truth—he was devastated," Sarah explained, knowing how difficult it must be for Oliver to hear what they were telling him.

"I know they were friends," Oliver acknowledged, pensive. "My father often spoke of him."

"Professor Hainsworth told us when we were at Canterbury Cathedral," Sarah continued. "He then explained everything on the ferry ride to Calais."

"But it's not just the professor," Tom added. "Dr. Beagleswick has all kinds of information about your father's involvement."

Oliver plopped down on the couch, crushed. "I know I don't get along with my dad, but . . ."

"We're so sorry to tell you this," Sarah conveyed sympathetically.

"Are you absolutely sure?" Oliver questioned, desperately searching for an explanation.

"Gowerstone had done a lot of research. He was pretty certain."

Oliver sat back, considering everything Sarah had just said. He just couldn't believe it. He didn't want to believe it.

"What do you really know about your father?" Sarah probed, eager to learn more.

"My father doesn't really talk about his past, although I know he came from a middle-class family."

"But your family has a title, doesn't it?"

"There's a Windsor connection, but it's distant."

"Is there anything out of the ordinary you can think of?" Sarah persisted.

At first Oliver resisted the absurd accusations about his father as he searched his brain for an alternative answer, but he started remembering people his father knew and discussions he had overheard.

"I guess there have been a few incidents, but I just thought it was part of his job: late-night meetings at our house with people I've never seen before and foreigners telling him what to do," Oliver recalled. "It seemed odd, given his position."

"I agree," Sarah nodded.

"There were also conversations I overheard about cash payments he received or had to give to others," Oliver disclosed. "I confronted him a few times, but he dismissed it as politics, said I wouldn't understand."

Oliver rose and began to pace the room, considering his past and gradually putting things together.

"I know when he was younger, everything suddenly changed. He went from receiving a common education to being accepted at Eton, an exclusive boarding school," Oliver recounted. "Then he went to Christ Church, Oxford, which is nearly impossible to get into unless you're part of the aristocracy or extremely well-connected."

"It sounds like others were helping him," Sarah said, riveted by what she was learning. "Anything else?"

"I suppose there was his swift rise in the government and his enormous wealth. It all came so quick. He went from a man with strong opinions to a man who did what others told him, from principled ideas to pushing false agendas. It seemed so hypocritical."

Oliver paused, sudden stricken by a thought.

"Take his painting collection," he began. "How does a man on a government salary collect priceless works of art? He said he bought a few at auctions and that the rest were gifts from friends."

"Who gives million-dollar gifts?" Tom said astutely.

"Perhaps that's how he was bribed, or at least one of the ways," Sarah speculated.

Oliver covered his face with his hands and rubbed his throbbing head. He felt empty and lost.

"This is just awful. All these years I've been living in a lie," he moaned, heartbroken yet angry. "What should I do? Should I confront him?"

"Maybe, but for now we really need your help," Sarah pleaded.

Oliver looked at them, a sense of purpose resurfacing. "What can I do?"

"We need to finish what we've started—locate Tom's parents and find out if he's really a Britfield," Sarah said passionately. "We also need to gather more proof about the Britfields."

"After our visit to the Louvre, I'll make sure you both get to the Loire Valley and Chambord," Oliver pledged, his eyes bright with newfound resolve.

"What about your job, your internship?" Tom wondered.

"I'll take the week off, tell them I have a family issue," Oliver replied.

Oliver rubbed his tired eyes and glanced at his watch.

"It's getting late," Oliver said, mentally drained by the whirlwind of thoughts that filled his head. "Let's talk more about this tomorrow. For now, I have a guest room with two twin beds you can use."

"Sleep does sound nice," Tom sighed, feeling completely spent.

"You'll be safe here tonight," Oliver said confidently.

"Are you certain?" Sarah asked, apprehensive.

"We're five stories up, with security cameras throughout the building and a doorman downstairs," Oliver assured them.

"Why all the protection?"

"There are quite a few important people living here. That's why my father chose the location," Oliver explained. "Anyway, no one knows you're staying with me."

6
CONFRONTATION

Inspector Fontaine sat in her modest, third-story apartment, located in Marais, on the Right Bank in Paris. She skimmed computer screens.

After discovering that her access codes had been suspended, she used Gustave's password to enter the Interpol database. Fontaine had reviewed hundreds of British passports, trying to find a match for the mysterious young man: names, faces, and descriptions. Working from the evening into early morning, she had only covered *A* through *G*, and was now on *H*. It was a daunting task.

Clicking through each picture, she came across Oliver Horningbrook: six one, blond hair, junior at Christ Church, Oxford University. She stopped. Instinct told her this was their guy.

Fontaine browsed the documents Detective Gowerstone had provided on Tom and Sarah: escaped from Weatherly Orphanage, Yorkshire; intercepted by the detective at Leyburn railway station; escaped in a hot air balloon over central England; crashed at Oxford.

"That's it," Fontaine said aloud. "That's the connection."

She returned to the screen. Oliver had been in France since the third of June; internship at the Louvre; mother was Catharine Horningbrook, socialite; father was Richard Horningbrook, prime minister of Great Britain.

Fontaine froze, eyes wide open.

"His father is the prime minister," she whispered, dumbfounded. "But this doesn't make any sense. What's the prime minister's son doing with Tom and Sarah? Is he working for his father?"

Fontaine leaned back in her chair, staring at the screen, then scrolled down to an address: 33 Rue de Caumartin, Suite 513, Paris.

Immediately standing, she printed the profile page, threw on her coat, and left her apartment.

Once outside, Fontaine walked over to a nearby convenience store and purchased a disposable cell phone. Exiting the building, she dialed.

"Gustave, I know it's early, but I've located the college student. It's Oliver Horningbrook . . . Yes, I'm sure of it. He's right here in Paris. Meet me at 33 Rue de Caumartin . . . I know you're on the other side of town, just get there as soon as possible."

After hanging up, Fontaine hopped into her light blue Mini and took off.

* * * * *

At 6:00 a.m., Oliver's phone rang. Still wearing clothes from the previous day, he stumbled out of bed and scrambled to answer it.

"Hello, Oliver speaking," he mumbled, half awake.

"Sir, this is the front desk. There are two men on their way upstairs," said the doorman, unsettled.

"Who are they? Why did you let them in?" Oliver questioned.

"I had no choice," he replied anxiously. "They had government IDs."

"What branch?"

"Nothing I've ever seen."

"Okay, thanks for letting me know." Oliver took a deep breath.

Now awake, Tom and Sarah wandered into his room.

"Is everything all right?" Sarah asked, heavy-eyed and sleepy.

"We've got to get out of here," Oliver exclaimed with urgency. "Two men are headed up to my flat right now."

Sarah's eyes widen. "I thought it was safe."

"So did I."

Seeing the look on Oliver's face, Tom and Sarah knew he was serious. Already dressed, they put on their shoes and started for the front door.

"Not that way—it's too late," Oliver warned them.

Oliver grabbed his jacket, wallet, and cell phone, then motioned Tom and Sarah toward the balcony.

"We'll have to exit through here," Oliver indicated, opening one of the French doors. "Just follow my lead."

"Your lead to where?" Sarah questioned, glancing at the street below.

"You'll see," he replied.

Oliver stepped onto the balcony, climbed over the railing, and balanced on a small ledge above the pavement.

"I'm sorry," Oliver apologized, feeling rather guilty. "I know this isn't what you planned."

"Don't worry," Tom said, shrugging his shoulders. "We've been in situations like this before."

Once all three were standing on the ledge, Oliver leaned over and closed the glass door behind them. As they waited outside, they could hear a knock at the front door. It was followed by a second, more aggressive knock.

All three of them stood motionless.

"What should we do?" Sarah asked, willing herself not to look down.

"Start moving toward the end of the building," Oliver replied, guiding them the best he could.

Suddenly the interior door smashed open. Two men, a tall Italian and a burly Romanian, both dressed in charcoal suits, entered. The Romanian clutched a photograph of Tom and Sarah.

"Search everywhere!" the Italian ordered, gesturing toward the bedrooms with his Beretta M9 handgun.

Scooting along the ledge, Oliver, Tom, and Sarah worked their way toward the corner, the sounds of Paris humming around them.

"Where are we going?" Sarah whispered as a gust of wind rocked her balance, causing her to shift her feet.

"There's a downspout at the end. I think it'll work.," Oliver tried to reassure her, knowing his makeshift plan was risky.

"Work for what?" Sarah asked, puzzled.

"To climb down. I do it all the time at school."

"Five stories?"

"It's actually only four."

"That doesn't help," Sarah mumbled.

Inch by inch, all three shuffled to the corner of the building.

Tom stepped forward. "I'll go first," he volunteered.

"Good lad, that's the attitude." Oliver moved aside and helped Tom into position. "Just take your time and be careful."

"I'll go next," Sarah offered.

Grabbing the copper pipe, Tom climbed on and started downward, methodically choosing each handgrip as he positioned his feet on something sturdy below.

When he was halfway down, Sarah followed, copying his actions. The added weight caused the downspout to creak and loosen.

"Perhaps this isn't such a good idea," Oliver whispered down to them, searching for an alternative option.

"Now is not the time to be telling us that," Sarah grumbled under her breath.

"I'm not climbing back up," Tom protested, almost at the next floor down.

"Understood, just keep moving," Oliver murmured.

Hand under hand, they gradually descended and reached the next level, carefully balancing on the ledge.

"All right, Oliver, it's your turn," Tom called up as he grabbed the pipe to stabilize it.

With cat-like agility, Oliver effortlessly descended to the fourth floor, then glanced below at the street and reevaluated his plan.

"This is going to take too long," he realized. "I've got a better idea."

Scanning the windows, he did a mental count and promptly moved to the third one.

"Let's try this," Oliver suggested, delicately tapping the glass.

A minute later, it popped open.

"Oliver? What're you doing out there?" a young man with an Austrian accent inquired, shocked yet not surprised.

"Good morning, Bernard," Oliver replied as casually as possible. "We seem to be in a jam. Might we come through your living room and exit by your door?"

"Be my guest." Bernard laughed, moving away from the opening.

"Excellent, truly obliged." Oliver nodded.

Glancing out from the window above, the Italian spotted all three of them. "They're on the ledge below," he yelled to the Romanian. "Get downstairs and cover the main entrance. I'll head to the fourth floor."

"We need to go," Oliver urged, motioning Tom and Sarah through the opening.

"You owe me big-time," Bernard stressed in his baritone voice, his brows furrowed.

"Yes, I do." Oliver chuckled halfheartedly, embarrassed.

All three entered the apartment, continued to front door, and rushed down the back stairwell.

"Who was that guy?" Tom asked, amazed by their good fortune.

"He's an ambassador's son. He works at the Austrian consulate," Oliver replied.

"More importantly, who are those men in your apartment?" Sarah asked anxiously.

"No idea," Oliver admitted, feeling a growing sense of tension. "Being a prime minister's son, I'm usually well protected. Whoever they work for, I don't think it's the French government."

While Marcel waited in a van parked around the corner, Tom, Sarah, and Oliver snuck along a side street to Rue Auber, a congested boulevard buzzing with morning activity. Vehicles zipped back and forth as pedestrians raced to work.

Suddenly, the two men appeared at the end of the block.

"We better move fast," Sarah exclaimed, pointing behind them.

"Follow me," Oliver yelled, searching for an opening in the traffic.

They dashed across the street, weaving in and out between the cars. Brakes were slammed, horns were honked, and obscene gestures made.

Seeing them reappear on the other side, both men broke into a run. As the Romanian charged between the vehicles, he was hit by a Fiat sedan, rolled off the hood, and slammed onto the pavement. Incapacitated, he waved the Italian on.

"Just get them!" he shouted, clutching his side and trying to stand.

Oliver, Tom, and Sarah walked quickly along the sidewalk, pushing through the dense crowd. The Italian was close behind.

* * * * *

Fontaine pulled up to 33 Rue de Caumartin and surveyed the neighborhood. She checked her weapon and exited her vehicle.

Concealed in the van, Marcel watched her march to the front entrance. Once she entered the building, he followed.

Fontaine flashed the doorman her badge and took the elevator to the fifth floor. As she approached suite 513, Fontaine noticed the damaged door hanging loosely on its hinges. She immediately pulled out her Glock 9mm and cautiously proceeded.

"Oliver," she hollered. "Oliver Horningbrook, are you in there?"

Hidden behind the wall, Fontaine peeked inside, advancing slowly with her weapon held in front. She skillfully maneuvered through the space, thoroughly searching each area.

After confirming the apartment was empty, Fontaine walked back into the main room and glanced out the window. From the corner of her eye, she saw a man standing at the doorway. He fired two shots.

Fontaine jerked backward as the bullets grazed her jacket and shattered one of the windows. She crashed into a mahogany armoire, then fell to the floor, twisting around and unloading half a magazine toward him.

Marcel threw himself on the ground, stunned by the rapid response. Bullets sprayed the wall and entryway, splintering the door casing and pulverizing the plaster. Traces of smoke and the smell of gunpowder filled the room.

Uninjured, Marcel jumped to his feet and bolted down the hallway. Fontaine swiftly recovered and chased after him.

Marcel moved from doorway to doorway, firing sporadically. A barrage of bullets whizzed back and forth, peppering the corridor and shattering light fixtures. Both stood their ground, exchanging rounds.

Marcel fired again and ran down a staircase.

* * * * *

He's gaining on us!" Tom yelled, looking over his shoulder at the man chasing them.

Frantically searching for a safe place to hide, Oliver recognized the Hotel Pierre.

"Let's go inside," he suggested, ducking into a revolving door with Tom trailing behind.

Sarah was halfway through when a hand clutched her shoulder.

"You're not going anywhere," the Italian fumed, his beady eyes glaring at her.

Frightened, Sarah mouthed to the others for help, pounding on the glass.

Now inside, Oliver and Tom grabbed one of the louvers and yanked the door, slamming the man's arm. He groaned in agony yet maintained his grip on Sarah.

Oliver gave the door another swift tug, decisively whacking the man in the face and crushing his arm. The man let go and dropped to his knees, his nose bleeding. Sarah quickly emerged from the door.

"Thanks," she gasped, rubbing her shoulder.

"You okay?" Oliver checked.

"I'm fine," Sarah nodded, rattled by the encounter.

"Let's get out of the lobby and find somewhere to hide," Oliver urged them.

They raced to the staircase and swiftly mounted the steps. Reaching each floor, they tried a variety of doors, but everything was locked. With nowhere else to go, they continued up the stairs until they reached the tenth floor. Exhausted, they stopped to catch their breath.

"We are on the last floor," Tom griped. "Where do we go now?"

"Should we go down in the elevator?" Sarah asked, feeling trapped in the hallway.

"Someone might be watching the lobby," Oliver cautioned. "We could walk into an ambush."

"What about the roof?" Tom proposed, motioning toward the door.

Reluctant, Oliver agreed. "It looks like our only option."

They hurried through the exit and onto a small deck, Paris glistening through the morning haze. Surrounding them was a complex jungle of interconnecting rooftops, copper valleys, stone chimneys, and glass skylights—a deadly obstacle course suspended over the city.

Sarah glanced back and forth, contemplating the terrifying choices.

"Which direction?" she asked, unnerved.

"I have no idea." Oliver shrugged. "Let's pick the least dangerous."

"It all looks dangerous," Tom muttered.

As if he were playing an intricate game of chess, Oliver skillfully evaluated the different options and chose the best route.

"Follow me and proceed with caution."

Each of their steps was carefully planned. They gripped anything available and balanced as well as they could.

They warily climbed over a steep roof peek and slid down a metal slope until reaching a flat area. They progressed along a narrow catwalk, ducked under a railing, and navigated around a variety of deteriorating chimneys and smokestacks until they reached a precarious section covered in tile.

"You know this outfit isn't the best for climbing," Sarah commented, tugging her blouse free from an exhaust pipe.

"If we make it to safety, I'll buy you a new one," Oliver promised.

"Did you say *if*?"

Scrambling over a brick firewall, Tom lost his footing on the wet surface and landed on his back. When he tried to stand, his feet gave way, and he was whisked down a copper valley. He flailed his arms as he tried to grab onto something, but the slick surface only increased his speed.

"Help," he cried out, trying to stop his slide.

"Tom?!" Oliver shouted as Tom vanished into the skyline.

"Do something," Sarah exclaimed, watching in horror.

"Like what?" Oliver felt powerless.

"I . . . I don't know."

As Tom sped toward the roof's edge, all he could see was the horrifying drop below.

"Don't let me die," he prayed aloud, closing his eyes and waiting for the impact.

The roof began to level out, slowing his pace before he slammed into a metal guardrail, making a deafening thud. Disoriented, Tom rubbed his throbbing arms and examined his body for injuries.

While Oliver and Sarah searched for him, Tom peeked over the edge at the sidewalk a hundred feet below.

"Thank you, God," he whispered under his breath, exhaling deeply.

"Where are you?" Oliver shouted.

"I'm down here," Tom grumbled, now covered in soot.

"Are you okay? Can you make it back up here?"

"I think so."

"O-Oliver," Sarah stammered, frozen in place on a massive skylight.

Oliver turned, his eyes widening. The glass began to crack, creating popping noises and splintering like a spider web.

"Don't move an inch," he warned her.

"I-I won't," Sarah murmured, paralyzed.

Oliver slowly approached, securing his footing near the edge. "Take my hand," he said anxiously, extending his arm.

Sarah reached out and grabbed hold just as the skylight collapsed, her legs dangling. Oliver yanked her from the opening, debris tumbling into the apartment below.

Sarah stared at him, white-faced. "That was close," she whispered.

"Too close," Oliver gasped, gently setting her down and wiping the sweat from his forehead.

Meanwhile, Tom painstakingly worked his way up the roof to where they stood.

"I see Sarah found a skylight," Tom mused under his breath.

She stared at him, tight-lipped. "I almost fell in."

"Almost," he grinned.

Suddenly, a bullet whizzed by and ricocheted off a nearby chimney, barely missing Tom. Instinctively, all three dropped to the ground and crawled behind a stone firewall.

"Jeez, these guys are serious," Oliver vented. "This is what you've been going through?"

"Yep," Tom answered gravely.

"You didn't tell me about the gunfire."

"We sort of left that part out," Sarah confessed.

"If my father is involved with these people, why are they shooting at *me*?"

"They're not," Tom explained. "They're trying to hit us."

* * * * *

Fontaine chased the man down the stairwell, leaping several steps at a time.

He ran out the front entrance, fired a few shots at her vehicle, then jumped into his van and sped away. By the time Fontaine aimed her gun, he was gone.

"Blast it," she cursed, lowering her weapon.

She then turned to her Mini, noticing the flat tires.

"Perfect. No one carries two spares."

A few minutes later, Gustave parked his black Porsche 911 and rushed over. "What happened?" he asked, a troubled expression on his face.

"I saw the man who is after Tom and Sarah," Fontaine replied, her temper boiling. "He shot at me."

"I can see that," Gustave acknowledged, gesturing to her jacket.

"I'm fine, the bullets just grazed me," she said dismissively.

"You could have been killed," he stated. "You should have waited until I got here."

"There wasn't time."

Gustave shook his head. "I'm your partner," he asserted. "We work together. That's why you call for backup."

"You're right," Fontaine agreed, relenting. "I should've waited."

"Where's he now?" Gustave asked, scanning the area.

"Long gone, headed east."

"Did you get a good look at him?"

"Not really," she replied, agitated. "Nothing we didn't already know."

"Tom and Sarah?"

"Missing."

"And Oliver?"

"Probably with them."

"How do you know?" Gustave questioned, trying to follow her analysis.

"Because the killer wouldn't waste time shooting at me if he already had the children," Fontaine reasoned.

"Maybe *you're* a target."

The comment unsettled her. "Maybe."

"We should report this to the chief," Gustave advised. "We need his help."

"I'm not sure that's a good idea," Fontaine said, shaking her head.

"Why not? It's standard procedure."

Fontaine walked closer, her voice serious. "Because I think Interpol is compromised."

"Compromised how?" Gustave asked bluntly, surprised by her remark.

"Someone there is working against us."

"What makes you so sure?"

"I've had my suspicions for a while," Fontaine revealed. "Like the way this case is going—it's clear someone's undermining it."

"It's possible," Gustave considered. "Do you have any proof?"

"Well, they shut off my phone and access codes," she declared. "How much more proof do you want?"

"Did you check on it?"

"Yes," Fontaine replied, annoyed. "They're supposedly investigating it."

"There have been some irregularities, I'll give you that," Gustave agreed. "When I checked some of the other building's security cameras around Notre-Dame, sections of footage were missing. Then I ran the plate from the van by the Eiffel Tower, but nothing came back in our system."

"Gowerstone warned me not to trust anybody. I just didn't think he meant my own department."

Fontaine gave Gustave a grave look. "We must keep this quiet for now," she insisted, gauging his reaction.

"Are you asking me to disobey Interpol?"

"No, of course not, at least not completely," Fontaine replied. "We just can't do everything by the rules, not until I find out more."

"You'll need to report in at some time."

"I know—I'm just not sure who's involved, and who I can trust."

Gustave rubbed his head, uncertain how to proceed.

"I know this is difficult," she sympathized. "I understand if you can't help."

"I didn't say I wouldn't help," Gustave conceded, aware that both their careers were at risk. "We'll play by your rules, at least for now."

"You're a good man, Gustave." Fontaine smiled.

"What do you want me to do?"

"I need you to drive in an eight-block radius and see if you can locate Tom, Sarah, and Oliver," Fontaine instructed. "Ask around and interview the neighbors. Someone must've seen something."

"What about you?"

"I'll search the area on foot and question the doorman." She wrote on a card and handed it to him. "This is my new cell number. Don't share it with anyone."

*****

"We need a plan," Tom whispered, glued to the wall as another bullet whizzed by.

"Like not getting shot," Sarah said dryly, huddled next to him.

"That goes without saying," Tom grumbled. "I mean, how do we get off this roof?"

Oliver carefully glanced over the top, searching for the gunman. "We obviously can't go back the way we came."

"What about over there?" Sarah pointed at a fire escape ladder about seventy feet away.

"That could work, if we could get to it," Oliver agreed. He peeked over the top again.

"I've got an idea," Oliver began, taking a deep breath. "Wait for my signal, then run as fast as you can. Once you get to the ladder, climb down until you reach the bottom."

"What about you?" Tom asked, puzzled.

"I'll be right behind, but he's not likely to shoot me, given my father's connections," Oliver presumed, hoping he was right.

"That's a heck of a risk," Tom stated, stunned by his bravery.

"And one I'm willing to take."

Sarah's eyes brightened, and Tom nodded.

"Keep your head down and run when I say," Oliver told them as he steadied his nerves. Tom and Sarah crouched by the wall, waiting for his cue.

A few minutes that felt like an hour passed. Oliver slowly peeked over the edge again. The gunman was preoccupied, struggling over a rooftop while trying to get closer.

"All right, go," Oliver whispered loudly.

Running flat-out, Tom and Sarah bolted for the fire escape with Oliver two steps behind. They slid to the rusty railing and hastily clambered down one by one until they reached a deserted alleyway.

By the time the Italian looked over, they had vanished.

* * * * *

Twenty minutes later, Oliver, Tom, and Sarah sat in a café, guzzling water and devouring croissants. They had cleaned up in the restrooms, washing their hands and faces and wiping the dust and soot off their clothing as best they could.

As Sarah sipped her water, she noticed Oliver's expression, his eyes distant. "Are you okay?" she asked.

"Yeah, it's just a lot to take in," Oliver admitted, overwhelmed. "Finding out that my father is corrupt, being chased from my apartment, and getting shot at—all in less than twelve hours."

"Welcome to our world," Tom declared, an exasperated look on his face.

"How did they know you were staying with me?" Oliver questioned, still shocked by the encounter with the gunmen. "It's barely been one day since we met at the Eiffel Tower."

"These are powerful people who seem to know everything," Sarah said through a mouthful of croissant. "They're always one step ahead of us."

"I'm beginning to see that," Oliver realized, trying to understand who they were up against.

"This is what we've been going through. No matter where we go, they seem to find us," Tom added in a frustrated tone.

"Knowing my father and how ruthless politicians are, I can only imagine what a threat Tom and the Britfield Dynasty would be to the balance of power," Oliver concluded, comprehending their dilemma.

"If you don't want to continue, we understand," Sarah said. "We don't have a choice, but you do."

Oliver leaned back and laughed; his mood lighter. "Just when things get exciting, you want to get rid of me."

"No, we just—"

"Don't worry; we're all a part of this now," Oliver confirmed his allegiance. "I'm with you until the end. Let's find what you need and get to Chambord."

"And your father?" Sarah asked, knowing it was a delicate issue.

"I'll deal with him later."

"Are you sure? I have a feeling it's only going to get worse," she projected. "The more we uncover, the more dangerous our situation becomes."

"Then we'll get through it together," Oliver said with a grin.

Tom and Sarah were relieved. Having Oliver's help was crucial at this point.

"What's next?" Oliver asked.

Sarah began reviewing what they knew, skeptical about their plan to get into the Louvre. "If they found Oliver's apartment, it means they're after all of us."

"What's your point?" Tom prodded.

"They'll know everything about him and that he works at the Louvre."

"But I'm not scheduled to work until tomorrow," Oliver interjected. "They wouldn't be looking for me today."

"It's still risky," Sarah warned.

"But you need that information. If we can get into the private area, I think we'll find what you're looking for," Oliver assured them, undaunted.

Sarah turned to Tom. "What do you think?"

"It's worth the risk," Tom agreed.

"Then it's settled," Sarah concluded, rising from her chair.

"We should wait until this afternoon, when the Louvre is busy," Oliver suggested. "More people, more confusion—it's easier to hide in a crowd."

7
THE HIDDEN CODEX

By 2:00 p.m., Tom, Sarah, and Oliver were standing outside the Louvre. It was an imposing structure; Tom felt as if they were about to trespass on an imperial fortress.

The four-story, weathered sandstone bastion was U-shaped, with the entrance in the center. An eleven-foot-high archway covered the first floor, capped by two stories of leaded-glass windows and a slate roof with granite chimneys. Every eighty feet a square tower with a mansard rooftop hovered over the main structure.

Originally constructed around 1190 as a citadel to protect Paris from Viking raids, King François I transformed the building into a Renaissance palace in the 1540s. During the French Revolution, the National Assembly decreed that the Louvre should be used as a museum, and it was officially opened to the public on August 10, 1793. Thirty-five thousand objects that dated from prehistory to the twenty-first century were on display in 650,000 square feet of galleries.

Entering the property, a pea gravel promenade led to the Arc de Triomphe du Carrousel, a sixty-three-foot-high monument celebrating Napoleon's 1805 military victories. It was topped by a bronze sculpture of *Peace Riding in a Triumphal Chariot*.

As Tom, Sarah, and Oliver continued toward the main entrance, they crossed over a brick esplanade until they reached architect I. M. Pei's glass and metal pyramid, a modern triangular skylight that allowed sunlight to reach below ground level. It is surrounded by a shimmering reflecting pool and playful fountains.

The atmosphere was a synthesis of international cultures, clothing, and languages blended in a noisy, colorful tapestry in and around the museum's entrance. Students, families, and tourists converged on the museum, eager to glimpse the priceless masterpieces and rare artifacts on display.

While Tom and Sarah surveyed the awe-inspiring architecture, Oliver waited in a snakelike queue to buy tickets.

"One student and two children," he told the female attendant, handing her his credit card.

"Is that you, Oliver?" she asked, pleasantly surprised.

"Oh, hello, Dominique," he replied fondly. "I didn't recognize you."

"Not working today?"

"Nope, just a tourist."

"Put your credit card away. You're covered," Dominique insisted, giving him a flirtatious smile. "We have to take care of our own, right?"

"Right," Oliver agreed.

"Here are three VIP passes. That'll get you into all the good exhibits."

"Cheers," he said appreciatively.

Oliver handed the tickets to Tom and Sarah and whispered, "We should probably look around for a while before we make our way to the private section."

"I don't mind." Sarah was ready to explore everything.

"I'm game," Tom agreed, curious what all the fuss was about.

"Then prepare yourselves for a carnival of objects, priceless artifacts, and spectacular paintings," Oliver enticed them.

They entered through a revolving door and descended a curved staircase, the glass pyramid soaring above.

"Where should we start?" Sarah wondered, simmering with anticipation.

"What would you like to see?" Oliver asked. "The collection is divided into different sections, such as Egyptian and Eastern antiquities, Greek and Roman, sculpture, paintings."

"Let's start with the paintings," Sarah said.

"How about the Italian section?" Oliver suggested. "There's one masterpiece I'm sure you'll enjoy."

Sarah's eyes widened as if she were about to open an enormous present.

They walked through connecting hallways and entered a room with a dazzling barrel-vaulted ceiling, a mosaic marble floor, and a variety of paintings filling the walls.

Tom spun around, viewing the pictures. It was a kaleidoscope of colors, shapes, and styles. "This is pretty cool," Tom confessed, enjoying the vivid realism captured by the artists.

"See, I told you art isn't that bad," Sarah murmured under her breath.

Oliver motioned them to a small painting of a half-smiling woman, protected by bulletproof glass. A group of people crowded around the object.

"This is Leonardo da Vinci's *Mona Lisa*," Oliver stated proudly.

"I've always wanted to see this," Sarah expressed, standing by the world's most famous painting.

"This?" Tom questioned, unimpressed.

"Yes, this." Sarah stood transfixed, gazing at the object. "It's amazing, simple yet mysterious."

"Hmm." Tom frowned. "It's just a small picture of some woman."

"Is that all you see?"

"Yep."

"Study it for a minute," she encouraged him. "Look at the technique Leonardo used with the light and shading, how real her eyes appear, her smile. Is she happy or sad?"

Tom leaned in closer and stared.

"Back away from the painting," a guard chastised him, then marched over. "And stand behind the line."

"Right," Oliver interjected, remembering the protocols. "You need to keep a distance."

"What line?" Tom questioned, perturbed by the guard's rudeness.

"In every room, each floor has a border that runs around it, three feet from the wall. Just stay behind that."

"Well?" Sarah continued, nudging him on. "What do you think?"

Tom looked again, straining his eyes. "I just don't see what all the excitement is about."

"I give up," Sarah sighed, throwing up her arms.

"It's okay, Tom," Oliver said understandingly. "There's much more to look at."

As they walked through the different rooms, Oliver played the perfect guide, offering insightful commentary on everything they saw.

Each space was its own tour de force. One room was washed in a tranquil blue with Greek statues and lavishly framed Dutch paintings by artists such as Rembrandt and Vermeer. The next section had a domed ceiling with Italian murals and paintings by Botticelli, Michelangelo, and Raphael. Another area was designed like an imperial ballroom with gilded moldings, a mahogany floor, and a glass ceiling that flooded the room with sunlight. Every imaginable era was meticulously represented: Greek and Roman, Middle Ages, Renaissance, Classical, Impressionist, and Modern.

Although Tom knew little about art, he appreciated beauty and couldn't help but be transported by the exquisite colors and images. He was inspired by David's heroic *Oath of the Horatii*, encouraged by the patriotism of Delacroix's *Liberty Leading the People*, stirred by Rembrandt's *Jeremiah Lamenting the Destruction of Jerusalem*, and intrigued by Caravaggio's *The Conversion of St. Paul*. For a brief moment, he had forgotten his problems and was able to enjoy all the grandeur and splendor the art had to offer.

Sarah was elated. She closely studied each painting and object. Entering the sculpture section, she examined every curve of the life-size marble statues, bronze busts, and golden figurines. She was captivated by

Antonio Canova's romantic *Psyche Revived by Cupid's Kiss*, transported in time by the *Venus de Milo*, intrigued by Michelangelo's eerie depiction of the *Slave*, and left speechless by the *Nike of Samothrace*.

"What do you guys think so far?" Oliver asked keenly.

"Brilliant," Tom replied, impressed.

"It's wonderful," Sarah announced with delight.

After a few hours in the galleries and a quick lunch in the cafeteria, they headed down four flights of stairs, where some of the twelfth-century foundations were preserved.

"The private area is down this corridor," Oliver said quietly. "It's watched by cameras and always guarded, so follow my lead."

Tom and Sarah nodded, wondering what they'd gotten themselves into.

Now deep underground, they entered a hallway where signs read "Restricted Area." The illuminated corridor was about a hundred feet long and had surveillance cameras strategically placed. At the end, an older, heavyset guard stood by a vault door and a young guard sat at a desk, monitoring computer screens.

As Oliver, Tom, and Sarah approached, the heavyset guard spoke to his younger colleague. "I'm going to grab something to drink. You want anything?"

"Coffee, black."

"You got it. I'll be back in a few minutes." The heavyset guard walked by and continued down the hallway.

Oliver confidently approached the desk. "Good afternoon," Oliver said politely. "I would like to—"

"This area is restricted," the young guard stated venomously. "Turn around and go back the way you came, or you'll be escorted out of the museum."

* * * * *

Mid-afternoon, Gustave met Fontaine on Rue Daunou in the Opera Quarter, a few miles from 33 Rue de Caumartin.

"I've searched every street and boulevard in an eight-block radius, but I didn't see them," Gustave reported, discouraged.

"After questioning some of the local shop owners, I spoke with the doorman," Fontaine began. "He said two men dressed in suits and presenting government identification showed up around 6:00 a.m. They then proceeded to Oliver's flat."

"Since when do government officials start work so early?" Gustave questioned.

"That's what I thought. It sounds like an extraction."

"Any idea what branch or section?"

"No, but everything was logged in at the front desk of Oliver's apartment complex, so I have copies of their identification and photos," Fontaine replied, handing him the pictures.

"That's a bit careless, don't you think?"

"Or just overconfident—maybe they think they're untouchable."

"This is getting stranger by the minute," Gustave mumbled, perusing the information. "I'll see what I can find out. Anything else?"

"There was an accident two blocks from the apartment. A man in a suit was struck by a car, but he got up and ran away."

"It was probably one of the men chasing them," Gustave reasoned. "Do you know what direction Tom and Sarah went?"

"They disappeared into the Hotel Pierre," Fontaine replied, noticing that Gustave seemed preoccupied. "What is it?"

"The chief called earlier—he wants me to bring you in," Gustave informed her. "He says you've gone rogue."

"Rogue," Fontaine repeated indignantly. "That's absurd."

"I know, but he wants to question you."

"About what?"

"He didn't say."

"Typical," Fontaine scoffed, disgusted. "Our case has been compromised, and now I'm a suspect."

"You have to go in at some point," Gustave continued. "In the next twenty-four hours, it'll be *you* the police are searching for."

"We need to buy some time," Fontaine said. "Tell the chief I'll be in later, but for now, let's find Tom, Sarah and Oliver."

Fontaine paced back and forth, meticulously analyzing the facts and trying to predict what was going to happen next.

"If Tom and Sarah haven't been caught, where would they go?" she thought aloud.

"They can't go back to the apartment," Gustave

speculated. "And as far as we know, they have no other contacts in Paris."

"*I* was their contact," Fontaine said, dispirited.

"I can put a trace on Oliver's credit cards," Gustave suggested. "If he uses any of them, we'll have a location."

"Also, get a couple of agents to watch the Louvre. I doubt he'll show up, but it's worth a try."

"I know a few officers we can trust," Gustave said. "They're reliable and will report only to me."

"The best thing we can do right now is research. See if Oliver has any relations in Paris—friends, schoolmates, girlfriends, relatives, aunts, uncles," Fontaine rattled off. "Then extend your search across France. Affluent people always have connections."

"I'll let you know what I find and call you later."

* * * * *

Oliver was taken aback by the abrupt reply, but he kept his composure. "My good man, I work here," he said coolly.

"It doesn't matter," snapped the young guard, abrasive.

"Just so we're clear, I'm Oliver Horningbrook," he trumpeted, presenting his identification. "My dad had shown me this section before, and I need to go in for a few minutes."

"Yes, I'm familiar with your father," he gulped, his voice softening. The guard keyed in the data while staring at Oliver.

"Mr. Horningbrook, I see your father's name on the list but not yours."

Oliver leaned over and whispered, "I'm giving a private tour to a British ambassador's kids as a favor to my father. Do you believe that, on my day off?"

"This is an ultra-restricted area. I could get into real trouble."

"Look, we'll just be a few minutes," Oliver said smoothly. "I need to make a good impression, if you know what I mean."

Oliver slowly removed a hundred-euro bill from his wallet and stealthily slipped it into the man's hand.

"Can you help me out?" Oliver asked with a wink. "If you know who my father is, you know I'm well connected and can always return a favor."

The young guard hesitated for a moment but quickly relaxed. "I suppose a few minutes wouldn't hurt. Just be quick, and don't touch anything."

"We'll be back in a flash."

"You better, or we're both in trouble."

Pushing a button, the young guard released the door's locking system, creating an orchestra of sounds.

"Just stay in the front rooms where some of the newly acquired objects are," the young guard ordered. "The kids will enjoy looking at the rare pieces."

"Sure," Oliver nodded, smiling.

Oliver opened the thick metal door and escorted Tom and Sarah into the first room.

The entire area was chic and modern, with stainless steel walls, plasma screens, and computer terminals offering virtual reality viewing and 3D holograms of artifacts displayed in midair. It seemed more like a futuristic space station than a museum archive.

They continued to a glass door that opened automatically as they approached and slid shut behind them.

"How did you know he'd let us in?" Sarah asked, her voice dropping to a murmur.

"I didn't," Oliver confessed, a slight trace of perspiration on his forehead.

"I don't like being watched." Tom glanced at one of the security cameras.

"Don't worry," Oliver conveyed in a whisper. "The private area where we're headed doesn't have any cameras."

"Why not?"

"Too many important people looking at things no one knows exist."

Following Oliver, they quickly moved through a few rooms, down a set of stairs, and into an enormous library. The area had endless rows of glass-covered shelves filled with leather books of varying sizes and colors.

"What is this?" Sarah asked, admiring the displays.

"First edition books, the original copies," Oliver replied.

"Can we look—just for a minute?" she inquired eagerly.

"I take it you like to read?" he asked, recognizing a fellow bookworm.

"That's all we did at Weatherly," Sarah reflected soberly.

"The orphanage had a library?" Oliver questioned, surprised.

"Only the books we took from the Grievouses' house," Sarah answered.

"You mean *borrowed*." Tom was quick to correct her.

"Yes, of course, borrowed," she restated.

"I see." Oliver chuckled. "I suppose we could look for a few seconds."

He removed a pair of white gloves from a nearby container, slipped them over his hands, and lifted the protective glass, delicately picking up a book.

"This is a first edition of Victor Hugo's *Les Misérables*."

"I love that story," Sarah remarked, hastily putting on some gloves. "Jean Valjean is one of my favorite characters."

"And this is Victor Hugo's original manuscript," Oliver continued, gently removing the document. "You can see his personal notes in the margins."

"That's so cool," she whispered.

Tom hurriedly put on a pair of gloves so as not be left out. He searched the books until he recognized a title.

"Over here, *The Count of Monte Cristo*," Tom said animatedly. "One of the best books I've ever read."

"Epic story," Sarah agreed. "Well chosen, Tom."

"And perhaps a fitting narrative," Oliver indicated, "given that you were falsely condemned to a prison, or in your case an orphanage, and have now escaped to reclaim justice."

"I've never thought about it that way," Tom admitted, pondering the similarity. "I like that version of events."

They spent a few minutes perusing the list of French authors: Honoré de Balzac, Alexandre Dumas, Gustave Flaubert, Marcel Proust, Jean-Jacques Rousseau, Voltaire. Then they moved onto playwrights: Descartes, Molière, and Jean Racine. It was a treasure of some of the finest stories ever written.

"This is just the French section," Oliver informed them. "There are books and manuscripts from around the world—even an original Gutenberg Bible, and works by Aristotle and Virgil."

"Shouldn't we be looking for something about the Britfields?" Tom reminded them, quickly tiring of the literary distraction.

"Yes, let's be about our business," Oliver agreed, hastening on to the next section.

All three continued through a maze of offices, storage vaults, and restoration rooms until they came to an isolated hallway.

"This looks familiar," Oliver remembered, trying to recall where his father had taken him.

"What happens if we get caught?" Tom wondered aloud, the idea suddenly becoming more real.

"Let's not think about it," Oliver stressed.

They continued down the hallway until they noticed a distinctive door. It had Latin lettering around the frame, a keypad, and two enormous deadbolts. Oliver stood with a vacant look in his eyes.

"That's going to be a problem," he mumbled, dismayed. "My father had the key."

"Which you don't have?" Tom said in a deflated voice.

"No, I don't," Oliver replied, flustered. "Although I do remember the keypad combination from watching my father. It's my mother's birthday. I can get us that far."

Oliver punched in the combination, deactivating the alarm and other internal locks.

Tom turned to Sarah. "Do you mind?"

"I'll take a crack at it," she responded deviously.

"Really?" Oliver questioned, intrigued by Sarah's clandestine skills.

"Two years at an orphanage, and you learn a few things," Sarah said coolly, removing two clips from her hair.

"Just give her a minute. She's a natural," Tom affirmed.

"Hmm," Sarah murmured, carefully studying the locks.

She wiggled the clips around, working them back and forth until she had opened them both.

"Extraordinary," Oliver expressed as he opened the door.

When they entered the room, it had an eerie atmosphere, as if an unnatural presence lingered in the air. Although spacious, the room was cold and dimly lit. The floor was covered with oriental carpets woven with pictures of Egyptian pyramids and strange symbols. The thirteen-foot walls were decorated with abstract paintings and mounted heads of wild animals. There were life-size Roman statues, medieval weapons, and antique torture devices. In the middle, rawhide couches were arranged in a circle. A nine-foot, eleven-inch-high golden sculpture of the Tower of Babel stood in the center.

Sarah clasped Tom's hand, her arm trembling slightly.

"Okay, now I'm freaked out," she confessed, expression blank, mouth open.

"Is it just me or does this place give you the creeps?" Tom asked as an oppressive feeling overcame him.

"It's a bit weird, isn't it?" Oliver agreed, recalling his earlier visit.

"What kind of people come here?" Tom questioned, examining the disturbing surroundings.

"People like my father," Oliver replied uncomfortably. Oliver stepped forward and turned on some more lights. "We've come this far. Let's check it out," he encouraged.

Tom and Sarah timidly nodded, their mood altered.

Oliver shut the door, and all three moved toward a set of mahogany bookshelves. There were round tables draped in burgundy tablecloths, carved wooden chairs, and antique reading lamps.

"How much time do we have?" Sarah asked tentatively.

"None, so let's move quickly," Oliver responded. "Look for anything that says Britfield."

They split up and rummaged through all types of books and manuscripts, climbing up the shelves and searching through antique cabinets. They discovered strange artifacts, Latin books on alchemy, Greek manuscripts on occultism, and Hebrew texts on esoteric beliefs.

Ten minutes later, Tom discovered a large chest tucked in one of the corners. It was covered with a beautiful purple cloth that had fine stitching along the outer rim. He removed the covering, revealing a golden crest and a crimson *B* on the front.

"This looks promising," Tom announced, pointing at the large *B*.

Oliver hurried over and was joined by Sarah.

Tom knelt to investigate: The chest had a worn leather surface and tarnished brass clips. Parts of the outside were tattered and frayed. Within the letter *B* was a keyhole.

When Tom tried to lift the cover, it wouldn't budge. "Would you mind?" he asked, glancing up at Sarah.

"Not at all," she said smoothly, leaning down and working the lock with a hair clip until it clicked.

"She's *definitely* a natural," Oliver emphasized approvingly, marveling at her expertise.

Tom gave her a gentle nod and opened the lid. The interior was lined with purple silk and contained stacks of ancient books, maps, and manuscripts. On the front of each document was an embossed *Britfield*. Tom stared in disbelief.

"Goldmine," Sarah gasped, her eyes wide.

Just as Oliver reached for one of the texts, they heard the scuffling of footsteps from the outside hallway.

"Someone's coming," Oliver exclaimed, shutting the lid.

Oliver desperately searched the room while Tom and Sarah clumsily threw the purple cloth back over the chest.

"What should we do?" Tom asked, scanning for a place to hide.

"Climb under one of the tables," Oliver motioned. "I've got an idea."

* * * * *

Marcel anxiously waited on a quiet street by the Left Bank, his immense confidence shattered.

A black town car with diplomatic plates and tinted windows drove up. Marcel approached the vehicle as the back window lowered a few inches.

"The children escaped, and Inspector Fontaine found

Oliver's apartment," Marcel timidly informed the older man in the car, his face scarcely visible.

"We know," the older man stated, his voice contemptuous.

"I tried to contact the extraction team, but I couldn't locate them."

"They've been taken care of."

"Reassigned?"

"Eliminated."

Marcel paused, the last comment resonating. "I see."

"Do you?" the older man asked, incensed. "Perhaps now you know how we reward failure and that your future is depending on this."

Marcel swallowed hard, bowing his head in shame. "I completely understand."

"You're supposed to be one of our best assassins. Should we hire someone else and dispose of you?"

"No," Marcel responded quickly. "I'll take care of everything."

"This is your last chance. They are just children—get rid of them."

"Yes, sir," Marcel answered obediently.

"And terminate that meddlesome inspector," the older man instructed. "Just make sure it looks like an accident."

* * * * *

Shoving through the door, a husky guard marched into the private room. Oliver sat calmly at one of the tables draped in a burgundy cloth. Tom and Sarah hid underneath, motionless.

"I heard voices," said the guard sharply, scouting around.

"It's just me," Oliver conveyed, casually reading a book. "I tend to talk to myself. It's a bad habit I picked up at Oxford."

"What are you doing in here?"

"Research."

"I can see that," the guard sneered irritably as he walked closer. "But this room is restricted."

Oliver chuckled. "It might be restricted to others," he stated confidently. "But I'm Oliver Horningbrook. My father is—"

"I know who your father is," the guard squawked. "He also knows the proper protocol and should have called ahead to set up a visit."

"That's been taken care of."

The guard glared at Oliver, searching for signs of deception, one hand firmly on his weapon.

"How did you get into this room?" the guard asked suspiciously.

"It was unlocked."

"I doubt that," he countered.

"I've been in here before. You can check at the front desk," Oliver challenged him. "It was called in and approved."

"We'll see about that. Wait here and don't move," the guard told him, then swaggered out the doorway.

Oliver rushed to the door and shut it, latching both locks, along with separate bolts on the top and the bottom on the inside of the door.

"Okay, guys, we've got to move fast," Oliver voiced under the table as Tom and Sarah reemerged, hearts pounding.

"I have a feeling we're in real trouble," Tom murmured.

"Just stay calm," Oliver rallied. "I got you into this, and I'll get you out of it."

"But there's only one exit," Sarah observed, curious how he was planning their miraculous escape.

"Not necessarily," Oliver hinted. "There may be another way out, but let's first see what's in the chest."

Encouraged by his tenacity, Tom and Sarah returned to the chest and opened the lid. Oliver rummaged through several texts until he grabbed a heavy, thick book with the words *Britfield Codex* etched on the front. The precious treasure was encased in silver and had two leather straps securing it.

Oliver unlatched the leather bindings and gently opened it. The first date he saw was AD 1066 on an old map of England. As he delicately turned the pages, Tom and Sarah looked on, transfixed.

"I don't understand any of it," Tom said.

"Languages are definitely not my specialty," Oliver confessed, knowing he was beyond his depth.

"Most of it's in Latin or Old English," Sarah clarified, squinting as she tried to read the words. "From what I can make out, it seems to be the history of England."

They continued flipping through an assortment of documents, signed agreements, and territorial maps.

"Look at this, the English royal lineage, with Britfield at the top, followed by names and royal titles," Oliver said excitedly, skimming down one of the pages.

"What does all of this mean?" Tom asked, intrigued.

"I'm no expert, but it seems to confirm the Britfields' rightful claim to the British throne, including the distribution of land and estates," Sarah replied, her mood ecstatic.

They turned to another page that displayed the topography of England, Wales, and Scotland.

Oliver leaned back, amazed. "This shows the entire British continent and Britfield is written all over it," he stated, staggered by the implications.

"That's a lot of land," Sarah gasped.

"Can you imagine the wealth?"

They kept skimming through until they reached the final page.

"It ends in 1837," Tom sighed, disappointed.

"What's the date on the decree?" Oliver inquired, making the connection.

Sarah removed the document from her purse.

"It's dated 1837, signed at the bottom by Queen Victoria," Sarah replied, thinking back to what she had been told. "Wasn't that when Lord Torrington, Queen Victoria's guardian, had the Britfields murdered?"

"I remember Professor Hainsworth and Dr. Beagleswick talking about that," Tom confirmed.

"Under Queen Victoria, the ruling dynasty began to erase the Britfields from history and destroyed any legitimizing documents," Sarah recalled, trying to make sense of everything.

"And we're holding actual proof," Tom realized.

"Do you guys have any idea how devastating this book

would be to the British Empire?" Oliver declared, fully aware of the gravity of what they were holding.

"And to the current royal family," Sarah added perceptively. "No wonder it's been hidden for all these years."

Their thoughts were suddenly interrupted by a parade of footsteps marching toward the room. It sounded like a stampede of wild animals galloping closer.

"They're coming," Oliver exclaimed, quickly rising.

The door erupted with thunderous knocking.

"Open this immediately," hollered one of the guards. "You're trespassing on private property and will be arrested!"

"Probably a good time to find that other exit." Tom sprang to his feet.

"Right," Oliver concurred, quickly surveying the room. "When my father was here, he told me about another way out. That's how the elite members entered and exited without detection."

"Any idea where it's located?" Sarah asked, hastily searching around.

Oliver pointed to the north wall. "My dad was standing right there and motioned to the tapestry."

Woven of fine silk and depicting famous battles of antiquity, a ten-foot by twelve-foot tapestry hung on the wall, an antique armoire in front of it.

The guards continued pounding on the door. "Open this now or we'll break it down," one of them yelled.

"Help me move the armoire," Oliver stressed, hustling over.

They gathered around the object and pushed. It eased to one side.

"It's on rollers. That's a good sign," Oliver said, encouraged.

Sarah pulled back one end of the tapestry and peered behind. "You're right, there's a door."

"Thank goodness," Oliver exhaled, his hope bolstered. "Grab the Britfield Codex and slide the trunk to where it was."

Tom and Sarah grabbed the Codex and tried to put everything back exactly the way they found it.

Suddenly, the room went dark and a loud siren blared, followed by flashing floodlights.

"What happened?" Sarah asked, covering her ears against the ear-splitting noise.

"They've activated the main alarm," Oliver exclaimed. "The entire museum is on lockdown."

8
A WOMAN OF WISDOM

After diligently searching Oliver's flat for clues, Fontaine decided to work from her apartment.

She was frustrated. After coming so close to finding Tom and Sarah, she had no idea where they were. In a city of two and half million people, it was a troubling scenario. Although Fontaine was shocked by her chief's absurd accusations, she was not surprised. In her experience, the guilty always blamed someone else. Fontaine would confront him sooner or later, but for now, finding Tom and Sarah was the priority.

Sitting at her computer, Fontaine did extensive research into Oliver's past. She reviewed all his known associates, friends, and relatives. After hours of investigating, she finally discovered an uncle who lived in the town of Chartres, about an hour southwest of Paris.

"If Oliver leaves the city, he might go there seeking help," she thought aloud, knowing it was her first promising lead.

As Fontaine wrote down the new information, she heard a faint crackling sound coming from inside the walls. The room temperature became warmer as the distinct odor of burning wood filled the atmosphere.

Alarmed, she glanced around the room and noticed a hazy smoke floating over the floor. She covered her mouth and began to cough, choking on the fumes. Within an instant, the apartment burst into flames.

Remembering her training, Fontaine lifted her shirt above her nose and dropped to the ground. The purplish-yellow flames licked the walls as they rapidly devoured everything in their path. Now engulfed in a prison of fire, parts of the ceiling began to topple down, igniting the carpet and furniture. Within seconds she was surrounded by a raging inferno.

* * * * *

Tom, Sarah, and Oliver covered their ears as the museum siren blared.

"So much for our secrecy," Tom murmured.

"And my internship," Oliver remarked as he opened the door inward, revealing a dark corridor built of granite and curved at the top.

"Any idea where it leads?" Tom asked, boldly peeking inside.

"No, but it'll get us out of here," Oliver responded in an anxious fervor.

"There's a light switch on the wall," Sarah noticed, reaching for the button.

"Wait," Oliver cautioned her. "I'm not sure what's at the other end. We don't want to alert anyone."

She nodded, slowly lowering her hand.

"But we can't see a bloody thing," Tom commented, blinded by the darkness.

"Here, this will help." Oliver turned on his cell phone to use as a light. "And let's cover our tracks."

Tom and Sarah promptly moved the armoire to its

original place, then reached under the tapestry and pulled it close to the wall.

"That's good enough," Oliver acknowledged, firmly shutting the door behind them. "Let's hope this leads out of here."

Oliver went first, followed by Sarah, then Tom, who held the heavy Codex under his arm. Frosty and damp, the corridor inclined upward as they marched forward.

* * * * *

Meanwhile, the guards continued to pound on the exterior door until they forced it open. Weapons drawn, they funneled in and looked around.

"It's empty," one of them remarked, lifting each tablecloth.

"Search everywhere," the senior guard ordered.

"That won't be necessary," a deep voice interrupted. "No one needs to look in this room."

The senior guard turned as a man stepped forward. The tall stranger had dark, oily hair, a hollow complexion, and spoke with an Israeli accent. He was wearing a black tailored suit and polished leather shoes and conveyed an air of military training.

"Two children and a young man broke in," the senior guard explained, intimidated by the man's imposing presence.

"I'm aware of that," the Israeli replied, an icy gaze in his eyes.

"What would you like us to do?"

"Turn off the alarm, exit the room, and lock the door. I'll handle it from here," he instructed in a hostile manner. "And if anyone speaks of this or what they've seen, it won't just be their job that's eliminated."

The guard's face turned pale as he swallowed. "Understood, not a word."

The Israeli scanned the room and noticed the armoire was slightly out of place. He shook his head in anger and rapidly dialed his cell phone.

"Someone has breached our chamber and is now in the passageway. Intercept the intruders and bring them to me."

* * * * *

Fontaine frantically crawled to her desk to retrieve her firearm and the files on Tom, Sarah, and Oliver. She stuffed the items into her purse and threw the strap over her shoulder.

The intense smoke and heat were nearly unbearable as she edged toward the front door, feeling her way along the wood paneling. It was blistering hot. She backed away as the front door burst into flames.

Trying to remain calm, Fontaine maneuvered toward the kitchen and grabbed a chair from the table. She stood up and threw it at the back window. The glass shattered. Although the cool air felt good in her lungs, it fueled the fire.

Fontaine glanced out the opening. Two flights down was a brick patio, an organic vegetable garden, and a pottery shed.

She took a breath, walked back a few paces, then leaped toward the shed, crashing through the rooftop and falling into an array of shelving, terracotta pots, and bags of compost.

The apartment exploded, dislodging burning debris in every direction. A black funnel of smoke billowed into the sky.

Half-conscious, Fontaine was awakened by a concerned neighbor standing over her.

"Are you all right?" he asked, brushing dirt from her face.

Fontaine opened her eyes. Her skin had cuts and bruises. "I don't know," she coughed, disoriented.

"Can you move?"

She nodded.

"Let me help," he offered, lifting her upright.

Fontaine grabbed her purse, now coated in ash.

"I've called the fire department. They should be here soon," the man informed her.

"T-thank you," Fontaine murmured, dizzy and lightheaded.

"What happened?"

"I-I have no idea," she gasped, continuing to cough.

The man guided her out of the shed and away from the apartment. Sirens wailed in the background. "Do you need anything?" he asked. "I can—"

"No, I'll be fine, really," she answered. "Just see if anyone else needs help."

The man left and walked back toward the complex. Fontaine rested for a minute, then grabbed her cell phone and dialed.

"Gustave, it's me. My apartment just caught on fire—the entire place is ablaze... No, I'm not kidding... Yes, I'm all right, but I don't think it was an accident. Someone's trying to kill me... No, you don't need to come over. Continue with your research, and we'll meet up later... Don't worry, I'll be okay. Just be careful, and I'll call you in a few hours. There's something I need to do."

She hung up, took a breath, and made another call.

"This is Fontaine. How soon can you get to Paris?"

* * * * *

"We seem to be walking uphill," Tom noticed, his legs strained.

"It's because we were four stories underground," Oliver explained. "Hopefully this leads to the street level."

As they continued, the overhead lights came on. Every hundred feet was an alcove with a metal door.

"What happened?" Sarah asked, suddenly feeling exposed.

"They know we're in here," Oliver responded, a tension in his voice.

"Are they behind us or in front of us?"

"Could be both."

"Then we're trapped."

"It seems that way."

"Maybe this leads out," Tom indicated, advancing toward one of the alcoves and examining the latched door.

Oliver and Sarah rushed over.

"Let's try to open it," Oliver instructed as all three pulled and pushed on the corroded latch.

"It won't budge," Tom grunted, his hands covered in rust.

"Stand back," Oliver advised, then kicked the latch with his foot.

It moved slightly.

"It's working. Kick it again," Sarah encouraged him.

Oliver kept kicking until the latch gradually shifted to one side.

They yanked on the handle and the door squeaked open. An overpowering stench seeped through, stinging their eyes and nostrils.

"Yuck," Sarah gasped, covering her nose.

Tom waved his hand in front of his face.

Oliver peeked inside. "It looks and smells like the Paris sewer system," he observed. "It must lead under the city."

The dark, humid interior had patches of light filtering down from the overhead manholes. Old cast-iron pipes and wiring crisscrossed the vaulted ceilings, stained by centuries of sewage. Both sides had a narrow concrete platform with a river of polluted water flowing through the center. The smell was ghastly.

"Should we go in?" Tom queried, a bit hesitant.

"Really?" Sarah questioned, her nose scrunched up.

"I don't think we have a choice," Oliver indicated.

Hesitant, all three stepped onto the raised platform, glancing back and forth.

"Which direction?" Tom asked, wondering if it mattered.

Oliver looked around, trying to get his bearings. "Let's go right."

They carefully moved along the slippery platform, covering their noses and clearing the path of cobwebs. Enormous rats swarmed everywhere, scavenging for food. Sarah's eyes widened as she clutched Tom's arm.

"I thought rats didn't bother you," Tom said, recalling their previous escape through the tunnel at Weatherly Orphanage.

"They do when they're the size of large cats," she clarified, cringing at the massive creatures.

* * * * *

A group of men dressed in suits ran through the secret corridor, searching for the intruders. They came from both directions and eventually met in the middle, baffled that no one was there.

"Where are they?" a stocky Frenchman asked, holding his weapon at his side.

"We didn't see anyone," another man replied.

"Well, they didn't just disappear," the Frenchman snapped, viewing the metal doors along the hallway. "They must have gone into the sewers."

"I thought those doors were welded shut."

"They should have been," he stated angrily, grabbing his walkie-talkie. "They're not in the corridor, sir. We think they've escaped into the sewer system."

"Hunt them down and bring them to me," the Israeli bellowed back.

* * * * *

An hour later, Sarah, Tom, and Oliver were still roaming the sewers, desperately seeking a way out. They zigzagged through a confusing network of tunnels, venturing up one way and coming down another. With dizzying effect, the repugnant smell continued wherever they traveled.

"It seems like we've been in here forever," Sarah moaned, exhausted. "What time is it?"

"Almost seven," Oliver answered, glancing at his watch.

In the distance, a symphony of voices echoed off the barrel-vaulted walls.

"They're behind us," Oliver warned, urging them forward.

Hustling along one of the platforms, Tom spotted a metal ladder that led up to a manhole, the last traces of daylight visible around its edges.

"What about this one?" Tom asked, still clutching the Codex under his arm.

Oliver shrugged his shoulders. "It's worth a try. I just hope it's not sealed like all the others," he replied as he gripped the ladder. "Let me go first this time."

He climbed up twenty feet and pushed on the manhole. With great effort, it moved. Easing the cover to one side, Oliver popped his head up and scanned the area.

"It seems clear," he notified them.

"Thank goodness, I couldn't take another minute down here," Sarah gagged, feeling faint from the fumes.

"No kidding," Tom blurted, desperate for fresh air.

One by one they exited onto Place des Vosges, a secluded road surrounded by luxury townhouses. In the center was a tree-lined park with manicured gardens and wooden benches.

Tom spun around, looking at the different buildings as street lamps flickered on. "Do you recognize anything?"

"I think we're near the Right Bank, about twenty minutes east of the Louvre," Oliver guessed.

After pushing the manhole cover back into place, they wiped their shoes on the nearby grass and plopped down on a bench. The evening breeze was invigorating as they took deep breaths.

"What should we do with this?" Tom wondered, setting the heavy Codex on his lap.

"Let me take a look at it again," Oliver said, curious.

He carefully examined several pages, trying to decipher the information, then handed it back to Tom.

"Even if I could read this, I wouldn't understand what it means," Oliver conceded.

"Do you know anyone who could?" Sarah inquired.

Oliver pondered the question. "There's a professor at the Sorbonne, right here in Paris," he remembered. "Last spring I did a semester abroad and attended one of her history classes. She's brilliant."

"Can we trust her?" Sarah questioned, skeptical.

"I don't know, but we can go there tomorrow. Right now we need a place to stay. There's a quiet hotel not far from here," Oliver recalled from a past visit with his friends. "It should be safe, at least for now."

Fifteen minutes later, all three stood in the lobby of Tartuffe, a boutique hotel off Rue de Bretagne. It was a fusion of French Renaissance and modern sophistication, with contemporary artwork covering the walls.

"I need two rooms for tonight," Oliver told the young female attendant. "One room with a king-size bed and the other with two twins."

"Adjoining?" the attendant asked.

"Yes, please."

She checked her computer. "We have something on the fourth floor."

"Perfect," Oliver agreed, eager for a good night's rest.

"That'll be three hundred and sixty-five euros," she informed him. "Will that be cash or credit?"

"Credit."

Oliver grabbed his wallet, then hesitated, gently nudging Tom and Sarah away from the counter.

"I was just thinking," Oliver whispered, his voice troubled. "These people you mentioned, they have vast resources, right?"

"They found us and your apartment," Tom replied frankly.

"Then they know everything about me," Oliver assumed, showing them his credit card. "If I use this, they'll know where we are."

"We didn't think about that," Sarah admitted.

Oliver held up his cell phone. "And they can track me."

Tom and Sarah glanced at each other, suddenly aware of the digital prison they inhabited.

Oliver turned back to the counter, removing money

from his wallet. "I'd rather pay with cash," he told the attendant. "What do you have for one hundred and fifty euros?"

She tapped the computer keyboard. "That'd be one small room on the bottom floor," she replied. "It has two twin beds."

"I'll take it," Oliver said gladly.

He removed the battery from his cell phone and handed the phone and battery to Tom.

"Do me a favor," Oliver requested. "Take these across the street and toss them into a trash can. From here on out, we'll need to be more careful."

* * * * *

Early the next morning Fontaine waited at the Eurostar train station in central Paris. She kept checking her watch as she sipped a cup of hot tea.

Finally, a bright yellow and white streamline train pulled up. The doors opened, and hundreds of travelers exited. Fontaine glanced back and forth, studying each passenger.

"Are you looking for me?" whispered a calm voice from behind.

She turned and smiled, relieved. Standing in a blue Burberry trench coat was Detective Gowerstone, holding a leather case and a black umbrella.

"Thank you for coming," Fontaine said gratefully.

"It's been a while."

"Yes, it has," she reminisced, her voice indicating an unresolved past.

Gowerstone gazed into her eyes and gently inhaled. "You're wearing Fleur by Floris," he noticed. "I remember that fragrance fondly."

"You should," she stressed. "It was a gift from a friend, who said he would call."

Gowerstone's head dipped slightly. "I'm sorry. I should have."

"There's no reason to bring that up now," Fontaine sighed, her voice delicate. "What's done is done. I'm thankful you came."

Moved by her breathtaking beauty, Gowerstone continued to stare at her. "Yes, we should focus on finding Tom and Sarah," he agreed, intense emotions masked by his businesslike tone.

"Let's find somewhere to talk, and I'll fill you in."

* * * * *

After leaving the hotel the next morning, Oliver, Sarah, and Tom briskly walked to the College de Sorbonne, France's most prestigious university, built in 1253 by Robert de Sorbon.

Situated in the Latin Quarter, on the Left Bank, the small campus was a collection of historical limestone buildings with ivy-covered walls and dormered rooftops. A simple two-story domed church sat in the middle, a symbolic reminder that the school was founded for underprivileged theology students.

After browsing the directory, Oliver located Professor Beauchamp's classroom. All three waited in the corridor, peeking in the doorway as she finished her summer class.

Dr. Josephine Beauchamp wore a vibrant floral dress, her long golden hair tied with a colorful ribbon. Vivacious and charismatic, she mesmerized her students.

"Remember, it takes discipline and hard work to compose a compelling narrative," Josephine said with conviction. "But no one can tell you what to write. You need to trust your instincts, because the truth will come from within."

Josephine looked at each student.

"Life is the ultimate adventure, but you have to experience it in order to write about it."

As the bell rang, a few students lingered behind to speak with her.

"I like her already," Sarah voiced admiringly.

"She's amazing, isn't she," Oliver commented, captivated once again.

After the last students left, they entered the room.

"Professor Beauchamp," Oliver prompted.

"Call me Josephine."

"Josephine, I had the privilege of attending one of your classes last spring."

"Yes, Oliver, I remember you," Josephine said with an energetic smile. "How's your novel? I recall you were working on a spy thriller."

Oliver frowned, staring at the wooden floor. "Not as well as I hoped," he confessed. "I tend to get distracted."

"That's all right," Josephine sympathized. "When the time is right, you will find your voice."

Josephine strolled over to greet them. "Who are your delightful friends?"

"Tom and Sarah," Oliver replied. "They're more like family."

"Such young scholars," Josephine said as she shook each of their hands. "You've brought them to the right place."

Oliver laughed, impressed by her wit.

"What can I do for you?" she asked inquisitively.

"We have an old manuscript we'd like you to look at," Oliver replied. "Do you have a minute?"

"Of course. Please, sit down," Josephine offered.

They gathered around her desk, and Tom placed the Britfield Codex in front of her. Observing the name embossed on the cover, Josephine swallowed hard.

"Where did you get this?" she asked, clearing her throat.

"It's, ah, borrowed," Oliver responded clumsily.

"Tom, would you mind closing the door?" Josephine asked.

"Sure," he obliged, walking over and shutting it firmly.

"Do you know what you have here?" Josephine inquired in a serious tone.

"We think so," Oliver answered uneasily.

Josephine gave Oliver a hard look. "Do you have any idea what kind of trouble you're in?"

* * * * *

Outside of Paris in the secluded Ravencliff castle, the Committee sat at the round table. Wearing black robes, all thirteen members were present.

"This is a serious situation," the Italian declared.

"It's a catastrophe," the Egyptian vented.

"What was taken?" the Master questioned, his eyes soulless.

"The Britfield Codex," the Italian replied apprehensively.

"I thought those documents were destroyed," the Master thundered.

"Not all of them."

"What was it doing in our private chamber?"

"Some of the members like to preserve relics from the past," the Italian tried to explain, terrified.

"Fools—that book should have been burned," the Master stated, his malevolent voice piercing their ears.

The other members started arguing among themselves.

"Quiet!" the Master demanded, his voice rumbling through the chamber.

The group went silent, bowing their heads in obedience.

"You're telling me three people passed through the security, broke into our sacred chamber, and wandered off with this Britfield Codex," the Master summarized, his temper seething.

"Y-yes, sir," the Egyptian answered in a quivering voice.

"The same three you have failed to eliminate."

The room went deathly still, each member frightened for his life.

"Do you know where they are?" the Master asked.

"No, not yet, but—"

"We have unlimited resources and you still can't find this Tom, Sarah, and Oliver. Is that what you're telling me?"

The group remained motionless, stricken by fear. The Master stood, adorned in a maroon robe and shaking with rage.

"If this Codex gets out to the public or is exposed by the media, many of our secrets will be discovered," the Master roared. "The last thing we want is for the public to question the false history we've forced on them."

"But we own the media, sir," the Austrian member interrupted. "The broadcasters only report what we tell them."

"We don't control everyone, at least not yet," the Master emphasized. "There are too many journalists who think of themselves as patriots. And this worldwide internet has been a disaster for hiding the truth."

"If any of these journalists speak out, we will silence them," the British member proposed.

"We would if we could find them," the Master countered.

The Master slithered behind each member, the candlelight catching a glimpse of his demonic face.

"All twelve of you report to me," he began, his tone harsh. "I must report to someone else. What will I tell *my* master?" He slammed his hand on the table. "That a couple of children have jeopardized our plans for a One World System?"

The men shuddered, concerned for their own lives.

"We've spent centuries hiding the truth," the Master continued. "We won't fail now. Understood?"

"Yes, sir," they answered in unison.

"Although you're here through family bloodlines, don't think you're irreplaceable," the Master threatened. "Eliminate the children and burn that Britfield Codex!"

The group stood. "Yes, Master. As you command."

The Master settled back in his seat. "What about that troublesome inspector?"

"She's been dealt with," the Egyptian reported. "The apartment was torched, with her in it."

"Good. At least one thing has been accomplished," the Master stressed, pleased. "Now get that Codex and eradicate those children."

"Even Oliver Horningbrook?"

"All of them."

* * * * *

Oliver, Sarah, and Tom stared at Professor Beauchamp, unsettled by her comment.

"Then you recognize it?" Oliver asked with reservation. "You know about its significance?"

"I've heard about the Britfields in whispered conversations," Josephine revealed guardedly. "But it's not something we openly talk about."

"Can you help us?" Oliver pleaded.

Unnerved by the request, Josephine carefully contemplated her answer. "Why do you have this book?" she queried.

"It's a long story."

"Perhaps you could enlighten me."

Oliver turned to Tom. "Do you mind?"

"Not at all," he replied. "Should I start at the beginning?"

"That might be best."

Tom spent the next thirty minutes telling Josephine everything he'd gone through and his connection to the Britfields. Sarah added commentary and filled in some of the details.

"That's an incredible story, Tom," Josephine empathized. "I understand why you're determined to find your parents, if they are your parents."

"I also discovered this when we were trapped at Mont-Saint-Michel," Sarah interjected, handing her the decree signed by Queen Victoria.

Josephine carefully examined the document, feeling the texture and holding it up to the light. She then removed a magnifying glass from her desk and studied through every detail: writing style, language composition, historical data.

"Fascinating," Josephine marveled. "To think something like this exists."

"Then it's authentic?" Sarah inquired, encouraged.

"Yes, it's authentic," Josephine confirmed. "And it makes perfect sense that you found it at Mont-Saint-Michel."

"What do the monasteries have to do with it?" Tom wondered.

"Everything, but that would take some time to explain," Josephine replied. "The history goes back centuries."

"We don't mind," Oliver asserted, settling back in his seat. "Tom, Sarah?"

"Please," Sarah agreed happily. "I'm only starting to understand all of this."

Tom nodded, leaning forward in his chair.

Josephine took a deep breath and gathered her thoughts, contemplating where to start.

"After the decline of the Roman Empire in the 400s, Europe entered what many historians have called the Dark Ages, which lasted about eight hundred years. It was a time of barbarian invasions, lawlessness, and cultural collapse. Governments were overthrown, towns ransacked, and cities pillaged. Countless books and literary documents were lost or burned."

"You mean great works of history?" Sarah asked.

"Yes, centuries of philosophy, science, mathematics, and historical plays were destroyed," Josephine answered, saddened by the loss.

"So how did anything survive?"

"It was the dedication and sacrifice of the monks."

"The monks?" Tom repeated, amused by the thought.

"Correct," Josephine affirmed, smiling. "During this turbulent period, Christianity was rapidly spreading. Inspired by great theologians such as Saint Augustine and Saint Jerome, monasteries flourished. Monks committed their lives to not only copying the Gospels but preserving ancient texts."

"That must have been a lot of work," Tom reasoned.

"It was," Josephine acknowledged. "In fact, we can thank Ireland for saving most of the literary masterpieces, from Homer and Plato to Aristotle and Virgil."

"Ireland?" Sarah doubted, finding the concept peculiar.

"Yes." Josephine laughed. "Isolated from the European continent, Ireland became a center for Christian scholars.

Relatively safe from outside influences, the monks painstakingly copied manuscripts and recorded history. Soon after, they shared these texts with monasteries throughout the world."

"So the Irish saved civilization," Sarah theorized.

"That's one hypothesis, but you're not too far off," Josephine validated, pleased by her curiosity.

"How did the decree end up at Mont Saint-Michel?"

"As an island fortress, Mont-Saint-Michel was ideal for storing literary treasures," Josephine explained. "It still houses one of the largest collections of medieval manuscripts in France, outside the Sorbonne and the Louvre."

"That explains their extensive library I had to organize," Sarah remarked with a trace of bitterness.

"I know it was a difficult time for you, but what a wonderful opportunity to read original works that no one else has seen," Josephine said.

"I never considered that," Sarah admitted.

"With the rise and fall of empires, these fortified monasteries became a perfect place to hide important documents," Josephine continued.

"So how did the Britfield Codex end up at the Louvre?" Oliver asked pointedly.

"Over the centuries, many priceless manuscripts were taken from the monasteries and moved to royal castles and palaces," Josephine replied.

"You mean stolen."

"That's one way to put it."

"But what does that have to do with the museum?" Tom questioned, confused.

"The Louvre was a royal palace before it was a museum," Josephine answered.

"Then you're aware of the Britfield history?" Oliver inquired, trying to get back on topic.

"In my decades of reviewing authentic documents, I've come across the Britfield story," Josephine divulged, her voice dropping. "Although evidence is scarce, the manuscripts I've read confirm the truth about the family's existence and their historical claim. It is a tragic tale hidden from society."

"Authentic? What do you mean?" Sarah probed.

"Most of history is written by those who control it, those who are in power. What you're taught today is only a fragment of the truth," Josephine reveled.

"Even at a school like Oxford?" Oliver inquired, astounded by the implication.

"Especially at Oxford or Cambridge," Josephine stressed with an undercurrent of resentment. "If these people can brainwash the youth with their fabricated history, then they can influence or change the next generation. That's why it's so important to question everything you read and to do your own research."

"Why hasn't anything been done?" Oliver asked candidly.

"These are powerful people who control governments. I'm just an academic, like most scholars. What can I do?" Josephine concluded, unsettled.

Oliver leaned forward. "You can help us."

* * * * *

Hobson Wexbury, mid-forties, short and nicely dressed, parked his Bentley around the corner from 10 Downing Street, London. He flashed his credentials to security and continued through the main entrance.

As Hobson entered, the prime minister turned, startled.

"What are you doing here?"

"I needed to speak with you," Hobson stated urgently.

"You should never come to this office—it's too risky," the prime minister berated him.

"It couldn't wait."

"What's so important?" the prime minister asked, lowering his voice and closing the door.

"We've lost Gowerstone," Hobson informed him. "We were tracking him last night, but he's disappeared."

"That's a problem," the prime minister agreed. "What about his car and his cell phone?"

"Gowerstone removed the GPS system from his car, and he's using an encrypted satellite phone."

"You have all this technology and resources at your disposal, including MI5 and MI6, yet you've lost the one man who can bring down my government," the prime minister vented, his temper mounting.

"That's correct, sir," Hobson said regrettably.

"I told you we should have dealt with him sooner."

"We'll find him," Hobson promised.

"You better," the prime minister threatened. "I want to know where he is and what he's up to. Once Gowerstone's popularity has faded, we'll arrest him on false charges and send him to one of our prisons outside of Britain."

"What charges?" Hobson asked, knowing Gowerstone had an impeccable record.

"Whatever we invent—enough to put him away for life."

Hobson nervously paced the room, not sure how to broach the next subject.

"Is there more?" the prime minister asked, annoyed.

"It's your son."

"What about him?"

"Yesterday Oliver entered the secret chamber at the Louvre and took the Britfield Codex," Hobson conveyed, his voice shaky. "He tricked one of the security guards into allowing him entry by using your name."

"He did what?" the prime minister exploded.

"He had two children with him."

"Not—"

"Yes, Tom and Sarah."

"So they're alive."

The prime minister walked to his chair and plopped down, shocked by the disclosure.

"I thought those meddlesome children had sunk with the ferry. This is terrible news," the prime minister mumbled to himself. "And how does Oliver know them?"

"We're not sure," Hobson replied. "It appears they met in Paris, and he's been helping them ever since."

"That stupid boy," the prime minister griped, shaking his head in disgust. "He shouldn't be mixed up in this."

"I agree, sir."

"This is a disaster, an absolute disaster." The prime minister slouched forward, rubbing his head. "I've done everything I can to shield that boy, and now he's on the wrong side."

"What would you like me to do?"

"I'm not sure." The prime minister paused. "Once the Committee finds out—"

"They already know," Hobson disclosed. "They want to meet with you tomorrow morning."

* * * * *

Taking a moment to reflect, Josephine walked to a window and glanced out.

"You have all entered an extremely dark area," she began, uncertain how to proceed. "I understand it wasn't your choice. None of you asked for this. The question is, do I risk everything to help you?"

"We didn't mean to put you in danger," Oliver confessed, feeling guilty. "I guess I didn't realize the risks in coming here."

"It's all right," Josephine reassured him. "I understand you meant well."

"Would you like us to leave?"

"Let me continue," Josephine replied, trying to express her thoughts. "You made a good point earlier. Why hasn't anything been done? Why doesn't anyone stand up for what they believe in? We all live in a shadow of fear, afraid to defend the truth and fight for justice."

Josephine walked back and sat down. "I've been a professor for twenty-five years," she said reflectively. "Teaching is my entire life. It's all I've ever wanted to do."

"What would happen if they discovered you helped us?" Oliver asked, concerned for her safety.

"The least of my problems would be losing my tenured position at one of the finest universities in the world." Josephine gave them a grave look. "The worst would be a tragic incident that looked like an accident."

"You're talking about these secret groups?" Sarah whispered.

"Yes, exactly. They're everywhere, and they are well-financed and connected," Josephine elaborated. "Even some of our faculty are members of the Masons or the Tavistock Institute, influencing decisions and distorting the truth. It's hard to know whom to trust."

"We can go, Professor. We'll find someone else," Oliver said.

All three stood up.

"I didn't say I wouldn't help," Josephine stated, motioning them to stop. "I just needed a moment to think about the consequences."

"Then you can help us?"

"Leave the Britfield Codex here and meet me at my office at four o'clock this afternoon."

9
AN UNCLE OF VALOR

Gowerstone and Fontaine sat outside a café on a quiet street on the Left Bank. There was an awkward tension between them, an unresolved past neither knew how to address. The detective sipped his tea as they talked.

"I don't know who started the fire," Fontaine continued. "It was all I could do to escape."

"And your entire apartment blew up?" Gowerstone queried, amazed by her bravery.

"Yes, everything I own was destroyed."

"Were you injured?"

"A few cuts and bruises, but I'll survive," she answered. "Let's focus on the case."

Gowerstone stared at her for a moment, emboldened. *What an extraordinary woman*, he thought to himself as he reviewed the case files.

"Is this all the information?" he asked, handing back the folders.

"It's everything I have."

"And the prime minister's son is involved?"

"Yes, although I believe he's helping Tom and Sarah," Fontaine said.

"How ironic that his father is the one man I want to arrest and bring to justice."

"You mentioned your history with the prime minister," she addressed, knowing the topic was sensitive. "Friendship can often blind us from the truth."

"Indeed," Gowerstone replied. "Nevertheless, this means Oliver is in danger."

"Won't he be protected by his father's connections?"

"Not necessarily. The fact that Oliver is helping Tom and Sarah will be seen as a betrayal, regardless of the circumstances," Gowerstone explained. "These people won't let anything get in their way."

Gowerstone paused and leaned closer to Fontaine. "You believe Interpol has been compromised?"

"Absolutely," she stated unequivocally.

"How much do they know?"

"I've shared all the files you provided and routinely updated the chief inspector," Fontaine replied, shaking her head in dismay.

"And you think he's involved?"

"Without a doubt," she answered heatedly, disgust etched on her face. "Everything I've done has been undermined."

"I know the feeling," Gowerstone sighed, reflecting on his past. "How have you left things with Interpol?"

"The chief wants to speak with me."

"Don't," he warned her, his voice sharp. "The second you're exposed, they'll finish you."

Fontaine reclined in the chair.

"What we're dealing with is bigger than just politics or runaway orphans," Gowerstone began. "If Tom is the heir to the British throne and the truth is revealed, it won't just damage the government or even the monarchy."

"What do you mean?"

"This involves centuries of fraud, corruption,

and murder. We are talking about royal families and multinational organizations," Gowerstone continued, recalling his months of research. "It's not just the royal claim to the throne that's being questioned but deeds entitling the Britfields to vast land and property worth trillions of pounds."

Fontaine's eyes widened as she slowly swallowed. "That explains a great deal. With that kind of money and power, you could do anything."

"Exactly, which is why they want the truth suppressed."

Gowerstone noticed her worried look. "I'm sorry for bringing you into this," he said softly. "I had no idea it was this serious."

Fontaine reached over and tenderly grabbed his hand. "It's all right, Detective. I'm a big girl, I can handle it."

"I just needed to get Tom and Sarah out of England. They weren't safe there," Gowerstone reasoned. "It wasn't until the last six months that I discovered how far this coverup extends, the people involved, and these secret organizations that control so much."

"What's our plan?"

"First, stay away from anything familiar, places you frequent, friends, associates—everyone and everything will be watched."

"Basically, stay out of Paris," Fontaine realized.

"We just need to be careful."

"What about my partner, Gustave?"

"Do you trust him?"

"I do," she replied confidently. "He's a good man, faithful and reliable."

A hint of envy crossed Gowerstone's face. "Are you involved?" he asked, bothered.

"Why, are you jealous?"

Gowerstone looked away.

"No, for your information." Fontaine laughed, interpreting his unspoken words. "Are you happy?"

"It's none of my business," he replied nonchalantly. "I just need to know facts."

"Of course you do," she added with a smile.

"Second," Gowerstone continued, avoiding the awkward moment, "we need to locate Tom and Sarah. What's their last known location?"

"I was confronted by the assassin at Oliver's apartment, so I must have just missed them. Gustave and I searched the area but found nothing."

"Anything else?"

"I researched Oliver's friends and relatives. It seems he has an uncle living outside of Paris."

"Tom and Sarah are smart. I would know, I chased them across half of England," Gowerstone said dryly, sipping his tea. "There's nothing left for them in Paris, and their ultimate goal is the Loire Valley. By now Oliver knows he's in danger and can't return to his apartment."

"You think they'll head to the uncle's home?"

"If I were Oliver and needed a place to stay while I looked for answers, it's where I would go," Gowerstone deduced.

"We should meet with Gustave and see what he's uncovered," Fontaine suggested. "He can continue the search here, and you and I can locate the uncle."

"Good, that sounds like a plan." Gowerstone stood, ready to leave. "What about your cell phone?"

"It's a disposable. They can't trace it without the number," Fontaine replied, cautious. "What about you?"

"No one knows I'm here. That's one advantage we have."

* * * * *

Late that afternoon, Oliver, Sarah, and Tom returned to the Sorbonne and went to Josephine's office three flights up in the main building. Oliver lightly knocked on her door.

"Who is it?" Josephine asked cautiously.

"Oliver."

Josephine rose from her desk and unlocked the latch. "Come in."

All three entered the room and glanced around. Her office walls were lined with scholarly books and ancient texts packed into walnut shelves. A leaded glass window looked down on a courtyard. Behind her hung numerous degrees, certificates, and academic awards.

"Please, have a seat," Josephine said politely.

They sat on a leather couch tucked underneath the window. Returning to her desk, Josephine appeared unsettled, her mood changed.

"I've read through the Britfield Codex," she began. "I'm astounded that this document has survived."

"Is the Codex authentic?" Sarah inquired.

"Yes," Josephine answered, revealing a slight smile.

"I've never seen a more complete or well-assembled family history."

"What does it all mean?"

"It's a detailed account of the Britfield dynasty. Starting in the early 1100s, it covers centuries of history that shows their lineage, marriages, and titles to property," Josephine explained. "There are deeds to land all over Europe, including almost fifty percent of England."

"Half of Britain," Oliver exclaimed, stunned by the ramifications. "If that's true, the royal gentry would lose most of their property."

"Their property, titles, and wealth," Josephine stated.

"That would cause absolute chaos."

"And undermine the very fabric of Britain," Josephine affirmed, her voice uneasy. "It would reallocate wealth, bring down the government, and destroy the monarchy, including impacting most of Europe. It would also expose centuries of corruption and rewrite history."

"Just from that Codex?" Oliver questioned.

"Yes," Josephine responded gravely. "Now you understand my apprehension."

"I guess that's why certain people would kill for it," Sarah realized.

The room went quiet, each of them grasping the magnitude of what they had found.

"What else does it say?" Sarah pressed.

"It provides legal documentation verifying the Britfields' rightful claim to the British throne." Josephine paused, her voice strained. "From my experience, it's indisputable evidence."

"So everything we've heard is true?" Sarah asked with a mixture of excitement and foreboding.

"Correct. All the rumors are real, and all the speculation is fact," Josephine replied confidently. "I've known about the Britfields for years. I've just never come across such a complete anthology of material."

"Does the Codex explain what happened?" Tom inquired.

Josephine leaned forward. "Everything is here, from ancestors and descendants to the opposing families. There are even names of occult groups and secret organizations that fought to undermine the Britfields."

"I remember Professor Hainsworth mentioned the Stuart dynasty. Why is that important?" Sarah wondered, thinking about her Scottish ancestry.

"It gets complicated," Josephine said, catching her breath. "In 1603, James Stuart, known as James VI of Scotland, was crowned James I, King of England. The Britfields were outraged. When the Tudor dynasty ended with Elizabeth I, the Britfields were ready to inherit their rightful claim, so they assembled at one of their southern castles. When James was informed of their plans, he ordered his Stuart knights to surround the castle and executed everyone inside. James then signed a decree to have any remaining Britfields captured and removed."

"What happened?" Oliver asked, intrigued.

"The Britfields were mostly taken by surprise," Josephine answered. "Some escaped to different parts of England, and others fled to France. Many were imprisoned, and others were murdered."

"Couldn't they fight back?" Tom questioned, clutching his fists.

"Yes, there were a few heroic battles, but James I controlled the army, which now included England and Scotland. Nevertheless, the Britfields remained resilient and formed strategic alliances," Josephine continued, pausing to take a drink of water. "However, as the Britfields prepared to take the English crown, the Civil War erupted in 1641. Oliver Cromwell, a military leader, took power in 1649 and abolished the royal sovereignty. Ironically, the Stuart dynasty was returned to the throne eleven years later."

Tom and Sarah listened intently, impressed by the professor's encyclopedic knowledge.

"Then in 1714, the House of Hanover inherited the British throne," Josephine resumed. "Their royal bloodline was mostly German, not English. The Britfields were determined to seize the throne, so they gathered together from across Europe. They brought in renowned historians, scholars, and lawyers, offering irrefutable documents and proof."

"But they didn't win, did they?" Oliver asked skeptically.

"No, and the controversy raged on," Josephine replied. "You see, the Britfields believed in improving people's lives. They wanted to abolish oppressive laws, distribute some of their land back to the farmers, support local industry, and offer education to the masses. They were ahead of their time. They believed freedom was a gift from God that no one could take away."

"And the other royal families?" Tom inquired.

"Their philosophy was to keep the masses ignorant and poor," Josephine stated with resentment. "What Rome called 'bread and circuses' became a creed for royalty—keep the public distracted and docile while you destroy their lives through unjust laws, oppressive taxes, and false wars. This is still true today."

"Why does everything end in 1837?" Sarah inquired, coming back to that date.

"That's when Queen Victoria came to power, and her guardian, Lord Torrington, destroyed any evidence that the Britfields had ever existed," Josephine clarified. "He then hunted down and killed the Britfields. Their lawyers were imprisoned and tortured. Their scholars were arrested and hung from the public scaffolds. However, few know about this, because it was never recorded. Like I said, whoever controls the power controls history."

"Yet some of this evidence was saved and placed into the Britfield Codex," Sarah realized, understanding its importance.

"That's correct," Josephine acknowledged. "Although most of the documents were destroyed, this Codex remarkably survived."

Oliver leaned forward. "What's the Britfield connection to France?"

"All dynasties are connected, either through marriages or alliances," Josephine asserted. "It's the way power is consolidated and protected. Remember, many of the Britfields were of Norman descent."

"Is there anything recent about the Britfields?" Tom asked, hopeful.

"There's a rumor of a second Britfield Codex, one that continues from 1837 until recent times," Josephine disclosed. "Where it's kept or if it exists at all, who knows. Nevertheless, I've come across a few documents, which I've saved."

Josephine walked to a cabinet, unlocked a drawer, and pulled out a bulky file. Everyone looked on with excitement as she flipped through the pages.

"The last known Britfield family lived in Kent, Southeast Britain," Josephine announced, reading from a document.

"That's what the Archbishop of Canterbury told us," Sarah concurred.

"Then you know about the Britfields' only son, whom you believe is Tom?"

"Yes," Sarah replied, her voice confident.

"He's the last heir to the Britfield dynasty," Josephine confirmed, showing them a detailed record. "Although the Britfields' son was kidnapped over a decade ago, he was never found. Born May 2, if he is alive, he would now be thirteen years old."

Tom pondered the revelation. In his whole life, he had never known his birthday.

"If I'm their son," Tom began, developing his thoughts, "then that means I'm older than Sarah."

"So?" Sarah glanced at him with an amused look in her eyes.

"So I'm older than you."

She laughed under her breath. "Maybe in age but not maturity."

Josephine sat down and stared at them with a solemn gaze. This vibrant woman looked scared.

"This book could destroy many prominent people," she told them, her voice intense. "As you know, there are those who would do anything to silence the truth."

"You mean these secret societies?" Oliver guessed.

"Yes, centuries old, these influential groups hide in the shadows but wield an enormous amount of power," Josephine validated, then came to an abrupt conclusion. "It's not safe for you to remain in Paris, especially with the Codex."

"What can we do?" Sarah asked, distressed by the warning.

"Leave the city as soon as possible," Josephine emphasized, worried about their welfare.

"I have an uncle who lives about an hour from here. I'm sure he could help us," Oliver suggested.

"He may prove a reliable ally, but be careful who you trust," Josephine cautioned, her tone stern.

"We can't thank you enough," Oliver expressed, standing and shaking her hand.

"You're welcome," Josephine said, handing him the Codex. "Just be vigilant. The Britfield Codex could change history."

Oliver nodded, taking her advice seriously.

"I wish you all the best, but I don't think it's a good idea to contact me again," Josephine stressed, sensing that she'd already revealed too much.

"I understand," Oliver acknowledged graciously.

Tom, Sarah, and Oliver walked toward the door.

"I hope you're successful," Josephine added. "We need the truth exposed, so be safe and Godspeed."

A few minutes later, all three stood in the university's quad, pondering their next move.

"What an extraordinary woman," Oliver said. "I never realized how much she knew."

"That was quite a meeting," Sarah admitted, still processing the overload of information.

"We have definitely gone down the rabbit hole," Oliver stated as his eyes drifted to a nearby payphone. "I should call my uncle and see if it's all right to visit. He always disliked my father, and now I know why."

"How can we get there?" Tom wondered.

"I'll rent a car," Oliver replied.

"But if you use your credit card, they'll know where you are," Sarah interjected.

"They might know I've rented a car, but they won't know where we're headed," Oliver rationalized. "Anyway, we need transportation."

Oliver walked to the payphone and called his uncle. After a lengthy conversation, everything was set. All that remained was finding a car rental and leaving the city.

* * * * *

Hours later, Oliver drove a silver S550 Cabriolet Mercedes swiftly through the outskirts of Paris and into the countryside. The moonlight shrouded the rural landscape as they transitioned from cramped city blocks to patches of purple lavender fields and rolling hills dotted with farms and cottages.

Sarah nestled in the front seat, gazing at the quaint towns and villages. Tom sat in the back, watching Paris transform into a postcard silhouette.

"Love the car," Sarah said approvingly.

"I second that," Tom added as he felt the smooth leather seat.

"If we're going to travel, we might as well travel in style," Oliver declared with a grin. "We should be at my uncle's estate around 10:00 p.m."

"When was the last time you saw him?" Sarah asked, curious about their relationship.

"It's been about three years."

"Do you like your uncle?"

"Very much," Oliver replied warmly. "He's a true gentleman, kind and generous. In the summers I'd spend weeks at his estate, and we'd drive around the countryside. They're some of my fondest memories growing up."

"But your father doesn't like him?"

"No, which is why I haven't seen him in so long," Oliver replied. "They couldn't be more different. My dad was always driven by politics, regardless of what it took. My uncle was more conservative, always adhering to his principles."

"Did someone say estate?" Tom inquired, emerging from the back.

"You'll see." Oliver laughed. "You won't be disappointed."

They continued along the road and through Chartres, passing its fable-like setting: cobbled streets, brick storefronts with blue shutters, and rows of three-story houses, their moss-stained rooftops covered in red tiles.

The Eure River gently flowed through the medieval town past aged willows, abandoned mills, and ruined castles overgrown with vegetation. Elegant villas and chateaux graced the outskirts. Dominating the skyline was Chartres Cathedral, a 120-foot Gothic structure with over 150 stained glass windows.

A few minutes later Oliver pulled into a gravel driveway, protected by a canopy of towering oak trees. The car stopped at a massive iron gate, with the initials *HH* in the middle. Below was the Latin phrase: *A vaillant Coeur, rien impossible.*

Tom peered through the window, glimpsing the massive stone wall surrounding the estate. "Wow, is your uncle rich?"

"He's well off," Oliver replied, amused by Tom's reaction. "He owns a shipping company—exports wine and imports technology from all over the world."

"And the *HH*?"

"Henry Horningbrook."

"What does the Latin phrase mean?" Sarah asked, attempting to decipher the wording.

"It's our family motto—*To the valiant heart, nothing is impossible.*"

Oliver rolled down his window and leaned toward the voice box, two digital cameras mounted above. "It's Oliver. I'm at the front entrance."

The gate slowly opened as additional lights flooded the area. It was like an entire city coming to life. The extensive grounds had exotic plants, box hedges encircling rose gardens, and immaculate lawns bordered by lofty trees. A tiered waterfall gently cascaded into a pond filled with fish and covered with giant water lilies. In the back were tennis courts and a riding stable.

Tom's and Sarah's eyes were glued to the front window, speechless.

Oliver continued up a long driveway until he came to the roundabout, a white marble fountain dominating the center. Behind was a breathtaking chateau, its ivy-covered granite façade flanked by five towers. The six-story masterpiece had spiraling chimneys, cantilevered balconies, and a horseshoe-staircase climbing one flight to the front door.

"This is someone's house?" Tom questioned, gawking at the architecture.

"I told you he was rich," Oliver chuckled.

"You said well off."

After parking the car next to a 1959 Rolls-Royce Silver Cloud and a pristine XJ Jaguar, all three walked up the staircase to an imposing wooden door that opened as they reached the top step.

"Good evening, Mr. Horningbrook," said the butler.

Dressed in a traditional black-and-white outfit, Stevens was the personification of old-world tradition. In his late-fifties with neatly trimmed gray hair, he stood at attention, his face stern.

"Hello, Stevens. How are you?"

"Quite well, thank you," Stevens replied cordially. "Who may I inquire are your guests?"

"This is Tom and Sarah."

"It's a pleasure to meet you," Stevens acknowledged, slightly bowing his head. "Please, follow me to the study."

They entered the main foyer, which was elegantly decorated with Corinthian columns that extended three stories to a Baroque mural depicting Napoleon's Battle of Waterloo. Medieval knights guarded each corner, valiantly grasping their swords and shields. Etched into the marble floor was the family coat of arms, a red dragon on one side and a golden lion on the other.

They continued down an arched hallway to a library adorned with period furniture, leather-bound books, and family portraits, mostly of Oliver and his uncle. Displayed on the walls was an impressive collection of classical French and British paintings, along with sixteenth-century Italian tapestries. An enormous fireplace danced with cedar-scented flames.

Stevens motioned them to a group of Chippendale chairs covered in royal blue silk. "Please, be seated. I'll inform the master you've arrived."

"Thank you," Oliver said as all three situated themselves.

Stevens bowed and left the room.

"Master?" Tom inquired, finding the term odd.

"Stevens is a traditional butler," Oliver explained. "He believes in the hierarchy of position. He accompanied my uncle when they left England twenty years ago."

A moment later, Sir Henry Horningbrook gracefully entered. Mid-sixties and heavyset, he had piercing blue eyes and a cheerful persona. His clothing was dapper, his manner refined.

Oliver promptly stood to greet his uncle. "Sir, it's an honor to see you again." Oliver firmly gripped his uncle's hand. "Thank you for having us."

"Oliver, just call me Henry," he conveyed politely. "The title was neither asked for nor wanted."

"Yes, sir, I mean Henry."

"And these two delightful children are your friends, Tom and Sarah."

"My adopted family," Oliver was quick to add.

"Good evening," Henry welcomed them in a robust voice. "I appreciate that you've been looking after my nephew while he is in France."

"I think it's the other way around," Sarah corrected as she stepped forward to meet him. "He's been a true lifesaver."

"Oliver's a good lad, isn't he?" Henry smiled admiringly.

"And a great friend."

Henry looked at Tom, carefully studying his appearance and features. "This must be the true heir to the British royal bloodline," Henry proclaimed with a trace of excitement.

"I'm not sure about that, sir," Tom mumbled awkwardly.

"From my understanding, you're carrying quite a responsibility on your shoulders," Henry sympathized.

"I guess so."

"I'm familiar with the Britfield story—one of the finest families in Europe."

Stevens appeared in the doorway.

"Dinner is ready, sir," he announced, standing at attention.

"Excellent." Henry grinned, patting his stomach. "I figured you'd be hungry after your journey, so I took the liberty of having a late supper prepared."

"Brilliant," Tom blurted, famished.

Sarah elbowed him. "Where are your manners?" she whispered with a glare.

"It's fine, Sarah. I appreciate a young man with a hardy appetite," Henry acknowledged, gesturing to the doorway. "Shall we eat?"

They sat at a grand mahogany table decorated with golden candelabras and china vases overflowing with fresh sunflowers. Four place settings were meticulously arranged at one end of the table. A dazzling chandelier hovered overhead.

Oliver and Henry had a glass of vintage Bordeaux, while Tom and Sarah sipped sparkling water from crystal goblets. They ate prime rib, chicken, and vegetables. The family crest decorated the delicate Wedgewood plates. Freshly baked bread, a variety of fruit, and local cheeses were plentiful.

"So, you're in a bind?" Henry began as he indulged in the feast.

"Yes, quite," Oliver replied timidly. "Actually, a bit overwhelmed, to be honest."

"You shared some of the details on the phone. I'm sorry you had to find out about your father this way. I suppose it was inevitable."

"You've known all along?"

"I have," Henry replied with a touch of remorse.

"It's like I've been living in two worlds," Oliver confessed, feeling the weight of what he knew. "One world that's real and the other that's hidden behind the scenes."

"The area you've entered, all of you"—Henry

motioned to Tom and Sarah—"is extremely dangerous. Unfortunately, you're in it now, so it's best to understand what you're up against."

"How are you connected?" Oliver asked, surprised by his uncle's straightforwardness.

"Like your father, I was approached at a young age by a secretive group," Henry answered, his tone rigid. "I had a choice to make. I could have anything I wanted but lose my soul, or I could take the hard road."

"And work for what you believe in," Oliver clarified, proud of his uncle.

"Yes, exactly. It hasn't been easy, but I've never had to compromise my ethics or morals," Henry maintained.

"How did our family become part of this?" Oliver queried.

"When recruiting candidates, these groups usually focus on certain bloodlines. The Horningbrook name goes back centuries in British history, and there's a distant royal connection," Henry explained.

"What happened after you turned them down?"

"They approached your father. It was an offer he couldn't refuse," Henry replied, his expression melancholy. "I observed the sudden change that overtook him. He was different. His refined character transformed into arrogance with a ruthless sense of entitlement. Since then I've been interested in finding out more about these people and their objectives."

"There's so much we don't know," Sarah admitted.

"Few do," Henry acknowledged. "These people have created a hidden world behind the reality we live in."

Oliver leaned forward. "How much do you know about these secret organizations?" he asked bluntly.

"Practically everything," Henry replied, sipping his wine. "I've been researching them for over forty years."

"Why devote so much of your time to learning about them?"

"Because I want to expose them so the rest of the world can know what's going on," Henry revealed, his voice resolute. "When a group of wealthy and powerful people conspire to control the world, it makes me angry. The harm they've done to humanity is deplorable: unnecessary wars, famines, economic crises. They've orchestrated all of it."

"How far back does all of this go?" Tom wondered.

"Thousands of years, to ancient times," Henry answered.

"You mean like Egypt and the Middle East?" Oliver asked, unconvinced.

"Yes," Henry confirmed. "It's always been a battle of good versus evil, right versus wrong, God against the ungodly. Although the locations have changed, the lust for money and power has not."

"These people are linked all the way back to antiquity?" Oliver challenged, finding it improbable.

"They believe so. This nefarious group consists of thirteen European families, connected through bloodlines and marriages. Some are from royal dynasties, and others are wealthy bankers. They believe themselves to be special, different from the rest of society—chosen to rule over us," Henry articulated. "Analogous to the pyramid symbol seen on corporate logos, they have placed themselves at the top."

"How many people are involved?" Sarah asked, uneasy.

"At the center, there are no more than a few hundred, but those closely connected are in the thousands. Not many when you consider that they control most of the wealth in the world."

Henry poured another glass of wine, took a hearty sip, and continued. "Each bloodline is a member of the Committee, a secret society carried down from generation to generation. Members frequently gather to discuss and plan the outcome of the world. From this circle of influence arose numerous global institutes, corporations, foundations, and think tanks. Most of these organizations seem innocent on the surface but are evil at the core."

"How does my father fit into all of this?" Oliver inquired tensely.

"These groups recruit young people they believe they can use and control: brainwashed puppets who are placed in prominent positions to influence society."

"Even a prime minister?"

"Especially a prime minister, or a president, or an influential leader."

"But why my dad?"

"Your father was always ambitious—too ambitious for his own good," Henry answered resentfully. "He wanted everything now and was willing to cut corners to obtain it."

Oliver bowed his head, dismayed by the conversation. Henry leaned over and gently touched his shoulder.

"I know this is hard to hear, but it must be said," Henry conveyed with compassion. "These are ruthless people who play for keeps."

"I appreciate knowing," Oliver asserted. "Please continue."

"When he was in his late teens your father was recruited by the Committee and was immediately moved to Eton. He then transferred to Christ Church, Oxford—a bastion of influential members. From the beginning, they prepared him for politics. He was charismatic, likeable, and he didn't ask too many questions—the perfect candidate for public office."

"They invested all that time in him?" Oliver wondered aloud.

"These people plan things twenty, fifty, even a hundred years ahead," Henry explained. "And when a decision has been made, it's final."

Tom and Sarah had stopped eating, a glazed look in their eyes as they nervously listened.

Henry noticed their distressed faces. "Why don't we finish our meal, and we'll talk more in the library."

* * * * *

Later that evening, Gowerstone and Fontaine met Gustave in Montmartre, an artists' community overlooking central Paris. The winding cobblestone roads encircled Sacré-Cœur, the white Neo-Romanesque church that dominated the village.

All three quietly sat at Au Lapin Agile, a local café

and renowned haunt for artists and writers. Fontaine could feel the tension between these two seasoned professionals, each one sizing up the other. Gustave was dressed in a chic Italian suit and leather loafers. Gowerstone embodied the British Empire with his attire: a Burberry trench coat, a Kilgour tweed jacket, a crisp white Gieves & Hawkes shirt, and a royal blue Turnbull & Asser tie.

"How do you know Inspector Fontaine?" Gustave inquired, a hint of envy in his voice.

"Fontaine and I worked on a case years ago," Gowerstone replied.

"Was it successful?"

"All my cases are successful," Gowerstone stated matter-of-factly. "But Fontaine's instincts and natural abilities were indispensable."

Gustave studied him closely, not sure what to think. "Why involve her now?" he questioned, wary.

"She's the best agent I know, and I'd trust her with my life," Gowerstone replied firmly.

Fontaine smiled at Gowerstone, sipping her wine as she tried to relax.

"Since she's been *assisting* you, she's almost died twice," Gustave declared, his tone threatening. "You've put her in grave danger."

"It's nothing I can't handle," Fontaine interjected, hoping to defuse the hostility. "It goes with the profession."

"But is it also worth losing everything?" Gustave asked.

"What do you mean?"

"After the fire at your apartment, the chief is convinced you're behind it, that you're trying to destroy evidence," Gustave shared.

"That's ludicrous," Fontaine snapped.

"He's made you a suspect, and I've been ordered to bring you in."

Gowerstone grasped the handle of his Glock, ready to draw. "That won't be necessary," he warned Gustave, his tone steely.

"I'm not planning to," Gustave assured him, holding up his right hand to back Gowerstone down. "I know the accusations are false. I'm just letting you know where things stand."

"And where do you stand?" Gowerstone questioned.

"With Fontaine," Gustave replied adamantly. "She's my partner, and I'd also trust her with my life."

"I'm a fugitive," Fontaine said cynically, a bitter inflection in her voice.

"Unfortunately, yes," Gustave confirmed. "And I'm not the only one the chief has notified about arresting you."

"The rest of Interpol?"

"And the local police."

"Classic transference. Blame the innocent to cover your own guilt," Fontaine vented, stunned by the audacity.

"It also puts you on the defensive," Gowerstone added.

"You mean instead of finding Tom and Sarah?"

"Exactly," Gowerstone affirmed.

Fontaine gulped her wine and sat back, disheartened. "What can I do?"

"We stick to our plan," he responded evenly. "We leave tomorrow and track down the lead."

"Lead?" Gustave inquired, feeling excluded.

"Oliver's uncle who lives about an hour southwest of here," Fontaine whispered, surveying the room to see if anyone was listening.

"What if he's part of this whole conspiracy?" Gustave theorized. "You could be walking into a trap."

"A chance we're willing to take," Gowerstone stated.

"It's our only lead and we're running out of time," Fontaine stressed, anxious to leave Paris. "Have you discovered anything else?"

"The two men who broke into Oliver's apartment," Gustave began. "Their bodies were pulled out of the Seine this afternoon."

"Who were they?" Fontaine wondered.

"We have no idea," Gustave replied. "There was no identification. We ran their fingerprints and DNA but came up with nothing."

"And the assassin?"

"He could be anywhere."

"So that's how these people deal with failure," Gowerstone interjected. "They murder their own."

Fontaine was troubled by the revelation.

"I know this is overwhelming, but we must get to Tom and Sarah before they do," Gowerstone insisted, resolute.

"I agree," Fontaine asserted.

"When you leave Paris, I can stay behind and follow up on any leads," Gustave offered. "I'll let you know what develops and keep you updated."

"What will you tell the chief?"

"That I couldn't locate you and have no idea where you are," Gustave answered.

"If you continue to help me, you'll be risking your career," Fontaine cautioned him. "You wouldn't just lose your job—you'd be arrested."

"I'm willing to take that chance for you."

* * * * *

After dinner, Henry, Oliver, Tom, and Sarah sat in the library by the warm fire. Henry reclined in his leather chair and lit his pipe.

"You mentioned that Dr. Beagleswick and Professor Hainsworth spoke about World War I and World War II," Henry began, hoping to return to the conversation.

"A little," Sarah recalled vaguely. "Is it important?"

"Everything's important because everything's connected," Henry explained. "Those two wars were started and controlled by the Committee. They orchestrated the events and worked both sides of the conflict."

Oliver straightened in his chair, baffled by the absurdity of their actions. "But why do something so horrific?"

"Wealth and power," Henry stated unequivocally. "They say they make more money in one day of war than in a year of peace."

"That's awful," Sarah commented, repulsed by the thought.

"I agree, and it goes much deeper than that. Wars are strategically manufactured to break down the will of the people while reorganizing the global system. They create a conflict, then they offer their own solutions. Their motto is *Ordo ab Chao*, which means 'Order from Chaos.'"

Sarah listened intently. "Where were the Britfields in all of this?"

"They were still trying to return to their rightful place in power, but with two world wars involving millions of people, little could be accomplished. During all this confusion, members of secret societies continued to find and eliminate any remaining Britfields."

"I've never read or heard anything about this," Oliver admitted, flustered by his lack of knowledge.

"Why would you? The Committee owns most of the media and publishing houses—you read what they print. They also influence most of the colleges and universities, what's taught and what's not, what's deemed important and what's discarded," Henry informed them. "They're always pushing some false agenda."

"What happened after World War II?"

"A new era of tyranny began under communism, which was just another manufactured ideology to create terror and oppress millions of people," Henry answered, leaning forward in his chair. "The Committee wants us to live in constant fear—if there isn't a problem, they'll create one."

"How does all of this tie in with the Britfields?" Tom inquired, anxious for answers.

"Most of the world is ruled by the British monarchy. Although they appear as figureheads, their fortune is estimated to be in the trillions of pounds," Henry answered. "Britain still controls over twenty-five percent of the world's landmass."

"You mean like India and Australia?" Oliver questioned, astonished. "I thought they were sovereign nations."

"Although South Africa, India, Australia, and Canada were eventually given back to the people, it's just a façade," Henry clarified. "The British monarchy dictates their laws and influences their decisions."

Oliver, Tom, and Sarah listened with interest. Though they were overwhelmed with information, they appreciated receiving honest answers to their questions.

"While Britain may appear weaker than it once was," Henry continued, building to a crescendo, "it controls most of the world's money and power, centered in the City of London, which is a cesspool of corruption."

"You mean the banks and banking system," Oliver inferred, starting to see the financial connection.

"Yes," Henry replied, then took another puff on his pipe.

Sarah edged forward in her seat. "What about the United States?"

"After America won its independence in 1783, British secret societies infiltrated the government, manipulated politicians, and influenced most of the presidents. They also took over the entire monetary system in 1913. The Federal Reserve is a private bank owned by thirteen families, mostly European."

"Again, it's about the money," Sarah asserted. "Did America have any good presidents?"

"A few, but as you may know, they were either shot or assassinated. The Committee was quick to eliminate any ideas of real independence."

"With Britain as powerful as it once was, a true claim to the monarchy would be devastating," Oliver concluded, envisioning the chaos that would ensue.

"Yes," Henry corroborated. "From what I've gathered, Tom's appearance at Windsor Castle over six months ago threw the Committee into a panic."

"You've been following this?" Sarah asked, surprised by his familiarity.

"From a distance," Henry replied, carefully gauging his answer. "I have an alliance of contacts, patriotic men and women who know what's going on and are committed to stopping the Committee."

"What about these other groups?" Oliver asked. "When I was at Oxford, I heard a few secret societies mentioned."

"There are hundreds of these organizations. Some you've heard of, and many you haven't," Henry elaborated. "Each one has its own agenda and carries out specific orders."

"Like the Masons?"

"Precisely," Henry validated, proud of his nephew's knowledge. "Centuries old, the Masons appear to be a simple organization, carrying out noble endeavors. However, as you progress up the hierarchy, their goals become more sinister. Few ever reach the top level of thirty-third degrees or beyond. The details of their real beliefs and activities are hidden in secret books and practiced at clandestine rituals."

"W-what do you recommend we do?" Sarah asked timidly.

"As you mentioned earlier, you need to get to the Loire

Valley and locate Tom's family to confirm that he's a Britfield," Henry emphasized. "Once you're there, they'll protect you."

"And the Codex?"

Henry puffed on his pipe, contemplating. "May I see it?"

"I'll get it," Oliver said, leaving the room.

He quickly went to the car and returned a few minutes later, placing the Codex in front of Henry.

"I've heard about this book," Henry said, admiring the priceless object. "I knew it existed. I just can't believe you found it."

Henry spent thirty minutes gently turning the pages, mumbling to himself and shaking his head in astonishment. Meanwhile, Tom noticed Sarah's worried expression. He gently reached over and grabbed her hand.

"It's going to be okay," Tom promised, his eyes confident. "We'll get through this together."

Sarah smiled, her fear melting away. "I know," she sighed deeply. "It's just a lot to think about."

Henry finally finished and looked up. "This is extremely thorough," he asserted. "I've never seen anything so complete."

"We had it authenticated," Oliver added proudly. "Professor Beauchamp at the Sorbonne confirmed it's genuine."

"You've done well," Henry stated. "But you must guard this Codex."

Oliver looked at Tom and Sarah with trepidation. The risks and responsibilities were weighing heavily on him.

"Can you help us, Uncle?" Oliver asked.

Henry paused, mulling over the request. Silence descended as everyone eagerly awaited his answer.

"Of course I will," Henry answered wholeheartedly. "I'm a part of this now, just like you."

"What can we do with the Codex?"

Henry walked over to the fireplace mantle and poured himself a brandy, swirling it around and taking a sip.

"If handled correctly, there's enough information here to expose centuries of corruption and establish the Britfields as the rightful heirs to the British throne. There are thousands of patriots waiting to rise against this tyranny. Tom could be the spark that ignites the hearts of millions. Just as Victor Hugo once wrote, 'All the forces in the world are not so powerful as an idea whose time has come.' I believe this time has come."

"I'm curious," Oliver wondered. "I mentioned on the phone that we escaped from the Louvre into a private corridor. Where does it lead?"

"The French prime minister's office," Henry replied succinctly. "As I said, all the heads of state are involved, one way or another. If they're not bought or bribed, they're blackmailed or removed."

Henry yawned and looked at his watch. "It's almost one in the morning. Perhaps we should get some rest."

"Good idea," Oliver agreed, his heart heavy and his eyes weary.

"I've had Stevens prepare three bedrooms. He'll show you upstairs."

"Thank you again. I didn't know who else to turn to," Oliver acknowledged in a downtrodden tone.

"Don't worry," Henry assured him, impressed by his initiative. "We'll figure out what to do."

Henry stood, picking up the Codex. "If you don't mind, I would like to lock this in my safe tonight."

"That's a good idea, Uncle."

"I wish everyone a good night's sleep."

Henry disappeared through the doorway as Stevens entered.

"I'll show you to your rooms."

10
THE UNEXPECTED GUESTS

Early the next morning, the British prime minister was chauffeured to Pall Mall Street, London, a prominent boulevard known for its private clubs, including the Athenaeum, the Carlton Club, and the Institute of Directors. With the current crisis escalating, the prime minister was summoned by the Committee to meet two of its representatives.

The PM was dropped off at the Oxford Club, escorted by his security staff. After checking in, he took an elevator to a private suite on the third floor. His bodyguards waited outside as the prime minister entered and shut the door.

The oak-paneled room was decorated with nineteenth-century oil paintings depicting collegiate rowing matches along the River Cherwell. A picture window looked toward St. James Park, where Londoners hustled back and forth to work. Two middle-aged men sat at the far end of a long table.

The first man, Leopold, spoke with a French accent and wore a tailored burgundy suit. He was unusually tall, with blond shoulder-length hair. His persona was cold. Dorian, the second man, spoke with an Italian accent. He was heavyset, had long black hair tied into a ponytail, and was dressed in a crisp charcoal suit.

"Sit," Leopold ordered.

The prime minister took a deep breath, tightened his tie, and sat at the other end of the table, his throat dry, his hands shaky.

"I was just informed that—"

"Quiet," Leopold interrupted. "You'll not speak until you're spoken to. Is that understood?"

The prime minister nodded submissively.

"Not only has the Britfield Codex been stolen from our sacred chamber at the Louvre, but it was taken by your son," Leopold vented feverishly.

"Your own flesh and blood betrayed you," Dorian sneered, a look of loathing in his malevolent eyes. "The question is, why is Oliver with Tom and Sarah?"

"I have no idea, sir," the PM replied clumsily, a look of shock on his face.

"No idea," Leopold repeated in a mocking tone. "The one book and one child that could bring down the British government, and you're unaware of how this transpired."

"Y-yes, completely," the PM stuttered, fearing for his life.

"We've retrieved camera footage from Oxford showing that Oliver not only met Tom and Sarah at Christ Church over six months ago, but he provided them a safe place to hide when the police were looking for them," Leopold revealed, waiting for a reaction. "Now he's once again assisting them."

The prime minister was flabbergasted. "I'm completely unaware—"

"Quiet," Leopold bellowed, rising from his seat, his face inflamed with anger.

"We're still trying to piece together how this happened, but for now, our only objective is to retrieve that Codex and eliminate the children," Dorian said as he searched the prime minister's face for any traces of deception.

"Know this, Prime Minister," Leopold began, "as of this morning, all of your assets have been frozen. Your money, property, and stock holdings have been transferred to one of our Swiss accounts. Everything you owned is now ours."

Stunned by this information, the prime minister didn't dare speak or oppose their actions.

"As far as your position as prime minister, we'll see if you live to the end of the week," Leopold contended, seething with rage. "Is that understood?"

"Yes, sir," the prime minister groveled.

"Now it's time for you to be useful again. We need to find your son," Leopold continued, relentless. "Where would he go outside of Paris?"

Instinctively, the prime minister knew the answer but withheld the information.

Leopold marched around the table and hovered over him. "You have something to tell me?"

"I think, perhaps, Oliver may have gone to my brother's estate," the prime minister confessed reluctantly.

"Yes, your brother. He once refused our invitation to join us and we've never forgotten. However, he's elusive, and we haven't been able to locate him. Do you know where he is living now?" Leopold asked as he opened his jacket, revealing a Cougar .45 caliber pistol.

Terrified at what they would do to him, the prime minister yielded.

"I can furnish you with the address," he whispered regrettably.

"Good," Leopold said as he walked back to his seat.

"What are you going to do to my son?"

"Right now I'd worry about your own life."

* * * * *

After a solid night's rest, Tom awoke to a bright sunny morning. He eased out of his comfortable sheets, slipped on a silk robe that had been placed bedside, and glanced around his room. Even though Tom didn't know anything about antiques, he could tell the space had been decorated with the finest.

The decor was a tour de force of antiquity: Persian rugs, Spanish antique cabinets, medieval statuary, French satin drapes, and a Tudor-style four-poster bed with an embroidered canopy.

After washing up and dressing, Tom wandered into the hallway and down the stairs to the kitchen. Henry stood at the stove frying eggs. Oliver and Sarah were already sitting outside.

"Good morning, Tom," Henry greeted him cheerfully. "Would you like two eggs or three?"

"Three," Tom replied.

"Excellent. You have a hearty appetite," Henry added with a chuckle. "Why don't you join the others in the garden and I'll be out shortly."

Tom went outside, where Sarah and Oliver sat at a table near the pool. Stevens poured Tom a tall glass of freshly squeezed orange juice and gently placed a linen napkin on his lap.

"How did you sleep?" Oliver asked, his worries briefly forgotten.

"That's the first good night's rest I've had in months," Tom sighed.

"Me too, although I had some wild dreams," Sarah added.

"Anything interesting?" Oliver asked, his curiosity peaked.

"It was the last forty-eight hours all mixed together," Sarah replied in a heavy tone.

Oliver laughed. "What do you think of my uncle's home?"

"Are you kidding me? This place is amazing," Tom responded as he gazed around the breathtaking estate.

Now visible in the sunlight, the property was surrounded by formal gardens, flagstone pathways, and neatly trimmed shrubs. A tree-lined esplanade stretched to the nearby pond, and cascading fountains poured into marble basins. Apple orchards, olive trees, and rolling fields with hedges enclosed an array of thoroughbred horses and patch-eyed cows.

Henry approached the table carrying several plates of gourmet treats: thick bacon slices, fresh farm eggs, strawberry crepes, and blueberry pancakes. "Help yourself," he said proudly.

"I take it you like to cook?" Sarah asked, admiring the generous portions.

"Although I'm British, French cooking is the only way

to live," Henry professed. "When you're on your own, it's an important skill to master."

"You never married?" Sarah inquired.

"No," Henry mumbled to himself, remembering his earlier life. "However, I came close."

"Please continue, Uncle," Oliver interjected. "I don't know this story."

"It was too many years ago, Oliver. Perhaps another time," Henry said dismissively. "Right now we need to discuss our strategy. Chambord is only a few hours south of here, and we should leave as soon as possible."

* * * * *

Late that afternoon, Henry was in his upstairs office with Tom, Sarah, and Oliver. An opened titanium briefcase sat on the desk. Next to a black umbrella a beige Burberry trench coat was draped over an armchair.

Henry was hastily finalizing details when he paused at a sixteenth-century Baroque painting. As he gently pressed the frame, the three-by-four-foot canvas sprang open. Hidden behind was a safe.

"So that's where you stored the Codex last night," Oliver observed, peering on with interest.

"Along with other necessities," Henry said mysteriously.

Henry fiddled with the complex locking system, dialing right and left, then inserting his thumb in a digital scanner. The six-inch-thick steel door eased open. Henry removed the Codex, some sealed folders, and a USB flash drive. He carefully placed these items inside separate compartments in his briefcase.

"What's all this for?" Sarah wondered, staring at the briefcase.

"Valuable information that will expose these despicable organizations and dishonest people," Henry replied with conviction. "Your visit has inspired me. It's time to rise up and fight together."

Henry returned to the safe, removing a Beretta 9mm, a handful of cartridges, a satellite phone, and bundles of hundred-euro notes.

Tom and Sarah glanced at Oliver, who was staring at the pistol. "Is that loaded?" Oliver asked, followed by a gulp.

Henry shoved in a cartridge. "It is now."

A loud knock at the front door echoed through the house. Everyone froze.

"That's odd," Henry remarked, disturbed. "I'm not expecting anyone, and the front gate is locked."

Steven's voice came over the intercom: "Sir, there's someone at the front door. They bypassed our exterior fencing and security cameras. Should I alert the local police and take precautionary action?"

All four stared at each other, anticipating the worst.

"No, that won't be necessary," Henry replied calmly. "Go see who it is but wait for me."

"Yes, sir."

"And, Stevens, be careful."

Henry cocked his gun, loading the chamber. "Stay here and don't make a sound," Henry instructed. "If something happens, take the briefcase and escape down the back stairwell."

"Yes, Uncle," Oliver said, nodding nervously.

Henry left the office and walked down the hallway to a second-story terrace that overlooked the front door. Designed with marble steps and a decorative iron railing, the staircase descended from both sides. Henry held his pistol upright and motioned to Stevens. The butler cautiously approached the entryway.

"Who is it?" the butler asked in his signature monotone.

"Inspector Fontaine," a woman answered. "I need to speak with Sir Horningbrook. Is he in?"

Hearing her voice, Tom's and Sarah's eyes widened. As they entered the hallway, Henry glanced over. "Who is she?" he asked in a loud whisper.

"She's our contact in France," Sarah replied, bewildered as to how she had found them. "She was assigned to protect us."

"What happened?"

"Everything," Sarah said dryly, throwing up her hands.

"I see." Henry nodded, mulling over how to proceed. "Stay where you are, and I'll make sure it's safe."

Henry glided down the staircase and positioned himself several feet behind the door.

"How did you get through our front gate, Inspector?" Stevens asked loudly. "That's breaking and entering."

"I apologize. It's an occupational hazard."

"Meaning?"

"I'm used to getting into places."

"You're trespassing on private property."

"I understand, but it's vital that I speak with Sir Horningbrook."

Henry steadily raised his weapon and signaled to Stevens to open the door.

Once the butler unlatched the various locks, Fontaine entered. She was dressed in khaki pants, a black turtleneck, and a brown windbreaker. Her long auburn hair was pulled back and tied over her left shoulder with a tartan ribbon.

"Thank you," Fontaine said respectfully.

"That's far enough, Inspector," Henry warned her. "If that's who you really are."

Fontaine slowly turned, staring directly at the gun's barrel, then made eye contact with Henry. She removed her identification badge and held it so he could see.

"How do I know that's legitimate?" Henry questioned. "With the current technology, you could have bought it or made it yourself."

"I suppose you're right," Fontaine admitted, trying not to provoke him.

"What do you want, Inspector?"

"I'm looking for your nephew, Oliver," she replied with urgency.

"Why, what's he done?"

"Oliver may be in danger."

"Explain," Henry pressed.

"I'm not at liberty to discuss the details. I'll need to speak with him directly," she maintained, knowing the subject was sensitive.

"What makes you think he's here?"

"We know he was staying in Paris, but he's missing. You're his nearest relative."

Oliver walked in sight on the upper landing. "I know who you are, Ms. Fontaine," he said, wanting to reassure his uncle that she was not a threat.

Fontaine looked up, startled but relieved. "Then you know who I'm looking for and the danger they're in. Have you seen them?" she pleaded. "Are they with you?"

Without a sound, Gowerstone emerged from behind an interior wall, his gun aimed at Henry. The detective was wearing dark pleated slacks, a navy pullover sweater, and a black Barbour wax jacket.

"Put down your weapon, Sir Horningbrook."

"Who are you?" Henry demanded, surprised as he turned.

"I'm Detective Gowerstone, Scotland Yard."

Henry squeezed his grip tighter, ignoring the request. "You're a long way from London, Detective."

Recognizing his voice, Tom and Sarah excitedly joined Oliver on the landing. "Detective Gowerstone," Tom exclaimed.

Seeing Tom and Sarah alive and unharmed, Gowerstone let out a heartfelt sigh. "Thank God you're both safe," he declared.

"It's okay, Sir Horningbrook. He's with us," Sarah confirmed, her face aglow.

Henry lowered his weapon, exhaling slowly. Tom and Sarah rushed down the staircase and were embraced by Gowerstone.

"Fontaine and I were so worried," Gowerstone said, hugging them tightly. "You gave us quite a scare."

"We've a lot to tell you," Tom conveyed. "It's been crazy since the ferry in Dover."

Seeing Sarah and Tom in person for the first time, Fontaine's eyes brightened. After months of searching, she had finally found them.

Gowerstone nodded to her. "Good work, Inspector."

"Thank you, Detective." Fontaine turned to Sir Horningbrook. "We appreciate you watching over Tom and Sarah. We're indebted."

"It was my pleasure," Henry said chivalrously, then motioned to the other room. "Perhaps we should sit. There's much to discuss."

They all went into the library and sat around the fireplace: Henry on his comfy leather armchair; Sarah, Tom, and Oliver on a high back French sofa; Fontaine and Gowerstone on Chippendale chairs. Stevens brought refreshments on a silver tray.

"I've been searching for you two for over six months," Fontaine declared with a hint of relief.

"It's not our fault," Tom reacted. "So much has happened."

"I want to hear it all," Fontaine insisted. "Start with the ferry from Dover."

Two hours later, Tom and Sarah had covered their time since leaving Dover on the Ferry in late December. Oliver added details about his involvement and what he knew about his father. Henry, Gowerstone, and Fontaine shared what they had uncovered: the Committee, the thirteen ruling families, secret societies, and other nefarious groups. It was a complex puzzle that was finally starting to fit together.

The afternoon sun dipped into the horizon, staining the clouds a deep pink and purple.

Exterior and interior lights switched on all over the estate. The fireplace glowed, flames roaring and logs sparking.

Sarah and Fontaine had an instant connection. Graceful and intelligent, the inspector was the older sister Sarah never had. They chatted in French, sharing bits of their past and hopes for the future.

Stevens rolled in a silver cart filled with goat cheese, stuffed mushrooms, minced beef with potato puree, egg custard with caramel sauce, and fruit tarts.

Henry enjoyed a glass of Louis XIII cognac as he listened intently to the conversation. For years he had felt alone, and now he had trustworthy allies. He glanced at Gowerstone. "My brother has mentioned you. How long have you known him?"

"Since we were students at Eton," Gowerstone answered. "I first met him when I was sixteen. However, he had a private side to him I never understood."

"Yes, my brother has many secrets," Henry revealed. "Some I'm aware of, and others I'm not."

"He joined the elite clubs at Eton and Oxford, groups that met in private rooms and underground chambers," Gowerstone recalled. "I never had an interest in them, so I suppose our friendship was more surface than solid. Yet I always respected him. Until now."

"There's a part of your past that my brother spoke of, one I'd like to learn more about," Henry hinted, approaching the subject tactfully.

Gowerstone became quiet, staring at Sir Horningbrook. "I wasn't always a detective, if that's what you mean."

Surprised, Fontaine leaned over. "Do tell, Detective," she prodded.

Gowerstone shifted in his chair, the topic unpleasant.

"Which intelligence agency was it?" Henry inquired, discerning Gowerstone's evasiveness.

"MI7," Gowerstone responded guardedly.

"I've heard of MI5 and MI6, but I've never heard of MI7," Fontaine said, fascinated. "Could you elaborate?"

"When I graduated from Oxford, I was young and ambitious," Gowerstone began. "At the time I had no idea what I was getting into."

"Why did they approach you?" Henry asked.

"I fit their profile. Prestigious schools, top of my class, multilingual, no brothers or sisters, and I was driven to succeed," Gowerstone answered.

"You never mentioned this," Fontaine said, feeling excluded.

"We're not allowed to speak of it. Once you're in, you never really leave," Gowerstone explained.

Henry propped up in his chair, eager to hear more. "How long did you serve with them?"

"Seven years, six months," Gowerstone replied.

"From my understanding, that's a lifetime."

"Yes," Gowerstone conceded with a trace of animosity. "The things I saw, what we had to do. People can't imagine the power of MI7 and what they're behind."

"Such as?" Oliver inquired, engrossed in the conversation.

"The organization is involved in countless operations, not just in Britain, but globally. They're usually behind the disasters we read about, including instigating wars and destabilizing countries, like the Middle East at present. You see, it's important for them to keep the public distracted and dependent on the government. If there's not an enemy, they'll create one."

Gowerstone paused, collecting his thoughts. He sipped a glass of water, then continued. "MI7 also controls MI6, which was instrumental in creating America's CIA and Israel's Mossad, two of the world's largest intelligence agencies. MI6 still controls them both," Gowerstone explained.

"I thought America and Israel were sovereign nations?" Fontaine questioned, puzzled.

"With MI7, there's no independence, only dependence. If you pull back the curtain and look hard enough, everything is connected."

Gowerstone was relieved to share what he knew. Years of carrying around these secrets had taken its toll. Now he was with friends, people he could trust.

"How does this tie into the Committee or the other thirteen families?" Sarah asked, trying to link the pieces together.

"The Committee was instrumental in forming these organizations. Many of their members serve at the top levels. Intelligence is everything—what others know and what they're hiding. MI6 and MI7 are behind countless endeavors, such as government overthrows and the war on terrorism. The terrorist groups we are supposedly hunting were actually created by the CIA and MI6."

"To justify wars and control other countries," Fontaine realized.

"Exactly. If a dictator deviated from the Committee's agenda, they claimed he was a threat and got rid of him. If they want the resources of another country, they destabilize it and then take everything. Although I had my suspicions, I didn't discover this until recently. When you work for these groups, you're usually compartmentalized."

"Compartmentalized?" Tom inquired, unaware of the term.

"Isolated from others," Gowerstone clarified. "When you're hired, they train you for a specific field. All you know is your assignment. You do what you're told and never ask questions. Only the top people understand what's truly going on."

Sarah and Tom leaned back, distressed. This was far more than they imagined, a nightmare that was becoming a reality.

"How did you get out?" Fontaine asked.

"It wasn't easy, but I finally left," Gowerstone replied ambiguously. "MI7 knew I didn't have the stomach for it, but I was loyal and would never betray them. They still keep surveillance on me. But I know their tactics, so I've been careful."

"And now?" Henry questioned.

"That loyalty has ended," Gowerstone stated decisively.

"What did you do when you left?" Fontaine inquired, wanting to learn more.

"I became a detective," Gowerstone answered proudly. "I wanted to help others, which is the reason I focused on missing children and runaway orphans. I thought it was a noble pursuit, a way of compensating for all the things I was forced to do."

Henry was enthralled by what he was hearing, a story that was finally making sense. "What happened over a decade ago in Kent, England?"

"Known as the last location of the Britfields, the house was plundered, and their son was kidnapped," Gowerstone responded. "From that day I committed myself to finding their son."

"But you ran into problems?" Henry asked, already familiar with the case.

"Yes," Gowerstone recalled with bitterness. "Every time I got close to finding a clue or a connection, someone interfered or sabotaged my work. Important documents were stolen, and witnesses vanished. After two years of investigation, I was forced by my superiors to drop the case."

"Who was behind the kidnapping?" Henry probed, suspicious of his brother.

"From what I discovered, the Committee orchestrated most of it, along with the British prime minister. He betrayed me and the Britfield family."

"And their son?"

"He was never found and presumed dead—that is, until now." Gowerstone smiled at Tom, a tender devotion in his eyes.

"For a long time I've known about my brother's activities," Henry disclosed. "There was little I could do, except gather information and seek the help of trusted allies."

"I was clueless; I couldn't see past our friendship," Gowerstone admitted. "I didn't find out that the prime minister was involved until Professor Hainsworth informed me at Canterbury Cathedral. Since then I've been dedicated to researching these malicious people and bringing them to justice."

"The prime minister, my brother, is really just a puppet controlled by the Committee. He follows their direct orders."

Oliver reflected on his father, saddened by what he was hearing. It was still hard to believe.

"They really have that much power?" Oliver questioned, struggling to accept the truth.

"Yes, complete power," Henry articulated. "Every important position in the Western world is influenced by the Committee: in politics, governments, corporations."

"Who controls them?"

"The Committee takes its orders from the British royals and other ruling families."

"They are connected to all this?" Sarah questioned.

"They are at the center of it," Henry announced with certainty.

"I always thought they were just a figurehead, a tourist attraction who represented a historical past," Sarah expressed, surprised.

"That's exactly what the royalty wants you to believe. They appear powerless but hold all the power," Henry explained. "It's all smoke and mirrors. They make you see one thing while they do another—they create global initiatives based on lies and false science to invent a problem and generate fear. Then they collect billions of dollars to solve the fabricated crisis."

"That's terrible," Sarah voiced, struggling to understand.

"Another one of their tricks is to create worldwide charities, promote their false causes, then pilfer the money," Henry continued, diving deeper into the subject.

"You mean like nonprofits that advocate for a certain disease and ask for donations," Fontaine inquired, repulsed by what she was hearing.

"Yes. They funnel millions through these organizations and use the money for their own clandestine projects," Henry confirmed. "When you search deep enough, you'll discover this entire group is based on occultism, supernatural beliefs and practices. They're heartless entities that have sold their souls."

There was an eerie silence; a malevolent presence pierced the air as if an unwelcome guest had suddenly arrived.

"It all sounds so hopeless," Sarah confessed.

"It's never hopeless," Henry insisted, his voice rising. "Regardless of how dark it may seem, there's always hope. Many people around the world know what's going on. They know they've been deceived. The blinding veil of ignorance is slowly lifting, and the truth is seeping through. There are thousands, millions who would rally around a true cause. Returning the Britfields to the throne could be the spark that ignites a revolution of liberty over tyranny."

Tom gazed at the fire, listening to the discussion. He

felt overwhelmed as he began to comprehend his place in all this. He was a simple orphan who was now destined for greatness.

Henry looked over at Tom. "It's a lot to take in, isn't it?"

"You think?" Sarah interrupted, a bit uneasy. "A thirteen-year-old boy now heir to the British throne, a global conspiracy, and a potential revolution."

"Sometimes it's not what we choose but what chooses us," Henry professed.

"I just want to find my family," Tom said earnestly. "That's what's important to me."

"And we will," Fontaine vowed, her voice encouraging. "Tomorrow we'll make sure that you and Sarah get to the Loire Valley and Châteaux Chambord."

Oliver looked at his uncle. "What about the Codex?"

"That's right," Henry remembered. "Oliver, go to my office and bring down the briefcase."

Oliver jumped up from his chair and rushed up the stairs. A moment later, he returned with the titanium briefcase. Gowerstone and Fontaine watched intently as Henry opened it.

"What's all this?" Fontaine inquired, glaring at the ancient book encased in silver.

"It's a complete history of the Britfields from their beginning until 1837," Sarah answered proudly. "It has documents, deeds, legal papers—everything."

"Where did you get it?"

Sarah paused as she considered her response. "We . . . found it at the Louvre."

"Found it?" Fontaine asked suspiciously.

"Borrowed it," Oliver interrupted, realizing they were in the presence of a French inspector and a British detective.

"Well, it's really Tom's, isn't it?" Sarah countered.

"Don't worry. I'm not here to arrest anybody," Fontaine asserted, smiling warmly at Sarah.

Gowerstone leaned in closer, analyzing the text. "This is extraordinary," he acknowledged, carefully turning the pages. "Finally, a complete anthology of proof. Has it been authenticated?"

"Yes, sir," Tom answered readily. "Oliver introduced us to a professor at the Sorbonne. She agreed that it's real."

"There's more, Detective," Henry continued, grabbing his folders and USB flash drive. "I've been gathering this information for decades: names, dates, photographs, linked events—indisputable evidence of this global conspiracy. It should be everything you need to expose these people and their corruption."

Gowerstone looked approvingly at Henry. "This is exactly what I've been searching for."

"It's my life's work," Henry expressed with a heavy sigh. "I trust you can use it."

As Gowerstone reached for the documents, the alarm keypads started flashing, followed by a warning sound. Henry looked over, startled. "Someone's on the property."

The entire house went dark, except for the glow from the fireplace.

"Everyone, get down," Gowerstone shouted.

They all dropped to the floor. A second later, the front door exploded with a bright flash, scattering fragments of wood and stone everywhere. Shouting erupted as the rumble of footsteps approached.

"What's happening?" Henry asked in disbelief that his house was being overtaken.

"We've been compromised," Gowerstone deduced, his instincts sharp. "You must get Tom and Sarah somewhere safe."

"Understood, I know where to go," Henry said, leaning up and putting the documents back in the briefcase.

Henry closed the lid, but before he could grab the briefcase, a cacophony of gunfire erupted. Bullets pierced the walls, peppering the ceiling and shattering priceless objects.

Gowerstone glanced at Fontaine. "Are you ready?"

"Always," she replied, her adrenaline pumping.

They swiftly removed their weapons and turned around so their backs were against each other.

From every section of the house, men dressed in black tactical gear approached the library. Wearing infrared goggles, they tracked their targets with a green laser attached to their weapons. The glowing beams shifted back and forth.

Gowerstone nodded to Henry. "Go! We'll keep them busy."

Hastily crawling over the wooden floor, Oliver, Tom, and Sarah followed Henry to another part of the room.

The fireplace flames lit the area as shadows jumped around. Tracking one of the figures, Gowerstone let loose three rounds. The man stumbled backward and fell. Fontaine targeted another man and released two rounds, hitting him in the chest. Their senses alert, Fontaine and Gowerstone methodically fired again, clipping one man and neutralizing another.

"They're everywhere," Fontaine exclaimed as a volley of shots ripped across the floor and shredded the sofa. Flashes of gunfire illuminated a snowfall of feathers drifting in the air.

Meanwhile, Henry had crawled to the library cabinets and tapped a hidden switch. A side panel popped open, revealing a cavity.

"Where does it lead?" Oliver asked, peering inside.

"To my private wine cellar," Henry replied, his voice shaky.

The garden windows smashed inward as two men entered. Fontaine and Gowerstone ducked down and moved in opposite directions.

Now inside, the main assault team scoured each room, searching for its prey. One of the men tossed a flash grenade into the middle of the library.

"Close your eyes and cover your ears," Gowerstone yelled from across the room.

There was a loud bang and a flash of light. Windows shook in their frames and cracked.

Disoriented, Henry crouched, trying to recover his senses. Tom and Sarah leaned back, holding their ringing ears. Oliver struggled to regain his equilibrium.

One of the men spotted Tom and grabbed his ankle, dragging him backward.

"Help," Tom gasped, scratching at the floor.

Bending down, the man pulled him closer. "Stop resisting me," he growled with contempt.

"Never," Tom vowed, fighting with all his strength.

Suddenly a china vase smashed over the man's head, knocking him out.

"Not on my watch," Sarah stated, a defiant look in her eyes.

"T-thanks," Tom mumbled, grateful for her intervention.

"Don't mention it," she said coolly as she grabbed his hand and scurried back toward the hidden door.

Henry recovered from the initial shock. "Let's get to my wine cellar," he stammered, still lightheaded.

"What about the briefcase?" Oliver asked, pointing toward the table.

"It's too dangerous," Henry warned, waving him into the cabinet opening.

"We can't just leave it," Oliver declared.

Before Henry could object, Oliver was gone.

The entire room had turned into a war zone as bullets whizzed back and forth. Small fires started burning, creating a hazy smoke.

Scrambling along the floor, Oliver made his way back to the table and searched for the briefcase. Glancing around, he saw it had been knocked to the ground and swiftly grabbed the handle. Firmly tucking the briefcase under his arm, he crawled back through a wasteland of debris toward the secret panel.

"Here you go, Uncle," Oliver said breathlessly, his face covered in sweat. "It's too valuable to leave behind."

"Good lad—that was very brave," Henry exclaimed, stunned by Oliver's courage.

"Where's Stevens?" Oliver wondered.

"I don't know," Henry replied, struck by the thought. "Take the briefcase below with Tom and Sarah. I'll meet you at the bottom. There's a flashlight right behind the panel."

Taking out each man with precision, Gowerstone remained cool and methodical. As figures appeared, he released multiple rounds. One man fell in his tracks, while another man was blown back into a wall. One by one, Gowerstone lessened the odds against them.

Spotting Gowerstone crouched in a far corner, one of the men carefully aimed his weapon. Before he could pull the trigger, a wooden object clobbered him in the head and he crumpled to the floor.

Stevens marched forward, holding the butt of his Remington 870 Tactical shotgun, angered by the intrusion. Gowerstone glanced over and nodded thanks.

Surrounded by four armed men, Marcel entered through the front door of the house and scanned the rooms leading from the foyer.

"Spread out and find those children," Marcel ordered ferociously.

As the men dispersed, Marcel spotted Fontaine in the library through the hazy darkness. "She's still alive," he murmured to himself, shocked.

Fontaine looked over—their eyes locked.

Fontaine advanced around the room, trying to get to him. As she lined up Marcel in the sight of her Glock, another man grabbed her from behind, lifting her off the floor. He squeezed tighter, forcing her arms to tense, and she dropped her weapon.

Fontaine intuitively switched to self-defense mode, slamming her head back into the man's face. Dazed, he loosened his grip. She smashed her right heel into his toe, making him release his hold. She then arched forward, knocking his stomach. As he bent down, she twisted around and slapped his ears, stunning his reflexes. She then pulled his head down as her right knee came upward, knocking his face and throwing him backward. She followed with a high kick to his forehead and a roundhouse to his neck, which sent him flying to the ground. He was immobilized.

As Fontaine reached for her gun, someone smacked her from behind and she fell to the floor.

"You should be dead," Marcel declared, holding his weapon.

Seeing Fontaine from across the room, Gowerstone aimed his Glock at Marcel, but before he could pull the trigger, a barrage of bullets flew his way.

Gowerstone leaped behind the sofa, firing as he jumped. A bullet clipped Marcel's arm and spun him around, causing him to drop his weapon.

By the time Fontaine grabbed her Glock, Marcel was gone.

"Detective, Inspector, over here," Henry hollered, hunkering by the hidden panel.

Gowerstone and Fontaine quickly maneuvered through the smoky wreckage of the once pristine library.

"Quick—get inside," Henry urged. "Take the stairs to the wine cellar."

"What about you?" Fontaine questioned, her breathing heavy.

"I'm waiting for Stevens," Henry replied.

Fontaine went first, shadowed by Gowerstone. They descended a twenty-foot spiral staircase and met Oliver below. Everyone was on edge, their faces pale, their clothing soaked in perspiration.

"Is anyone hurt?" Fontaine asked, a worried look in her eyes.

"We're okay," Oliver confirmed, holding up the flashlight in his right hand and the briefcase in his left hand.

"Tom? Sarah?"

"We're fine," they mumbled from the shadows, still traumatized.

Gowerstone gently touched Fontaine's shoulder. "What about you?"

"A bit shaken," Fontaine admitted, her expression intense. "I didn't see that coming."

"None of us did," Gowerstone conveyed, angered. "I'd better check on Sir Horningbrook and Stevens."

Gowerstone reloaded his weapon and went back up the stairs.

Before reaching the safety of the bookshelves, Stevens had been shot in the leg. He cringed in pain as he crawled toward Henry.

"I-I don't think I can go much farther," Stevens gasped, putting pressure on his wound. "I'll hold them off as long as I can."

"I'm not leaving you," Henry promised, his face etched with devotion. "You've served me for thirty years. Now it's time that I serve you."

Henry leaned over and grabbed Stevens from behind.

"Hold on to me," Henry directed, lifting him upright and dragging him behind the panel.

They were met by Gowerstone, who gently assisted Stevens down the staircase. Closing the panel, Henry followed behind.

When they reached the bottom, Henry flipped on the lights. Rows and rows of wine bottles ran the length and breadth of the entire basement.

"Wow, I knew you loved wine, but this is borderline crazy," Oliver exclaimed, handing Henry the briefcase.

"I've been collecting for twenty years," Henry announced with a sense of accomplishment.

Fontaine diligently tended to Stevens, ripping fabric from her coat and wrapping it firmly around his wound. She then slid a wooden stick through the material and turned it, creating a tourniquet.

"Keep this tight. It'll slow the bleeding," Fontaine instructed, her voice soothing.

"Yes, Inspector," Stevens acknowledged.

"Is there another way out?" Gowerstone asked, searching for an alternative exit.

"There's a door at the other end," Henry replied. "It leads to the east garden and tennis courts. I have a bungalow about a half mile from here."

"But won't they search the entire property?" Oliver questioned.

"Trust me, nephew."

"We should move," Gowerstone insisted, his voice stern. "It won't take them long to figure out where we are."

* * * * *

Marcel surveyed the room, his right arm hanging from a temporary sling of ripped fabric, his left hand grasping his weapon.

The walls were riddled with bullet holes. Shredded paintings hung in their gilded frames, and shattered furniture was strewn everywhere. The small fires continued to burn, engulfing the house in smoke.

"They disappeared," one of the men reported, a bewildered look on his face.

"No one disappears," Marcel thundered back. "They're hiding somewhere. Rip this house apart and find them. We'll torch the entire place if we have to. That'll force them to come out of hiding."

* * * * *

Henry led the way toward the other side of the wine cellar, the titanium briefcase firmly in his hand.

The subterranean environment was a colorful collection of priceless vintages: Château Lafite 1865, Romanée-Conti 1945, Penfolds Grange Hermitage 1951, Château Mouton-Rothschild 1945, Château d'Yquem 1811, Château Margaux 1787.

Unable to help himself, Tom grabbed a bottle as he walked by. "Sir Horningbrook, what would something like this cost?" he asked.

"That one would go for around 280,000 pounds, or about 180,000 euros."

Tom gulped, his hand trembling. "Just for a bottle of wine?"

"It's not just a bottle of wine. It's a historical treasure, like a vintage car or a classical painting."

The others stared at each other, realizing the enormous value of his collection.

"Perhaps you should put that back," Sarah whispered, gently guiding Tom's hand to return the bottle.

They zigzagged through towering shelves, unable to see more than ten feet in front of them. Footsteps thundered from above, moving quickly throughout the house. It sounded as though objects were being hurled to the ground as the château was thoroughly ransacked.

"They're not going to quit until they find us," Fontaine commented, staring at the ceiling.

"It's only a matter of time before they discover the basement," Henry warned.

They marched down another corridor of bottles, turned a corner, and finally reached the end. Henry moved some empty wine barrels, revealing a stainless steel door and digital keypad.

"This tunnel was already here when I bought the estate. The aristocracy always built an escape route in their mansions in case they ever needed to get away," Henry informed them. "I replaced the old door when I upgraded my security system."

Henry tapped in a combination, which released the locking mechanism.

Grabbing the massive door, Oliver pulled it opened and shined the flashlight into the breach, revealing a narrow hallway that faded into the dark.

"At the other end is a set of stairs that leads up to the tennis courts, but it's been a while since I used it," Henry remarked ominously.

Oliver stared at him, eyes raised. "Meaning?"

"Hopefully the door at the other end still opens."

* * * * *

Marcel meticulously checked each wall in the library, scanning every wooden seam and panel.

"How did you escape?" he mumbled to himself, his fury mounting. "It's got to be here somewhere."

Marcel continued plundering the room, ripping paintings and tapestries from the walls. He tapped the paneling, listening for any hollow sounds. His men stood by, weapons ready.

Marcel reached the book cabinets. Most of the shelves were now empty, leather-bound books carelessly tossed about. Delicately moving his hand over the woodwork, he noticed a gap between two sections.

Marcel knelt to examine the intricate carvings along the edge and saw a discrepancy in the configuration. He pushed the section and a small panel popped opened, revealing a staircase.

"I knew it," Marcel stated, a sinister smile creeping across his face.

He glanced at his deputy, Maxwell. Six feet tall with a shaved head, Maxwell was built like a rock.

"This must lead to another exit from the château," Marcel indicated. "Gather a group of men and search the perimeter."

"Yes, sir," Maxwell said and hurried outside.

Standing by the bookcase, two men reloaded their guns.

"Get after them," Marcel ordered.

The two men nodded, yanked open the secret door, and entered.

Below, Fontaine could hear footsteps rattling the metal staircase.

"They've found the entrance," she whispered loudly. "We're out of time."

"Sir, should I implement the backup plan?" Stevens asked, knowing what was at stake.

Surveying his prized wine collection, Henry nodded sadly. "Flood it."

11
RESISTANCE

Stevens removed a brick of C4 explosive and a digital timer from the inside pocket of his overcoat.

Tom was mesmerized, impressed by the butler's resourcefulness. "Talk about being prepared," he said with admiration.

"It's a butler's creed to always be ready—anticipate the unexpected."

Stevens placed the explosive on a twelve-inch water pipe that ran along the basement wall. He set the timer for two minutes, then pulled a lever, closing all the floor drains.

"But your wine collection," Oliver protested, sadden by his uncle's sacrifice.

"Lives are more precious than possessions," Henry responded in a stoic manner. "Now let's get to the bungalow."

Using the flashlight as a guide, Oliver entered the passageway, shadowed by the others. Henry helped Stevens through the entrance, flipped off the basement lights, and shut the door, sealing it tight.

One by one, they followed the glowing flashlight: Sarah first, then Tom, Fontaine, Henry, and Gowerstone, who helped Stevens navigate the uneven brick floor.

Meanwhile, two men clamored down the staircase, guided by searchlights mounted under their weapons.

Side by side in military fashion, one man checked the left as the other checked the right.

As they turned one of the corners, a blistering explosion engulfed the basement, echoing loudly and rattling the wine bottles. A warm blast of wind knocked them off their feet. Blinded by the flash, their ears rang and their eyes stung.

"What happened?" one of the men shouted.

"I don't know," his teammate mumbled, trying to get to his feet, his legs wobbly.

He slowly rose, brushing off glass particles. As he bent down to retrieve his weapon, he could hear the distant sound of rushing water. The shelves started crashing together and knocking over.

"What the—"

Before either man could move, a tidal wave overpowered them.

The basement filled quickly, the men struggling to the surface, gasping for air.

Hearing the loud explosion, two more men had hurried down the metal staircase and had started searching the smoke-filled cellar for their comrades. They saw the oncoming flood and made a dash for the staircase.

It was useless. Before they touched the bottom step, the water reached them. All four men drowned.

* * * * *

Oliver came to a set of stairs. "We're here," he announced, guiding the flashlight to a ceiling hatch.

Henry stepped forward. "Let me go first and make sure it's safe."

Still clutching the titanium briefcase, Henry climbed the steps. He unlocked two side bolts and forced the stainless steel hatch up and over onto the ground.

"Is it clear?" Oliver asked anxiously.

Henry popped up his head and scanned the area. "I don't see anyone. Let's move quickly."

Everyone hurried up the stairs and onto the tennis courts, a small set of bleachers on each side and a chain-link fence surrounding the area. At one end was a white pergola with Greek columns supporting a terra cotta rooftop.

Rows of poplars and orange trees dotted the sprawling grounds, releasing a sweet aroma in the air. Bathed in moonlight, the east gardens were tranquil, the leaves covered in a bluish light.

They glanced back at the château. Flames were flickering in some of the rooms. An occasional flashlight skimmed the interior walls and jumped across the windows.

Oliver grabbed Henry's shoulder, motioning toward the distance. "They're coming."

About fifty yards away, a group of flashlights moved through the gardens.

"Follow me," Henry prompted.

Everyone trailed behind, their brisk walk morphing into a sprint.

* * * * *

Using a large spotlight, one of the men methodically combed the area, pausing on anything that looked suspicious. Maxwell stood close by. The beam glided across the hedges, occasionally stopping on a life-size statue before continuing.

Maneuvering the light across the tennis courts, he caught a glimpse of seven figures darting off in the opposite direction. The man steadied the light on the backs of the shortest two.

Startled, Sarah turned, the beam blinding her.

"It's them," the man yelled as he grabbed his rifle. "They're over here."

Suddenly four other flashlights pierced the blackness, illuminating the east garden.

"They've spotted us! We have to move faster," Henry emphasized.

Everyone darted toward a jungle of trees in front of them. Gowerstone held Stevens on one side while Fontaine grabbed him on the other, practically lifting him off the ground as they sprinted across the grass.

"Get the Hummers and track them down," Maxwell ordered, turning to one of his men. "Take one vehicle to the south side and the other to the north. We'll cut them off in the middle."

"Yes, sir," the man acknowledged, rushing to the Hummers parked by the château.

"The rest of you, this way," Maxwell shouted as he ran, followed by four other men.

* * * * *

Although it was difficult to see through the thickly knitted trees, Henry led the way, instinctively remembering the topography of his property. Oliver shadowed behind, attempting to hold the flashlight.

"This way," Henry recalled, making a sharp left turn.

The branches lashed their bodies, stinging their bare skin.

"To the right," Henry yelled, making another sharp turn as he pushed his way through the foliage.

Everyone abruptly switched directions, sliding along the moist ground. They could hear the group of men closing in, the sound of their galloping footsteps approaching.

"It's not far from here," Henry encouraged.

They continued through the trees until they came to a sprawling lavender field, its hypnotic fragrance floating on the breeze.

"*Achoo*," Sarah sneezed, her nose tingling. "Pardon me."

"Which way?" Oliver asked.

"Across the meadow on the other side of the wall," Henry gasped, struggling with exhaustion.

With the enemy right behind them, they quickly caught their breath and rushed across the meadow. Each one was now a moving target, exposed by the moonlight glowing on the blossoming lavender.

Observing the running figures, the men stopped at the edge of the field. One knelt and positioned his rifle. He aimed and let off a flurry of rounds, while the other four men continued the foot chase.

* * * * *

Back by the château, two black Hummers sped across the estate, annihilating everything in their path. The vehicles knocked over statues, smashed into fountains, and shredded the pristine gardens.

The Hummers split, with one heading north and the other heading south.

* * * * *

Henry ran up to a rock wall, its granite stones soaring twelve feet overhead. Oliver was next, followed by Sarah, Tom, and finally Fontaine and Gowerstone, carrying Stevens, whose face was pale and sweaty.

Henry moved along the wall, searching for the gate.

"Oliver, point the light over here," he instructed.

"Won't they spot us?" Oliver asked, afraid of being seen.

"They might, but I can't see a bloody thing," Henry grunted, flustered.

Oliver panned the light until it shone on a large medieval gate, its thick oak planks held together with rusty bolts.

Henry tried to open it, but it wouldn't budge. "Brilliant," he blurted out, hopelessly rattling the door.

"Stand back," Gowerstone warned. He pulled out his Glock and fired a single shot that shattered the lock.

"Well done," Henry approved, yanking open the gate and guiding everyone through.

They tracked along a gravel pathway until they reached the bungalow, a rustic straw-and-plaster dwelling with pane glass windows and a cedar shake roof. Overgrown bushes covered the walls and climbed up the sides.

Henry tried the front door but it was locked.

"I'll handle it," Gowerstone said calmly. He walked over, fired once at the keyhole, and kicked in the door.

Everyone entered. A musky smell permeated the sparse surroundings.

"Who lives here?" Oliver inquired, surprised by the deserted interior.

"The gardener," Henry replied. "He quit about six months ago."

"I don't blame him," Oliver murmured.

Noises from outside silenced them.

* * * * *

Maxwell and his team surrounded the bungalow, taking up strategic locations around the perimeter.

Both Hummers screeched to a stop, one from the south, the other from the north. The outside was now completely flooded with lights.

Pleased with the situation, Maxwell took out his walkie-talkie and radioed Marcel.

"Sir, we have them trapped in a small house," he reported. "What are your orders?"

"Annihilate them—all of them," Marcel ordered in a cold, calculating voice.

*****

"We're completely surrounded," Oliver exclaimed, noting the lights from every direction.

"Have some faith, nephew. I've prepared for this," Henry assured them, a stalwart tone in his voice.

"What's the plan, Henry?" Fontaine asked, her patience thinning.

"I have a vehicle stored in the garage."

"Then show us the way," she said with a sense of urgency.

Gowerstone stood still, aware of the sudden silence outside.

"What is it?" Fontaine questioned, noticing his expression.

"Everyone, hit the floor and cover your head," Gowerstone yelled, grabbing Tom and Sarah.

Fontaine pulled Stevens down with her as Henry and Oliver dropped to their stomachs.

A second later, bullets tore through the building. The windows shattered, and the walls were riddled with holes as chunks of plaster fell onto the concrete floor.

Henry swiftly crawled to a door and turned the knob. "Over here," he shouted in a strained voice.

All six of them slithered across the floor. Projectiles continued to shred the walls, ricocheting erratically.

Henry maneuvered down eight steps to the garage and crouched at the bottom. Sarah was first, trailed by Tom, Oliver, and then Stevens, who was being supported by Fontaine and Gowerstone.

Henry flipped on a light. Constructed of thick stone, the windowless garage acted as a fortified shelter. Parked inside was a black Range Rover with massive chrome bumpers and oversized tires.

"It was custom built, with a few modifications," Henry remarked.

"I always wanted a Range Rover," Oliver whispered, admiring the vehicle.

Henry squeezed Oliver's shoulder. "If we get out of here, it's yours."

"If?" Sarah questioned with a glare, her heart pounding loudly in her ears.

"*When* we get out of here," Henry corrected himself.

Henry quickly opened the back hatch and lifted two folding seats, placing the titanium briefcase on the floor.

"All right, everyone in," Henry instructed. "Tom and Sarah can sit back here. The side and rear panels have reinforced steel."

Tom and Sarah climbed in and buckled their seatbelts, nervously glancing at each other. The constant thunder of gunfire was heard above.

"Keep your heads down," Henry cautioned them.

"It looks like you were anticipating something like this," Fontaine observed.

"Knowing the type of people I've been researching, it was only a matter of time before this happened."

Oliver opened the passenger door for Fontaine, who helped Stevens into the back seat and buckled him in. Gowerstone entered the other side, while Henry and Oliver hopped in the front.

* * * * *

"Hold your fire," Maxwell instructed, raising his hand and making a fist.

The men stopped but maintained their positions.

The bungalow façade was obliterated: empty window frames, walls pockmarked, and exposed oak beams underneath the tattered plaster.

Maxwell motioned south and north with his fingers, indicating that his men should approach from each side in pairs.

Both teams stealthily advanced toward the house, their backs against what was left of the walls as they edged toward the openings. One man tossed a stun grenade through a window. It made a loud bang, followed by a flash.

Two other men approached the west side of the building, walking down a steep embankment. They stood by a wooden garage door.

One of the men stopped, listening to a low humming sound.

"What is that?" he asked, perplexed.

"I'm not sure," the other man mumbled.

The sound started to build, revving louder. Their eyes widened as they realized what it was.

"Back away from the door!" one of them yelled.

Before either could react, the Range Rover smashed through the door, knocking both men to the ground.

The vehicle sped across the pea gravel driveway, sliding back and forth until Henry switched gears and accelerated, heading for the paved road twenty yards away.

One of the men got to his feet. "They're getting away!" he cried, reaching for his weapon. "They're going toward the north road."

Maxwell hurried around the corner just in time to see the car disappear. "Get the Hummers," he exclaimed, furious.

"Should I notify Marcel?" one of the men asked.

"No," Maxwell responded sharply. "Let's get them first."

Both Hummers pulled up, fully loaded with men. Maxwell got in the first vehicle and they sped off.

* * * * *

As Henry drove along the twisting road, slivers of moonlight sliced through the oak trees forty feet overhead. The estate was massive, including a lake, farmlands and rolling hills draped in sunflowers.

"They're right behind us," Oliver stressed, peering back at the four headlights tailing them.

"Where are we going, Henry?" Fontaine asked impatiently.

"I have a secluded villa in Tours, along the Loire River," he answered loudly so the others could hear. "The property is not registered in my name. No one knows I own it."

"But then what?" Oliver asked. "We can't hide there forever."

"We rest and regroup. In the morning we continue to Chambord," Henry asserted, undaunted by the circumstances.

Fontaine leaned forward. "What about the car's GPS?"

"It was never installed, and the vehicle is registered under another name," Henry responded. "As I continued my research, I discovered that anyone who got close to the truth didn't last long, so I've taken all the necessary precautions."

"Since I began this journey six months ago, I've lost two good friends and four associates," Gowerstone said bitterly.

The Range Rover raced along the narrow country road as both Hummers edged closer. Although Henry accelerated, it was hard to navigate at high speeds.

"Everyone, keep your heads down," Fontaine cautioned as she removed her weapon.

Gowerstone lowered his window and pulled out his Glock.

As the Hummers gained, two men started firing automatic machine guns. Bullets peppered the Range Rover, riddling the sides and blowing out the back window. Tom and Sarah were jolted by the shock but remained crouched over.

Henry swerved from side to side as he tried to avoid the gunfire, but the bullets kept hitting the car.

He turned onto a dirt path through a grassy field and over a wooden bridge. Undeterred, the Hummers advanced and tried to slam into the Rover.

"Enough of this," Fontaine declared as she leaned out the window and unloaded a clip into one of the vehicles.

She pierced the hood and shot out the front window. Smoke billowed from the engine, blinding the driver.

Fontaine reloaded and emptied another clip in rapid secession.

Aiming straight for the driver as he leaned out the window, Gowerstone fired his Glock.

The driver faltered, swerving back and forth. He lost control and skated down the embankment, crashing into a massive chestnut tree. A few seconds later, the Hummer burst into flames. The other Hummer rammed into the back of the Range Rover, throwing it off-kilter.

"Hold on," Henry yelled, struggling to stabilize of the vehicle.

Everyone in the car braced for impact. Oliver buttressed himself against the dashboard. Gowerstone and Fontaine gripped the interior ceiling straps. Tom and Sarah crouched lower, covering their heads.

As the Range Rover started to skid on the wet ground, Henry worked feverishly to control it, turning the steering wheel back and forth.

The men in the Hummer opened fire again, showering the vehicle with bullets.

Regaining control, Henry pulled onto a paved road and accelerated over a hilltop. He sped up and hooked a hard right into a wall of Laurel Hedges seven-feet tall.

"What are you doing?" Oliver questioned, his eyes glued to the seemingly impenetrable barrier.

"Trust me—I know every inch of this property," Henry assured him.

The Range Rover crashed through the branches and disappeared into a forest of poplars. The driver slammed on the Hummer's breaks and quickly backed up.

Henry navigated between rows of trees that were scarcely six feet apart. He grasped the steering wheel with white knuckles, beads of sweat glistening on his forehead. The uneven ground caused the vehicle to shift, knocking against the tree trunks and denting the side panels.

Oliver gulped as he watched trees whizzing by his window.

"Are they still back there?" Henry asked, his concentration fierce.

"About fifty feet behind us," Tom yelled, glimpsing the headlights.

The Range Rover scraped against a poplar, crushing the right door and snapping off a side mirror. Low-hanging branches whacked the front window, causing a cascade of cracks.

"Are you sure this is a good idea?" Oliver gasped, bouncing in his seat and holding on for life.

"It's the only one I have . . . ," Henry confessed, his voice trailing off.

As they got closer to the edge of the forest, all they could see was the sky dotted with stars: no visible road, trees, or objects. The moon revealed a poppy field.

Henry began to increase his speed, mentally timing the distance to the horizon.

"W-what's ahead?" Oliver stammered, eyes bulging.

"Something they're not expecting," Henry replied.

"We're not headed toward the cliffs, are we?"

"Sort of."

At the last possible second, Henry yanked the steering

wheel, making a sharp left and following along the edge of a ravine.

Though the driver frantically tried to turn, it was too late. The Hummer continued straight ahead, flying off the cliff and into a lake. The vehicle crashed with a thunder. Water rapidly filled the interior, pulling the Hummer underneath the surface.

"Nice move," Oliver breathed, looking back in disbelief.

"Well done, Henry," Fontaine approved. She turned around to check on Tom and Sarah, who were both sitting in stunned silence.

Rattled and shaken, muddy and cut, they glanced over at each other. Sarah's hair was a tangled mess. Tom carefully brushed pieces of broken glass off his shirt.

"Any injuries?" Fontaine asked.

"I don't think so," Tom muttered, still dazed as he examined his body.

"I'm all right," Sarah sighed heavily, then turned to Fontaine with an admiring gaze. "All of you were incredible."

"I second that," Tom added earnestly.

Fontaine looked at Gowerstone, who remained quiet, lost in his thoughts. "You're safe," Fontaine continued, smiling. "That's all that matters."

"Well done, Uncle," Oliver acknowledged, patting him on the shoulder.

"I never expected an entire assault team to come after Tom and Sarah," Henry admitted, astounded by what had transpired. "I suppose if we ever needed confirmation of Tom's royalty, we just got it."

"They'll keep coming," Gowerstone warned. "Their failure tonight will only amplify their resolve."

"Then we'll disappear for a while," Henry avowed.

He made his way to a paved road and headed toward the southern part of his estate.

Using a first aid kit from the car, Fontaine tended to Stevens's injury. With Gowerstone's help, she removed the bullet lodged in his leg, disinfected the wound, and wrapped it with a temporary bandage. Stevens took some aspirin but was still feverish, drifting in and out of consciousness.

"Stevens will need medical attention," Fontaine said, gently wiping his forehead with a cloth. "Gunshot wounds are reported to the police, so we can't go to a hospital."

"I know a doctor who lives on the outskirts of Tours. He's discreet and can help us," Henry said with confidence.

"I'm fine, sir," Stevens mumbled, worried that he had become a burden.

"You've done so much," Henry commended him. "We're all grateful for your help."

Fontaine tenderly rubbed Stevens's arm. "You're a good man, Stevens. Good men are rare these days."

"Now that we're all targets, what'll happen to Stevens if we leave him with the doctor?" Gowerstone asked.

"I have a network of people who can help," Henry replied, somewhat elusive. "They'll get him to a safe house and look after him."

Oliver leaned over. "What about my father?"

"We'll deal with him in time," Henry promised.

Ten minutes later, they reached an iron gate in the brick wall surrounding the estate. Henry pushed a remote control that opened it. He drove onto the main road, glancing at his watch.

"It's late," Henry realized, exhausted. "We have a two-hour ride ahead of us. Everyone should try to get some rest."

* * * * *

Back at the chateau, Marcel and his men continued plundering the rooms, searching for information. Shelves were cleared, furniture knocked over, and the contents of dresser drawers dumped on the floor. Marcel knew Sir Horningbrook was more than he appeared, and he wanted answers.

As Marcel moved around the master suite, his walkie-talkie buzzed. "Sir, it's Maxwell."

"Have they been eliminated?" Marcel asked.

There was a long pause.

"They got away," Maxwell reported, his voice shallow. "One of the Hummers is totaled and the other is at the bottom of a lake, but we can—"

Marcel tightened his grip on the radio, crushing it in his hand. He was dumbfounded that two agents, an old man and his servant, a college student, and two children had not only outmaneuvered a trained assault team but had once again escaped. Marcel's future now hung in the balance.

He was contemplating his options when his cell phone rang. Marcel dreaded answering it.

"Yes, Master," he said obediently.

"Update," the morbid voice demanded.

Marcel's throat was dry.

"We've had another setback," Marcel conveyed, his hand quivering. "My team took control of the chateau and secured the estate, but the children got away. They couldn't have traveled far, so we're going to—"

"That's enough," the morbid voice stated.

"Sir, give me—"

"We'll handle it from here. Clean up the situation and return to the castle."

The line went dead.

* * * * *

About two hours later, Henry pulled into a residential neighborhood on the outskirts of Tours. He had called his doctor, who agreed to look after Stevens. The doctor was generously paid for his help and his silence. Everyone bid Stevens a heartfelt goodbye, knowing that his bravery had contributed to their successful escape.

After leaving, Henry drove to the Loire River and over Pont Wilson, a bridge that led to the town of Tours. Dating to pre-Roman times, Tours was once a prosperous silk-producing metropolis.

Although deserted at this early hour, Tours was still a vibrant city under the lights: the four-story town hall had rows of majestic columns and a large clock underneath its copper tower. Medieval buildings lined the cobblestone streets, ancient statues towered above the sidewalks, and the fifteenth-century Renaissance cathedral dominated the skyline.

Henry drove through the city towards the eastern outskirts, eventually reaching a private roadway leading to his villa. Large trees and bushes covered the area, keeping it hidden from the road and surrounding property. For a simple hideaway, the house was exquisite: the two-story home was built of rose-colored brick and granite stone, with a gambrel roof covered in faded shingles, weathered green copper gutters, and two tall chimneys.

Just down the hill was the Loire, France's longest river that begins up north and flows 634 miles to the Atlantic Ocean.

Parking in the garage, Henry closed his eyes and took a deep breath, thankful they had made it safely. Although he carried himself well, displaying a refined confidence, Henry was worried. In the past, he had always remained anonymous, collecting his research in secret. Now he was known by the enemy, his magnificent estate had been destroyed, and his future was in question.

Oliver had dozed off but was awakened by the sudden stop. Gowerstone and Fontaine remained attentive, trained to stay alert. Tom and Sarah were napping when Henry opened the back hatch.

"We're here," Henry announced, gently helping them out of the car. "Once we're inside, you can wash up and get some real sleep."

"Thank you," Sarah mumbled, rubbing her weary eyes and guiding Tom toward the front door.

Oliver exited the car and Henry grabbed the titanium briefcase. Oliver appraised the nearly demolished Range Rover.

"On second thought, you can keep the car, Uncle," he half joked, dismayed by its appearance.

"Understood, nephew." Henry chuckled.

Turning off the alarm, Henry unlocked the front door and flipped on the lights.

The maple-paneled rooms were filled with Empire-style furnishings, rustic landscape paintings, and colorful Asian rugs covering the hardwood floors. The ceilings had exposed oak beams and modern lighting.

Everyone gathered in Henry's study, a treasure trove of artifacts displayed on antique tables and glass shelves. Sanskrit tablets, prehistoric statutes, and an assortment of ceramic pottery were covered with hieroglyphics. The walls were a collage of complex diagrams, charts, and timelines. The group stood in awe, examining all the images and information.

On one side was a detailed map of ancient Mesopotamia, including the dates of its monarchs, starting in 4200 BC, and a picture of the Tower of Babel circled in red. A large arrow pointed to a historical chart of events in Egypt beginning in 3800 BC and showed the date of each ruling pharaoh.

In one corner were pictures of pyramids and information indicating all their locations and astrological alignments. Numerous arrows were drawn from Egypt to Asia Minor, Eastern Europe, Greece, Rome, Italy, the island of Malta, and then continued to the south of France, with a large crimson circle around Rennes-le-Château and the word *Merovingian*.

From Rennes-le-Château another arrow continued

north to southern Germany, with a circle around Bavaria and the date 1776. It was an enormous puzzle with hundreds of pieces that were somehow connected. The attention to detail was extraordinary.

On another wall was a large pyramid sectioned into eleven layers. At the top was Nimrod, with an ancestral lineage of noble families underneath. Below that were the Egyptian pharaohs, followed by world empires and their rulers. Beneath that were the Knights Templar, then the thirteen ruling families, followed by names of secret societies, and finally European kings and queens. Next to the pyramid was a Bible verse:

> *"So the LORD scattered them abroad from thence upon the face of all the earth: and they left off to build the city; Therefore, is the name of it called Babel; because the LORD did there confound the language of all the earth: and from thence did the LORD scatter them abroad upon the face of all the earth."*
> Genesis 11:8–9

A third wall showed the last fifty years of world history: dictators, presidents, wars, and catastrophic events, all with dates and descriptions, all remarkably connected.

"This is incredible," Oliver marveled.

"I told you I've done my research," Henry remarked, his tone serious. "It's forty years' worth."

"Yeah, but..."

"All these connections, ancient bloodlines, and secret societies are the intricate fabric that make up the Committee. They are convinced that only they can understand the enlightened truth from ancient manuscripts and mystical teachings. Going back thousands of years, this hidden knowledge is passed on from family to family. It's the foundation of their belief system and what they live by."

"What's your conclusion?" Oliver wondered, a chill running through his body.

"The Committee and its members think they are the chosen rulers of the world, the masters of humanity," Henry answered. "However, it's all a lie."

"Very troubling," Sarah interjected, a shudder in her voice.

"It's horrible," Fontaine declared as she studied the elaborate charts. "Yet it helps explain how these groups consolidated power and why they orchestrate such terrible events."

"They're pure evil, living in the darkness and blind to the truth," Henry concluded. He rubbed his aching forehead and sighed. "It's late, and we've had another long night. Why don't we get some sleep, and we'll talk more tomorrow."

"I'm all for that," Tom agreed, yawning loudly.

"And the bath?" Sarah inquired.

"Yes, of course," Henry acknowledged. "I'll show you where it is."

"I'll make sure the building is secure and take the first watch," Gowerstone offered, starting to check the windows and exterior doors.

Fontaine stepped forward. "I'll take the second watch."

* * * * *

On the outer edge of Paris, the Committee was meeting at Ravencliff. The underground vaults were lit by flickering torches and ceremonial crimson candles. A dewy smoke from incense crept along the stone floor. A frigid, lifeless sentiment pervaded the interior.

Standing at the center of a circle of thirteen, Marcel faced his peers. Strauss stood by his master, watching. This unnaturally proportioned, seven-foot-tall giant remained silent but observed everything.

"Maxwell and my team?" Marcel inquired, his voice shaky.

"Liquidated," the Master declared, emotionless.

Marcel bowed his head, saddened by the loss of his colleagues. "May I explain what happened?" he asked apprehensively.

"Silence," the Master shrieked, his eyes ablaze. "We're aware of your failure tonight, but we will not fail in our mission."

"Yes, Master," the other twelve members chanted in unison.

"Let's drink to the elimination of Thomas Britfield and the Britfield bloodline."

They each took a crystal goblet of aged Rothberg Bordeaux from the table.

Walking through an opening in the circle, an elderly servant carried a golden tray with a single goblet of crimson wine. Marcel stared at the glass and slowly picked it up, his hand trembling.

"To our future success," the Master vowed.

The thirteen raised their glasses and drank. Marcel hesitated, taking a deep breath.

"I said drink!" the Master screamed in a hideous tone.

Marcel took a sip.

"All of it," the Master commanded.

Marcel took a large gulp and waited. A moment later, he was gasping for air. He dropped the glass and fell dead to the ground.

The Committee was unfazed as they sipped their wine.

"You know what needs to be done?" the Master asked Strauss.

Strauss nodded, fanatically determined.

"Then do it and don't fail," the Master ordered.

12
A VEILED SECRET

With rest and the devoted care of the villagers, Professor Hainsworth eventually awoke. His first thoughts were of Tom and Sarah. He hoped against hope that they were still alive.

Hainsworth was still weak and could barely walk, but he was determined to get well and search for the children he had promised to protect. His wallet and other information were lost at sea, so the Presd'eaux, a kind family, had volunteered to watch over him during his recovery.

As Hainsworth slowly improved, he tried to call Detective Gowerstone but was unable to reach him at New Scotland Yard. When asked to leave his name and number, Hainsworth hung up, not knowing whom to trust. The professor was aware that the prime minister was corrupt and was suspicious of what had happened on the ferry. He had heard a loud explosion before the boat sank. Hainsworth needed to be extremely careful, because nothing was what it seemed.

Determined to stay in France in case Tom and Sarah appeared, Hainsworth contacted the only person he trusted, his ex-girlfriend Anna, who lived in Paris. Surprised to hear from him after years of silence, she immediately took a leave of absence from work and drove to see him.

* * * * *

It was late morning as Fontaine searched every room in the villa, making sure the house was secure. The sky was clear and sunny, promising a better day.

Fontaine continued into the study, where Gowerstone rested on a leather chair, a woolen blanket covering his legs. She gazed at him fondly, remembering the past: an assignment that became a close friendship that had blossomed into more. It was a wonderful time that had ended abruptly.

Gowerstone awoke, catching her staring at him. Startled, Fontaine looked away, rather embarrassed.

"How long was I asleep?" Gowerstone asked.

"About four hours," she replied, recovering her composure. "You needed the rest."

Gowerstone glanced at his watch. "It's already past ten. How are the others?"

"They're fine, upstairs asleep. Henry left about an hour ago to get some groceries and supplies."

Gowerstone slowly rose from the chair, a disquieting expression on his face. "How are you holding up?" he inquired delicately.

"Good," Fontaine replied, desperate to have a deeper conversation but unsure how to proceed. "You know I'm trained for this kind of work."

"I know," he said, impressed by her fortitude. "You're the best agent I've ever worked with."

Gowerstone paused for a moment, his composure softening. "Last night was a close call. I didn't expect that."

"Neither did I," Fontaine confessed. "I don't know how they made the connection to Henry."

"It's hard to say."

"You don't think the prime minister betrayed his brother?" Fontaine speculated.

"And his own son?" Gowerstone leaned forward and pondered the question. "I suppose it's possible. These people have no empathy. They don't function like normal people."

Fontaine took a deep breath, the stress of the last few days clearly visible in her face. "If anything were to happen to Tom or Sarah . . . ," she began.

"We won't let it," Gowerstone promised.

Fontaine nodded, then glanced affectionately at him. "Is there anything else you want to talk about?" she asked, moving closer.

Feeling cornered, Gowerstone tensed. He knew the conversation had switched from last night to ten years ago, sensing an undercurrent of unresolved issues.

"I should have called you. It's inexcusable," he apologized.

"You're right, you should have," her voice rising. "Why didn't you?"

"After we finished our assignment in Paris, I was called back to England and immediately given a new case. It was of the highest priority—one I couldn't talk about."

"And?" she persisted.

"The days turned into months and months—"

"Turned into years," Fontaine interrupted.

"I guess I got caught up in the assignment," Gowerstone admitted."

"That was a decade ago. Just like before, you put your job before people."

"I do my job to protect people."

"Strangers, not those close to you," she interjected, trying to break through.

"It's how I am. I don't know how else to act."

Gowerstone became flustered. He could handle an army of assassins, but he didn't know how to deal with a relationship. "I thought about you," he added quickly.

"You did?" Fontaine asked, her tone warming.

"Not a day has passed that you weren't on my mind."

"Go on."

Gowerstone cleared his throat, trying to compose his thoughts.

"And I missed you," he revealed.

"That's much better." She started thinking about what he had said, about the case ten years ago. "Wait a second. That assignment you were given, it wasn't the kidnapping of the Britfields' son, was it?" Fontaine asked, looking up toward the bedrooms where Tom and Sarah were sleeping.

"Yes, I spent over two years investigating it until I was removed by the prime minister. Although I never stopped searching. It was the only case I was unable to solve."

"And then over six months ago, a twelve-year-old boy by the name of Tom escaped from Weatherly Orphanage."

"When I read his file and saw the picture, I hoped, I knew, that I had found the missing child, the last Britfield heir."

Fighting a mixture of emotions, Fontaine looked at him compassionately. "I understand now."

As Fontaine's tough exterior began to melt away, Henry came through the front door, weighed down by shopping bags.

"I was just picking up supplies in town," he announced, briskly walking into the kitchen.

Gowerstone and Fontaine shared a silent gaze, then broke off.

"Good thinking, Henry," Fontaine said, wandering into the kitchen.

Rebounding from the awkward moment, Gowerstone trailed behind.

Fontaine helped Henry unpack the groceries: fresh bread, eggs, fruit, cheeses, meats, pastries, and an assortment of other goods.

"What's in the other bags?" Fontaine asked.

"A change of clothing for Tom and Sarah," Henry answered. "After last night, it's the least I could do. Plus, the new outfits will help them blend in with the local scene."

Henry removed a package of disposable cell phones, handing one to Fontaine and one to Gowerstone.

"It's time we take more precautions," Henry instigated. "Make sure you destroy your current phones and anything else that can be traced back to you."

"Yes, of course," Fontaine agreed, removing the battery from her cell phone and tossing it into a trash can.

Gowerstone did the same. Although he had an untraceable satellite phone, he wasn't willing to risk it.

"Brilliant," Henry commented. "If you make a call, only use the cell phone once. Then remove the battery and dispose of it. Once they lock into a position, they can trace you, even if the phone is turned off."

"We're both familiar with how these surveillance systems work," Fontaine informed him. "I've used them many times to track suspects."

"And don't use any of your credit cards," Henry continued. "They're already tagged. Only use cash."

"I've been using cash for the last six months," Gowerstone said.

Henry opened a bag of coffee and began spooning it into a coffeemaker. Although he appeared cheerful, he was distressed, not only worried about Tom and Sarah, but concerned for Oliver's safety.

"No tea?" Fontaine inquired amusingly. "And you being British?"

"I can't stand the stuff." Henry laughed. "You know we were drinking coffee before tea. Tea wasn't introduced to our coffeehouses until the 1660s." Henry glanced at his watch. "Is anyone else up?"

"I figured they needed the rest," Fontaine replied. "Should I wake them?"

"Please. We should have something to eat and get moving."

* * * * *

After a late breakfast, everyone sat in the living room planning their next steps. Tom and Sarah were dressed in their new clothing, modest outfits in blues and grays. Sarah wore a periwinkle cotton dress, and Tom had on a pair of jeans with a light gray pullover shirt. They each wore a pair of blue sneakers.

"So the last known Britfields left Kent, England, about eight years ago and moved to Chambord. Is that correct?" Henry inquired.

"That's what the Archbishop of Canterbury told us," Tom replied, trying to remember the details.

"And you trust him?"

"Absolutely."

"Did he indicate if they'd still be there or if he would notify them you were coming?" Henry asked as he considered their strategy.

"No, he didn't," Tom answered, wishing he had more to offer.

"It's not going to be easy," Henry theorized, addressing the others. "If the Britfields are there, I'm sure the chateau is well guarded."

"Nor will they know if we're friend or foe," Gowerstone added. "We're strangers who will appear as intruders."

Tom removed a worn, folded document from his pocket and handed it to Henry. "The archbishop gave me this before we left Canterbury," he said, hoping it would help.

Henry closely examined it. "This is good, very good," he affirmed. "It's an official document signed by the archbishop. He's a wise man to have provided this."

"Besides the document of introduction, how would the Britfields know for certain that Tom is their son?" Fontaine asked, foreseeing the dilemma.

"I suppose when it comes down to it, a DNA test would offer conclusive evidence," Henry replied, then smiled at

Tom. "But a mother usually knows her son—maternal instinct."

Tom's heart swelled at the thought of seeing his real mother and father. Suddenly everything he and Sarah had gone through felt worth it.

"Why would the Britfields come to France?" Oliver asked, aware of the risks. "It's so close to England."

"Yet miles apart," Henry responded philosophically. He poured another cup of coffee and continued. "The French and English have always despised each other. Although they were allies during World War I and World War II, they prefer to stay apart."

"Could you explain?" Tom asked. "Since we're in their country, it would be good to know."

"That's a great deal of history to cover." Henry laughed. "To start with, the Normans from Normandy invaded England in 1066. In a decisive engagement, Duke William II defeated the Anglo-Saxon king Harold II at the Battle of Hastings. Although William claimed the throne was his, Harold disagreed. Nevertheless, the English didn't have a choice once Harold was killed in battle and their army was defeated. Eventually the Anglo-Saxons accepted their Norman ruler and the families intermarried, uniting England."

"So it ended well?" Tom guessed.

"Hardly," Henry said, rolling his eyes. "After Henry II, William's grandson, inherited the English throne in 1133, he married Eleanor of Aquitaine, who was from France. Her dowry entitled him to Anjou, a large territory in the lower Loire Valley. This provided Henry a legitimate claim to other parts of France, which infuriated the French king, Louis VII. After two centuries of territorial battles, the Hundred Years' War began in 1337. England invaded France and eventually controlled almost half of the country. But a century later, the English were defeated and lost most of their gains."

"What about the Scottish piece of the puzzle?" Sarah interjected, recalling her history. "There's a connection, right?"

"Very astute," Henry acknowledged. "In 1558, Mary, Queen of the Scots, married Francis, the Dauphin of France, who eventually ascended to the throne. When Mary Tudor, Queen of England, died without an heir, Mary, Queen of Scots, believed she had the rightful claim over Queen Elizabeth, the illegitimate daughter of Henry VIII, based on bloodlines and marriages. Conflict once again erupted."

"It's all so confusing," Tom murmured, desperate to understand.

"That's politics," Henry maintained. "When power and control are at stake, people will do anything to seize it."

Henry rose from his chair, pacing as he spoke.

"There's always been tension between France and England," he elaborated. "During the American Revolution, the French joined the colonists and helped defeat Britain at the Battle of Yorktown, Virginia, in 1781. When Napoleon came to power in 1804, he tried to conquer Britain but was stopped by Lord Horatio Nelson at the Battle of Trafalgar in 1805. Napoleon was finally defeated by the Duke of Wellington in 1815 at Waterloo, Belgium.

"I get it now. France was probably the best place for the Britfields to hide," Tom concluded, his mind spinning with details.

"Yes, that's true, although the Committee is not based in one country. These people are global."

"After their failure to capture Tom and Sarah at your chateau, do you think they'll stop?" Oliver inquired, still unnerved from last night.

"No," Henry replied candidly. "As Detective Gowerstone stated, they'll only be more determined."

"I can't imagine it getting any worse," Sarah interjected.

"I'm afraid it will," Henry sighed, a solemn directness in his voice.

"'What does 'it' mean exactly?'"

"From my understanding, until Tom appeared at Windsor Castle over six months ago, the Committee believed he was dead. They thought their royal problem was solved. Once they realized Tom was alive, they knew their plans were in jeopardy."

"How?" Oliver asked, disconcerted.

"Tom's claim to the English throne could be enough to encourage others to rise and fight."

Everyone was quiet for a moment, reflecting on what Henry had shared. They weren't just endeavoring to reunite a child with his parents; Tom's presence would inspire a slumbering populace to fight for their future. Tom felt the weight of the burden he was carrying.

Henry grabbed the titanium briefcase and sat down. Fiddling with the locks, he opened it and removed the Codex.

"Now we have proof. Along with the information I've gathered, it's enough to dislodge these criminals who control society. Communicated through the proper media channels, the world will know the truth."

"I can handle that," Gowerstone asserted. "I have someone who can take this information global."

"That will be critical," Henry emphasized.

Oliver squirmed in his seat. "You were talking about Windsor Castle and how the Committee realized Tom was still alive."

"Yes, thanks to Gowerstone's timely intervention, Tom and Sarah were able to get out of England," Henry continued. "Yet for over six months, no one knew where they were or if they had perished in the English Channel."

"Then the two of them appeared at Notre Dame," Fontaine added, wishing she could have gotten there first.

"Once Tom and Sarah resurfaced, the Committee resumed their hunt," Henry elaborated. "The Committee not only knows that you're somewhere south of Chartres, but that you're in France for a reason."

"Do you think the Committee knows we're headed to Chambord?" Sarah inquired, uneasy.

"I don't know," Henry answered. "It's possible."

"Which makes it even more risky," Fontaine implied.

"But I have to get there," Tom exclaimed, more determined than ever.

"Yes, of course, we're still going," Henry stated. "All I'm saying is that we don't know what awaits us."

Henry sipped his coffee, quiet for a moment.

Gowerstone stood and began pacing the room, assessing their predicament.

"What are your thoughts, Detective?" Oliver asked, trusting Gowerstone's instincts.

"Henry's right. We don't know what awaits us. These people are well informed and well connected," Gowerstone replied. "It's not just law enforcement we're up against, but practically every other agency in the country."

"From what I've experienced at Interpol, the corruption is at the highest levels, including the chief inspector," Fontaine stated, shaking her head in resentment.

"They're all connected," Henry articulated. "Interpol was specifically created to help carry out the Committee's illegal activities. These organizations only exist to support the Committee's agenda."

"I wish I knew that before I joined," Fontaine remarked, feeling foolish.

"You couldn't have known. Everything is compartmentalized," Henry explained. "I'm sure you did well arresting criminals. Although it also removed the Committee's competition while making the public believe that justice was being served."

"When, in fact, the most dangerous criminals have been running the show," Oliver realized, finally comprehending how the system worked.

"Precisely," Henry acknowledged.

"Which means the Committee has already alerted each law enforcement agency in France," Fontaine concluded. "I'm sure by now every organization has our photographs."

"They've probably been told that we're criminals," Oliver said, shocked by the idea.

"More likely we've been branded as terrorists," Henry stressed. "Once this information is programmed into their computers, it becomes official, whether it's true or not."

His comment sent a chill through everyone.

"Most policemen are just doing their job," Henry continued. "Each one is given an order and executes it without question. If we're labeled as terrorists, we'll be treated as terrorists."

"So just driving on the roads is risky," Oliver reasoned.

"Yes, they will have a description of my vehicle and the license plate number. With thousands of digital cameras around the country, we wouldn't get very far."

"We have the same system in Britain," Gowerstone interjected. "There are over two hundred thousand cameras from Southampton to Scotland. It's more of a police state than a democracy."

"So much for privacy," Oliver vented, feeling exposed and violated.

"We're now living in a technocratic society, ruled by those who control the technology," Henry conveyed. "They like watching and recording our every move."

"Couldn't we put a different license plate on the car?"

"By now they have a digital signature of my car, a precise schematic of the vehicle."

"So how did we avoid detection last night?" Oliver questioned.

"No one was looking for my Range Rover, because everything happened so quickly," Henry rationalized. "I also took precautions while driving, so I think we were able to avoid most of the surveillance."

"First thing this morning, standard procedure would be to study all the cameras in that area," Fontaine explained. "I'm sure they captured enough information to at least know what direction we headed."

"It's not just the cameras we need to be concerned about, it's the satellites," Gowerstone added. "These sophisticated systems can read the date on a coin."

"From space?" Tom asked in disbelief.

"Yes. You can't imagine the advanced technology these organizations have: high-powered telescopes, thermal-imaging, and voice recognition that can be detected from thousands of miles away. The public is only aware of about ten percent of the technology that really exists. The rest is secret, classified."

"He's right," Henry confirmed. "Most of the money received from taxes is diverted to these black projects."

"Black projects?" Oliver inquired.

"Activities that are done in secret without any oversight or the public's knowledge," Henry answered. "Instead of spending tax revenue on schools and infrastructure, they build advanced weaponry, underground bases, and other things that serve their nefarious agenda. Most of their technology is at least fifty years ahead of what's available to the public."

"How much are we talking about? Like millions of euros?" Oliver probed, fascinated.

"Try trillions."

"That explains why nothing ever improves, such as

education, crime, or poverty," Fontaine reflected with a hint of anger.

"It's all by design," Henry maintained.

"But we're still going to Chambord, right?" Tom interrupted.

"Absolutely," Henry replied, his resolve resurfacing. "Detective? Inspector?"

"Without a doubt," Gowerstone stated.

"Yes, of course," Fontaine agreed, unwavering in her commitment.

Henry walked closer to his nephew. "Oliver, my lad?"

"I'm in, regardless of the consequences," he answered decisively.

"What about you, Sarah?" Tom asked, wanting to honor her opinion.

"I'm with you, whatever you decide," she replied, her courage mounting. "We've come this far—let's see it through."

"Then it's settled," Henry confirmed. "We'll leave shortly."

"If we can't use the Range Rover, how are we going to get there?" Oliver wondered aloud.

A grin spread across Henry's face. "I have a boat."

"That might work," Fontaine ventured. "As I recall, Chambord is only a few miles inland from the Loire. The river may be our safest route."

"Before leaving, we'll need to restock. I'm low on ammunition," Gowerstone stipulated, checking his Glock.

Fontaine pulled out her weapon. "I only have three rounds left."

"That won't be a problem," Henry assured them.

Everyone followed Henry to his cellar. He approached a steel door and typed in a ten-digit code. The door depressurized and eased opened.

Henry motioned everyone into a large room that resembled a military supply depot: camouflage jackets and pants, survival gear, night vision goggles, and an assortment of knives. The walls were covered with handguns, rifles, and semiautomatic machine guns.

"Cool," Tom murmured, immediately perusing the shelves.

Oliver's eyes bulged. "I had no idea."

"No one does," Henry said. "I've been stocking up for years, just in case."

Gowerstone examined all the weaponry. "There's enough here to equip a small army. You can't be working alone."

Henry paused as he thought about his response. "I collaborate with a group of patriots who share my belief in freedom and liberty."

"How many?" Fontaine asked, wondering about his network.

"There are thousands throughout Europe, ready and waiting," Henry answered proudly. "You don't think that the enemy is the only one who is well organized."

"Frankly, I don't know what to think," Fontaine admitted, still trying to process everything.

Henry opened a few bottom cabinets, taking out more weapons and placing them on a long table.

"Take whatever you need," he encouraged them. "We may not be back if things go sideways."

"Sideways?" Tom repeated in an incredulous whisper.

"Disastrous," Oliver explained with a touch of foreboding.

Henry started filling a beige backpack with a compass, binoculars, a survival knife, metal canisters, and a variety of weapons.

Fontaine picked up ten clips for her Glock, loading each one with hollow-point bullets. Gowerstone followed suit and tucked two throwing knives into his belt. Scanning the rest of the arsenal, they each grabbed a Taser Stick, able to deliver 800,000 volts of electricity.

Sliding one of them into her jacket, Fontaine turned to Gowerstone. "These could come in handy. Not as lethal as a gun, but still effective at close range."

"Agreed," Gowerstone nodded, admiring the object.

"Why do you use the Glock 10mm?"

"It's more powerful and deadly. You only need one shot to drop someone," Gowerstone explained. "Why the 9mm?"

"More accurate."

"True, the 10mm has a stronger recoil."

After they finished, Fontaine walked to the exit with her cell phone. "I should contact Gustave and let him know we're okay. See if he has discovered anything useful."

"It's never been more important to have someone on the inside," Gowerstone stressed. "Anything he can provide is helpful. We need to know what they know."

Fontaine nodded and walked outside toward the river.

She reached Gustave but kept the conversation brief, focusing on the essential facts. When Fontaine finished, she removed the battery from the phone and disposed of both. She then rejoined the others waiting by the front door.

Gowerstone pulled her aside. "What did he say?"

"Nothing was reported about the assault on Henry's chateau," Fontaine replied. "Gustave said that the chief inspector was visited this morning by two men. After the meeting, one man stayed behind. Whoever he is, it looks like he's running the show now."

"It's just as we speculated—Interpol is controlled by an outside group."

"There's more," she noted, her face tense. "Our assumptions were correct. Before I was wanted for questioning. Now I've been classified as a threat to national security and branded a terrorist."

"Based on what?"

"Whatever they've made up," she declared with animosity. "You've also been added to Interpol's Most Wanted List, and there's an arrest warrant for Henry on some trumped-up charges."

Gowerstone was unfazed. "Oliver?"

"Wanted for questioning."

"Tom and Sarah?"

"They wouldn't dare mention their names."

"So if they're captured, no one will know."

"Exactly," Fontaine confirmed. "All my case files have been seized, and any research I've done on Tom or Sarah has been erased."

"Do they know where we are?"

"Gustave didn't have that information. He said he'll

keep searching for answers, but it's difficult under the circumstances. He doesn't want to raise any red flags."

"Understood," Gowerstone acknowledged. "It's a complicated situation."

"If only we could stay a few steps ahead."

"Interpol's just one institution," Gowerstone expounded. "We now have to contend with all of them. Not just MI5 and MI6, but organizations without accountability, mostly black ops and ex-military."

"We're completely outnumbered," Fontaine vented, wondering how they stood a chance.

"The good guys usually are."

"So much for my career," she sighed heavily. "You spend your entire life working for what you believe in, only to have everything taken away by the click of a computer."

Gowerstone rested his hand on her shoulder. "We'll get through this," he assured her. "I promise."

Henry joined them. "Is everything all right?"

"We'll fill you in later," Gowerstone replied. "Let's stay focused on our mission."

After Henry secured the Britfield Codex and other important information in his room safe, they all left the villa and walked down a pathway toward the Loire. At the river's edge sat Henry's boathouse, a fieldstone building with discolored roof tiles and a copper weathervane.

A Sheerline 955 Aft Cockpit cruiser floated in the river. It was bright white with a royal-blue bottom. In the back were two Nanni 4.60HE 60hp diesel engines that provided enormous horsepower for navigating the river.

Tom admired the boat. "This looks fast."

"Very fast," Henry said.

"I think I'll take this instead of the Range Rover," Oliver jested, half-serious.

"You have expensive taste, nephew," Henry remarked, amused. He escorted them to the bow.

"All right, everyone onboard. Be careful getting in, and make sure you're always holding on to something in case the boat shifts."

They boarded the cruiser and stood on the main deck. Henry started both engines, the tremendous power vibrating the boat. He confidently steered out of the boathouse and headed east on the river.

Trying to remain inconspicuous, Henry hugged the shoreline where the boat could remain hidden among the tall trees and overgrowth.

Although everyone felt the seriousness of the situation, they enjoyed the warm sunshine, cool breeze, and breathtaking scenery.

Known as the "Garden of France," the Loire Valley was blanketed in vineyards and fruit orchards. The picturesque hills were sprinkled with church steeples and glimpses of spectacular chateaux hidden behind trees. A variety of sailboats glided back and forth. Scattered overhead was a patchwork of colorful hot air balloons.

Tom and Sarah glanced up, remembering their harrowing journey over half of England in a balloon: the freezing temperature, the helicopter chase, the thunderstorm, Heathrow Airport, and the final crash into the Serpentine Lake in Hyde Park.

"Fond memories?" Oliver asked dryly, a slight grin surfacing.

"That's one way to put it," Sarah murmured.

"What's another?"

"Terrifying," she replied bluntly, a sudden shiver running down her spine.

"I thought it was exciting," Tom chimed in.

"You weren't afraid of heights."

"That's true," he conceded. "And now?"

"Trust me, I'm cured."

Tom tapped Henry on the shoulder. "Sir Henry, have you ever visited Chambord?"

"Please, call me Henry," he said calmly as he navigated the river. "Yes, several times. It's the most magnificent chateau I've ever seen."

"How were you able to get into the castle?"

"It's open to the public, or at least part of it is," Henry answered. "Little did I know that the true royal family of Britain was hiding inside."

This last phrase gave Tom chills. To hear these words about the family he hoped was his was encouraging. Now only a few miles away, in another country with a group of strangers who had become friends, he felt very close to home.

"I don't understand how the Britfields could hide in plain sight," Sarah interjected. "Wouldn't that be dangerous?"

"It will always be dangerous for the Britfields," Henry maintained. "However, it's actually brilliant. They're using the same tactics as the enemy, hiding in plain sight. Not many would suspect it.

"Why not?"

"It's assumed that the Britfields are deceased."

"But what if they're seen?" Tom questioned.

"They wouldn't be," Henry reasoned. "Chambord is enormous. When the chateau is open to the public, only a small section can be visited, such as the main entrance hall, the grand dining room, and a few bedrooms. Everything else is kept sealed off."

"So they could be living in one area and never see any outsiders," Tom concluded.

"That's correct. A hundred years ago, opening one's estate to the public would have been absurd, but today it's common practice."

"It's like the manor houses in England," Oliver explained. "Part of the house is open to tourists, while the family lives in another section. They use the money from admissions to pay for the upkeep."

"The cost associated with maintaining an estate is astronomical," Henry explained, knowing from his own experience. "With the decline of the aristocracy, they needed to earn money somehow."

"Who are the Britfields staying with?" Tom wondered. "I mean, who owns the property?"

"That's a good question," Henry admitted, although he had an idea. "Obviously it's someone loyal to the Britfields."

"The place must be well guarded, with a contingency plan in case they're discovered," Fontaine surmised.

"There's probably an entire tunnel system underneath Chambord that leads off the estate," Henry conveyed with a suggestion of foreknowledge.

"But who protects them? Who would take that risk?" Fontaine asked as if she were interrogating a suspect.

Henry hesitated. "I might know."

This was one of Henry's last secrets, perhaps his greatest. It was the reason for his meticulous research and why he was in France. However, if Henry could trust anyone, he knew it was Tom, Sarah, Oliver, Fontaine, and Gowerstone.

They all stared at Henry, waiting for him to answer.

"Well?" Sarah asked impatiently.

"The French Resistance," Henry replied in a restrained tone.

"The French Resistance?" Oliver repeated, stymied. "I thought that was just during World War II."

Henry weighed his response. "It started in World War II, but it didn't end when the war was over," he revealed cryptically.

"You're telling me that they're still around?" Oliver questioned.

Attentively steering the boat, Henry shifted in his deck chair, considering where to begin.

"After Nazi Germany invaded France in 1940, the French people united behind a common purpose. They were ready to work together to win back their freedom and expel the Germans. The idea of fighting for their country, fighting for their future and their children's future, became a singular goal. No longer did politics or opinions matter, whether you were educated or ignorant, rich or poor, aristocratic or working class. There was a bond among the people, a band of brothers and sisters forged together. The nobility fought next to farmers;

merchants helped academics; doctors collaborated with shopkeepers. The clergy finally stood behind their words and picked up rifles; pastors defended their people. Although they fought against the greatest mobilized army in history, they had an invincible force: a faith in God and a willingness to sacrifice their lives for one another."

"Wow," Sarah and Tom whispered in unison, stirred by the narrative.

"But didn't the Americans land in Normandy to free the French?" Oliver asked, recalling his schooling.

"D-Day, right?" Sarah remembered.

"That's correct. The Americans and the British helped liberate France, but the French Resistance made it possible," Henry continued. "The Resistance worked feverishly for months before June 6, 1944, the day of the D-Day landings, cutting phone lines, blowing up railroads, and causing chaos. They also passed along valuable information about Nazi gun placements and troop movements."

Oliver rubbed his forehead, perplexed. "I thought the French Resistance was disbanded once France was liberated."

"Although France was free from the Nazis, tyranny soon reigned again in a different form. The globalists and bankers swooped in to seize power, forcing their socialist agenda."

"Globalists?" Tom asked, unacquainted with the term.

"They are the same immoral people we've been talking about. The ones in the shadows, pulling the strings of their puppets. They don't care about individual rights or a country's sovereignty. They want a one-world government, where they dictate all the rules and control everyone's lives."

"So the French Resistance stayed together," Oliver realized.

"Yes, they were well organized and still shared the same basic beliefs: freedom and the protection of individual rights."

"And they're still active today?"

"They've never been stronger."

"I've heard rumors of a resistance group taking down dirty politicians and exposing fraudulent organizations," Fontaine recollected. "But we've never been able to produce conclusive evidence. They're careful to cover their tracks and seem to work in small groups."

"How do you know so much about this organization?" Gowerstone asked Henry, still skeptical.

Henry took a deep breath as he contemplated his reply. "I've been a member for over two decades," he said gallantly.

Oliver was taken aback, his eyes wide open. Fontaine was stunned. Gowerstone was not surprised. Tom and Sarah looked on with admiration.

"That explains a great deal," Gowerstone stated, his mind reviewing everything Henry had shared.

Just then a black helicopter buzzed overhead.

"That doesn't look local," Fontaine noticed. "The windows are tinted, and there aren't any markings."

"The countrywide search for us has begun," Henry informed them, immediately increasing the boat's speed.

"Chambord's not far. Once we dock, it's only a couple of miles inland."

Henry glided along the Loire, consulting his map and staying close to the river's edge. Twenty minutes later, he located a small dock with a few fishing boats moored to one side. Gently lifting the throttle, he eased into a clear spot.

"Oliver, do you mind?" Henry requested, motioning to the starboard side.

With lightning speed, Oliver threw two rubber bumpers over the side, leaped onto the dock, and securely tied the vessel.

Everyone disembarked and marched along the weathered planking until they reached the shore. Local birds were busy with their mid-day activities. A light breeze fluttered through the ancient elms overhead.

Henry checked his compass. "This way."

They followed a dirt path across a field of wildflowers until they emerged on Quai de la Loire, a main roadway. A few cars raced by as they crossed over to Route de Chambord, a long boulevard leading to the Château de Chambord.

They stayed back from the road, hiding among the overgrowth. Henry led the way, and Oliver trailed behind, scouting the area. Gowerstone and Fontaine searched vigilantly for anything suspicious.

Tom and Sarah were excited. Their long journey from Weatherly was hopefully coming to an end.

"How much farther, Henry?" Oliver asked as he whacked branches with a stick.

"It's still a good mile," Henry answered, studying his map.

"We'll need to watch for security cameras around the estate," Gowerstone advised. "And the outer perimeter will be well guarded."

"From my understanding, security will be tight but not observable," Henry relayed. "If it were obvious, people would suspect something."

Finally, they reached a twelve-foot-high brick wall capped with beveled granite. Every hundred feet there was a stone plaque with an odd creature prominently displayed.

"What is that thing?" Tom asked, squinting at the object.

"It's a salamander, King François I's personal emblem," Henry answered. "The castle is covered with them."

"A lizard?" Sarah questioned, surprised. "What a peculiar thing to represent your family."

"Symbolizing fire and ice, the salamander is a mythical creature that could survive in fire while simultaneously extinguishing the flames with its cold body."

"It looks like a dragon," Tom observed, touching the elaborate carving.

"Spooky, if you ask me," Sarah mumbled to herself.

"The royalty tends to be eccentric, entertaining many superstitions and occult beliefs," Henry explained, his words hinting at a darker side.

Moving along the wall, they reached the main entrance where a prominent marble sign read "Parc de Chambord." The boulevard was jam-packed with cars.

"It's so busy," Tom commented, watching a line of vehicles parading by.

"Chambord is one of France's most popular tourist destinations," Henry explained. "It attracts thousands of people from around the world."

"Should we just walk in?" Sarah wondered, noticing people strolling along the sidewalks.

"Why not?" Henry proposed. "We'll simply act like tourists."

"Listen." Gowerstone abruptly stopped, looking upward. He searched the sky, his senses on high alert. There was a humming noise, and it was getting louder.

"I hear it," Fontaine said.

"Let's get out of the open," Gowerstone instructed, guiding everyone under a tree, its canopy acting like an umbrella.

A few hundred feet above, a white object flew by. It had a narrow body and long wings.

"What is it?" Oliver asked, peering through the leaves.

"It's a surveillance drone," Gowerstone answered. "A military-grade, remote-controlled aircraft. It's probably searching for us."

13
A RENAISSANCE MASTERPIECE

Oliver was busy tracking the object with Henry's binoculars. "Does the drone have cameras?"

"Cameras and thermal imaging that can detect heat from the human body," Gowerstone answered.

"Even through the trees?"

"Through trees, cars, and the walls of most buildings."

"I know Interpol uses drones," Fontaine mentioned. "It's illegal to survey the public, but they do it anyway, mostly at night."

"As do the other agencies," Gowerstone added. "I've spotted them flying over parts of England. We have an entire department dedicated to this technology."

"And now one of these drones just happens to be soaring over Chambord," Oliver conveyed, skeptical that this was a coincidence.

"They must know we're here," Gowerstone concluded, uncertain how to proceed.

"We could be walking into a trap," Fontaine cautioned.

Henry let out a deep sigh. "How do they know about Chambord?"

"They could just be searching the general area," Oliver suggested. "They knew we were headed south."

"The south is vast. This location is too specific. They must know something," Gowerstone rationalized.

"I have a bad feeling about this," Fontaine said as she continued to scan the sky.

Tom and Sarah looked distraught, their optimism diminishing.

"Do we continue?" Henry asked. "Our only advantage was that they didn't know where we were."

Gowerstone turned to Tom with a stern yet compassionate look. "Tom, we're responsible for you and Sarah, and I don't want to jeopardize your safety. However, the decision is yours."

Tom glanced at Sarah. "What do you think?"

"I haven't come this far to stop now," Sarah replied, determined. "I think we should continue with the plan."

Tom looked at Gowerstone. "Let's move forward," he said firmly.

Gowerstone nodded, admiring Tom's bravery. "Okay, but we need to be more alert."

"And take some precautions," Henry added, realizing how exposed they were.

Henry opened his backpack, removing several baseball caps and handing them to Tom, Sarah, and Oliver. All three put on the caps. Henry then handed Gowerstone and Fontaine sunglasses.

"Let's try to blend in," Henry recommended. "It's a simple tactic, but it will help hide our facial features on camera."

"Not a bad idea," Fontaine said as she slid on the glasses. She took a colorful Hermès scarf from her coat pocket and covered her hair.

"We should also walk in two groups," Gowerstone

suggested, putting on a wool cap he had tucked away in his coat pocket. "Fontaine and Tom can go with me, while Sarah can walk with Henry and Oliver."

"Just like two families," Sarah said playfully.

Fontaine gazed at Gowerstone, enjoying the idea.

"Something like that," Gowerstone murmured as he slid on his sunglasses.

They continued up the road in two groups, merging with other tourists heading toward the chateau. They turned at a bend in the road and looked through a clearing of trees. They stood in awe.

Across a pristine grass field was their first glimpse of Château de Chambord. The four-hundred-forty-four-room castle was three hundred feet wide and five stories high. The rooftop resembled a city skyline with eleven different towers and three styles of chimneys. The upper terrace had spires, shell-shaped domes, and richly sculpted gables. Centered was a one-hundred-twenty-five-foot lantern, crowned by a Fleur de Lys, the emblem of French royalty.

Started in 1518 by François I, the interior contained eighty-four staircases and three hundred and sixty-five fireplaces, one for each day of the year. A twenty-mile wall encloses the property, protecting thirteen thousand acres of woodlands—approximately the size of Paris. On the north side of the estate sat stables that once housed twelve hundred horses. Long gravel pathways bordered a crystal blue lake, reflecting the magnificent château.

"It's massive," Oliver gasped.

"It's brilliant," Tom remarked, mesmerized.

"It looks like a beautiful city hidden in the countryside," Sarah whispered.

After admiring Chambord from a distance, they continued toward the main entrance, where a line had formed.

Gowerstone observed three pairs of men, all dressed like vacationers. Gowerstone noticed their serious expressions, short haircuts, and military mannerisms. They were obviously trained operatives.

The detective whispered to Fontaine, smiling as if he were saying something funny while trying not to draw attention. "Do you notice the teams of two?" he asked in a whisper.

"All three." She smiled back, followed by a fake chuckle. "What are your thoughts?"

"We play it cool for now. They haven't noticed us yet."

"And if they do notice us?"

"We take them down."

Gowerstone purchased three tickets with cash and escorted Fontaine and Tom inside the chateau. Henry, Oliver, and Sarah waited in line, gazing over their brochure map of Chambord.

Once Henry bought his tickets, he had to check his backpack at the front counter, but he quickly removed a few items and stuffed them in his pockets.

Fifteen minutes later, they all met in the main foyer, crowded with dozens of tourists.

Tom and Sarah stared up at the coffered ceiling twenty feet above the marble entry hall. Carved salamanders and golden symbols decorated the frieze running around the room. An enormous marble fireplace dominated one side, and a variety of historic oil paintings covered the other walls.

The decorations and ceiling designs represented three different monarchs: the letter *F* and the salamander for François I, crescent moons for Henri II, and the letter *L* and sunbursts for Louis XIV, the Sun King.

Straight ahead was a miracle of Renaissance engineering: a spectacular double-helix open staircase with each stairway superimposed on the other, so that people could climb or descend simultaneously without ever seeing each other. It was rumored that the complex design had been created by Leonardo da Vinci while he was employed by François I.

Tom was busy examining the multifaceted staircase, struggling to decipher the mysterious design. Sarah was enamored by the vibrant tapestries that displayed royal hunting scenes and life at court.

"Where do we even begin?" Oliver wondered, overwhelmed by the sheer size of the château.

"We should take one of the tours," Henry suggested, studying his map. "When the group continues to the next section, we'll break off and explore the private areas."

"But there are cameras and security guards everywhere," Fontaine interjected. "I don't think we'll get very far."

"That's what I'm counting on."

"Pardon?" she questioned.

"At some point we'll need to contact those behind this façade, the men in charge of protecting the Britfields."

"That makes sense, in a dicey, dangerous sort of way," Oliver mumbled.

"The security personnel are highly trained and know who they're protecting," Henry explained. "Once they see Tom and the letter from the archbishop, they might give us access to the Britfields."

"Might?" Sarah inquired dubiously.

"We have no idea how they'll react, but it's our best option."

They followed a tour group around the first floor, making their way into the grand ballroom.

The space had an ambiance of a forgotten era: the exquisite craftsmanship, the intricate parquet floor, the arched windows with burgundy drapes, the walnut coffered ceiling, the crystal chandeliers.

Sarah mused about what it would be like to waltz across the ballroom in a beautiful dress at a midsummer night gala. She squinted at Tom, trying to visualize him in a tuxedo.

"What?" Tom asked, noticing her gaze.

"Nothing." She laughed, putting the idea out of her mind.

The group passed through the royal bedrooms of Louis XIV and his wife, Maria Theresa, their portraits staring down at the unwanted intruders. Each decadent room had a massive four-poster oak bed with a purple silk canopy and a royal crest stitched onto the material. Divinely crafted antique furniture and bronze statues of Greek gods complemented the space.

They continued to the former lodgings of François I,

which included his bed chamber, private rooms, and an atrium with sculpted ceilings displaying symbols of François I: the letter *F*, knotted rope motifs, and salamanders spitting water at evil fires.

The tour guide would occasionally stop to point out important paintings or artifacts.

Searching his map, Henry tried to figure out where the Britfields might be residing. He casually strolled over to Gowerstone and Fontaine, motioning around the room like an inquisitive tourist.

"The map indicates that the west wing houses a private chapel in the corner tower," Henry conveyed in a subtle whisper. "Adjacent are private apartments on the third and fourth floor. If they're anywhere, it's probably in this section."

"That sounds promising," Fontaine whispered.

"Let's stay with the tour and see how close we can get," Henry instructed.

The group continued through the first story and ascended the double-helix staircase to the next floor.

A seemingly endless corridor led to a variety of bed chambers. Evoking the French grandeur of royalty, each suite was a masterpiece: crimson satin drapes, Napoleonic blue wallpaper with golden bees, Persian rugs covering mahogany floors, Ming Dynasty sculptures, and intricately carved marble fireplaces.

After viewing the different bedrooms, the group went up the stairs to the third floor and turned right down a hallway. Some of the rooms were open, but others were locked.

As they moved down the corridor, they noticed certain sections roped off with signs saying "Private: Do Not Enter." Each restricted area had security personnel guarding the entrance. The men were muscular and fit, with military-style haircuts. They each wore a small receiver in the left ear and the bulges under their jackets indicated that they were carrying weapons. Cameras were visible in every corner.

Henry moseyed over to Gowerstone as Fontaine and Tom surveyed another room.

"The Britfields are probably on one of these top floors," Henry speculated. "According to the map, most of the west wing is private."

"We'll need a distraction," Gowerstone proposed.

"When we leave the next bedroom, I'll create a diversion," Henry said provocatively. "It should keep the security personnel occupied."

Henry meandered back to Oliver and Sarah, who were listening to the tour guide.

Fontaine motioned to Gowerstone. "We have a tail."

"You mean the two men behind us, trying to blend in while reading their maps upside down."

"What branch do you think they're from?"

"Probably black ops or hired mercenaries. We'll take care of them in due course," Gowerstone replied, revealing the taser tucked in his jacket.

The group entered the King's Private Chambers, now packed with tourists gazing at the spectacular views from the windows. The tour guide pointed to different objects, commenting on each piece and its historic significance.

The two men stood by the doorway, partially blocking the entrance.

Gowerstone nodded to Fontaine then Henry, who reached into his pocket and discreetly removed a silver canister.

Following his signal, Fontaine abruptly grabbed her stomach and bent over, coughing dramatically.

"Are you all right?" Gowerstone asked loudly, trying to draw attention.

"I-I don't know," she replied faintly. "I need to get some fresh air."

"Let's get you outside."

Gowerstone put his arm around her, escorting her toward the exit. The two men standing by the doorway looked on suspiciously.

"Excuse me, let us through," Gowerstone said, maneuvering his way around a sea of tourists.

As they approached the doorway, Fontaine and Gowerstone swiftly thrust their tasers into the side of each man, delivering 800,000 volts. Both men dropped to the floor, immobilized.

Henry flipped the switch on the canister and rolled it under an enormous canopy bed. A grayish smoke emerged from underneath, rapidly filling the room.

"Fire," Henry yelled, causing an instant panic.

The frightened tourists stampeded toward the doorway. Two security guards hurried into the room, passing the exiting people, along with Fontaine, Gowerstone, Tom, Sarah, Oliver, and Henry.

The smoke crept into the hallway as three additional security guards ran down the corridor.

"Where to?" Fontaine asked.

"We need to get to the fourth story and over to the west wing," Henry directed.

Following his lead, they hurried around the corner to a stone staircase. It was roped off with a sign: "Restricted Area." Henry, Gowerstone, Oliver, and Fontaine stepped over the rope while Tom and Sarah ducked underneath.

As they ascended the steep flight of steps, a deafening fire alarm sounded. Red boxes attached to the walls started flashing. There was the rumble of footsteps as hundreds of tourists began leaving the different floors and bolting for the exits. Thunderous shouts echoed off the walls, creating further pandemonium.

"You set off the fire alarm," Oliver said, startled by all the chaos. "Was that your plan?"

"Part of it," Henry replied. "This will help clear the chateau."

"Is that a good idea?"

"It causes confusion and distracts the guards."

"It also alerts the outside authorities and brings attention to Chambord," Gowerstone pointed out.

"I know, but we needed a distraction."

"I think you got one," Sarah added.

They climbed the stairs, turned right down a deserted hallway and continued until they reached another restricted area.

Two security personnel appeared out of nowhere. Roland, mid-forties, tall and brawny, and Fredrick, late thirties, medium height, marched toward them. These men were different from the others—more intense and visibly armed.

"My name is Roland and this is Fredrick. You're in a restricted area," Roland announced. "Turn around and head back down the stairs."

"I'll escort you to the exit and out of the building," Fredrick stated, his voice hostile.

In a flash, Fontaine and Gowerstone drew their guns and aimed them at the guards.

"We're not going anywhere," Gowerstone stressed, tired of the games they were playing.

The two men started to reach for their weapons.

"Don't," Fontaine warned, her eyes deadly serious. The guards paused, slowly lowering their hands.

"We mean you no harm," Gowerstone assured them. "We're here to speak with the Britfields."

The guards looked surprised.

"They know who I am," Gowerstone continued, his voice sincere.

"And who might that be?" Roland asked, unimpressed.

"I'm Detective Gowerstone, New Scotland Yard."

"I'm afraid I can't help you. I've never heard of the Britfields," Roland said.

"We know they're here," Fontaine interjected, agitated.

"You're mistaken and have made a grave error," Fredrick threatened, his glance intimidating.

A loud rumbling came from the ceiling as two barred walls suddenly descended on both sides of the group, one in front and another in back, trapping them in a ten-foot-by-ten-foot cage-like structure.

"That's inconvenient," Oliver mumbled to the others.

"Didn't see that coming," Tom whispered.

From both directions, armed guards entered the corridor, their M16s held upright.

"Now lower your weapons and put them on the floor," Roland ordered, his tone harsh.

Gowerstone glanced at Fontaine and nodded. They gently placed their guns on the ground.

Tom and Sarah were crestfallen, their hopes seemingly dashed. However, Henry appeared calm.

"May I presume you're the ones who ignited the smoke bomb in the King's Private Chambers and tasered two men," Roland inquired.

"Yes, it was us," Fontaine admitted grudgingly. "But we have a good reason. We—"

"I'm not interested," Roland interrupted. "You have no idea the trouble you're in."

Henry boldly moved forward, face-to-face with Roland on the other side of the steel bars.

"*Dieu, vie, liberté*," Henry stated with conviction.

The guard's expression immediately changed, as if the words had triggered a programmed reaction.

Oliver and Tom promptly turned to Sarah. "God, life, liberty," she whispered.

The guard looked straight at Henry.

"*Famille, amitié, indépendance.*"

Tom and Oliver glanced back to Sarah. She rolled her eyes. "Family, friendship, independence."

"It's worth fighting for," Henry continued, his spirit lifted.

"And dying for," Roland emphasized.

"These are the God-given rights of every man, woman,

and child. They must be protected and defended at all costs," Henry concluded.

Henry lifted his shirt collar to reveal an emblem of a white dove and a silver sword with a lion in the background. Oliver and the others watched this odd exchange, baffled by what was transpiring.

"You may speak freely," Roland said, his attitude softening.

"We're here to see the Britfields on urgent business," Henry informed him, turning to Tom. "Would you mind sharing your document?"

"Not at all," Tom mumbled.

He reached in his pocket and handed over the letter through the bars, his hand a bit wobbly. Roland carefully reviewed it, looking overwhelmed by the revelation it held.

"Is it possible?" he whispered, staring at Tom.

Roland motioned to the other security guard. "Frederick, lower your weapon and raise the gates," he commanded.

The metal bars slowly rose, disappearing into the ceiling. The security team disengaged and stood at attention.

"Can someone tell me what's happening?" Sarah asked, trying to comprehend the sudden fortuity.

"The French Resistance," Henry broadcasted. "You asked who could be trusted to guard the Britfields. I give you this loyal band of brothers."

Gowerstone and Fontaine exchanged a look of relief as they reached down to retrieve their weapons and put them back in their holsters.

Roland spoke to Fredrick, who promptly walked to a keypad and shut off the fire alarm.

"Can you assure me that there will be no more smoke bombs or tasers used?" Roland asked Henry cordially.

"Yes, on my word."

"Good, let's get to work. There's quite a bit of protocol we will need to cover."

They shadowed Roland down the corridor to a secure room, where people in uniforms were sitting in front of several rows of computer screens.

For almost an hour, Henry, Oliver, Gowerstone, Fontaine, Tom, and Sarah were questioned, given extensive background checks, fingerprinted, and verified through facial recognition software.

"Okay, we're done here. Everything appears valid, exactly as you've stated," Roland confirmed. "Please follow me."

Fontaine turned to Henry. "Bravo," she declared, astonished that his plan had worked.

"Are they going to take us to the Britfields?" Tom whispered to Oliver.

"I'm not sure, but it seems like we're headed in the right direction."

"And we're not in a steel cage or surrounded by machine guns," Sarah added.

They continued down another hallway, where there was a fortified titanium door every fifty feet. As they passed through each section, Roland tapped in a different code and placed his thumb over a digital pad and stared into a biometric retina scanner that read the unique patterns on his retina.

"This is some security," Oliver whispered to Henry.

"It's cutting-edge technology," he replied, impressed. "I've read about it, but I've never seen it."

"I think it was easier breaking into the Louvre," Oliver said under his breath.

"You might want to keep that to yourself," Henry advised with a stern look.

They finally came to a majestic arched doorway that led to an enormous suite. Roland went through the same extensive security protocol, but this time he had his entire face scanned and spoke into a voice recognition system using a passcode in Latin. He waited patiently until the door opened.

As Roland entered, everyone followed behind.

The interior was luxurious yet businesslike: a row of modern office desks, a glass boardroom table, and massive plasma screens. Another area had twelve-foot tapestries depicting the Britfield coat of arms: a crest with a golden lion on one side and a white horse on the other. A Latin phrase wrapped around the interior crest with the words *Arte et Marte; Consillio et Animis*. Enormous windows offered breathtaking views of the estate and the distant horizon. In each section of the vaulted ceiling was a painted royal crest with a golden *B*. Men and women dressed in business attire rushed about, seemingly unaware of the visitors.

"Please wait here," Roland instructed as he left the room.

"I think we're in the right place," Oliver said as he spun around, viewing the interior.

"It's like a twenty-first century royal court," Sarah remarked, impressed by the sophisticated surroundings.

"What does that say?" Tom asked, pointing to the Britfield crest.

"I told you, my Latin isn't very good," Sarah replied, wishing she knew.

"By skill and valor; by wisdom and courage," a voice thundered in a thick Scottish brogue.

Sarah's ears perked up at the familiar accent. Everyone turned as an older gentleman entered.

In his late fifties with broad shoulders, deep blue eyes, and short, silver hair, the six-foot-tall man wore a tailored pinstriped suit. His manner was refined yet disciplined; his rigid stature conveyed a military past.

"And the bottom phrase?" Sarah inquired, intrigued.

"By love and faith," he answered reverently. "These are the words that the Britfields live by." Appearing mesmerized, the man marched over to Tom and knelt by his side, staring into his eyes.

Feeling a bit awkward, Tom glanced at Gowerstone and Fontaine for guidance.

"It's all right, Tom. You can trust him," Henry assured him.

After a moment, the man stood to address the others. "I apologize for my abruptness," he stated politely. "My name is Alistair. It's been eleven years since the Britfields lost their child. To think that this might be their son is a bit overwhelming."

"We understand," Henry acknowledged, amazed that their plan had succeeded.

"Pardon me, sir," Sarah interrupted. "What part of Scotland are you from?"

"Sterling, my lass. And you?"

"Edinburgh."

"The finest city in Britain," Alistair professed. "It's refreshing to see another Scot among us."

Sarah beamed, feeling a kindred bond with her countryman.

Alistair scrutinized each one of them, studying their expressions and features. He recognized Gowerstone.

"You were there at the beginning," he said, walking over and firmly shaking his hand.

"And at the end," Gowerstone said coolly.

"Yes, we heard about your chase from Yorkshire to Canterbury," Alistair revealed. "You stayed with this case for over ten years. That's remarkable. We owe you a debt that can never be repaid."

"You owe me nothing," Gowerstone responded. "It has been a privilege."

"Do you know Henry?" Fontaine asked.

"We're aware of Sir Horningbrook," Alistair replied. "Although I've never had the honor of meeting him, he is one of us, united by a common belief. The information he has provided over the years has been vital to understanding the enemy."

"The Committee?" Fontaine tried to confirm.

"They're the top organization, but there are many others."

"You mentioned Detective Gowerstone's chase, so you must have known about Tom," Henry said, curious how much he knew.

"Our organization monitored what was happening," Alistair informed them. "We have agents everywhere."

"Why didn't you help us?" Sarah inquired, disappointed that no one had come to their aid.

"We did," Alistair contended, his voice resonant. "There were others after you, unseen and behind the shadows. Our men kept them there."

"You mean you took them out," Oliver clarified, raising his brow.

"Yes, in a manner of speaking."

"Couldn't you have rescued us when we escaped from Weatherly and made our way to London?" Sarah continued, reflecting on everything they had endured.

"Once we heard the news about Tom, we immediately tried to intervene," Alistair began, his voice animated. "But you two were hard to find, as I'm sure Detective Gowerstone will attest to, covering half of England by foot, car, balloon, cab, subway, and train. We got close but never close enough."

"Were you notified that Tom might come here?" Henry asked.

"The Archbishop of Canterbury contacted us," Alistair replied. "We were astounded by the news."

"But you didn't act on it?" Fontaine questioned, assessing his commitment.

"We had two teams waiting to meet Tom and Sarah in Calais and escort them to Chambord," Alistair replied, his eyes radiant.

"You had my back?"

"Yes, Inspector, we had your back."

"But someone got to the ferry?"

"A Committee assassin detonated a bomb that sunk the vessel," Alistair disclosed, a trace of bitterness in his accent. "We weren't sure if Tom and Sarah survived. Like you, Inspector Fontaine, we searched the entire coastline and country. We've been searching ever since."

"How long have you known they were alive?" Fontaine queried, enlightened by what she was learning.

"Shortly after the episode at Notre-Dame. We only wish we could have intervened sooner," Alistair confessed, clutching his fists.

"Are the Britfields here?" Sarah asked as she surveyed the room.

Alistair paused, all eyes on him. "They left six weeks ago," he replied, noticing Tom's disappointment. "It was too dangerous for them to stay at Chambord any longer."

"But they're alive?" Fontaine asked, hopeful.

"Yes, alive and healthy," Alistair announced, smiling. "It's my job to keep them that way."

On hearing the news, Tom became melancholy. After all these years, he just wanted to see his parents. Alistair promptly leaned over to comfort him.

"Don't worry, you'll meet them soon. That is once we confirm that you're their son," he said, hoping to encourage the boy, then, turning to Gowerstone, he asked, "If you don't mind, may we verify Tom's rightful heritage?"

"That would be expected," Gowerstone agreed. "You've the means?"

"We have a complete medical facility onsite and have been prepared in case Tom arrived."

"How exactly will you confirm Tom's identity?" Sarah questioned in a protective manner.

"It will be confirmed through his DNA."

"From a sample of his blood?"

"Yes, it's relatively painless and won't take long," Alistair explained reassuringly to Tom. "Would that be all right?"

Tom looked to Gowerstone, the one man he trusted above all others. "What do you think, Detective?"

"You need to know for certain," Gowerstone said approvingly.

"Will you go with me?"

"I would insist."

"Good, then we can proceed," Alistair confirmed.

Walking to a nearby desk, he pressed a button on an intercom.

A few minutes later, a man and woman entered from another room. Mid-thirties, they wore long white medical coats and had a friendly demeanor.

"If you follow them, they'll perform the proper tests," Alistair conveyed pleasantly then motioned three guards to accompany them and make sure Tom remained protected.

Gowerstone gently rested his hand on Tom's shoulder. "Are you ready?"

"Yes, sir."

As they left the room, Sarah watched intently, not knowing what to expect. She felt a mixture of excitement and uncertainty, happiness and foreboding. After all the things they had gone through, it came down to this one moment.

"Please, feel free to sit while we wait," Alistair suggested, glancing toward the fireplace. "I'll have some refreshments brought in."

There was a glow in Alistair's eyes. Instinct told him that Tom was the Britfields' lost son.

"What about the men we disabled at the doorway?" Fontaine questioned.

"They've been taken care of," Alistair answered, his voice telling.

"We also counted three other teams embedded with the tourists, and I'm sure there are more," she added. "We believe they're here for Tom."

"Our men have had them under surveillance since they arrived," Alistair replied evenly. "If we apprehend them now, it will confirm that Chambord is a safe house. Henry's smoke bomb allowed us to evacuate the chateau without anyone becoming suspicious. But this ruse won't last long. I believe our time here has come to an end. We will need to relocate soon."

"Do you think you've been exposed?" Fontaine asked.

"That's why we moved the Britfields," Alistair explained. "Since Tom resurfaced at Notre Dame, thousands of the Committee's minions and trolls have been looking for him. There are spies and traitors everywhere."

They stood motionless, evaluating what Alistair conveyed. It was hard to know whether a friend was an enemy or an ally was a spy.

"And the teams outside?" Fontaine continued, feeling on edge.

"We'll deal with them soon enough. We're on high

alert, and our security protocols are in place," Alistair answered, motioning them to sit.

They walked over to a large marble fireplace and sat on two opulent sofas covered in turquoise silk. The mood was tense as a whirlwind of thoughts and emotions raced through their minds. For the first time since they were together, they remained silent, thinking about Tom and what his news might bring.

14
KIDNAPPED

An hour later, the door opened. Tom entered first, his expression serene and confident. Gowerstone followed, his eyes distant.

"Well?" Sarah asked anxiously, standing from her seat.

"It was conclusive," Gowerstone replied, delighted. "He's a Britfield, the last royal heir and part of the true bloodline to the British throne."

Henry sprang to his feet and vigorously shook Tom's hand.

"That's marvelous, my young friend," he exclaimed, overcome by emotion. "This is an exciting time to be alive."

"I can't believe it," Oliver blurted out, grinning from ear to ear. "That's incredible."

Sarah was momentarily speechless, relieved by the revelation, but unnerved by what it signified. She was all too aware of the dangers that lay ahead. Half-smiling, she approached him.

"So this scrappy little orphan, with his brash attitude and obnoxious behavior, is actually royalty?" she teased.

Sarah stared at Tom for a moment, a glimmer in her eyes.

"Who would've guessed that this benevolent boy, who befriended me on my first day at Weatherly, was a future king; this kind, generous lad, who always protected me. I guess I've always known you were a prince, regardless of noble titles or royal bloodlines."

She put her arms around Tom and hugged him tightly. "It's been a difficult journey, but thank you for taking me along," she said softly, her heart warmed by his friendship.

"I never would have made it without you," Tom whispered in her ear. "You were my reason to keep going."

His heartfelt sentiment touched her deeply; many unspoken words and silent understandings had created their unbreakable bond.

"And now we're so close to finding your real family." Sarah smiled confidently. "It's just a matter of time."

Fontaine approached Gowerstone, her head tilted upward as she gazed at him. "You always knew, didn't you?"

"I always hoped," Gowerstone stated.

"Congratulations, Detective. I suppose this means your record is perfect," Fontaine stated, thrilled by the revelation. "You found the Britfields' lost child."

Alistair stood motionless, stunned by the results. Years of hoping and searching had finally come to fruition—his faith had been rewarded. He was now in the presence of a rightful heir to the British throne.

"There's the issue of getting Tom to his parents," Fontaine said, eager to leave Chambord.

"Yes, of course," Alistair mumbled, clearing his throat, eyes almost teary.

He looked at Tom and gave a slight bow. "Your Royal Highness."

"Please, it's still Tom, and always will be."

"As you wish," Alistair obeyed humbly, overwhelmed

with joy. "If you'll excuse me, I must retrieve the proper documents."

Alistair briefly left the room, then returned with a sealed folder, the Britfield crest on the outside. He handed the documents to Gowerstone.

"Your parents have been moved to a safe house near Lake Como in Italy, but we don't have much time," Alistair informed them.

"Italy?" Sarah asked, wondering exactly where.

"Northern Italy, close to the Swiss border," Alistair responded, intentionally vague. "However, they won't be there for long, and I don't know their next location."

"Why is that?" Fontaine inquired, wanting to understand their procedures.

"The Britfields will be transferred to the next in command. Someone who assumes my role in Italy. Only they will have that information," Alistair replied. "It's how we keep them safe."

"Then we should leave at once," Gowerstone stated, buttoning his jacket and checking the exits.

"I'll notify the Britfields of our wonderful news and that we're on our way," Alistair said, still marveling at the revelation.

As Alistair walked over to speak with Tom, a thunderous explosion rocked the room. The windows shook as pieces of plaster fell from the ceiling, tables toppled over, and lamps crashed to the floor. Startled, everyone was thrown off balance.

"What the heck was that?" Oliver exclaimed, his heart pounding.

"It sounded like C-4, controlled detonation," Gowerstone replied, his Glock drawn as he stepped closer to Tom.

Fontaine swiftly drew her weapon and pulled Sarah to her side.

The door from an adjoining room swung open as ten guards rushed in and fanned out.

"Barclay, what is going on?" Alister asked, panic rising.

"We're under attack, Commander. We've been breached," the leader of the unit reported.

Short with broad shoulders, strawberry blond hair, and a neatly trimmed beard, Barclay had been a member of the Resistance for ten years. A tech-savvy genius and fluent in five languages, he was a valuable ally.

"What section?" Alistair asked, his mood altered.

"They're coming from all sides. We need to initiate Code Eagle."

Alistair's calm manner snapped into military mode as he tapped his two-way wireless ear comm: "All units, Code Eagle. Alert local teams to descend on Chambord and prepare for evacuation."

Alistair motioned his men to encircle Tom, forming a protective barrier.

"Code Eagle?" Tom asked.

"It's time to fly, Lord Britfield," Alistair responded firmly.

"Leave this place," Sarah whispered.

"Yeah, I got that part," Tom murmured.

Hearing a loud rumble, everyone looked out the back windows. Two black helicopters buzzed overhead, encircling the estate. A third helicopter landed by the east gardens, rapidly unloading an assault team in dark gray uniforms. The remaining tourists scattered, running to their cars or taking shelter under the nearby trees.

"This is crazy," Oliver gasped, watching all the chaos.

"Who is that?" Fontaine questioned.

"With this type of firepower, it must be the Black Cult of Horus, also known as BCH or the Brotherhood of Death, the Committee's private army," Alistair answered, his tone sharp. "They have thousands of members and secret bases worldwide."

"Mercenaries?"

"Mostly ex-military and specially trained forces," Alistair articulated.

"Commander, are you ready to descend?" Barclay asked, standing at attention.

"We'll leave directly," Alistair replied, his temper mounting. "Continue to update our organization. We'll need reinforcements immediately."

"Yes, sir," Barclay complied, dialing his satellite phone.

"How many Resistance members will come?" Henry inquired.

"There are hundreds spread throughout the Loire Valley, but it will take time for them to assemble. This engagement could be over in a few minutes."

"What's your current unit strength?" Gowerstone questioned, assessing the circumstances.

"We have a team of thirty specially trained operatives throughout the estate."

"It appears that the enemy has twice that amount, along with heavy weaponry," Gowerstone observed, seeing that they were outnumbered.

"Normally we have over a hundred men, but since the Britfields left, we've reduced our numbers," Alistair maintained. "We're organized and well trained, but this malevolent cabal has access to unlimited resources."

"We've experienced them already," Fontaine noted, recalling the previous night.

"How secure is this room?" Gowerstone asked as he studied the layout.

"It's reinforced concrete, but nothing's impenetrable," Alistair replied. "There's also a steel-encased stairwell. It descends five floors to a tunnel system under Chambord, with three separate extraction points—one to the west, another to the east, and a third to the south."

"It's time we utilize that escape route," Gowerstone stressed.

Outside the chateau, the battle raged between the Resistance and the Black Cult of Horus: good versus evil. The assault teams approached from all sides, systematically firing at anything that opposed them. The Resistance sealed off the interior hallways and floors, preparing a counterattack.

Alistair nodded to Barclay and the other guards, who moved toward the adjoining room.

"Ready?" Alistair questioned, drawing his Desert Eagle .50 caliber revolver.

"Always," Gowerstone replied, his expression like stone.

Exiting into another room, they arrived at a vault door. Alistair quickly punched in a series of codes, laid his hand on the digital fingerprinting pad, then leaned forward for the eye scan. An instant later, the massive door clicked open.

"There will be an extraction team waiting at each exit point, ready to escort us to a secure location," Alistair notified them.

"When we get to the bottom, which way should we go?" Henry asked, wondering if one was better than the other.

"South," Gowerstone stated instinctively.

"Why?" Fontaine questioned.

"We came from the west, which is well covered by the enemy. The east traps us in the heart of France."

"And the south?"

"It leads to Italy and the shoreline. The coast provides more options," Gowerstone continued, methodical as always. "If we can't fly, drive, or take a train, we can commandeer a boat."

"I agree, we'll head south," Alistair said, impressed by Gowerstone's analysis.

Alistair switched on the lights, exposing a spiral staircase with steep metal steps.

"Hold on to the railing," he instructed.

Two guards went in first, then Henry and Oliver, followed by Fontaine, Tom, Sarah, and Gowerstone. Two guards went down the stairs behind them.

"Keep us informed," Alistair ordered Barclay, who remained in the suite, his voice stern. "We'll report our progress. Make sure no one breaches these rooms."

"Understood, sir," Barclay acknowledged, his face a portrait of resilience.

Once everyone was through, Alistair closed the door and locked it.

Step by step they rapidly descended, the narrow interior cold and musky. Sarah became dizzy from the repetitive turning, gripping tightly to the railing. Although the small enclosure made Tom claustrophobic, he took a deep breath and proceeded.

Halfway down, another explosion shook the chateau, causing the walls to crumble and debris to fall.

"I don't know what kind of explosives they're using, but I've never experienced anything like this," Fontaine declared.

"It's platinum magnesium thermite, military grade," Alistair conveyed, recognizing the intensity. "It's lethal, designed to bring down large buildings, even skyscrapers."

"I've never heard of it," she admitted, perplexed.

"No one has," Alistair stated. "It's one of the Committee's Black Science Projects, secretively developed in underground research labs."

They maintained their descent in a snakelike procession, swiftly turning as fast as possible. When they were nearly at the bottom, three more explosions detonated in rapid secession. Louder than the others, they rocked the entire château.

Massive chunks of stone broke free and collapsed into the stairwell. Losing their balance, everyone knocked into the metal railing and fell onto the stairs.

Gowerstone quickly shielded Tom, and Fontaine covered Sarah.

"Look out!" Oliver shouted, yanking Henry away from a piece of falling granite. It missed Henry's head by inches, but he lost his balance and tumbled over the rubble.

Raining debris hit the metal staircase, causing a shockwave of vibrations and loud pings. A jagged stone dislodged and clipped Gowerstone's shoulder, slamming him against the wall. He quickly braced himself, his shoulder cut and throbbing with pain. Another piece fell on a guard and knocked him unconscious.

A minute later, the echoing stopped, followed by silence. Engulfed in a cloud of chalky dust, the lights began to flicker, then slowly went dead.

"Your Highness, are you safe?" Alistair asked, searching the area.

"Yeah, just a bit shaken," Tom mumbled, the darkness around him oppressive.

"Stay calm and don't panic. We'll take care of this," Alistair promised.

Flashlights sprang on, first by Alistair, then by Gowerstone, who instantly checked on Tom and Sarah, as well as Fontaine and the other guards.

Everyone was in shock as they saw all the debris had fallen into the stairwell. It was a miracle no one had been seriously injured.

Gowerstone helped Tom to his feet and brushed him off. "You're not hurt, are you?"

"No, sir," Tom answered, checking his body for cuts and bruises.

Fontaine attended to Sarah, lifting her from the metal platform. "Are you all right?" she inquired in a worried voice, searching for injuries.

"I think so," Sarah stammered, coughing as she wiped her clothing.

Fontaine moved her light over to Gowerstone. "Detective, are you hurt?"

Holding his injured shoulder, Gowerstone shrugged it off. "We're good," he answered, unfazed.

"Henry, Oliver?" Fontaine continued, gliding her flashlight around the stairwell.

"We're fine, Inspector," Oliver responded as he helped Henry to his feet.

Alistair shined his flashlight down the steps. The entire area was packed with fallen stones. "It's completely sealed off," he stated, flustered.

"Is there another way down?" Gowerstone asked.

"We have two more emergency stairwells," Alistair replied. "One is centrally located in the chateau, and a third is on the east side. However, it will be nearly impossible to safely get to them."

"It's imperative that we leave Chambord with Tom and Sarah," Gowerstone insisted, his patience waning.

"Understood, Detective," Alistair acknowledged, instigating the next protocol. "We'll use a rooftop extraction."

He tapped his ear comm. "Barclay, report."

Static came out of the receiver as Barclay's voice faded in and out.

"Sir, sectors one, two, and three are besieged. Floors one and two have been compromised. We're still holding floor three and the upper sections. We're overwhelmed by their numbers and firepower, but we'll prevail, over."

"Barclay, we need a rooftop extraction in the west wing."

"Yes, sir. We'll get our birds in the air and make it happen, over."

"And get another team to the Britfield suite for an escort."

"They'll be here directly. *Dieu, vie, liberté*, over."

Oliver and Tom glanced at Sarah.

"God, life, liberty," she answered, annoyed. "Don't you guys remember anything?"

"We've been a bit distracted," Tom muttered under his breath.

Alistair turned to Gowerstone. "Let's make our way back up. There's an escape ladder in the Britfield suite that leads to the rooftop."

"I've seen the roof. It's an obstacle course," Gowerstone remarked, questioning his plan. "Is there anywhere safe to land?"

"No, but when our helicopters get close, they'll drop a harness that can remove two people at a time," Alistair answered, well aware of the risks.

"It's dangerous and exposed, but I understand we're running out of options," Gowerstone agreed, his expression strained.

With weapons drawn, Alistair and Gowerstone led the way back up the stairwell, trailed by Henry, Tom, Sarah, Oliver, Fontaine, and the other guards, two of whom carried the injured man.

The ascent was strenuous as they wove their way around fallen chucks of stone until they finally reached the metal door. After undoing the locks, Alistair cracked the door open and checked the interior. His other men were standing by with their weapons ready.

Alistair entered first, his mood controlled, his manner stoic. "The stairwell is completely sealed off."

"Then let's get you to the rooftop and off this property," Barclay said confidently. "Three Bell 525 helicopters are en route."

"How long?"

"Five minutes, maybe ten," Barclay guessed. "They're coming from our base on the outskirts of Orleans."

"Armed?"

"Completely."

"Good." Alistair nodded. "We'll wait until our extraction team arrives before we move."

"I'm pulling them from the east wing," Barclay conveyed. "I'll start grabbing the rest of the files from the other rooms."

"Destroy what you can't remove."

Barclay confirmed the order and swiftly left the room.

Gowerstone diligently scanned the suite, making sure it was secure. He motioned to Fontaine, who entered with the rest of the group.

Gunfire continued outside and shooting echoed in the hallways.

"Move toward the interior walls and stay away from the windows," Alistair instructed. "The glass is bulletproof, but I don't want to take any chances."

They walked over to a set of couches and sat by the fireplace. A guard handed them bottles of water and towels to wipe their hands and faces. They waited patiently, their nerves on edge.

Alistair turned to one of his senior men and a

demolition expert, Mackenzie, who had just entered the suite. His clothes were torn and his face cut, but his eyes blazed with determination. Tall, slender, and highly intelligent, he was lethal when pushed.

"Mackenzie, where are the reinforcements?" Alistair questioned, exasperated.

"They'll be here shortly, sir. The word has gone out, and Resistance fighters are coming from all over the Loire Valley."

"Whatever you do, make sure Tom is not mentioned," Alistair cautioned, his tone serious. "We must keep this within our team. We'll let them know soon enough."

"Yes, sir."

"What's our current situation?"

"It started with about sixty highly trained BCH forces," Mackenzie reported. "Most of them entered the estate in M117 Humvees on the eastern side. The others were flown in on helicopters. We immediately detected them and engaged. We've brought the number down to about thirty."

"What's our strength?"

"We've lost seven men. Five others are injured but still fighting," Mackenzie continued, catching his breath. "The upper three floors are secure, and we're taking back floors one and two. I believe Barclay filled you in on the rest."

"Our surveillance?"

"Most of the cameras have either been destroyed or disrupted by the explosions," Mackenzie relayed. "They're also using a high-frequency transmitter to jam our communications, but I was able to circumvent it."

"And the power?"

"The main generators have been destroyed. We're currently on backup units."

"How does the outside perimeter look?" Alistair asked.

Crouching down, Mackenzie and another guard eased their way over to the southeast windows and peered out. They had a clear view of half the estate.

"It's complete pandemonium," Mackenzie stated. "We were able to evacuate most of the tourists, but some have been trapped inside Chambord or on the estate."

He removed a set of binoculars and scanned the surroundings.

"It appears that our men have secured parts of the south and west side, but I can count about fifteen BCH forces scattered throughout the grounds in teams of three. Two teams have set up offensive positions with rocket launchers," Mackenzie described.

The suite door opened, and the extraction team entered with six fully armed men. As they prepared to escort Alistair and his group from the room, they were suddenly interrupted.

"Get down," Mackenzie shouted, dropping to the floor and covering his head.

Everyone hit the ground as a small rocket slammed against one of the reinforced windows, causing it to explode inward and dislodging the entire casement. Glass shards sprayed everywhere.

Mackenzie and the other guard were blown back, injured but conscious. The suite was in disarray, furniture tossed and structural cracks forming on the walls. The window opening was charred and smoldering.

Alistair's composure evaporated as his fiery Scottish temper flared. Now provoked, his military senses were at their height. "Your Highness, are you injured?" he asked, rushing over to his side.

"I'm good, Alistair." Tom coughed as he shook himself free from the fragments.

Alistair scanned the room. "Is anyone hurt?"

"We're good," Fontaine replied, rattled by the explosion. "We were far enough away, and the couches protected us."

Moving around the room, Alistair checked on his men. He attended to their injuries and made sure their weapons were fully loaded.

Alistair then looked at Gowerstone, Fontaine, and Henry. "When this is over, we'll take the battle to the enemy."

"Indeed," Henry concurred, knowing the time to fight had arrived.

"For now, let's get Sir Thomas and Sarah safely off the estate."

Barclay entered from the other room with four additional men. His reaction to the destruction was masked by his resolve for revenge.

"We're ready, sir," Barclay told Alistair decisively. "It's time to move to the rooftop extraction point."

The ten Resistance fighters, plus Alistair, Barclay, and Mackenzie, were each prepared to sacrifice his life for Tom and his friends.

Leading the way to a corner of the room, Barclay pulled back an enormous tapestry, exposing floor-to-ceiling panels. He opened a panel, revealing a metal ladder that led to the roof.

"Four guards will go first to make sure it's secure," Alistair directed, motioning his men through the opening.

The guards climbed up, armed with semiautomatic rifles. A moment later, one of the men gave an all-clear signal.

Alistair went first, followed by Gowerstone, two guards, Tom, Fontaine, Sarah, Oliver, Henry, and the rest of the men. The forty-foot ladder ended inside a domed tower atop Chambord. It was a circular room with small access doors in the front and back.

They crouched inside and peered out the windows. The roof was an eccentric mishmash of architectural styles, including flamboyant Gothic and Italian Renaissance, that incorporated eleven different towers asymmetrically placed. The entire area was surrounded by richly decorated dormers and soaring chimneys. Centered above the double-helix staircase below was the lantern tower, topped with the fleur-de-Lys, the royal symbol of France.

Everyone descended a set of marble steps to the rooftop terrace, which encircled the chateau and offered a three-hundred-sixty-degree view.

Battles continued below with a barrage of gunfire and devastating explosions. On the north side, the Resistance gained ground, retaking an enemy stronghold by the horse stables. On the south side, the enemy pushed back, forcing the Resistance into defensive positions.

Alistair surveyed the situation, enraged by the onslaught. Although it was difficult to watch, his men's bravery and willpower evened the odds.

"We have no idea how anyone knew we'd be here," Henry uttered, consumed by guilt. "We took every precaution we could."

"The enemy would have attacked anyway," Alistair said reluctantly. "They've become bolder and more brazen. They're determined to destroy anyone who opposes their agenda."

"But how did they find out you were here?"

"Secrecy is a thing of the past," Alistair articulated. "Technology has invaded our lives and allows them to monitor our every move. There are surveillance devices everywhere and backdoor access into most computers. It's nearly impossible to stay one step ahead."

"Sir, I just got word. Three birds are close, maybe five minutes," Barclay informed him.

"I can see them on the horizon," Mackenzie observed, pointing at three approaching silhouettes.

Everyone looked across the sky at the tiny objects hurrying toward Chambord. Impatient to escape, their spirits were lifted.

"Let's get into position and prepare for extraction," Alistair ordered.

As they climbed up toward the top of the lantern tower, a black helicopter swooped down and hovered fifteen feet over the west rooftop. The cabin door slid open, revealing a dual barrel XM213 auto-cannon Gatling gun.

"Take cover," Alistair shouted.

Scattering to defensive positions, everyone ducked behind chimneys and stone outcrops.

Gowerstone pulled Tom into a protective recess while Fontaine sheltered Sarah, hiding in a narrow space behind a wall. A withering barrage of armor-piercing bullets shredded the rooftop, ripping through the slate shingles and slicing stones in half.

Pulling Sarah closer, Fontaine shielded her as bits of sharp masonry showered down. "Where are they getting these weapons?" Fontaine exclaimed, astounded by the firepower.

"Wherever they want," Alistair vented as he desperately tried to return fire.

While the 30mm rounds wreaked havoc on the rooftop, a team of ten BCH men slid down grappling ropes hanging from the helicopter and rapidly established offensive positions. They fanned out and advanced, firing at anything that moved.

The last man to descend was Strauss. Like a mythical Greek warrior, this soulless giant stood seven feet tall in his black body armor. A cultish pentagram with an Egyptian eye was centered on his vest.

Picked off by enemy snipers, two men guarding Tom dropped to their knees, injured but alive. Gowerstone pulled each man to safety, hastily wrapping torn fabric around their wounds to slow the bleeding.

A few Resistance fighters maneuvered in and out of the mazelike structure, firing at the enemy with razor-sharp accuracy. Three BCH men were fatally struck, and another one crawled for cover, dragging his injured leg behind him.

"We need to repel this assault," Alistair commanded, signaling his men into position. "What's our current arsenal?"

"Besides handguns, we have five M16s, three SA80 rifles, and a Heckler & Koch MG4, along with compression grenades," Barclay replied as he prepared the counterattack.

"Let's form a three-prong assault, with team A on the south side, team B on the north side, and team C cutting through the center," Alistair instructed, using his hands to illustrate. "Our primary team will guard Sir Thomas."

As a hail of gunfire pounded their positions, Gowerstone nodded to Fontaine. In one swift motion, she leaped up and fired directly at the helicopter, piercing the outer shell and cracking the windshield. The helicopter faltered but quickly stabilized.

Gowerstone twisted around and shot six rounds directly at the man operating the Gatling gun. Struck in the arm, leg, and chest, the man lurched forward and plummeted from the helicopter.

"Nice shooting, Detective," Fontaine called as she dropped back down to reload.

"Commence attack," Alistair directed, waving his men ahead.

They hurled a volley of grenades at BCH positions. The multiple explosions that instantly followed temporally stunned the BCH force and knocked them back.

"Let's move," Barclay ordered, taking the lead.

The Resistance teams sprang forward, advancing in tight formations and firing at will.

"Look, sir," Mackenzie exclaimed, shaking Alistair's shoulder.

Entering the estate was a caravan of vehicles, a combination of cars, trucks, and SUVs carrying hundreds of Resistance fighters.

"It's about bloody time," Alistair sighed, shaking his head.

Unfazed by the opposition, Strauss located Tom and marched toward him.

Seeing the demonic creature, Gowerstone sprang from his position and fired five shots straight into Strauss's chest. Protected by his thick body armor, Strauss barely flinched.

"What *is* that thing?" Fontaine questioned.

"If I had to guess, it's a one of the Committee's Super Soldiers," Gowerstone replied, unsettled. "It's a secret program to create invincible soldiers by merging man with machine."

"So he's not completely human?"

"No," Gowerstone replied bluntly.

Gowerstone unloaded three more rounds at Strauss, hitting his chest and left arm. Strauss just smirked as he reached over his shoulder and removed a rocket launcher. Gowerstone's eyes widened.

"Brace yourselves," he warned, shoving Tom into a stone crevice and covering him.

Fontaine and Sarah wedged between the steep roof tiles, preparing for impact.

Strauss fired directly at Gowerstone's position. The rocket hit a granite chimney, sending shockwaves across the rooftop and causing masonry to tumble. A thick cloud of smoke blanketed the area.

Blown back by the explosion, Fontaine was pinned under a stone. She lost her grip on Sarah, who slid down the roof tiles and crashed onto the observation deck fifteen feet below. Lying on her back, Sarah tried to stand but her knee was twisted.

Gowerstone checked on Tom. "Are you hurt?" he asked, clearing debris from his body.

"My ears are ringing, but I'm okay," Tom murmured, clearly in shock.

"Help!" Fontaine yelled, trying to dislodge the massive stone. "I'm trapped."

"I'm coming!" Gowerstone shouted, searching for her position.

"Get Sarah first," Fontaine insisted, her breathing shallow. "She fell down the roof, toward the north side."

"Alistair, guard Tom," Gowerstone hollered. "I'm going after Sarah."

Alistair crawled over, kneeling by Tom and using his body to protect the young prince.

"No one touches him," Gowerstone stated firmly.

"No one will," Alistair guaranteed.

Gowerstone descended a roof section, searching for Sarah. Gunfire was rapidly exchanged, ricocheting sporadically.

Seeing the oncoming Resistance vehicles, Strauss knew time was limited. His men were now outnumbered and losing ground. As he continued toward Tom, he was met with a salvo of bullets.

Determined to eliminate his target, Strauss removed a metallic object, a subatomic particle grenade. Pushing a button, he was about to throw it when his hand was pierced by a 10mm bullet. He looked over and saw the smoking barrel of a Glock.

The grenade dropped in front of Strauss. He quickly kicked it away as it burst into a fiery blaze of white light. Dormer windows shattered as the entire rooftop quaked. Strauss's clothing was charred, and his skin was blackened.

Barely conscious, Sarah was lying on the observation deck.

As Gowerstone edged toward Sarah, he heard a loud scream and quickly turned. One of the BCH men hovered over Fontaine with his rifle. She struggled to move but couldn't retrieve her weapon.

Gowerstone stormed the man, slamming him against a stone wall. The man crumpled into a heap, unconscious. When Gowerstone turned, he saw that Sarah had vanished.

"No!" he cried out, searching in every direction. Horrified, he saw Strauss carrying Sarah across the west terrace, draped over his shoulder.

"Tom!" Sarah shrieked, struggling to free herself.

A massive dual engine helicopter descended over the rooftop, releasing four harnesses. Strauss and the remaining men secured the belts and swiftly ascended.

Gowerstone ran toward the helicopter but was met by a hail of gunfire, pinning him down. Alistair and his men refrained from firing back, unwilling to risk hitting Sarah.

Seeing what was happening, Tom's heart sank. It was a surreal moment, happening in slow motion.

"Sarah!" Tom yelled out, desperate to help. He sprang to his feet but was firmly held back by Alistair.

"I'm sorry, Your Highness, but I can't risk your safety," Alistair declared.

"Let me go," Tom pleaded. "She needs me."

"You'll only get hurt or captured."

"I order you to release me."

"Not when it comes to jeopardizing your life," Alistair stated, unyielding.

For a split second, Tom's and Sarah's eyes met. Then in an instant the helicopter was gone.

15
THE RISE OF THE LION

Tom fell to his knees, devastated. He felt a deep pain, a powerful connection ripped from his soul, a bond suddenly broken. He was empty and motionless.

Gowerstone watched as the helicopter disappeared, shocked beyond words, enraged beyond belief. He returned to Fontaine, removing the heavy stone and helping her stand. Words couldn't describe the loss she saw in his eyes.

"We'll get her back," Fontaine professed, her conviction unwavering.

"If it takes the rest of my life," Gowerstone vowed.

Although his duty was to protect Tom, Alistair also felt responsible for Sarah's capture. But he knew he couldn't allow emotions to cloud his judgment. It was essential to keep a clear head and plan their next move.

Multitudes of Resistance fighters flooded the estate. Arriving from all directions, they created a perimeter around Chambord and slowly closed in. They overwhelmed the enemy by skill and numbers, driving them from their positions. The fighting was fierce, but soon the enemy was either captured or eliminated.

The three rescue helicopters arrived, hovering over the rooftop while providing a protective shield around Tom.

As Alistair reviewed the circumstances, one of his men called in. "Sir, we've contained the enemy. Their positions are being neutralized and all the floors have been cleared. An escort team is on its way up."

"Send two helicopters after Sarah and track her down. If possible, force the other helicopter to land. We must know where they're headed," Alistair ordered. "We're returning to the Britfield suite, so make sure it's secure."

"Understood," the man acknowledged.

Immediately, two helicopters banked to the left and traveled southwest, the last direction Sarah and her captors had been headed.

After securing the entire roof, Barclay approached Alistair with a silver box, strange hieroglyphics on its exterior.

"Commander, this was left by the BCH assault team." Barclay scanned the container for explosives and carefully opened it. Inside was a digital satellite phone, its screen glowing. "Perhaps they dropped it," he speculated.

"No, it's their way of communicating with us," Alistair surmised. "Unfortunately, the game has just begun."

Mackenzie walked over with a group of guards. "Are you ready to go down, sir?"

"Let's proceed," Alistair said, deep in thought.

Too weak to move, Tom was helped to his feet and escorted off the roof.

Oliver and Henry emerged from a protected alcove, covered in stone dust. They brushed themselves off and followed Alistair.

Everyone made their way down a staircase until they reached the Britfield suite. The heavily guarded room was in disarray, but a few men were already clearing the debris.

Tom was taken to a couch and tended to gently. A blanket was put over his shoulders, and he was given a glass of water.

Gowerstone knelt by Fontaine's side, wrapping her bruised wrist and cut arm.

"It's not your fault that Sarah was taken," Fontaine said, trying to comfort him. "If anything, it's mine. She was my responsibility."

"Don't blame yourself for something you had no control over."

Gowerstone finished wrapping her arm and walked over to Tom, firmly placing his hand on his shoulder. "I promise you we'll get Sarah back," Gowerstone said softly. "We'll find her, no matter what it takes."

Tom looked at Gowerstone. He nodded his head, too upset to speak.

Standing in the middle of the room, Alistair addressed everyone. "We can't stay here any longer," he began. "We must prepare to leave the estate and get Sir Thomas to his parents."

"And Sarah?" Fontaine asked, consumed with worry.

"We have two helicopters in pursuit. We'll use all our resources to track her down and bring her back safely," Alistair replied.

Barclay entered, looking distraught. "Sir, I've received an update. By the time our birds were in the air, the helicopter was gone, as if it had vanished into thin air."

"No trail or heat signature?" Alistair questioned, stunned.

"Nothing, but they'll keep searching."

Tom could hardly breathe. He felt an emptiness in his aching heart.

Alistair began to come undone as he tried to contain his temper. He took a deep breath and looked at Tom, who was close to tears.

"Sir Thomas, I'll stop at nothing to find Sarah," he pledged.

Tom faintly nodded.

"Every hour that passes works to our disadvantage," Gowerstone stated with mounting intensity. "We need a plan to strike back."

"The best defense is a good offense," Fontaine agreed, following his logic. "Keep the enemy guessing and off-balance."

As the debate continued, the satellite phone rang. Gowerstone answered and put it on speaker. "Yes," he said sharply.

"This is Strauss. We don't want the girl. We want the boy," he demanded, his voice harsh. "It's simple, one life for the other."

"I see you've moved from coldblooded murder to kidnapping," Gowerstone stated intensely.

"We do what's needed."

Fontaine walked over, anxious to intervene. "The girl is innocent in all of this," she pleaded, her voice tense. "She's no threat. Please, just return her, and no one else needs to suffer."

Strauss began to laugh, his callous chuckle void of empathy. "That's not the way it's going to work. I've texted the time and location that we'll make the exchange. The detective will escort the boy—no one else. If we identify anyone within ten miles of the site, the deal is terminated and the girl will be lost forever."

Fontaine was shocked. "You know we can't possibly—"

"You have exactly twenty-four hours," Strauss interrupted, angered. "If you don't show, you'll never see the girl again. Just the detective and the boy—no vehicles, helicopters, or police."

"The Committee owns most of the authorities anyway," Fontaine added with bitter irony.

"Only the important ones," Strauss mocked. "And don't bother tracing the call. Our technology is superior."

"We're aware of the Beast System, your D-Wave quantum computer in Belgium," Alistair interjected, his hands tightening.

"Then you know we monitor all your communications. Any attempt to undermine us will be futile," Strauss emphasized. "An innocent for the heir, the girl for the boy. It's your choice."

The line went dead. Alistair looked at Barclay, who nodded and left the room.

Fontaine stepped forward. "Can you trace it?"

"We're privy to some of their technology," Alistair replied. "They don't control everything."

Gowerstone picked up the phone to review the text.

"What does it say?" Henry asked, an anxious look on his face.

"Five p.m., the Café Pomerol in the town of Moulis, north of Margaux."

"That's in Bordeaux," Henry announced, finding the location odd.

"Why there?" Fontaine asked, confused.

"It actually makes sense," Gowerstone reasoned as he processed his thoughts. "It's in the middle of nowhere, with a small population, close to the River Gironde, and not too far from the Atlantic Ocean. It's simple to monitor and not landlocked, so it's easy to escape using a boat or other means, if necessary."

"By car, it's about four hours from here," Alistair estimated, familiar with the region. "To avoid detection, we won't use the main roads, so it'll take longer."

Barclay came in from another room with a sheet of paper. "We got it, sir," he said excitedly. "Our men tracked the exact place."

"Excellent," Alistair expressed with relief. "Where did the call originate from?"

"It came from the region of Medoc," Barclay answered, then hesitated. "It specifically came from the Grand Château Rothberg, Saint-Christoly-Médoc, fifteen miles from Moulis."

"The Rothberg estate?" Fontaine asked, shocked. "The Rothbergs are one of the oldest families in France."

"I came across the name Rothberg in my research," Gowerstone murmured as he paced the room. "Their family started centuries ago in finance, lending money to prominent families and eventually to the royalty. Based in London, they established a banking empire that reaches across the world. They're one of the thirteen families we spoke about."

"Then they're part of the Committee," Fontaine realized. "Don't you think it's a bit reckless to expose themselves like this?"

"It's arrogance—they believe they're untouchable," Gowerstone asserted.

"They must be holding Sarah at the estate."

"I'd bet on it," Gowerstone maintained. "She represents one of their trophies, until they can capture Tom."

"We'll need a complete layout of the property."

"I can provide that," Alistair interjected, ready to help. "But for now, we must get Sir Thomas to his parents. Our men will assist with Sarah's rescue."

"He's right," Gowerstone agreed. "We need to get Tom to safety."

As Tom listened, he began to feel stronger, his confidence returning. He didn't like being threatened or bullied. His grief and self-doubt were replaced with courage and resolve.

"I'll do it," Tom exclaimed, standing from his seat. "I'll give up my life for Sarah."

Alistair was stunned by the declaration. "Sir Thomas, I can't allow that to happen under any circumstances," he stated categorically, his tone strong.

"It won't work without me," Tom reasoned, determined. "We need to do this together. If I'm not there at five o'clock, they'll know it."

"Sir Thomas, if we don't leave now, we'll never get to the Britfields in time."

"Sarah's all that matters now," Tom declared. "She's my family."

"But you've waited your entire life to meet your parents," Alistair rationalized. "Isn't that what's important?"

"Not anymore," Tom answered firmly, his stance unmovable.

Fontaine and Gowerstone were deeply touched. Never had all three of them felt so united, as if a Divine force had instilled a sense of invincible strength.

"Sir Thomas, I must return you to your parents," Alistair persisted. "Those are my orders."

"If I'm a Britfield, then you must do whatever I tell you, right?" Tom proposed, realizing he finally had a last name.

Alistair hesitated. "That's correct."

"Then I order you to let me bring Sarah back," he advocated. "In fact, I demand it."

"It goes against every protocol and instinct I have."

"There is no way I am going to move forward without her," Tom claimed.

Alistair took a deep breath and backed down. "As you wish, sir."

"Okay, it's settled," Gowerstone realized, reluctant. "Although I don't agree with risking Tom's life, I believe it's his choice, and I will honor that."

"We'll need an airtight plan," Fontaine stipulated.

"Yes, of course," Alistair concurred, still surprised by the decision. "But first we must evacuate Chambord and get to our safe house twenty miles from here. It will have what we need. Barclay, let's break down everything. Remove all the files, information, and every trace of the Britfields. Initiate Code Enigma."

"Yes, sir," Barclay acknowledged. "The entire estate will be wiped clean."

"Code Enigma?" Oliver asked Henry in a whisper.

"As if they were never here," he replied.

Barclay instantly orchestrated a team to remove every computer and file cabinet as well as the Britfield tapestries. Rooms were cleaned, debris discarded, and broken windows replaced.

"It will be extremely difficult to attack the enemy head-on," Alistair began as he walked around the room, conceptualizing his plan. "We're dealing with the most ruthless organization in the world. Their intelligence and reconnaissance are superior. If they detect one other person or realize they've been deceived, it's game over."

"It sounds hopeless," Oliver mumbled, trying to mask his fear.

"Nothing is hopeless. There's always a way," Alistair encouraged him. "We just need to figure out what it is."

"And in less than twenty-four hours," Henry added.

"I need two teams to escort Sir Thomas, Detective Gowerstone, Inspector Fontaine, Sir Henry, and Oliver to our safe house," Alistair instructed. "Let's move quickly and take every precaution."

As they were escorted down the stairs, the entire estate was being painstakingly cleared and cleaned. Injured Resistance fighters were taken to a nearby compound, along with any wounded or deceased BCH forces. Tourists were attended to and removed from the property with the excuse that they had been caught up in a military exercise that had gone wrong. They were paid for their trouble in exchange for signing nondisclosure agreements.

A crack team of twenty-five Resistance carpenters and masons descended on the estate to repair walls, patch bullet holes and paint ceilings, hallways, and damaged trim. Gardens were replanted, wreckage was removed, and Humvee tracks were wiped clear. Within twelve hours, most of the estate had been restored to its pristine condition. Although rumors would surface, all traces of the previous day were gone.

Meanwhile, a convoy of vehicles and over one hundred Resistance fighters escorted Tom and his friends to a safe house outside of Orléans, close to the Loire River.

Overshadowed by the Cathedral of the Saint-Croix of Orléans, the quaint Romanesque town's narrow streets were lined with Renaissance buildings and four-story, half-timbered homes. First conquered by Julius Caesar in 52 BC, Orléans became an intellectual capital under Charlemagne, and by the tenth century was a prominent city. In 1429, Joan of Arc and her troops defeated the English and delivered the town back to the French. A bronze statue of Saint Joan on her horse dominated the main square.

By dusk the weary group had arrived at a manor house on the outskirts of Orléans, the sun fading into the night. A weathered fieldstone wall surrounded the property, helping it blend in with the countryside.

Two hours later, everyone was sitting in the main room, reviewing the plan. Alistair stood in the middle, addressing his men.

During the discussion, Fontaine leaned over to Gowerstone and whispered in his ear. "I'm going to call Gustave and see if he can come down," she said quietly. "He could provide us with updates, and he's an excellent marksman. I checked with Alistair, and he agreed that we could use the extra help."

Fontaine stood and walked over to Barclay. "Do you have an untraceable phone I can use?" she asked in a muted voice.

Alistair nodded to Barclay, who handed her an encrypted satellite phone.

Fontaine walked into an empty room and contacted Gustave, explaining what had happened since they last spoke. He was excited to hear from her and had been working hard gathering any information that could be useful.

"How soon could you meet me?" Fontaine asked with urgency. "It shouldn't take you more than two hours to get here."

"I'll leave directly," Gustave replied. "There's a great deal I need to tell you. Where are you located?"

"Drive to Orléans, and I'll pick you up in front of the cathedral. Trust no one, and make sure that you're not followed," Fontaine emphasized. "I'm sure you're being watched closely."

She hung up. Regardless of everything that had transpired, it felt good to speak with her partner again. Fontaine quietly returned to the group and sat down.

"Is everything all right?" Gowerstone inquired, concerned.

"Yes, Gustave is on his way here. He has some important updates."

Alistair continued to review their strategy. "If we do this, it must be all or nothing," he stated fervently.

"What do you mean, sir?" one of his men asked.

"Until now, we've always worked in the shadows. Few know of our existence or strength. If we attack the enemy at their own compound, it will trigger an all-out war. They'll stop at nothing to get retribution. However, I believe it's time we shine a light on their wickedness. Sir Thomas Britfield's presence tonight is a sign of hope and a new beginning for all of us."

Alistair looked at Henry, Oliver, Gowerstone, and Fontaine. "The people we're dealing with are brutal and ruthless. They'll come after your family and friends. You need to know what's at stake."

These words carried a dire warning: the enemy's cage had been rattled and was about to be opened.

After a moment of silence, everyone nodded in agreement, taking stock of their own lives and understanding what they were risking.

"Let's proceed," Alistair resumed. "We can start positioning some of our Resistance fighters in Bordeaux, Margaux, and Moulis. They'll play the role of either singles or couples who are out sightseeing, visiting the wineries, or boating along the Gironde. They'll appear as locals or tourists, enjoying the beautiful countryside."

"But you said their technology and reconnaissance are superior. Won't they detect your presence?" Fontaine wondered, apprehensive.

"It's at the height of summer, so the villages and vineyards will be flooded with people. Our men and women are experts in disguise and role-playing, blending in and remaining unnoticed. We're also using traditional Cold War spy techniques. No radios or earpieces until we've neutralized their surveillance and jamming devices. Remember, we've been doing this for over eighty years."

"And the location where the extraction is taking place?" Gowerstone questioned, needing more specifics.

"We'll quietly set up different teams in the town of Moulis: a couple walking their dog, a few masons working on a wall, a waiter or waitress at a restaurant. We'll have college students on holiday who are masters in martial arts; a romantic couple shopping along the street who are highly trained in explosives; an old man fishing who is a seasoned sniper. Our organization is diverse—young people, academics, artists, doctors, shopkeepers. Their training is lethal, and their commitment is absolute."

"It's risky," Gowerstone cautioned.

"It's all risky, but our people know what they're doing."

"What about getting Sarah back?" Tom interjected, longing to be reunited with his best friend.

Alistair stepped aside. "Barclay, would you mind?"

Barclay motioned to one of his men to turn off the lights and switch on a large computer screen behind him.

"We've been methodically studying the Rothberg estate. Using detailed maps of the chateau and after hacking into a military satellite we have a clear picture of what to expect." Barclay motioned to the screen with a laser pointer, indicating specific locations. "You can see with these thermals that the property is well protected. The reddish glows indicate people. They've stationed guards in teams of two or three throughout the estate."

"Is this in real time?" Henry asked, fascinated by the technology.

"Yes," Barclay replied. "We've counted sixteen men guarding the perimeter and twelve men inside the chateau. Not as many as we thought, and they're not expecting us."

Barclay clicked to the next picture.

"You can observe the detailed layout of the Rothberg chateau—a three-story building with an extensive cellar. In the northeast corner is reinforced concrete and what appears to be holding cells with a single image barely detectable. We're almost positive this is where they're keeping Sarah."

Seeing the screen, Tom's heart leaped. It was frightening watching his best friend reduced to a glowing image. He was more determined than ever.

"You can expect high-voltage wiring around the walls and fences, digital motion detectors at key areas, and a variety of surveillance cameras throughout."

"When will Operation Overload commence?" one of the men asked.

"Tomorrow morning at seven hundred hours we'll disperse our teams. We'll have over sixty of our people slowly surround the Rothberg estate, waiting for their cue. The enemy would expect large vehicles in an assault formation, so we'll use the same techniques we use in the town of Moulis: couples hiking and exploring the countryside."

"Why don't we attack the Rothberg estate first thing in the morning?" Mackenzie asked as he loaded his weapon.

Alistair stepped forward to address the question.

"Two reasons. First, we still can't confirm that Sarah

is there, which we'll continue to work on. If she's not, we may lose her forever. Second, there's a chance they'll bring her to the exchange tomorrow, where we'll intervene and rescue her. If they don't bring Sarah, it provides us with more time to confirm she is at the estate and get her out."

"Understood, sir." Mackenzie nodded, impatient to engage.

"Once we've neutralized the enemy and have Sir Thomas safely reunited with Sarah, we'll rendezvous in Lyon and head straight to northern Italy," Alistair summarized. "There will be three helicopters waiting at an extraction point."

Henry leaned forward and tapped Gowerstone's arm. "Would you like us to help?"

"Not with getting Sarah," Gowerstone replied. "We need you to retrieve the information at your villa."

"Oliver and I can head there in the morning, secure the Britfield Codex and other material, and meet you in Lyon."

"That's the best way to proceed."

"We have an important mission tomorrow. Let's get a solid meal and a good night's rest," Alistair concluded. "We'll reconvene at six hundred hours to finalize the details."

When the meeting was over, the men and women dispersed.

"Six hundred hours?" Tom asked Gowerstone.

"It's military time, based on a twenty-four-hour cycle. Six hundred hours means six o'clock in the morning. Seventeen hundred hours means five o'clock at night."

"I see, sort of."

"Don't worry about tomorrow," Gowerstone reassured him, noticing Tom's troubled expression. "I'll be right next to you, and I promise to keep you safe."

"Thank you, sir."

Unable to eat, Tom went straight to bed. Resting on a cot in one of the second-story bedrooms, his mind raced: *I can't believe Sarah's gone. What if something happens to her? What if everything goes wrong tomorrow? What if I never see her again?*

He tossed and turned until he conquered his anxiety. *No*, he decided. *I control my thoughts and fears. I just need to be strong; I need to be confident, and I need to have faith.*

* * * * *

Later that night, Fontaine met Gustave by Orléans Cathedral. He had been extremely careful, leaving his car a few miles back and hiking into the town through the countryside. Fontaine was grateful to see him, knowing the risks he was taking.

His eyes lit up when he saw her. "You look good."

"Liar. I look terrible." She laughed, knowing how exhausted she felt.

"You hide it well," he said, wanting to flatter her.

Fontaine smiled, appreciating his kind words. "What's the latest?" she asked anxiously.

"The chief is no longer running Interpol," Gustave revealed. "It's been overtaken by some government agency—people I've never seen before. Since we last spoke, many trustworthy friends and agents have been dismissed."

"It sounds like they're cleaning house," Fontaine theorized, troubled by the news.

"Anyone who questions their decisions has been removed or fired on bogus charges. I'm glad I came down when I did. I'll probably be next, if I'm not careful." Gustave paused as he collected his thoughts. "Interpol is collaborating with elements of the military, setting up roadblocks and perimeters throughout the country."

"Making it impossible to escape," Fontaine realized.

"Not impossible, but much more difficult," he explained, a trace of optimism in his voice. "They're also coordinating with the CIA and MI6."

"We're now up against the largest intelligence agencies in the world," Fontaine sighed, overwhelmed. "We should get back and update Alistair."

When they arrived at the safe house, Fontaine introduced Gustave to the group and told Alistair and Gowerstone everything Gustave had shared with her.

* * * * *

The morning couldn't come fast enough. When Tom woke up, he made his way to the main study. The house was buzzing with activity. Men and women of varying ages and backgrounds were hustling about as they prepared for Operation Overload. A tremendous amount of planning had gone into the mission, which was set to begin at 5:00 p.m.

Now over three hundred Resistance fighters were involved: some as scouts or reconnaissance; others monitoring computers and radio frequencies; some coordinating the extraction once Sarah was found. These trained spies and soldiers were now dressed like farmers, shopkeepers, and tourists.

Alistair entered the room and walked over to Tom. "Were you able to sleep, Sir Thomas?"

"Not really," he answered honestly.

"Me neither," Alistair confessed, then knelt by his side. "What you're doing today is extremely brave. You embody the Britfields' extraordinary valor. Their symbol is the lion, strong and courageous. Although it has been patiently waiting, the lion has risen and is embodied in you."

"I'm simply doing what needs to be done," Tom conveyed heroically.

Alistair nodded, overcome with admiration.

"Everyone has heard about the sacrifice you're making. You've brought an encouragement to our cause that we haven't felt in decades. These men and women would do anything for you."

Alistair gave Tom an affirming look and walked to their planning room to address the group. "Listen up," Alistair began, his voice forceful.

The room went quiet as everyone settled in their seats.

"Next to D-Day, this may be our most important operation. As discussed earlier, members of team A will take their positions in the town of Moulis. We already placed several units there last night, some staying at bed-and-breakfasts, a few working in local shops, others carefully positioned throughout the town."

"How many members, sir?" Mackenzie asked, ready to destroy the enemy.

"About thirty men and women in Moulis and sixty others around the Rothberg estate. We have a reserve team of thirty, three miles out."

"Then our attack strength is one hundred and twenty?"

"That's correct," Alistair verified. "As Detective Gowerstone and Tom approach the town, their car will likely be scanned by BCH forces to verify that it's them."

"So they'll know if they've been double-crossed?"

"Affirmative. We, on the other hand, will have our own team hidden with frequency scanners, checking *their* vehicles to confirm that Sarah is with them. At five o'clock, a BCH caravan will enter the town. By then we'll know if we proceed or immediately remove Tom," Alistair reviewed meticulously. "If Sarah is present, we'll neutralize their men, get her to the extraction point, and rendezvous in Lyon."

"Where will you be, sir?" Barclay inquired.

"Within fifteen feet of Sir Thomas, out of sight."

"And the chateau?"

"Led by Mackenzie, team B will surround the Rothberg estate on the outskirts of Margaux. Inspector Fontaine will provide support on the north side. At 5:00 p.m., they'll move in. I must emphasize how important it is to be on your guard and trust no one outside this room. The Black Cult of Horus will do anything to deceive us," Alistair concluded. "Godspeed."

After the meeting, Tom was fitted with a Kevlar vest under his shirt, just in case things went awry. Suddenly the danger became real. Although he was nervous, his courage was strong.

Gowerstone nodded to Tom that it was time to leave. They walked to a gray Mercedes-Maybach 560 sedan, reinforced with bulletproof windows, titanium door panels, and liquid-filled tires to prevent blowouts.

"You can still change your mind," Gowerstone said. "We can find another way."

"No, I'm ready," Tom stated decisively. "Of all the people to be doing this with, I'm glad it's you."

"I wouldn't have it any other way."

Gowerstone was moved, remembering how far they had come since Weatherly Orphanage, a spectacular chase that had transformed into a strong friendship.

Prepared to leave, Fontaine and Gustave walked over. Gowerstone embraced Fontaine and whispered in her ear, "Be safe and come back to me."

"I will," she replied tenderly.

Fontaine held on for another moment, finding it hard to let go. Gowerstone nodded to Gustave as a gesture of thanks.

Tom and Gowerstone climbed into the Maybach, buckled up, and drove down the driveway.

The game was on.

* * * * *

Henry and Oliver were escorted to a van, where they met Resistance members Geoffrey, Fredrick, Kurt, and

Nicolette, the team's leader. They were all athletic and heavily armed.

"We appreciate you risking your lives for strangers," Henry said graciously.

"You're no stranger, Sir Horningbrook," Nicolette acknowledged. "You're one of us. We know you've been in this fight for a long time."

"What's the plan?" Henry asked, anxious.

"Given the circumstances, we believe your boat is the safest way back to the villa," Geoffrey explained. "By now most of the roads are being monitored."

"Once we drive to the boat and secure the area," Nicolette continued, "Fredrick and Kurt will go on to the villa, while Geoffrey and I accompany you and Oliver along the Loire River to meet them."

"You don't think they've found it, do you?" Oliver wondered.

"The boat or the villa?"

"Both, I suppose."

"We don't know, which is why we need to check," she answered. "We can't be too careful."

Oliver entered the van, followed by Henry, who was eager to get back to his villa and secure the Codex.

* * * * *

About an hour later, they approached the dock. The boat appeared untouched as it bobbed in the water.

Henry handed Fredrick his keys. "It's the large white one with the blue bottom," Henry indicated.

Leaving the vehicle, Kurt and Fredrick carefully surveyed the area and walked onto the dock. It was quiet and peaceful.

While Kurt stepped into the boat and began scanning for explosive devices, Fredrick stripped down to a pair of swim trunks. He put on a pair of goggles, jumped in the water, and swam underneath the boat.

"You're sure thorough," Oliver commented, watching all the activity.

"We have to be. The people we're dealing with are evil," Nicolette stated. "One of their trademarks is explosive devices on cars, planes, and boats. They make it look like a malfunction or an accident."

A minute later, Fredrick emerged from the water and gave them a thumbs-up.

Kurt started the engine and revved the motor, waiting for a reaction, perhaps a delayed explosion. Although they had checked, there was always a chance they had missed something.

"All clear," Kurt breathed with relief, nodding to Nicolette.

Exiting the van, Oliver and Henry were escorted to the boat by Geoffrey and Nicolette. Kurt and Fredrick walked back to the vehicle, waiting for her signal.

Untying the ropes, Oliver pushed off the deck. Nicolette waved the others onward as Henry motored toward his villa.

Less than thirty minutes later, the boat eased into Henry's dock. Oliver remained sitting while Geoffrey jumped off and secured the vessel, his weapon drawn.

Nicolette called Kurt and Fredrick, who had arrived fifteen minutes earlier to search the property.

"Falcon, this is Swordfish. Is the nest safe?" she asked in a staid tone.

"It's all clear. The nest is empty," Kurt replied evenly.

Oliver glanced at Henry with an amused smirk, entertained by their codewords. Henry was relieved that all his precautions over the years had paid off, that it appeared no one knew about his villa.

Nicolette turned to Henry, her eyes serious. "We're clear, but we need to move fast. Things could change in an instant," she stated. "When you're done, we'll head to the safe house in Lyon."

"We'll move as quickly as possible," Henry assured her.

Everyone hurried off the boat and up to the house, keen to grab the Codex and other essential information.

* * * * *

Built on a curve of the Garonne River, Bordeaux encompassed approximately three hundred thousand acres, making it the largest wine growing district in France. Average harvests produced seven hundred million bottles per year, ranging from table wines to expensive vintages. Based on rigorous requirements and a complex grading scale, the château system was at the heart of monitoring quality. Some of the oldest vineyards were Margaux, Cheval Blanc, Gruaud-Larose, Vieux Château Certan, Palmer, and Château Rothberg.

After almost five hours of driving, Gowerstone and

Tom cruised into Moulis, Bordeaux. It was a popular stopover for tourists in search of food, quaint shops, or a place to rest. A country store was selling fresh fruits, vegetables, and homemade breads. Three antique dealers offered local artifacts and overpriced furniture. There were also two bed-and-breakfasts, three cafés, and a fourteenth-century Romanesque abbey.

Prior to the trip, Gowerstone had spent hours studying a map of Moulis and memorizing every building, street, and alley. He'd found eight escape routes and three potential choke points.

As they drove by, Gowerstone scrutinized each person and building. Twenty years of experience had given him a heightened sense of noticing anything odd or suspicious. He had learned that the slightest detail could mean the difference between life and death.

He glanced at his watch: 4:15 p.m. "How are you holding up?" Gowerstone asked Tom, his voice calm.

"A bit nervous, if I'm honest," Tom replied, tense.

"You're not the only one."

"You too?"

"Sure," Gowerstone answered candidly. "It's okay to be nervous. It means you're alert and ready."

"I didn't think about it that way."

"Regardless of age or experience, everyone feels nervous sometimes. Try to focus on something positive."

Alistair was close by, watching the town and searching for his strategically placed teams that were ready to attack on cue.

Gowerstone removed a satellite phone protected by

a waterproof case and handed it to Tom. "Put this in your pocket. If we get separated for any reason, call me immediately and I'll find you. My number is programmed in the contacts under *G* for Gowerstone."

"That sounds simple enough," Tom said, looking at the device. "I hope I don't need it." He stuffed the phone into his pocket, his hand trembling slightly.

"Shut your eyes and take a deep breath," Gowerstone suggested, noticing Tom's anxiety. "It will help you relax."

Tom closed his eyes and took a slow, deep breath. His heart was pounding, and his mind was racing. All he could think about was Sarah.

Gowerstone glanced at his watch again: 4:18 p.m.

The seconds felt like minutes, the minutes like hours. At this point, all they could do was wait.

* * * * *

Fontaine, Gustave, and six other Resistance members had driven for hours in a VW camper until they reached Saint-Estèphe, close to Médoc and the Rothberg estate.

Five other teams of eight men and women had already been dispatched in the area, each with their own instructions and mission. Some were watching the estate for heavy activity or a sudden exodus; others were ready to neutralize the guards around the chateau perimeter. A few highly trained teams were waiting to make their way inside, locate Sarah, and safely evacuate her. There would be no radio communication until 5:05 p.m., so everyone had to rely on the plan and precise timing.

The total strength of the assault and rescue teams was about sixty members, including singles, couples, and groups who blended into the countryside, riding bikes or photographing the breathtaking scenery. Each team was positioned about a mile apart, close enough to access the others but far enough away not to draw any attention.

Once the teams got close enough, they would cut the power to the estate. An advanced tech team using an electromagnetic jamming system would block all communications in and out of the chateau at 5:00 p.m.

Dressed in jeans and a T-shirt, with her hair pulled back into a ponytail, Fontaine exemplified the typical vacationer. Gustave wore a pair of khaki shorts, a polo shirt, and sunglasses, and pretended to be her boyfriend.

They both exited the van. Fontaine carried a trendy backpack that contained weapons, explosives, and ammunition.

"Are you ready?" Fontaine asked as she finished retying her shoelaces.

Gustave looked at a map. "Yes, we'll enter on the north side."

"Just past the horse stables and through the rose gardens," Fontaine confirmed, her senses alert.

Using a map and compass, they headed down one of the many trails that crisscross Bordeaux. The entire region was bustling with tourists and sightseers.

* * * * *

Before leaving the safe house, Gowerstone made

sure that he was well-armed. He had a Glock 20 10mm holstered under his left arm, a Glock 34 9mm tucked behind his back, and a Glock 23 9mm attached to his right ankle. In his left coat pocket were three explosive canisters, ready to deliver a powerful blast and a wall of smoke. He also had grenades and two throwing knives tucked in his waistband.

Although no one was using the radio, Gowerstone was wearing an earpiece so the Resistance team could notify him of Sarah's arrival and if anything was amiss.

At 5:00 p.m., three SUVs with tinted windows entered the town square, circled once, and parked about thirty feet away. The fronts of the vehicles faced the Mercedes.

Gowerstone's earpiece went live. "We've detected a young girl in the second vehicle but can't confirm that it's Sarah." He nodded slightly to acknowledge receipt.

Gowerstone coolly opened his door and exited the Mercedes, walking over to Tom's side. He stood patiently, his hands folded in front, waiting.

The front passenger door of the middle SUV opened.

Strauss exited, towering above the car. His presence seemed to cast an eerie shadow over the town. He glared at Gowerstone, trying to discern his face. Gowerstone was a portrait of calmness, his eyes like stone.

"Let's see the boy," Strauss demanded in a brazen tone.

Gowerstone stepped back and opened the door. Tom climbed out but remained behind the door panel as Gowerstone had instructed.

"Good, you brought him," Strauss scoffed, clearly pleased that his orders had been obeyed.

"Let's see Sarah," Gowerstone insisted, his patience evaporating.

All the SUV doors opened.

* * * * *

After hiking along a winding trail through fields of grapevines, Gustave and Fontaine were now strategically situated close to the Rothberg estate, its slate-covered mansard rooftop clearly visible. Cars and double-decker buses darted back and forth along the narrow roads.

On the exterior, the estate appeared to be a historical winery with acres of vineyards and a beautiful chateau hidden behind ivy-covered plastered walls. The eighteenth-century, three-story mansion was surrounded by sprawling lawns, pristine gardens, and rows of Sumerian statues. There was even an Olympic-size pool. It was the epitome of wealth, power, and prestige. However, it was also a fortified compound with guards, military weaponry, and advanced surveillance.

Gustave and Fontaine attached silencers to their weapons and snuck onto the Rothberg property. Staying low to the ground, they hid among the lush grapevines.

Fontaine popped her head above the foliage and scanned the estate with high-powered Swarovski binoculars. She observed guards dressed as farmhands, but they were wearing Kevlar vests and carrying sidearms as they worked among the vines. Each man was wearing an earpiece.

She crouched back down, dispirited.

"Last night Barclay said there were only eight teams of men patrolling the perimeter. There must be at least twice that many," Fontaine vented.

"Perhaps they reinforced their numbers this morning, just in case someone discovered where Sarah was hidden."

"We'll need to go around to the northwest side," Fontaine instructed, already certain something was wrong. "Although it'll take longer, it will be safer."

"Did you see any cameras or detection devices?"

"Quite a few," she replied, pointing. "Those small windmills have multiple cameras on top. You can't see them unless you're using the right equipment. As far as other devices, I'm sure they're there, but they're well hidden."

"We'll just have to be extra careful."

"Careful and invisible," Fontaine whispered.

* * * * *

From behind each car door emerged a BCH assassin wearing a tailored suit and sunglasses. They looked like mercenaries hired from foreign countries to perform nefarious activities.

As Gowerstone waited for Sarah, he had a gut instinct that something wasn't right. Over the years, he had learned to trust this sixth sense.

He slowly moved closer to Tom, with one hand on his shoulder and the other hand gripping a canister. Gowerstone made eye contact with a few Resistance members inconspicuously wandering toward the three SUVs.

Resistance fighters had already located and neutralized twelve BCH assassins who had been ready to ambush Detective Gowerstone. The Resistance had also quietly captured two snipers positioned on the abbey's rooftop.

"You're stalling," Gowerstone exclaimed. "I need proof of life. Let me see Sarah to confirm that she's okay."

"All in good time, Detective. We'll do this my way," Strauss stipulated, his tone cold.

"Then let's proceed," Gowerstone insisted.

"First have the boy walk toward me."

"That's not the way it's going to work."

"You're questioning my demand?"

"Yes," Gowerstone replied sharply.

The mood became tense, the air motionless. This shocked Strauss, who was used to getting his way.

"Then we seem to be at a crossroads, Detective."

"We do," Gowerstone stated, exasperated. "Now bring Sarah out of car."

* * * * *

Crawling along the vineyard grounds, Fontaine and Gustave stealthily made their way to the northwest compound wall, where the chateau sat close to the riverbank. They encountered two guard units patrolling the area and quickly overtook them, dragging their bodies out of sight, then tied them up and gagged them.

The entire operation hinged on the element of

surprise. If one shot was fired or someone yelled, the estate would be swarming with guards, and the mission would be compromised.

A few Resistance fighters had already silently breached the south compound wall and were quietly neutralizing unsuspecting guards as they searched for Sarah.

Fontaine checked her watch. It was 5:00 p.m. "Gustave, are you ready?"

"Yes, I've been waiting a long time for this," he said with a half smile, his eyes narrowing. "I wouldn't have missed it for the world."

Fontaine took a three-prong grappling hook and twelve feet of rope out of her pack. She tossed it over the wall until it caught at the top.

"You go first," Gustave suggested, motioning her ahead. "I'll cover your back."

"All right, let's do this." She took a deep breath.

As Fontaine stood up, Gustave struck the back of her head with his gun. She dropped to the ground, unconscious. He then grabbed her cell phone and communication equipment, crushing everything under the heel of his boot.

"You stupid, foolish woman," Gustave hissed, his good-natured façade fading away. "You're on the wrong side and always have been."

Dragging her body to the river's edge, he rolled her into the water face-up as the current whisked her away. He looked on, indifferent.

"Goodbye, Inspector," Gustave mocked. "Your days of meddling in our affairs are over."

Gustave removed the silencer from his weapon and fired two shots in the air, alerting the guards and exposing the operation. He then called in to the Resistance coordinator.

"This is Gustave. Shots have been fired, and they know we're here," he reported. "We should pull back and abort the mission."

"Negative," the coordinator insisted. "Proceed to the chateau, locate Sarah, and bring her back safely."

"Confirmed. I'll find the girl."

Gustave searched through Fontaine's backpack, removing additional ammunition and three weapon parts. Swiftly snapping them together, he assembled a high-powered sniper rifle, loaded a magazine, and headed toward the chateau.

16
THE WOLVES' DEN

Gowerstone was tired of playing games. "Bring Sarah out of the vehicle so we can see her," he demanded sternly.

Shocked by Gowerstone's audacity, Strauss stared at him with disdain. "As you wish, Detective." A malevolent grin crept across his face.

Two BCH assassins opened the passenger door. A blond-haired girl with a black scarf wrapped around her eyes was brought out of the SUV. Watching carefully, Gowerstone firmly held a canister in his hand, his finger on the switch

"Well?" Strauss asked impatiently. "Here's the girl—now give us Tom."

Tom's eyes focused on the figure. He knew instantly. "It's not her, Detective," he whispered, heartbroken.

Strauss noticed Tom's reaction and knew their charade had failed. "Get them," Strauss yelled. "Especially the boy!"

Gowerstone quickly activated the canister in his hand and then another one, hurling them toward the SUVs. They exploded with a succession of loud bangs, followed by an intense screen of grayish smoke. Three BCH assassins were knocked to the ground.

"Keep your head down, Tom," Gowerstone ordered, grabbing his Glock. "Quickly, get behind the car."

In an instant, the Mercedes was riddled with bullets; the front window deflected most of the projectiles.

Tourists scattered, taking cover behind trees and inside shops.

From every direction, Resistance fighters emerged, firing at the SUVs and dropping four men. Strauss was stunned by the sudden onslaught.

Alistair ran out from behind a nearby bush, guns blazing. He rushed over to shield Tom as Gowerstone returned fire, dropping a BCH assassin and wounding two others.

"We've planned an escape route. Let's move," Alistair advised.

With their heads down and Alistair leading the way, all three hurried around a building and down an alley. Alistair was covering Tom's left side as Gowerstone ran on his right.

The Resistance members closed in, taking down two more BCH assassins and disabling one of the SUVs with grenades.

Strauss was enraged by the counterattack. He had been certain his secretly placed teams would destroy any Resistance fighters who dared to show up. Now he was boxed in.

"Contact base and let them know we've been attacked. They can *eliminate* the girl," Strauss ordered, climbing into a vehicle. "Now hunt down that boy!"

* * * * *

After neutralizing three guard units patrolling the vineyards, Mackenzie, Barclay, and their team advanced to the chateau's north wall. They removed grappling hooks coated in rubber and tied ropes to the end. One by one, each man skillfully tossed them up the ten-foot wall and climbed over.

As the team landed on the opposite side, they were met by a shower of gunfire from the second- and third-story windows. Mackenzie's team fired back, then dove for cover, quickly regrouping.

"Take defensive action," Mackenzie yelled, removing a SMAW, a Shoulder-Launched Multipurpose Assault Weapon. "We'll see what they think of this."

Two of his men threw canisters at the chateau, creating a smokescreen. Two others tossed a handful of grenades, letting off a series of powerful blasts that shattered the first-floor windows.

"What are your orders, sir?" one of the men asked.

"On my countdown, fill the windows with bullets and take them out," Mackenzie instructed, inserting an 83mm rocket into the SMAW.

The men reloaded their weapons and waited for his cue.

Pinned under a withering barrage of gunfire, Mackenzie counted down. "Three, two, one!"

In unison, all six men lurched forward and opened fire. The windows were flooded with bullets, obliterating the glass and exterior.

Mackenzie launched the rocket, causing a huge explosion that blew a massive hole between the second and third stories. Billows of smoke enveloped the building as chunks of flaming debris tumbled downward.

*****

"Where's your team?" Gowerstone asked impatiently.

"Just ahead—they'll escort us to the extraction point," Alistair responded, pointing to the next street.

Across the road, eight Resistance men and women rushed toward them. They were followed by two heavily armed vehicles emerging from the bushes.

Just then an SUV smashed through a wooden fence, decisively cutting them off. Strauss and five BCH assassins opened fire in both directions.

"We're not going that way," Gowerstone exclaimed, swiftly maneuvering Tom behind a protective building. Gowerstone then fired four rounds at Strauss, each one a direct hit. Strauss was unfazed as his team retaliated.

"What's with that guy?" Alistair questioned, staring in disbelief. "Is he human?"

"I don't know, but nothing seems to stop him."

Gowerstone led Tom and Alistair through a backyard and onto another street. Sirens blared in the distance as police cars swarmed the town in response to the gunfire.

"We need transportation, and fast," Gowerstone shouted.

While Alistair called in their location, Gowerstone spotted an old beat-up truck parked across the street.

"Follow me," he instructed, grabbing Tom by the arm and running for the vehicle.

Gowerstone tried the front door, but it was locked. "Stand back," he warned as he used his elbow to smash the window. "Go to the other side!"

Gowerstone hopped into the front seat, leaned over, and flipped the door lock. Tom and Alistair hastily entered; Tom wedged in the middle.

"Keep your head down," Gowerstone instructed, reaching under the front steering wheel and fiddling with the wires.

Strauss and his men peeled around the corner and saw them sitting in the vehicle. Neighbors crouched behind walls and stayed out of sight.

"They're behind us," Alistair warned as he reloaded his weapon.

The engine started. Gowerstone cranked the gear shift and hit the accelerator.

Tom stared at him, astounded. "Where'd you learn all this?"

"Never mind that—just stay low," Gowerstone muttered under his breath.

They pulled onto the street and sped off, tires burning.

"Head for the extraction point two miles east of the Rothberg estate. The helicopters are waiting," Alistair conveyed as he continued speaking on his phone and providing updates.

Driving through the back roads of Bordeaux, Gowerstone carefully took each corner, accelerating out of the turn. He maneuvered his way down a narrow alley, over an intersecting street, and across an open field. Strauss's SUV was still following but was barely visible.

After a few more quick turns and a sharp corner, Gowerstone had lost him.

"Who was that girl?" Tom wondered as he looked back at the fading town.

"It's hard to say," Alistair admitted, troubled. "Could be someone working with the Black Cult of Horus or another prisoner they were using as a decoy."

Worried about Sarah, Tom became distressed. His nerves were raw, his hope dwindling.

"That didn't go as we planned, did it?" Tom asked, grief-stricken.

"I'm afraid not, Sir Thomas," Alistair replied, overcome with regret.

"What about Sarah?"

"I still haven't heard anything."

* * * * *

As they stormed the chateau, Mackenzie, Barclay, and their team confronted an onslaught of BCH guards. The fighting became frantic, often hand-to-hand combat.

After an intense exchange of gunfire, three Resistance members were wounded. The BCH had lost six men and pulled back to defensive positions.

One Resistance member stayed behind to attend to the wounded, while Mackenzie and Barclay stormed the house through a set of double doors. They covered each other as they entered the dining room. Suddenly, two guards rushed them, firing in all directions. Barclay and Mackenzie dove onto the floor, whipped around, and unloaded an entire magazine. Both guards dropped.

Mackenzie and Barclay got to their feet and continued the search. With time running out, they had to find Sarah.

* * * * *

After endlessly navigating through the heart of Bordeaux, Gowerstone, Alistair, and Tom could finally see the Rothberg chateau. The once immaculate estate looked like a battlefield blanketed in a haze of smoke.

They drove to where a group of Resistance fighters had formed a protective perimeter around three helicopters. Each member was heavily armed with either a submachine gun or a high-powered rifle.

Gowerstone parked close to the aircraft and quickly exited the vehicle, followed by Alistair and Tom. They were relieved they were safe but shocked by the outcome.

A team of four Resistance members hurried over to accompany them to the waiting helicopters. Alistair spoke with one of the men, explaining the situation and receiving updates on the rescue attempt. The expression on his face was revealing, his forehead tense and eyes sad.

Tom gazed across the field at the Rothberg estate, the sound of gunfire crackling in the air. It was unsettling.

"Sir Thomas, we need to leave," Alistair emphasized as he gently escorted Tom toward the middle helicopter.

Tom resisted, searching the area. "Where's Sarah?" he asked, worried.

"Sir, I'm sorry," Alistair began. "We haven't located her yet."

"She's not here?"

"I'm afraid not, but we're doing everything we can to bring her back," Alistair explained. "It shouldn't be much longer."

Shocked by the news, Tom became distraught. "I'm not leaving without her," he said obstinately.

"Sir Thomas, it's too risky to remain in Bordeaux," Alistair conveyed, his tone firm. "We must get you to Lyon as soon as possible."

"Detective?" Tom asked, pleading for guidance.

"He's right—you need to leave and trust that Alistair's men will find her," Gowerstone replied gently.

"Sir, we must get you to safety," Alistair urged, walking closer.

Tom felt conflicted, knowing he couldn't leave without Sarah. As they approached one of the helicopters, Tom turned and bolted toward the chateau, dodging past two Resistance men.

"Tom," Gowerstone yelled.

"Sir Thomas, come back here," Alistair hollered, mortified.

Continuing toward the estate, Tom ran into a vineyard and disappeared among the vines.

"Let's move," Alistair ordered. "Get two of those birds in the air and provide cover. We must locate Sir Thomas."

Grabbing a team, Alistair and Gowerstone frantically hurried after him.

* * * * *

Barclay and Mackenzie searched the chateau for access to the basement. Walking around the first floor, they tried every door and tapped on every wall, looking for a hidden entrance.

While Barclay provided cover, Mackenzie used a sophisticated scanner that penetrated wood and plaster, exposing the other side. Nothing seemed to lead downstairs; it was as if the basement didn't exist.

"There must be an entrance somewhere," Barclay exclaimed, frustrated.

"We'll rip this entire chateau apart if we need to," Mackenzie declared.

* * * * *

Running as fast as he could, Tom darted in and out of the grapevines, popping up every fifty feet to find his bearings. Unaware of what to expect, all he knew was that he had to find Sarah.

Close behind were Gowerstone and Alistair, desperately searching for Tom. The Resistance team split up into two groups and fanned out, quietly calling his name. Hovering overhead, two helicopters scanned the area.

As Tom got closer to the main compound, the sound of gunfire grew louder, and chaotic activity happening everywhere.

Approaching the south side, Tom stopped for a moment. Weary and disoriented, he bent over to catch his breath. He knew what he was doing was crazy, but he was acting on instinct, not reason.

After recouping his strength, he surveyed the ten-foot high wall.

"How am I going to get over that?" he wondered aloud, glancing down both directions for an opening in the wall.

About a hundred feet to the left was a small gap blown open by the Resistance. Encouraged, Tom rushed over and climbed through.

* * * * *

By now a full assault was underway on the Rothberg estate. Most of the exterior guards had been eliminated. Nonetheless, word had gone out that the chateau was being attacked, and more BCH forces were en route. The enemy's cage had been rattled, and they were now awake. The Committee was furious. The audacity that a small, ragtag group of men and women would dare challenge the most powerful organization in the world was simply unimaginable. It also made them nervous. If a small group of people could cause this much trouble, imagine what the masses could do if they ever woke up and took a stand.

* * * * *

Tom stood behind a tree, watching all the activity. The main building was about seventy feet away. The once beautiful exterior had been radically transformed: windows shattered, walls cracked, and the ground cluttered with debris.

From his vantage point, Tom could see the entire estate: flower gardens trampled flat, a gigantic pool filled with wreckage, and rows of hedges forming bizarre patterns of occult symbols.

Tom hunkered down and planned his strategy. He remembered from the briefing last night that Sarah *might* be on the east side of the basement, but which way was east? It was around 6:00 p.m. *If the sun sets in the west, which is over there*, he thought, *the east is on the opposite side.*

"Well, at least it's a start," he mumbled to himself.

Tom slowly crept toward the chateau, hoping to enter by one of the doors. Every few feet he hid behind a column or a nearby bush, trying to avoid detection. It took him ten minutes to cover about seventy feet, but when he arrived at the chateau, each door he tried was locked.

"Blimey," Tom murmured in frustration, shaking a doorknob.

As he moved to another door, a group of guards approached. Tom hastily dove into the bushes and hid. The men rushed by, cursing in German.

Emerging from the shrubbery, Tom spotted a trellis covered in lilac. He snuck over, grabbed hold, and began to scale.

Somewhere between the first and second story one of the pieces of wood snapped. Tom lost his footing and found himself dangling in midair, both hands firmly holding on.

*****

Thoroughly combing the vineyard, Gowerstone and Alistair couldn't locate Tom. It was unthinkable that he was on his own, unprotected. After checking in with the other teams, they concluded that Tom must have found his way to the chateau.

They approached the main entrance where a twelve-foot-tall iron gate had been blown open, twisted metal hanging to one side. The front guardhouse was a smoldering mass of flames, riddled with bullet holes.

Marching up the brick driveway, Alistair and Gowerstone headed toward the east side, followed by two teams of four men. Suddenly, they were ambushed from behind.

"Hit the ground," Alistair ordered as a spray of machine-gun fire hailed down on them.

Two of his men were wounded and crawled for cover.

"Prepare to counterattack," Alistair yelled, pulling three grenade pins and tossing them at the enemy.

Multiple BCH men were taken out by the explosions. The other guards faltered, stunned by the rapid response.

The Resistance team instantly hurled a volley of grenades with lethal effect and started fighting back.

* * * * *

With all his strength, Tom pulled himself up and secured his foot on the next step. He continued to climb until he spotted a small open window about six feet away. Maneuvering toward the ledge, Tom ran out of trellis, leaving a three-foot gap to get across.

"Figures," he grumbled under his breath.

Stretching as far as he could, he reached for the window. His arms burned as his grip loosened. Now thoroughly drenched in sweat, Tom stretched again and just managed to finger the window ledge. He consolidated his grip with both hands and pulled himself into a bathroom, tumbling onto the tile floor.

"All those years of sneaking around Weatherly definitely paid off," he whispered to himself. He got to his feet and eased open the bathroom door. The hallway was deserted, the walls decorated with ancient war shields and razor-sharp swords.

Entering the corridor, Tom hunted for a basement stairway but only found abandoned bedrooms, many left in disarray with papers tossed about. While he continued to check, he heard yelling from down the hallway and hastily entered one of the rooms, gently closing the door.

He turned and noticed a master suite with hardwood floors, a desk with a golden pyramid on top, and a mixture of odd Babylonian statues. The shelves were packed with Latin manuscripts and prehistoric tablets in glass frames.

The atmosphere in the room was unsettling, as if something unnatural lingered in the air. An oppressive feeling overpowered him, and he could hardly breathe.

"I've got to get out of here," he gasped, struggling to shake off the strange sensation.

Making sure no one was around, Tom reentered the hall. At one end was a door that was slightly different from the others. On closer observation, he discovered a steel panel painted to match the woodwork.

Tom tried the doorknob—it opened to a staircase. He hastily descended, passing the first story and two additional floors until he reached the bottom and pushed through another metal door.

Constructed of brick, the dimly lit basement was filled with storage crates and wine bottles. The fifteen-foot vaulted ceiling hovered above him. Even with all the activity going on in the chateau, the basement was quiet.

Tom entered and flipped a switch: the lights quenched the darkness. He saw what looked like prison cells at the east end. The thick steel doors had small barred access holes in the upper sections.

"This must be it," he said uneasily, his voice shallow. Tom rushed over to the first one. It was empty except for a rusty cot, an old mattress, and straw scattered on the floor.

"What kind of deranged people have cells in their basement?" he uttered to himself, confounded by what he witnessed.

Tom kept investigating, peeking into each one. "Sarah, are you here?" he cried out.

Every cell he checked was empty.

"Sarah," he called again, a bit louder.

Suddenly the silence was broken. He heard a scratchy voice say, "T-Tom."

He immediately ran toward the sound. "Sarah?"

"O-over here," she mumbled back.

Tom located her cell and glanced through the hole. It was Sarah, covered in a tattered blanket and peering out the front. When she saw him, her eyes brightened, and a slight smile surfaced.

"I knew you'd come, Tom. I knew you'd come."

"I'm sorry it took so long," he apologized. "Are you okay?"

"Just get me out of here."

Tom tried the door, but it was secured with a padlock.

"Give me a minute," he said frantically, rummaging around for a heavy object.

Tom spotted an assortment of tools in the corner and grabbed a sledgehammer. He dragged it over and awkwardly lifted it.

"Stand back," he gasped, his arms shaking.

Tom swiftly brought the object down, smashing the lock. He dropped the sledgehammer and swung the door open.

Sarah lunged into his arms, frail and weak. Her body was trembling as tears of joy ran down her cheeks.

* * * * *

After scouring the entire area, Strauss was informed that Tom and Detective Gowerstone had escaped. He was livid that his plan had failed. But he knew their victory would be short-lived.

Hearing about the assault on the Rothberg estate, Strauss organized what was left of his demoralized men and headed to the chateau. There wouldn't be any more games or negotiations. He would hunt down the Britfield heir and shoot him on sight.

* * * * *

Gowerstone, Alistair, and the two Resistance teams

were pinned down by gunfire. Remembering their training, they slowly undermined the enemy's flank, swinging around and maneuvering behind them.

The BCH guards were quickly overpowered and scattered in different directions.

Taking advantage of the moment, Gowerstone and Alistair assembled their teams outside the main entrance. The massive front door seemed impenetrable.

"When we enter, let's split up," Gowerstone strategized. "You take a team to the first floor, and I'll search the second."

Alistair nodded as one of his men removed two bricks of C4 and attached them to the door.

"Prepare for detonation," Alistair announced, motioning his men back.

Everyone moved to protected positions and covered their ears. Remotely triggered, the C4 blasted the door inward, knocking over everything in its path.

"Let's find Tom and Sarah," Alistair ordered with an unwavering sense of resolve.

They separated, Alistair searching the first floor and Gowerstone ascending the main staircase with a team of men.

As he entered a hallway, Gowerstone noticed Gustave exiting a bedroom. Both had drawn their guns. Recognizing one other, they slowly lowered their weapons.

"Where's Fontaine?" Gowerstone questioned, appalled that she wasn't with him.

"We split up to look for Sarah," Gustave replied quickly. "I'm searching the upper rooms."

"What about the basement?"

"That's where Fontaine went," Gustave lied, trying to remain calm.

"Unescorted?" Gowerstone asked, dismayed. "You shouldn't leave her alone. You need to stay together."

"That's what I told her, but she insisted," Gustave lied again. "She said we could cover more ground on our own."

Gowerstone gave Gustave a piercing stare, not sure what to think. Gustave's behavior was strange, but he knew Fontaine could be independent and stubborn. Grabbing his receiver, Gowerstone turned the dial to Fontaine's frequency and tapped his ear comm.

"Fontaine, are you there? Over."

There was no response.

"Fontaine, this is Gowerstone. Can you hear me? Over."

Gowerstone lowered his receiver, troubled he couldn't locate her.

"All right, Gustave, you stay with us," he instructed, suspicious. "We're searching for Tom and Sarah."

"Tom is here? What happened?"

"I'd rather not go into it. He's here and needs our protection."

"Yes, of course," Gustave replied. "Whatever I can do to help."

* * * * *

Firmly gripping her hand, Tom led Sarah to the stairwell and ascended the steps.

"It's very odd, but there's no access on the first story,"

Tom explained. "We'll need to go back up to the second floor."

Sarah nodded, still lightheaded. She was frightened as she glanced behind her, the traumatic experience leaving her disheartened.

They reached the second story and quietly snuck down the hallway when a compilation of voices echoed.

"Someone's coming," Tom whispered, freezing in his tracks.

"Should we head back?" Sarah asked, looking for an alternative exit.

"We don't have time."

With nowhere to run, Tom valiantly removed a sword from the wall. "We'll just have to confront them," he stated boldly, standing in front of her.

Although Sarah was impressed by his valor, he could barely wield the object. "Do you know how to use that?" she asked.

"How hard could it be?" Tom replied as he struggled to hold it upright.

"Just make sure the pointed end goes into your opponent."

* * * * *

When Strauss pulled up to the Rothberg estate, he was stunned. The entire building had been decimated, and many of his colleagues' bodies were strewn on the ground. It wasn't that Strauss cared about human life, or even the people he worked with—he just hated being outmaneuvered. Although Strauss had heard rumors about the Resistance, he had drastically underestimated their abilities.

Strauss exited the vehicle and opened the back, removing an M16A4 assault rifle with an M203 40mm grenade launcher and a bounty of ammunition. His team followed suit, arming themselves with a collection of advanced weaponry.

Strauss glared at his men. "Take the first floor," he ordered, seething with indignation. "I'll start on the rooftop and systematically work my way down. Leave no one alive."

* * * * *

"Tom," a familiar voice called.

"Detective?" Tom whispered, relieved when he saw Gowerstone turn the corner.

Gowerstone suddenly raised his weapon and aimed in their direction. Tom's and Sarah's eyes widened.

"Don't move an inch," Gowerstone declared, then fired twice.

Tom and Sarah shuddered, waiting for the impact as the bullets whizzed above their heads and struck two BCH guards coming from behind. Tom turned to witness both men dropped, lifeless.

"Nice shots," Tom mumbled, blinking is disbelief.

Gowerstone holstered his weapon and ran over to embrace them. "Never run away again. Understood?" he said sternly. "We stay together and work as a team."

Tom nodded, his head lowered.

"What you did was courageous," Gowerstone continued, harboring a trace of admiration. "But you could've been captured, or worse."

"I understand."

"Good, enough of that."

Gowerstone turned to Sarah. "Are you hurt?" he asked gently, noting her fragile condition and disheveled clothing.

"I'm just glad you found me," Sarah replied, her voice scratchy, her tone hardened. "It was awful, but now I'm with friends."

"Let's get you both to safety."

As they prepared to leave, German voices resonated from the main staircase.

"*Sie sind hier oben. Jeder von ihnen töten,*" one of them yelled in a coarse accent.

"They're coming up," Gustave warned as he pulled his weapon. "It sounds like six or eight men."

"What did he say?" Tom asked nervously.

"They know we're here, and they want to kill us," Sarah translated bluntly.

"We'll need another exit out of the chateau," Gowerstone stated as his team formed a protective wall around Tom and Sarah.

"I might have an idea," Gustave interjected. "Let's get to the rooftop. We can call for an extraction."

Gowerstone considered the suggestion and tapped his ear comm. "This is Detective Gowerstone. Tom has located Sarah. They're both safe and in our custody. We need an immediate rooftop extraction, over."

A static voice replied, "That's excellent news, Detective. We'll be there directly. Sending two birds, over."

"Has Inspector Fontaine reported in?"

"No. Whereabouts unknown, over."

Gowerstone was deeply disturbed by the news. Nevertheless, Sarah and Tom were his priority.

"How did you get to the basement?" Gowerstone asked. "It might lead to the rooftop."

"There's a staircase over here," Tom replied as he quickly retraced his steps.

Locating the large metal door, they opened it. Gowerstone peered inside and confirmed a set of stairs ascending to the roof. Gustave closely shadowed him.

"Okay, let's move," Gowerstone instructed. "You first," he said to two Resistance men, "then Tom and Sarah, and we'll follow behind."

As they entered the stairwell, a hailstorm of gunfire broke out. Eight BCH guards were at the far end of the hallway, shooting fanatically.

* * * * *

Still on the first floor, Barclay and Mackenzie continued to search the chateau's north side when they met up with Alistair and his team.

"Updates?" Alistair requested, pleased to see them safe.

"We can't find access to the basement," Mackenzie reported, dispirited.

"There's no need. I just received word that Gowerstone has Tom and Sarah," Alistair informed them, ecstatic.

"How are they?" Mackenzie asked.

"Safe," Alistair replied. "Remarkably, Tom found Sarah."

"What a brave lad," Mackenzie acknowledged, inspired. "I knew Sir Thomas had Britfield blood. He's going to be an extraordinary leader."

Alistair was stirred by the comments, a renewed sense of purpose empowering him. "The Lion has risen," he stated. "This is an exceptional time, men. Our fire has been reignited. They're headed to the rooftop, so let's get there as quickly as possible."

* * * * *

"Everyone inside the stairwell," Gowerstone ordered as he motioned Tom and Sarah behind the protective door.

The BCH guards approached as they were fired upon. There was a recklessness in their behavior, realizing they were losing the battle. Two Resistance men were hit and collapsed to the floor.

Rapidly firing his Glock, Gowerstone dropped one man and hit two others, causing them to stagger backward.

"Get Tom and Sarah to the roof!" he yelled as the two remaining Resistance men escorted them up the stairs.

Meanwhile, Gowerstone and Gustave tried to repel the attack. Bullets riddled the metal door, ricocheting off and littering the hallway.

Though he unloaded an entire clip, Gustave didn't appear to have hit anyone, which frustrated Gowerstone, who struck a man in the leg, causing him to stumble to the ground.

"We should join the others," Gustave suggested as he reloaded his weapon.

"Just a minute," Gowerstone said coolly. "I want to leave the Black Cult of Horus with a gift."

Gowerstone removed two high-powered grenades, pulled the pins, and tossed them into the hallway. Explosions rocked the corridor. They closed the door and hurried to the rooftop, joining the others by an exit.

"It seems clear," one of the Resistance men conveyed. "The helicopters should be overhead any minute."

"We can't stay in here—it's too dangerous," Gowerstone warned. "Let's move out with caution."

Exiting on the south end, Gowerstone took the lead while staying close to Tom and Sarah. The mansard rooftop was steeply pitched on both sides. In the center was a narrow catwalk, leading to an enclosed area rimmed by landing lights.

"That will work perfectly for the extraction," one of the men commented, gesturing to the flat section.

"It's probably where the Rothbergs' helicopter unloads its nefarious cargo," Gowerstone speculated. "But getting there will be challenging."

They paused to survey the estate. The Resistance had taken control of most of the property, but it was only a matter of time before BCH reinforcements arrived. Two Resistance AH-64E Apache helicopters approached, trailed by three smaller objects.

"What are those things?" one of the Resistance men asked, gesturing to the horizon.

Gowerstone removed a pair of binoculars. "They're

Black Sharks, Kamov Ka-50 Russian attack helicopters," he replied, his voice stressed. "They're fast and lethal."

The man looked through the binoculars. "What're they doing here?"

"Remember who we're fighting. The Black Cult of Horus has access to everything, including Russian helicopters."

BCH guards scrambled up the stairs, firing as they approached.

"We need to move to the helipad and set up a defensive position," Gowerstone commanded. "You go first, then Gustave."

Attempting to keep his balance, the Resistance man boldly scurried across the narrow catwalk. Sporadic gunfire came from below as a few BCH guards shot at the roof, shattering the slate tiles.

Gowerstone and the remaining Resistance member returned fire, taking out one man and pinning down the others.

"All right, Gustave, move," Gowerstone ordered, motioning him forward.

Gustave hurried over the catwalk, dodging erratic gunfire.

Gowerstone turned to Tom and Sarah. "Are you ready? Can you do this?"

Tom glanced at him with a roguish smile, recalling his years of exploring the Weatherly rooftops.

"We've got this, Detective," Tom boasted.

Gustave and the Resistance man made it safely to the helipad and provided cover fire. Gowerstone removed another grenade, pulled the safety pin, and carefully wedged the release lever between the doorknob and the doorjamb of the stairs.

"Okay, let's go."

* * * * *

Alistair, Mackenzie, Barclay, and a team of four men rushed through the chateau and up the main staircase, eliminating several BCH guards along the way. Thankfully the enemy's strength and numbers were dwindling.

When they reached the second story, they heard a loud explosion coming from behind a metal door. Two mortally wounded BCH men tumbled down the staircase, one man injured and disoriented.

"Gowerstone was headed to the rooftop. Find that stairwell," Alistair instructed.

Running to where the explosion came from, Mackenzie opened the door. He discovered several bodies lying at the bottom of the staircase. Meanwhile, a BCH guard was tucked in an upper corner of the stairwell, firing downward.

* * * * *

Gowerstone, Tom, Sarah, and the last Resistance fighter rushed across the catwalk. Shots zipped by as bullets chipped the slate, sending fragments of stone flying. They continued through a cloud of debris, keeping as low as possible.

As they reached the helipad, Strauss appeared from behind a brick chimney and fired on the group. Two Resistance men fell to the ground, wounded but alive.

"Not him again," Tom expressed with a mixture of anger and terror.

Sarah's eyes widened as she glimpsed her captor. Her body became tense, frozen with fear.

"You didn't think you were going to win, did you?" Strauss ridiculed Gowerstone with an arrogant scowl. "No one defeats us. You should know that by now."

Strauss cocked the grenade launcher and prepared to fire.

Gowerstone whipped around and unloaded an entire magazine directly at Strauss. One by one the bullets landed with precision: first in his chest, then his right arm, his left shoulder, his right leg, and finally his neck, a vital entry point that penetrated his skin.

Strauss glared in disbelief as he dropped his weapon and staggered backward.

Gowerstone removed the Glock 24 from behind his back and unloaded another magazine, each bullet striking with lethal effect.

Strauss let out a bloodcurdling scream that sent chills through everyone. He stared at Gowerstone for a few long seconds, an empty, soulless look in his eyes, then fell over the roof's edge, landing on a parked vehicle four stories below.

"That was awesome!" Tom exclaimed, his face ecstatic.

"Thank you, Detective," Sarah acknowledged quietly.

Gowerstone nodded, then promptly checked on the injured men.

Although the two Resistance helicopters were nearby, they had been intercepted by three Black Sharks and were engaged in an air battle.

The Black Sharks opened fire on one of the AH-64 attack helicopters, hitting its fuselage and sending it crashing into a vineyard. It skidded along the ground and burst into flames. The second Resistance helicopter returned fire, destroying one Black Shark and scattering the others.

As Gowerstone knelt to tend to the wounded men, Gustave pointed his weapon at Tom and Sarah. "Strauss was one of our best men," Gustave vented, bitter. "While he was only a prototype, he was extremely effective."

Defenseless, Sarah and Tom were astonished.

Gowerstone slowly raised his head. Now it all made sense. "So you sold out to the Committee."

"I wouldn't call it that," Gustave scoffed, amused by the comment. "However, I like being on the superior side, and they pay much better."

"What good is money when you've condemned your own soul?"

"Save your platitudes and patriotic nonsense for the ignorant masses," Gustave taunted, unimpressed. "I'm only interested in myself and preserving my future."

"What happened to Fontaine?" Gowerstone asked, fearing the worst.

"She was a burden and won't be interfering any longer."

Gowerstone glanced at his weapon. Its slide had recoiled, indicating that the last round had been discharged.

"You're fast, Detective, but not fast enough to reload," Gustave mocked in a challenging tone. "You should have saved a bullet."

"Let Tom and Sarah go," Gowerstone pleaded, aware he still had one concealed weapon strapped to his ankle. "You can do with me as you wish, but leave the children unharmed."

"It's not that simple. I have orders," Gustave stated coldly. "These children have caused us nothing but problems. It will be a pleasure to finish them."

"Evil will never prevail," Gowerstone avowed. "You can still walk away from this."

"It's fruitless to try and stop us." Gustave laughed. "We're everywhere, and we cannot be defeated."

Gowerstone watched Gustave closely, waiting for just the right moment.

"This brings an end to the Britfield Dynasty," Gustave gloated with pride.

As Gustave pulled the trigger, Gowerstone leaped in front of Tom and Sarah, knocking them to the ground. The bullet ripped through Gowerstone's shoulder as he hit the tarmac. He was bleeding but mustered enough strength to throw his empty weapon at Gustave, causing him to stumble when he moved to deflect it.

"Run, Tom and Sarah," Gowerstone yelled with a weakened voice.

They bolted onto the rooftop. While Gustave aimed again, Gowerstone grabbed the Glock 23 from his ankle holster and managed to get off one shot, striking Gustave in the knee.

"You imbecile!" Gustave hollered in a fit of rage. "Why won't you just give up?"

Tom and Sarah ducked behind a chimney and edged their way toward an iron ladder on the north side of the roof. Gustave fired at them but only chipped the chimney, unable to get a clear shot.

"You've accomplished nothing, Detective. Those two will be dealt with soon enough. Remember, there's an army of men on their way."

Gowerstone tried to grip his Glock, but he was too weak. The pain from his wound was paralyzing his arm and body.

Gustave walked over and pointed his gun directly at Gowerstone. "Goodbye, Detective."

Two shots rang out.

Gustave lurched backward, a distant gaze in his eyes. He stared in shock at what he saw, dropped his weapon, and fell face-first on the tarmac.

"Not on my watch, you traitor," Fontaine declared, emerging from behind Gowerstone.

Gowerstone glanced up at Fontaine, a slight smile on his face, even as his strength began to drain.

"What happened?" he questioned, overjoyed to see her.

"My *trusted* partner knocked me over the head and dumped me in the river," Fontaine replied, stunned by the betrayal. "Luckily, I awoke after drifting to the shoreline."

"Are you hurt?"

"I have a terrible headache and my pride is wounded, but I'll survive."

Gowerstone tried to stand. "We must get to Tom and Sarah."

* * * * *

Maneuvering to the ladder, Tom and Sarah peered over the roof's edge—the drop below was terrifying. They grabbed hold and managed to work their way down to the second story rooftop.

"There's no more ladder," Sarah announced, panicked.

"There must be another way off the roof," Tom presumed.

Searching back and forth, they desperately hunted for a way down.

"I don't see anything," Sarah uttered, becoming more stressed.

Tom crept closer to the roof's edge and peeked over. "What about jumping?" he proposed, pointing at the Olympic-size pool fifteen feet below.

"Why does it always have to be water?"

"It may be our only way down."

"That's quite a leap," Sarah observed, unconvinced.

"We can make it with a running start," Tom encouraged her.

Sarah nodded in agreement, knowing they were out of options.

"At least aim for the deep end and remember to find me when we land."

* * * * *

Seeing Gowerstone and Fontaine, Alistair and his men hurried over from the opposite end of the catwalk.

"The detective needs our help," Alistair stated, tearing part of Gowerstone's shirt and exposing the gunshot wound. "You'll be all right, my friend. We're not going to lose you."

Fontaine promptly stood. "We need to find Tom and Sarah," she emphasized with urgency.

"Which direction were they headed?" Alistair asked.

"The north side," Gowerstone mumbled, motioning toward the chimney.

"All right, let's go," Alistair instructed. "Inspector Fontaine, Barclay, and our team will locate them. Mackenzie will assist the detective."

"If I can stand, I can fight," Gowerstone asserted stubbornly.

"Understood." Alistair smiled, impressed by his bravery. "We'll communicate through our ear comms."

Gowerstone gave Fontaine's hand a gentle squeeze. "It's okay, I'll be fine. Go find them," he said as he let go of her hand.

Alistair, Barclay, Fontaine, and the remaining men left.

Mackenzie knelt by Gowerstone and removed a medical kit from his backpack. He took out a hypodermic needle with an anesthetic, disinfectant cream, metal clasps, gauze bandages, and an assortment of other tools.

Gingerly holding the detective's shoulder, Mackenzie administered a shot, numbing the area, then probed the wound and removed the bullet. Gowerstone cringed in pain yet retained his stoic demeanor.

Mackenzie applied disinfectant to the area, stitched the wound, and bandaged it. Using a gauze bandage, he then made a temporary sling for Gowerstone's arm.

"That should hold you for now." Mackenzie returned all the items to his medical kit and stuffed it in his backpack.

"It feels better. Thank you," Gowerstone said, noticing they were alone.

"You ready?"

Gowerstone stood, gripping his gun. "Ready."

* * * * *

With a running start, Tom went first, followed by Sarah. They jumped from the rooftop, soaring through the air and splashing into the pool. Their cannonball effect dislodged the water, causing waves to lap over the sides.

Tom swiftly resurfaced and swam toward Sarah, who was flailing under the water. He dove down and grabbed her arms, leading her to the surface.

She gasped for air, then took a deep breath, using Tom as a buoy.

"You good?" Tom asked as he paddled in the pool.

"I'm good," she replied, exhilarated by the jump. "I've learned to hold my breath longer."

"That's wise."

"How did you learn to swim?"

"The hard way," he answered, pensive. "When I was six, I was pushed into a pond at my first orphanage. I quickly discovered how to float and eventually how to swim."

They climbed out and wrung the water from their clothing. Although there was a whirlwind of activity around them, no one had noticed their death-defying leap.

"We need to get somewhere safe," Tom asserted, anxious to get moving.

"What about Detective Gowerstone and Alistair?"

"They don't know where we are," he reasoned. "We should try to get back to the Resistance camp. It's where I was before I came to rescue you."

Sarah felt overwhelmed by his sacrifice and bravery. She was eternally beholden.

"If we can get to the vineyards, I can probably find it," Tom contended, trying to recall the location.

With heads bent low, they crept across the north garden, searching for an exit.

Wherever they looked, BCH guards and Resistance fighters were still exchanging gunfire. The surroundings were a surreal apocalypse of raging fires, charred ruins, and plumes of smoke.

As Tom and Sarah scurried toward the north wall, they were spotted by a group of BCH guards.

"I see them," one of the men called, motioning to the others.

Frantically rushing through the garden, Tom and Sarah were soon ensnared in a jungle of thorny rose bushes.

"Ouch," Tom cried out, pulling a thorn from his arm. "These things are sharp!"

"This is ridiculous," Sarah grumbled, tugging on the hem of her dress now entangled in the barbed branches.

Attempting to free her, Tom yanked on the material, ripping it to shreds.

"I could have done that," Sarah winced.

Shots rang out as two of the BCH guards fired in their direction, bullets chipping the wall. With arms held low and faces cringing in pain, they wrestled through the last remaining forest of thorns and exited by an open gate.

"That was horrible," Sarah expressed as she examined her cuts.

"A bloody nightmare," Tom griped, rubbing the scratches on his arms.

They could hear the voices of the BCH men getting louder.

"We need somewhere to hide, and quickly," Sarah whispered.

"What about over there?" Tom gestured to a large barn with rows of horse stables.

"Good idea," she agreed, taking his hand and leading the way.

They dashed from one object to another, hiding behind a bush or a tree, until they made it safely inside and collapsed on a bushel of straw, exhausted.

"I don't think we'll make it out of here on foot," Sarah said as she peaked out one of the windows. "There're too many of them."

"I'm out of ideas." Tom threw up his hands.

Surveying the stables, Sarah noticed the prized collection of thoroughbred horses, a saddle hanging by each stall. The horses were restless, sensing the turmoil outside.

Sarah turned to Tom. "Do you ride?"

17
AN OLD ALLY

Tom stared at her for a long second, an exasperated expression on his face.

"What do you think?" he asked in an annoyed tone.

"I don't know," Sarah responded innocently. "That's why I'm asking."

"How many orphans do you know who ride horses?"

Sarah contemplated the question. "None, but you're not an orphan anymore," she rationalized, smiling.

"That doesn't change the point."

"Which is?"

"No, I don't," he huffed.

"That's all you had to say," Sarah sighed, shaking her head.

"And I suppose you do?"

"For five years in Scotland, hunter-jumper."

"I have no idea what that means."

"It means I can ride, so let's get out of here."

Sarah stood and examined the different horses. She chose the best-looking thoroughbred, walked over, and grabbed its saddle. "Are you going to help?"

Tom was perplexed. "How?"

"Hold the horse while I attach the saddle."

The chestnut stallion towered eighteen hands or seventy-two inches high. The animal was magnificent, strong and robust. It stamped its feet, eager to run free.

"He doesn't look too friendly," Tom noticed, apprehensive.

"You must be stern with these animals," she told him. "Don't let them know you're scared. They can sense fear."

"It's too late for that," Tom grumbled as he tried to calm the horse and hold it steady.

"That's good. Just gently stroke his neck," she instructed him.

With the finesse of an experienced equestrian, Sarah attached the saddle, halter, and bridle. She then adjusted the stirrups and leaped on, centering her body and firmly gripping the reins.

"Okay, open the stall."

Tom unlatched the horse's stall door and swung it open.

"Now climb on and hold my waist," Sarah said coolly as she calmed the horse with her hand, patting it gently.

"I'm not sure about this."

"Get on and stop complaining."

Tom tentatively approached one side of the towering beast.

"You singlehandedly rescued me from a fortified prison, but you're reluctant to get on a horse?" Sarah voiced, staring at him with bemusement.

"I see your point," he mumbled.

She glared at him as if to say, *Now*!

"All right, I'll get on," he said, sizing up the colossal animal.

With great effort, Tom climbed the wooden crossplanks and eased onto the back of the stallion. He then reached awkwardly around Sarah's waist.

"That wasn't so bad, was it?" Sarah asked.

"We're not moving yet."

"Hey, you two! Get off that animal!" a guard yelled as he entered the stable.

Two BCH men appeared by the barn entrance, their M16s aimed straight at Tom and Sarah.

"Of course. We'll do exactly what you ask," Sarah said, narrowing her eyes.

She sunk her heels deep into the stirrups, arched her back, and tightened her grip on the reins. "Hold on," she whispered.

Tom squeezed her waist, clutching on for dear life.

With one swift kick of her heels, the horse lurched forward with the force of a locomotive. Sarah smashed through the guards, knocking them to the ground. The horse bolted out of the stable like a thunderous storm and galloped toward the vineyards.

Another guard caught a glimpse of Tom and Sarah as they sprinted past. "They're getting away!" he shouted, amazed at the sight.

"Retrieve the vehicles and track them down," another man ordered as he watched the horse vanish into a field of grapevines.

Two guards quickly jumped on motorcycles, while another team commandeered a black Hummer parked nearby.

* * * * *

Alistair, Barclay, and a team of Resistance fighters scoured the rooftop, looking for Tom and Sarah. They searched around every corner, chimney, and dormer but couldn't locate them.

With one helicopter destroyed and the other engaged in a midair dogfight, Alistair ordered the third helicopter to scout the area and find them. He checked in with each Resistance team. Some had successfully overpowered the BCH forces, but others were still under siege. No one had seen Tom or Sarah.

"You don't think they fell off the roof, sir?" Barclay asked, glancing over the edge.

"No, we thoroughly surveyed the ground around the building," Alistair replied confidently. "They must have climbed down."

"Sir—you have to see this," one of his men yelled, perched on the rooftop with his binoculars. "It looks like two children on a horse."

"What?" Alistair questioned. "Give me those."

Alistair leaped up, swiped the binoculars, and took a hard look. "I don't believe it," he murmured.

Alistair turned, a proud glare in his eyes. "Barclay, send the third bird to the southwest vineyard to assist with cover fire and extraction."

"Yes, sir," Barclay acknowledged as he called the base.

"Also, have our command post initiate the assault jeeps with teams of four. Send three of them to the southwest vineyard about one hundred clicks from the chateau. Form a protective line and intercept Tom and Sarah. Send the others to pick us up in front."

* * * * *

Crouched over the horse's neck, Sarah was now in full gallop. Arched slightly forward and standing on her heels, she had a perfect rhythm with the stallion. She was in her element, becoming one with the horse and remembering her years of riding: the precision, the control, the freedom.

Tom, on the other hand, could find neither rhythm nor balance as he bounced up and down. He gripped her waist as tight as possible, completely at the mercy of her skill.

The vineyard was divided into a mazelike grid of six-foot high stocks, blooming with a variety of grapes. The rows were long and narrow, making them dangerous to navigate. Sarah continued to ride with an intense vigor, the vines whisking by.

Two motorcycles zipped after them, accelerating along the muddy paths. The guards observed Sarah in the distance, her head just above the foliage, her silhouette visible against the setting sun. The Humvee drove on the outer field, following along on a parallel road and closing the gap.

Occasionally glancing back, Sarah gauged the distance between her and the enemy. She couldn't outrun them, but she could definitely outmaneuver them.

Darting in and out of the rows, she headed straight for one of the five-foot barriers that separated the different fields. Tom's eyes sprung open at the oncoming obstacle.

"There's a *rather* large fence ahead," he cried out.

"That's the idea," Sarah asserted as she increased her speed.

* * * * *

Mackenzie helped Gowerstone down the stairs to the second floor. Although he was weakened by his wound, Gowerstone's determination burned strong.

Using his earpiece, Mackenzie communicated with Alistair, providing updates and strategizing their next move.

"Have they found Tom and Sarah?" Gowerstone asked, disquieted.

"They're on a horse riding into the southwest vineyard."

Gowerstone was relieved as the news settled in. "Then they got away—that's good."

"We have a helicopter en route, and Alistair is sending three assault jeeps to intercept," Mackenzie reported. "We'll get them back safely."

"What are your orders?" Gowerstone asked, eager to assist.

"Alistair wants this compound destroyed," Mackenzie responded, carrying a large backpack filled with explosives. "I have studied the architectural layout. With just a few well-placed devices, we can bring down the entire building."

"What's your background?" Gowerstone questioned.

"Biochemistry, engineering, and demolition," Mackenzie replied with a Cheshire grin.

"That's a lethal combination."

"I like to think so."

Rounding a corner, they were startled by a BCH guard

about to fire his weapon. Using his good arm, Gowerstone grabbed the knife tucked in his waistband and threw it with force. It struck the man in his chest, and he collapsed.

"Nice throw, Detective," Mackenzie approved, astonished by his accuracy. "Let's get to the basement and find the structural pillars."

* * * * *

"Hold on!" Sarah yelled as she prepared to jump.

Tom wheezed, his knuckles white, his eyes shut tight.

Remembering her training, she gradually rose from her seat and focused beyond the fence. In one swift stride, the horse leaped over, barely knocking its back hooves on the top plank. The animal landed with a firm yet fluid motion and continued to gallop.

"Wow, I've never jumped that high before," Sarah exclaimed, invigorated.

"You're telling me now?" Tom groaned, his legs cramped.

"Well done," she said triumphantly, patting the horse's neck as the animal gave its head a shake of victory.

"Thank you."

"Not you, the horse."

The two motorcycles approached the barrier and slammed on their brakes. One of the guards skidded along the ground and stopped short, while the other crashed into the fence and flew from his bike.

Sarah looked back with a smile, knowing they were on her turf.

The Hummer sped along the outer road and turned into the field, bouncing over the uneven terrain.

Sarah crouched down and continued galloping into the open countryside. Seeing a wooded area, she rode as hard as she could, avoiding obstacles and leaping over ditches.

The third Resistance AH-64E attack helicopter approached. It targeted the Hummer and released a lethal barrage from its 30mm cannons, ripping the vehicle to shreds. It then launched two Hellfire rockets with devastating effect, blowing the Hummer eighty feet into the air and reducing it to a blazing mass of molten metal. It was time for the Resistance to strike back, and they did it with a vengeance.

Tom and Sarah saw the explosion and felt a sense of relief as they dashed in and out among the trees. Although the Resistance helicopter pursued, the craft lost sight of them in the thick forest.

* * * * *

Standing next to the parked assault jeeps, Alistair, Barclay, Fontaine, and the remaining team met up with Gowerstone and Mackenzie.

Even though the Black Cult of Horus was temporally defeated, their setback would be short-lived. They were regrouping in masses.

Fontaine stood by Gowerstone, relieved to see him. Since their meeting in Paris, each event had brought them closer together. Fond memories resurfaced, and wounded emotions were forgotten.

Alistair rallied to the occasion, his Scottish fervor burning inside.

"All that matters now is rescuing Tom and Sarah. We have a royal prince who needs to be reunited with his parents—let's act like it."

Everyone nodded in agreement, their confidence bolstered.

"Detective, where's that thing you shot off the roof?" Mackenzie asked, glancing around the building.

Gowerstone walked over, taking a long look at the vehicle that Strauss had crashed into, traces of blood visible.

"Unbelievable," he mumbled. "I unloaded at least ten rounds into him."

"And he fell four floors. He couldn't still be alive, could he?" Mackenzie asked, puzzled.

"It's possible," Gowerstone considered. "The laws of biology and physics don't apply here. We're dealing with an entirely different species. Genetically modified with animal DNA and microchips, these things have unnatural abilities."

"Like what?" Mackenzie asked.

"From my research on the Super Soldier Program, I learned these creatures possess extraordinary ability to rapidly heal."

"How disturbing," Mackenzie expressed.

"Known as Black Science, it involves aspects of demonology. That's why these underground labs exist, isolating specific traits from animals and transferring them to humans, such as DNA from starfish to foster regrowth and from jaguars for endurance. Then there's the technology, which incorporates thermal imaging for the eyes, sound suppression for the ears, and fiber optics from the head to the fingertips."

"Then they're not really human," Mackenzie realized, aghast.

"No, they're not."

"We'll have to confront this problem soon enough. Right now we have to get Tom and Sarah," Alistair interrupted, trying to redirect the conversation. "Are the charges set?"

"Everything's in place," Mackenzie replied.

"Good, let's destroy this edifice of evil," Alistair said as he leaped into the first assault jeep.

Barclay and Mackenzie followed behind. The other team members entered the vehicles, Fontaine sitting next to Gowerstone.

A multitude of police cars and firetrucks approached as the assault jeeps sped away, heading southwest.

"Sir, I just got word that one of our helicopters spotted Tom and Sarah disappearing into a forest," Barclay relayed as he communicated with their base. "It's about seven miles from here."

"Then let's not waste time," Alistair urged.

The jeeps navigated around the estate. When they were about a hundred yards away, Alistair glanced at Mackenzie.

"Pull it," he ordered.

Mackenzie pushed a remote detonator. A loud boom shook the area as the support structures were vaporized, and the entire building dropped straight down into a heap of rubble. A fiery cloud of smoke billowed into the air, creating a skull-like image visible for miles around.

It was an awesome sight and a powerful statement that rang out across the world, a message to the Committee that a reckoning had begun. The light of freedom had awoken, and the Lion had risen.

"This will start a war like nothing we've ever experienced," Barclay forewarned.

"It's about time," Alistair declared. "We've been asleep too long."

* * * * *

Meanwhile, Tom and Sarah rode into Couquèques, a picturesque town surrounded by farmland and vineyards. As the sun slipped below the horizon, streetlamps flickered on. The sky transformed into a watercolor of bright pinks and oranges; a strong summer breeze rustled through the ancient treetops.

Sarah and Tom trotted down Rue Joseph Boye, trying to look inconspicuous on their massive stallion. The street was filled with gourmet restaurants and wine bars. Locals sauntered about, engaging in conversation and gesturing at Tom and Sarah.

"We kind of stick out," Tom whispered, his legs stiff.

"Perhaps we could find a place to tie up the horse," Sarah suggested, exhausted by their traumatic journey.

"And stand on solid ground again," Tom pleaded, rubbing his aching body. "My butt hurts."

"Mine too." Sarah laughed, sharing in his pain.

Continuing along, they were abruptly accosted by a local police officer, staring in bewilderment.

"What do you think you're doing?" he squawked as he strutted over. "Get your horse off the street. What kind of town do you think this is?"

"Yes, sir. Sorry, sir," Sarah quickly responded, stumbling over her words. "We'll take care of it right away."

"Where have you two been?" the officer questioned, taking in their muddy clothing and disheveled appearance.

"Oh, just galloping around the countryside," Sarah replied, searching for an excuse.

"And where are your parents?"

"Meeting us in town," Tom intervened swiftly, pointing in a general direction of the town square.

"Fine," the officer grunted, agitated. "Now remove that animal or I'll write you a citation."

"Yes, sir, whatever you say, sir," Sarah replied as she maneuvered the animal toward a grassy knoll.

She stopped under a sprawling oak tree and eased herself off the horse, then tied the reins to a branch. Feeling a sense of accomplishment, Sarah took a deep breath and pulled back her matted hair.

"Are you coming?" she asked, her hands on her waist.

"What's the best way down?" Tom wondered, looking back and forth.

"Lean on your stomach and kick your left leg to my side, then slide off."

Sarah walked closer, ready to assist. Tom followed her

directions, edging downward as Sarah guided his legs. He landed with a thud.

"Yikes," Tom gulped, trying to stand. "My body feels dreadful."

"It was a bit rough, wasn't it?"

"But worth it," he claimed, suddenly gaining his senses. "That was quick thinking and an incredible ride. You were amazing."

Sarah smiled, appreciating the compliment. With everything she had lost over the years, she had still retained her equestrian skills.

"What do we do now?" Sarah inquired, surveying the town.

Tom thought for a moment, suddenly remembering the cell phone Gowerstone had given him. "I've got this," he remarked smoothly, removing the phone. "It has the only number we need."

Tom opened the case, turned on the phone, scrolled to the contacts, and pushed Gowerstone's number.

"Detective?" Tom asked tentatively.

"Tom, where are you?" Gowerstone asked, delighted to hear his voice.

Tom turned to Sarah. "Where are we?"

"No idea," she answered with a puckered brow.

"Ask somebody," Tom asserted, motioning to the crowded sidewalks.

Sarah approached a stranger walking by. "*Excusez-moi, monsieur. Quelle ville est ce?*"

The man glared at her with indifference. "*Couquèques*," he replied tersely and continued on his way.

"Did you get that, Detective?" Tom asked, holding out the phone.

"We got it. Couquèques," Gowerstone confirmed. "We'll be there directly. Find a safe place to hide and stay out of sight. Also, keep your phone on, so we can triangulate your exact position."

"Yes, sir," Tom acknowledged, his hope strengthened.

They briskly walked over to a quiet area hidden by bushes, sat down, and waited. Tom told Sarah what had happened with the exchange, running through the town, the high-speed chase in the stolen truck, and trying to find her in the chateau. She was astonished by what had transpired.

Sarah then explained how she was whisked away by the evil Strauss, who seldom spoke. She was blindfolded, taken to the Rothberg basement, and thrown into a cell without food or water. She was questioned by a French interrogator, asking about Tom and the Resistance, but she played the fool and offered little insight. Her years at Weatherly Orphanage had trained her in wordplay and how to answer a question with a question or reply in vague analogies. They finally gave up and left her alone. Terrified the whole time, she had never prayed harder.

Twenty minutes later, a garrison of Resistance men arrived. Gowerstone was the first one out of the vehicle, trailed by Fontaine and Alistair.

"I can't believe what you accomplished," Fontaine exclaimed, marveling at their extraordinary escape. "That was some superb riding, young lady."

"I'm just glad it all came back to me," Sarah said modestly, overcome by the attention.

Gowerstone walked over, searching them for any injuries. "Are you both okay? That was a terrible ordeal."

"A little sore, but we'll live," Tom replied, grateful to be safe. "I know Sarah is starving. We'll need to get her some food."

"We have plenty in the vehicles." Fontaine smiled. "I'll make sure she's well attended to."

Alistair approached, shadowed by Barclay and Mackenzie. Their eyes glowed with reverence: Tom and Sarah had outsmarted the Black Cult of Horus. It was a remarkable feat that would become legendary in the Resistance. It is often small heroic actions that can inspire the hearts of many.

"Sir Thomas, I'm sorry we didn't get to you sooner," Alistair apologized.

Tom waved it off. "Don't worry. We're together again, and that's what's important."

"Sir, we should get to our next destination," Mackenzie stressed, aware of the scene they were creating. "We don't want to telegraph our position any longer."

Alistair agreed, and everyone entered the assault vehicles and headed toward their rendezvous point, where they switched to SUVs, then continued to Lyon, three hundred and fifty miles away.

Exhausted, Tom and Sarah eventually fell asleep, nestled in the back seats and covered with a blanket.

Sitting next to Gowerstone, Fontaine reflected on Gustave's betrayal. It hurt deeply.

"Gustave must have been the reason we were consistently compromised, from Notre-Dame to Chambord and finally Bordeaux," she realized, disgusted. "That little snake. The whole time we were together, he was informing the Committee of our location. I'm so sorry."

"Don't be," Gowerstone consoled her, sympathetic. "Often those closest are the most deceptive. I know firsthand."

"The prime minister?"

"Yes," he admitted. "While trust is important, you must always remain vigilant."

"At least Gustave will never bother us again."

"He made his choice, and his decision came at a high price."

Gowerstone shifted around in his seat, deep in thought. He knew the gathering storm was building and about to unleash mayhem.

* * * * *

Six hours later, the caravan arrived on the outskirts of Lyon and gradually made its way to a safe house in the city.

Situated on Rue de Vendôme, the Resistance base was three blocks east of the Rhône River and two blocks north of Parc de la Tête d'Or. It was a prime location between Paris and Marseille, yet close to the Swiss border.

Lyon was known for its historic landmarks, including Basilica of Notre-Dame de Fourvière and Place des Terreaux. A vibrant metropolis, the city had a global reputation for its fine cuisine and Michelin-star restaurants. Lyon was also the international headquarters for Interpol, which allowed the Resistance to monitor their activity more easily.

They parked the vehicles in a secluded alley and entered a four-story, medieval structure attached to other buildings. The unassuming façade had peeling paint and cracked plaster, masking the sophisticated, modern operations inside.

Tom and Sarah surveyed the interior: a high-tech complex with personnel dressed in business attire and working at computer stations. Overhead were lights, motion detectors, and digital cameras. Once they entered, Gowerstone was promptly attended to. His wound was examined and the bandages changed, and he was given a proper sling for his arm. After the medical staff finished with him, Gowerstone washed up and rejoined the others.

"It's quite impressive," Fontaine commented, amazed by the facility. "How extensive is your network?"

"We have compounds and safe houses throughout Europe, some as large as this and others smaller, hidden in office buildings, retail shops, and basements. Our members are everywhere, working at normal jobs but ready at a moment's notice. Each country has several primary headquarters and numerous bases, all well-equipped and connected to the others. However, any of them can be shut down instantaneously. This keeps us safe and mobile. There's also a hierarchy of leadership based on training and experience."

Henry and Oliver rushed over.

"I knew you guys would make it," Oliver trumpeted, leaning over to embrace Tom and Sarah. "They let us monitor some of the progress when we arrived. It was like listening to a suspense thriller."

"We're so glad you're safe," Henry interjected, beaming with excitement. "That was a daring mission. Who would have thought that showing up at my house would have set all this in motion?"

"You've been like a family to us," Sarah said, overjoyed to see them again. "We're so grateful."

"Wait until you hear about Sarah's riding," Tom added with a chuckle. "It was awesome."

"I can't wait," Oliver expressed, eager to hear about their adventures.

One of the men approached Alistair, pulling him aside and providing an update. Alistair listened intently.

"What is it?" Gowerstone asked.

"Our surveillance wires have been buzzing all night. It looks like our incident in Bordeaux has infuriated the enemy," Alistair announced, his manner composed. "The media are saying it was a terrorist attack, and the authorities are using it to implement further draconian protocols and to threaten martial law."

"What's that?" Tom inquired.

"It's an excuse for the government to turn France into a militarized country, oppressing the citizens and stealing their liberty," Alistair articulated, affronted.

"We should make haste," Henry recommended in a grave tone. "We just attacked one of the most influential families in the world, striking at the heart of their network. The Committee will come at us with everything."

"He's right, our time is limited," Alistair said as he motioned a few of his men to prepare for their exodus.

"What else?" Gowerstone questioned.

"The Britfields have been moved to a safe house in northeast Italy. Depending on the situation, we're not sure how long they'll be there."

"Which means the window of opportunity to get Tom to them is shrinking."

Hearing the news, Tom was disappointed but still had faith he'd see them soon. Sarah gently rubbed his back, providing an encouraging comfort.

"We need to leave," Alistair continued, taking the initiative. "Borders will be closed, and a nationwide search will begin."

"They have that much influence?" Fontaine questioned, still trying to comprehend the Committee's reach.

"They don't just control corrupt politicians and officials," Alistair replied.

"You mean the military?"

"Certain factions, mostly at the top," Alistair explained. "There's a dark side to the military few know about. While there are many good men and women serving, there are also bad ones."

Hearing about borders being closed and rogue military factions sent shivers through everyone. The web of darkness was massive and quickly closing in.

"I think it's a good time to split up and carry out our separate missions," Alistair stated. "We're too vulnerable right now, and every hour counts."

"He's right," Henry agreed. "We each have our own objectives, which are vital to our overall success."

Henry approached Gowerstone.

"You need to get this information to your resource

in England and make sure it goes public," Henry said, holding up the Britfield Codex, files, and flash drive. "This could go viral overnight. And right now the truth is the enemy's greatest threat."

"What about Tom and Sarah?" Gowerstone questioned, feeling responsible for them.

Fontaine stepped forward. "You put me in charge months ago. Let me continue. I'll protect them," she promised. "Now that I'm a fugitive, I won't be returning to Interpol. We can communicate using encrypted satellite phones, and Alistair can provide whatever is needed."

She looked to Alistair, who nodded in agreement.

"They are now under our protective care, Detective," Alistair interjected respectfully. "They're our responsibility to safeguard."

It was difficult for Gowerstone. Tom and Sarah had become an important part of his life.

"Sir, it's okay. Focus on getting the truth out," Tom urged.

"We'll be safe with Inspector Fontaine," Sarah added. "I'd trust her with my life."

While considering his answer, Gowerstone glanced at Oliver and Henry. "What about you two? Where do you go from here?"

"It's time to confront my father," Oliver replied, knowing the task ahead was challenging. "He's my dad, so I need to give him a chance to come clean."

"That might not be safe for you," Gowerstone cautioned.

"I know, but I have to try."

"And if he doesn't confess?"

"We have enough information to expose him and his colleagues," Henry alleged, his commitment unyielding. "I should have done it years ago. Tom and Sarah's visit has inspired me to take a stand."

Gowerstone stared at Oliver. "It's a brave thing you're doing, but you must be careful. The men who control your father are ruthless."

Oliver swallowed hard. "Yes, Detective. I will."

The mood in the room was suddenly quiet; everyone's eyes were on Gowerstone. He knelt by Tom, remembering all that they had gone through. Tom had brought purpose back into his life, sharpening his wit and strengthening his resolve.

"You know, Tom, we're quite similar," Gowerstone began.

"How's that?" Tom wondered, intrigued.

"I too was an orphan," Gowerstone revealed, smiling.

"Really?"

"I was adopted by a prominent family when I was young, but they raised me as their own," Gowerstone explained. "I was fortunate. They were kind and loving. Their position in society provided many opportunities."

Fontaine stared at Gowerstone, always surprised by his past. She didn't know the man completely, but she wanted to.

Tom rested his hand on Gowerstone's shoulder. "That makes us part of the same club, Detective."

"Which is?"

"The Orphans' Club."

"That it does." Gowerstone laughed, touched by the sentiment. "And I wouldn't have it any other way."

"I'll never forget what you've done for me," Tom said tenderly. "Next to Sarah, you're the best friend I've ever had."

For a moment, Gowerstone's rigid exterior softened; his soul was profoundly moved.

"It's mutual, Tom," Gowerstone nodded, shaking his hand. "Your character and integrity are an inspiration to all of us. Remain brave and watch over Sarah."

"Thank you, sir. I will," Tom said and hugged Gowerstone.

Gowerstone turned to Sarah, his eyes radiant. "Tom wouldn't have made it this far without you. You're his reason he continues. You give him strength."

Teary-eyed, Sarah felt proud of being a part of something bigger than herself. She gave him a firm hug, tears slowly running down her face.

"We'll never forget you," Sarah imparted, her words heartfelt. "We can never repay all that you've done for us."

"The debt is mine."

As Gowerstone stood, Henry handed him the Codex, files, and flash drive.

"This should be everything you need," Henry asserted. "By now I'm sure all the airports and ferries will be watched closely."

"Without a doubt," Alistair confirmed. "But don't worry, Detective. We'll get you on a boat to Dover. My best men will accompany you to Brittany on the western coast, then you'll need to drive all night. Once you're back in England, we'll connect you with other members."

"I'll get this information to my contact," Gowerstone agreed, then gazed at Tom and Sarah. "You're both remarkable children. It's a privilege to know you."

"Amen to that," Alistair exclaimed in his deep Scottish brogue.

"Keep that phone with you, Tom," Gowerstone insisted. "Call me if you need anything."

"Will we ever see you again?" Tom asked, saddened by his departure.

"Yes, God willing."

"I didn't know you're a believer, Detective," Alistair remarked, surprised by the reference.

Gowerstone chuckled, rubbing his chin. "I am now. Only God could have protected us through all that we've experienced."

He walked over to Fontaine. "Yes, Detective. Do you have something you wish to tell me?" she asked playfully.

Gowerstone shook his head. He knew affectionate glances and unspoken words were not enough anymore. It was time that he expressed his feelings to the woman whom he hoped embodied his future. Gowerstone leaned over and whispered softly into her ear.

Fontaine's face lit up as she whispered back, "Me too."

She had known how he felt all these years but needed him to say it, needed to hear those three precious words. He was a man of honor, so if he said it, he meant it.

"Wherever I go, you'll always be with me," Gowerstone added.

"I know that now," Fontaine whispered.

Gowerstone gave her a soft kiss. He straightened up, pulled his trench coat tight, and nodded to Alistair.

"It's been a pleasure working with you. Look out for these three. They're all I have in the world."

"I will, Detective," Alistair vowed, solidly shaking his hand.

Gowerstone took one final look around the room. "Let fear never dictate, nor your courage ever waver. Godspeed, my friends."

A team of four men escorted Gowerstone down a hallway and out a back door. A powerful emotion hung in the room; everyone had been touched by the steadfast devotion of Detective Gowerstone. His brilliance, his exemplary conduct, and his unwavering sacrifice had set a standard for all to follow.

Alistair stepped forward. "Henry, are you ready?"

"We are," Henry answered with a sigh. "But before we head to England, there's someone I need to meet in Paris, one of my most trusted contacts. He'll put everything into motion. We're not confronting the prime minister without the proper protocols in place."

"Understood. We can assist you in that area."

"That's what I'm counting on."

Alistair nodded to Mackenzie, who stood at attention.

"Take a team of four men and escort Henry and Oliver to Paris," Alistair instructed. "Stay with them as long as needed. Report all your movements and any problems."

Realizing they were leaving, Tom and Sarah hurried over to Oliver. He had become like a brother to them. They couldn't imagine what would have happened if he had not come into their life. What a true blessing he had been.

"Thanks, Oliver, for everything," Tom said appreciatively.

"We're going to miss you," Sarah added warmly. 'You're a true gentleman, brave and generous."

Oliver looked at them with a grin on his face. "You two sure know how to show a guy a good time," he joked. "I thought my summer was going to be boring."

They laughed as they bid him farewell.

"You've given my life new meaning," Oliver continued. "We're family, maybe not by blood or birth, but by an even stronger bond. I know I'll see you again."

He gave Tom a firm handshake, followed by an embrace.

"Like the three Musketeers, we're on an adventure of a lifetime," Oliver summarized poetically.

"Exactly," Tom agreed with excitement.

Oliver gave Sarah a firm hug. "Don't let this royal stuff go to his head," he whispered.

"You can count on that," she assured him.

"Thank you for coming into our lives," Henry articulated. "As Oliver said, we're family now."

Henry and Oliver bid everyone farewell and were escorted to a waiting vehicle.

"Sir Thomas," Alistair began, "why don't you and Sarah get washed up, eat a proper meal, and rest for a while. We'll leave Lyon at sunrise."

The thought of sleep was intoxicating. Tom and Sarah were utterly spent, physically and mentally. They agreed, looking forward to a hot bath, a warm meal, and soft sheets.

"Barclay, escort Sir Thomas and Sarah upstairs, and make sure they have fresh clothing."

All three entered an elevator and rode up to the third floor. Alistair remained busy organizing his team and preparing for their expedition to Italy.

Unbeknownst to them, criminal activities were in motion throughout France. The Committee had called an emergency meeting, demanding swift retribution and a nationwide search for Tom and Sarah. Every snitch, spy, and corrupt official was called upon. Not only were all their resources maximized, but satellites had been re-tasked to scan Southern France. Footage was gathered, information was examined, and resources were checked.

A sinister cloud was moving across the continent and hovering over Lyon.

18
DIVINE INTERVENTION

When Anna arrived at the Presd'eaux seaside cottage, her heart warmed at the sight of Hainsworth. She was deeply touched that he had asked for her assistance. Suddenly the years apart didn't matter—the arguments and disagreements vanished from memory. Anna noticed a transformation in the man she had last seen all those years ago. Before he was stubborn and selfish; now he embodied a peaceful humility, wiser and compassionate.

They sat outside in the cool summer breeze for hours. Hainsworth told her everything that had happened, starting with the cold December day at Oxford when Tom appeared on his doorstep with Sarah. At that moment, his life had changed. Something about the two frightened children spoke to his heart, and he knew he needed to help, regardless of the circumstances. Hainsworth's academic pursuits suddenly became trivial when these orphans entered his world.

Needing information, Hainsworth called the only other person he trusted, the Archbishop of Canterbury, who was ecstatic to hear from the professor. The archbishop immediately shared that Tom and Sarah were alive and somewhere in France. On hearing the news, Hainsworth wept with joy. Although the archbishop didn't know where Tom and Sarah were, he promised to do everything in his power to let them know that the professor was safe and looking forward to seeing them.

Still recuperating, Hainsworth decided to stay in the seaside village for a while, but he knew one day, perhaps soon, he would be reunited with Tom and Sarah.

In all the years Anna had known the professor, she never dreamed of the man he had become—selfless, courageous, and even adventurous. Tom and Sarah had transformed his cold, rigid nature into that of a loving, thoughtful, gentle man. Anna asked if she could stay as a guest of the Presd'eaux family, using one of their spare bedrooms. She would faithfully remain by Hainsworth's side and help him recover. Anna knew that she would never leave his side again.

* * * * *

At the first light of dawn, Tom and Sarah were awakened for their journey to Northern Italy.

Now dressed in a new set of clothing, they ate breakfast in the third-story kitchen and were escorted to the second-floor conference room. Tom wore a pair of jeans, a charcoal pullover shirt, a black Barbour waxed jacket, and hiking boots. Sarah wore brown pants, a tan turtleneck, an olive Barbour waxed jacket, and hiking shoes. Each carried a tartan scarf and a wool cap.

Tom was bursting with excitement. After thirteen years of being an orphan, he was only hours away from meeting his father and mother, a thought that was almost incomprehensible. What would he say? How would they act? Would they even recognize him?

When Tom and Sarah arrived in the conference room, Fontaine greeted them with a welcoming smile. She sat next to Alistair at a large circular table, sipping tea and reviewing maps of France and Italy. On the table was an assortment of fruit and pastries, as well as a hot tea kettle and china cups. The curtains were shut, and the overhead lights were on.

Barclay stood by, leaning over the table and pointing to different locations.

"Good morning, Alistair. Good morning, Inspector Fontaine," Sarah greeted them in a high-spirited manner.

"Please, just call me Fontaine.

"I can do that," Sarah agreed happily.

"Were you able to sleep?" Fontaine asked.

"I was out in minutes," Sarah replied. "What about you?"

"I had a hot bath and rested for a few hours."

Alistair promptly stood, greeting Tom with a slight bow. "Sir Thomas, Sarah," he said respectfully.

"Alistair, the bowing really isn't necessary," Tom said, still unsure how to respond to it.

"It's my obligation and an honor," Alistair insisted.

"Well, if you must," Tom relented, grinning at Sarah.

She rolled her eyes and shook her head with disapproval. Royalty or not, he would always be her Tom—the thoughtful, mischievous boy she had met at Weatherly two and a half years earlier.

"Jealous?" Tom asked in a whisper.

"Hardly," Sarah answered abruptly.

Tom and Sarah sat at the table and helped themselves to the pastries.

"We're discussing our plans to get to Italy," Fontaine began. "I know this has been a strenuous journey, but hopefully we're close to your final destination."

"All the main roads have been blocked," Alistair interjected. "They've established multiple checkpoints throughout Southern France."

"Already?" Sarah exclaimed, frustrated by the enemy's relentless pursuit.

Sarah was tired and just wanted to be left alone. Although Tom carried himself well, she could see the strain on his face.

"The Committee has responded quickly. I thought we'd have at least a few more hours before they acted," Alistair conveyed.

"Did Detective Gowerstone get back to England?" Tom asked.

"He is currently somewhere in the English Channel. Henry and Oliver are on the outskirts of Paris."

"If all the main roads are blocked, couldn't we just take a helicopter?" Sarah wondered, suggesting what she thought was an obvious solution.

"I wish it were that easy," Alistair answered. "Right now the air space is heavily monitored. We wouldn't get ten feet off the ground without being detected. I've heard police helicopters buzzing over the city all morning."

"Do they know we're here?" Tom questioned, glancing toward the window.

"They might," Alistair replied candidly.

"Then what's the plan?"

"Using the back roads, we'll drive toward the Swiss border and hike over the Alps to Italy. It's the only way."

There was a heavy knock at the door as it opened. A young woman entered holding three sheets of paper.

"Sir, a citywide lockdown has been declared. A bulletin with photos of a woman and two children suspected of terrorism is being distributed."

She handed them to Alistair.

"Police are already searching door-to-door," she continued anxiously. "We need to move immediately."

"Understood," Alistair acknowledged, perturbed yet calm. "Initiate Protocol Trinity. In five minutes I want everyone on the move and not a trace of our existence left behind. We'll exit through stairwell A."

She nodded and exited the room. Alistair showed Tom, Sarah, and Fontaine the photos.

"They're moving faster than I imagined," Alistair admitted. "We'll leave now and finalize the details on our way."

"Citywide lockdown?" Tom asked.

"It means no one gets in or out of Lyon without passing through checkpoints manned by police or other agents," Alistair explained. "More than likely, the military is involved."

"But how would they know we were here, in this city?" Fontaine questioned, then eased her hand over her Glock. "Southern France is enormous, and we've only been here for five hours."

Alistair's mind raced as he reviewed the last forty-eight hours, remembering small details and irregularities he had missed before. Everything suddenly became crystal clear.

"We've been betrayed by one of our own," he replied, staring at Barclay, who backed away from the table.

"I-I'm sorry, sir, I had to do it," Barclay confessed, his face a portrait of cowardice.

Alistair stepped in front of Tom and Sarah, rapidly drawing his gun. "How could you!" Alistair exclaimed, stunned.

"I had no choice. T-they got to my family," Barclay mumbled. "They found them and took them to one of their hidden locations."

Deceived by one of his best men, Alistair was rattled. From Chambord to Bordeaux and finally Lyon, too many compromises had occurred. While Gustave's betrayal explained many things, inconsistencies and unanswered questions had remained in his mind.

"I knew things were amiss," Alistair continued, furious. "How long have you been working for them? I need to know how much damage you've done."

"Since Tom and Sarah arrived at Notre-Dame. But I never dreamed that Tom and Sarah would find us."

"When did they kidnap your family?"

"Over six months ago, when the ferry left Dover. They notified me that my wife and daughter had been taken," Barclay answered, reaching for his firearm.

Before he pulled out his weapon, Tom grabbed the tea kettle and threw it at Barclay. The boiling water burned Barclay's hands and face. He screamed in pain.

"Hand over your weapon," Fontaine demanded, her Glock targeting his chest.

"If I don't complete my mission, I'll never see my family again," Barclay protested, desperate.

"Don't be foolish. You'll never leave this room alive," Alistair warned him, his temper blazing.

Just then the power in the building snapped off, and the lights and computers went dead.

Panicked, Barclay ran for the door, but Fontaine shot him in the leg. He tumbled to the ground and slammed into a table.

"Not so fast," Fontaine threatened. "You have many questions to answer. We need to know more about the Committee and who else has been compromised."

Emergency lights flashed on, illuminating the room. Alistair took Barclay's gun and tied his wrists together with a lamp cord.

"You've betrayed all of us. Not just Sir Thomas and Sarah, but our entire organization," Alistair vented. "You should have come to me. We could have helped your family."

A moment later, the door opened to a team of six Resistance members, their weapons drawn.

"Is everything all right, sir?" one of the men asked.

"We've discovered a traitor among us," Alistair responded. "As we evacuate the facility, transfer him to our Monte Carlo safe house for questioning. Locate and secure his family. They shouldn't have to suffer for his mistake."

"Understood, sir."

"Wait," Fontaine exclaimed as she stared at Barclay. "What's the plan? How much do they know?"

"They know you're here, in this section of town," Barclay answered. "But they don't have the address."

"What about Detective Gowerstone, Henry, and Oliver?"

"I haven't communicated with the Committee since we arrived in Lyon," Barclay murmured. "I didn't have time."

"How can we trust you? How do we know you're not lying?" Fontaine persisted.

Barclay looked up at Alistair. "Sir, it's the truth, but you must evacuate this building."

Alistair motioned to his men. "Take him out of my sight."

"I'm sorry," Barclay blurted, ashamed of what he'd done.

Two of the men fastened metal cuffs on Barclay's hands and feet and dragged him out of the room. The other four men formed a circle around Tom and Sarah, waiting at attention.

"They can turn off the power to an entire city?" Fontaine asked, astonished.

"They could shut down the entire country if they wanted to and blame it on an EMP or a terrorist attack. Through the Committee's interlocking corporations, they effectively own the electrical grids."

Fontaine walked over to Tom and Sarah, who both stood speechless.

"Quick thinking, Tom," Fontaine commended him.

"He seemed so nice and caring," Tom admitted.

"It's often those you least expect," Fontaine reflected, thinking about Gustave's treachery.

Alistair stood for a moment, appalled that the Committee had breached his highest level of security. There was no way of knowing how much damage Barclay had caused or what he had revealed, but for now, escaping from Lyon was all that mattered.

"Are we ready?" Fontaine asked, anxious to get Tom and Sarah to safety.

"Yes, time is of the essence," Alistair replied, trying to remain calm.

As they prepared to leave, they heard thunderous knocking on the first-floor exterior door.

"Open up! We need to search the building," a man yelled.

Alistair went to the window and looked down. The alley was swarming with police and military going door-to-door and canvassing the entire block.

"All right, follow me," Alistair instructed. "We have three separate escape exits. They can't cover them all."

Fontaine, Tom, and Sarah followed closely behind him.

Alistair went to a wall shelf, punched in a code on a keypad, and opened a hidden door that accessed a stairwell. He then radioed to his team: "Have all the personnel left the building?"

"Everyone's out," a voice responded. "Anything important has either been removed or destroyed."

"Have a team meet us in section A, and we'll rendezvous at our prearranged location." Alistair reached over and pressed a button. A red light activated and a digital display started counting down. "In five minutes, whoever enters this building will have a surprise. Unfortunately, we'll lose most of our equipment."

They entered the stairwell and descended three floors, where they were met by a team of ten Resistance members, prepared and well-armed. They had extra weapons, flashlights, and first aid kits.

Everyone rushed through a lighted tunnel leading under the adjoining buildings, up a set of stairs, and onto a deserted alley, a block from their base. The lane was relatively deserted, except for a few locals walking about.

"Fan out," Alistair ordered his men, motioning in different directions. "If we can't reach our backup vehicles, we'll leave the city on foot."

* * * * *

A few minutes later, the safe house door was blown open and a squadron of police swarmed in. The interior was in disarray with chairs knocked over, hard drives missing, and cabinets empty. No one was left to question or arrest. The Resistance had practiced this drill countless times and had carried it out with precision.

"Search every square inch," the police captain ordered, accompanied by two military men. "Inform the commander that we've found their base of operations."

As they moved through the interior, one of the men noticed a digital clock counting down from one minute. His eyes sprang open as panic seized his body.

"Get out of the building!" he screamed hysterically.

Everyone scattered for the exit, stumbling over each other as they frantically left the structure. As the last man ran through the doorway, the entire building was engulfed in flames, devouring any remaining evidence.

"Search the entire city. They can't be far," the captain directed, standing in the street as smoke streamed from the building.

* * * * *

Alistair marched along a cobblestone walkway, Tom and Sarah directly behind him, Fontaine covering their backs. Members of Alistair's team were placed in strategic positions around them to watch windows, rooftops, and suspicious individuals.

The patchwork of tall buildings created a daunting maze, with narrow passageways leading to private courtyards.

"Our other safe house is on Rue Bossuet, eight blocks north of here," Alistair informed them. "It's much smaller, but we can regroup and utilize the vehicles stored there."

"Did Barclay know about the second location?" Fontaine questioned, apprehensive.

"No," Alistair replied firmly. "But it's fully equipped in case our main location is ever compromised."

"Right now eight blocks seem far," Fontaine observed. "I'm sure they know we're on foot, and they'll be swarming this area shortly."

"It's an unfortunate situation, but we will prevail," Alistair said gallantly.

Along with the police and military, cheering crowds flooded the sidewalks. Many of them were dressed in traditional French clothing, and some waved blue, white, and red flags. Some men wore velvet trousers, patterned shirts, and blue Basque berets. The whole scene looked like a production of *Les Misérables*.

"*Vive la France*," one of the men hollered, lifting a mug to his lips.

"*Vive la république,*" a woman yelled as she lit firecrackers.

"What's going on?" Tom wondered, watching the crowds in bewilderment.

"I almost forgot. It's July 14th, Bastille Day," Fontaine recalled. "It's the day the Parisians stormed the Bastille in 1789 as an act of defiance against the tyrannical monarchy. It's a national celebration, like the Fourth of July in America."

"These crowds could work to our advantage," Alistair theorized, noticing all the chaos. "The more people, the more confusion."

As they approached the end of the road, a group of police marched by, then looked back.

"They're over here!" one of them shouted, blowing his whistle.

Another policeman pulled his weapon and radioed in their location.

"Find us a way out of here," Alistair ordered his men as they searched for an alternative route.

Everyone hastily backtracked and hurried across a street, dodging cars and trucks. More officers flocked to the area, and a police helicopter hovered above.

Four Resistance men stayed behind, engaging in a fierce gun battle. Bullets whizzed back and forth, and pedestrians scattered in terror. Although they were outnumbered, the Resistance men held their position, giving Alistair and the others time to escape.

Searching his phone's GPS, Alistair tried to navigate the labyrinthine streets, a mishmash of roads that either led to dead ends or twisted around to where they began. It was a matrix of mousetraps.

"I don't think we can make it to the other safe house," Alistair realized. "We'll head east and out of the city."

"Can't you call for an extraction?" Fontaine asked.

"No, it's impossible to get anyone in or out of Lyon right now."

Cutting through back alleys, they made their way to the Rhône River, where masses of individuals were celebrating and shooting off fireworks. Police were everywhere, some positioned on rooftops, others searching the crowds.

Pushing through a mob of people, they crossed over Pont de Lattre-de-Tassigny to the eastern side, rushed down the street, and turned onto Rue Royale, where military jeeps had set up barricades. The officers were holding up photographs and questioning each person who walked by.

"We can't go that way," Fontaine stressed, frustrated.

Desperate to find a secure route, Alistair searched the area. He then glanced at Tom and Sarah, who were unusually quiet.

"We'll get out of this," Alistair promised, his voice reassuring.

Frightened but feeling courageous, Tom and Sarah nodded.

Alistair checked his GPS and continued. "Down this street. It leads to Montée Saint-Sébastien and through the business district."

As they entered the boulevard, two policemen recognized them and began to pursue them.

"Over here," Fontaine yelled, rushing into a café with Tom and Sarah.

Alistair went next, followed by his men. They scurried around the tightly packed tables, bumping into customers and hurrying toward the kitchen.

"Hey, you can't go back there," one of the waiters yelled.

Alistair glared at the man and flashed his weapon. The waiter backed down, retreating behind a counter.

In the kitchen, they pushed their way past stacks of boxes and baskets of vegetables, startling the cooks. A second later, they exited onto an empty alley.

Alistair looked at his phone, turning around to find their location. "To the left. That should lead to Rue Rosset and over to Rue Henon, across the Saône River."

As they ran down the boulevard, they were confronted by a small unit of military personnel. Gunfire instantly erupted. Bystanders leaped into doorways and dove behind cars.

The Resistance men placed themselves in front of Alistair, Tom, Sarah, and Fontaine, using their bodies as shields. Two of them were hit as they returned fire.

Fontaine grabbed Tom and Sarah, pulling them behind a wall.

"There's got to be another way," Fontaine exclaimed, her nerves raw.

Alistair knew the best defense was a powerful offense. "Gentlemen, use your smoke canisters, then rush them. Attack their weakest point and undermine their position," he ordered. "We need to take away their advantage and break their confidence."

The Resistance men tossed cylinders, creating a thick curtain of smoke. They concentrated their firepower on the weakest point and pressed forward, pushing the military back and causing them to scatter, while two others remained with the group.

"That should buy us a few minutes," Alistair encouraged them. "Follow me, through here."

They hastened down a road that paralleled an ancient monastery, its barred windows a deterrent to unwelcome intruders. When they turned the corner, they were confronted by a dead end. Alistair was distressed but not discouraged.

The police started closing in, encircling the area.

"This doesn't look good," Fontaine remarked, glancing at a helicopter hovering overhead.

"We'll find a way," Alistair declared, then tried the handle on the massive monastery door. It was locked and bolted shut.

"We'll have to shoot it open," Alistair warned, stepping back.

Fontaine nodded, shielding Tom and Sarah.

As Alistair removed his weapon, the door swung inward.

"Can I help you?" an elderly monk asked calmly.

Tom's and Sarah's eyes sprung open, thunderstruck.

"Brother Gabriel?" Tom gasped, unable to believe his sight.

Gabriel smiled, not looking surprised to see them. "I had a premonition I'd see you again."

"But what are you—"

"Can you help us?" Sarah asked directly.

"Of course," Gabriel replied, motioning everyone inside.

They swiftly entered the monastery with the two Resistance men. Gabriel shut the door and bolted it.

"I don't believe it," Tom blurted, trying to grasp the coincidence.

Gabriel grinned, his eyes glowing with brightness. "Believe, Tom."

"I apologize for interrupting, but how do you know this man?" Fontaine asked, bewildered.

"Brother Gabriel helped us escaped from Mont-Saint-Michel," Sarah replied, looking at him fondly. "Without him, we'd still be there."

"That's good," Fontaine maintained. "We'll need his assistance again."

"You don't seem surprised to see us?" Tom questioned.

"I had faith there was a reason I was sent here."

"I have been wondering. How do you know about Tom and the Britfields?" Sarah asked, puzzled. "You mentioned that name just before we left."

"We monks might be humble, but we're also well educated. We know world history; in fact, we recorded most of it. The real history, that is."

"Yeah, but how did you—"

"I also know the Archbishop of Canterbury. When you left Dover, he contacted me, along with other trusted friends throughout France. He asked us to pray for you and help if we could. You see, there are really two factions in the church—those who are committed to God and those who serve something else," Gabriel answered candidly. "So you're in a bind?"

"Quite," Alistair stated, stepping forward. "We need a way out of Lyon."

"Then follow me," Gabriel instructed.

Gabriel led them through a hallway and down a set of stone steps, pitted and worn by centuries of use. They were met at the bottom by a young monk.

"Brother Michael, these are the two children I spoke of, Tom and Sarah," Gabriel said. "They need our help."

"Yes, Brother Gabriel," Michael responded eagerly.

"In a few minutes our monastery will be overtaken by the authorities. Stay calm and do your best to delay them," Gabriel conveyed.

Michael nodded and headed back up the stairs, locking the door behind him.

"This way, quickly," Gabriel continued as everyone descended another set of stairs.

Tom and Sarah exchanged confounded looks, still stunned by their good fortune.

After reaching the bottom floor, Gabriel flipped a switch, lighting the room. They surveyed the spacious cellar. Lining the ancient hay-and-plaster walls were rows of enormous oak casks, fourteen feet in circumference. The atmosphere was dry and cool, a delightful, sweet smell in the air.

"It's huge," Tom expressed, looking around.

"This is where we store our wine," Gabriel told them, gesturing his hand across the extensive surroundings. "Over six centuries old, this vault holds thousands of liters."

"But won't they find us down here?" Fontaine questioned.

"We're not planning to stay."

Gabriel walked them to the eastern corner and stood in front of one of the barrels.

"There's one casket you'll find particularity interesting." Gabriel turned the wine spigot counterclockwise three times until it clicked. "Would your men help me for a moment?"

"Of course," Alistair obliged, motioning them over.

The two Resistance men grabbed the corner and pulled. With great effort it squeaked open, hinged on one side and completely empty.

"That's handy," Tom commented, impressed by their ingenuity.

"I thought you'd like that." Gabriel chuckled. "I don't believe it's been used for decades."

"It makes a unique hiding place, but what if they search the barrels or just put bullets through them?" Fontaine asked, still skeptical.

"Have some faith, Inspector," Gabriel said. "It's only an access."

"Access to what?"

"To our underground tunnel system."

"I've heard about these," Alistair interjected, excited to witness one firsthand. "My organization has used them in other parts of Europe. We seem to have a shared connection, Brother Gabriel."

"Most of the Abbey tunnels were dug around the 1550s, during the reign of Henri II. He violently suppressed the Protestant Reformation and murdered thousands of innocent people," Gabriel explained. "Over the centuries, the structures have been improved and reinforced."

"There was a short-lived marriage between the king's son and Mary, Queen of the Scots, until she returned to Scotland," Alistair recalled, proud of his heritage.

"That's correct."

"I believe it was Gabriel de Montgomery, captain of the King's Scottish Guard, who fatally wounded Henri II in a jousting tournament."

"Yes, it was reported as an accident."

"It wasn't," Alistair clarified, hinting at the truth.

"Fascinating," Gabriel acknowledged, inspired to learn more. "You said you needed to get out of Lyon. Here's the way."

"Where does it lead?" Fontaine asked.

"Toward Geneva, Switzerland, which is close to the French border."

Alistair turned to Gabriel. "You're putting your life in grave danger," he warned. "Why are you helping us?"

"We've been protecting and hiding the persecuted for centuries," Gabriel responded bravely. "The battle you're fighting has been going on for millennia. The people and places may have changed, but the principles are always the same."

"Which are?"

"It's a war of good versus evil," Gabriel expounded. "We don't just fight against flesh and blood but against principalities, against powers, against the rulers of the darkness of this world, against spiritual hosts of wickedness in the heavenly places."

"That sounds fairly accurate," Alistair agreed, reflecting on the Committee.

"Sooner or later everyone will need to decide what they believe in, what they're willing to stand for, and what they're willing to die for."

Gabriel's convicting words had an etching effect on their hearts.

"You knew who we were at Mont-Saint-Michel?" Sarah inquired, searching for answers.

"Yes, I knew."

"But why did you take so long to help us?"

"When you first came to the monastery, you were both gravely ill and it took months for you to recover," Gabriel reminded them. "I was trying to get word out, but as you know, I was sent to solitary confinement. You've experienced how stringent the Order is regarding their punishments. While there are a few Godly men at Mont-Saint-Michel, the others are not."

"I understand," Sarah smiled.

Boisterous shouting and banging could be heard from above.

The monastery was now surrounded by police and military personnel trying to get into the building. A three-block radius had been cordoned off and two helicopters circled above, watching the extensive grounds and interconnecting buildings.

* * * * *

"I'm coming, I'm coming. Be patient," Michael called. He took a deep breath, walked to the door, and opened it.

The policed shoved past him and began searching the monastery. A senior military commander approached, his expression serious, his eyes cold.

"What's going on here?" Michael asked sternly.

"We have reason to believe you're harboring terrorists and other fugitives."

"This sanctuary was pure until you barged in," Brother Michael protested. "The only terrorists present are the ones you brought with you."

The military commander stepped closer and scrutinized Brother Michael, searching for any deceit or nervous movement. "Will you cooperate with us?" the commander asked coldly.

"Do I have a reason not to?"

"Are you hiding anyone in here?"

"What would make you think that?"

The military commander became flustered by the monk's refusal to respond. "Answer the questions."

Just then Strauss entered, dressed in an oversized police uniform. He towered above the others, pushing them aside. His face was scarred, his left arm appeared paralyzed, and he limped on one leg.

Michael stepped back, feeling the presence of pure evil. Overcome by fear, he wasn't sure what to do.

"I'll handle this," Strauss stated, showing the commander his ring with its Egyptian symbol, an emblem of a secret society.

"Yes, of course. I'm at your service," the commander replied.

Being in a holy environment made Strauss agitated and uncomfortable. He stood still for a moment, trying to concentrate on his surroundings.

"They're here," Strauss declared with certainty. "Tear this place apart and bring them to me."

* * * * *

Brother Gabriel stepped into the wine casket and walked to the rear. Even under these dire circumstances, he embodied an undeniable peace.

"There's a switch located in the back," he remembered, fiddling around. "Everyone in and close the front. It should latch automatically."

Taking his cue, Tom and Sarah went first, followed by Fontaine, Alistair, and the two Resistance men.

Alistair grabbed the casket door and firmly closed it, locking it in place. The interior was dark except for two tiny slits in front that let in slivers of light. An aroma of sweet wine with a hint of vanilla and oak filled the space.

Fontaine peeked through one of the cracks, and Sarah looked through the other.

Alistair flipped on his flashlight to assist in the search for the concealed button.

"I know it's here somewhere," Gabriel said calmly.

A moment later, they heard the rumbling of footsteps storming down the stairs. Soon it sounded like the room had been filled with more than a dozen officials.

"I told you, this is just our wine vault," Brother Michael emphasized, attempting to retain his composure.

"We'll see," Strauss declared, not trusting a single word the defiant monk uttered.

On hearing the deep, heartless voice, Sarah shuddered. She looked closer through the hole and spotted Strauss. Her eyes shot open. Fontaine swiftly clapped her hand over Sarah's mouth, fearing she would scream.

"Can I let go?" Fontaine asked in a low murmur.

Sarah nodded yes, her expression exhibiting terror as Fontaine gently removed her hand.

"I thought that thing was dead," Sarah whispered in a demoralized tone.

Strauss slowly surveyed the room, peering at each casket. "You say these containers only hold wine?"

"This is our winery," Michael replied, uneasy.

Strauss removed his silver-plated Remington .45 and fired at the first three caskets. Red liquid spurted from the bullet holes, spilling on the ground and forming large puddles.

Fontaine and Sarah slowly backed away from the front of the casket.

"We need to hurry," Fontaine stressed in a whisper.

"I think I've found the latch," Gabriel muttered, reaching down to the corner.

"You see, just wine," Michael said, hoping to lure them back upstairs. "Now please, leave our vault, and allow us to clean up the mess you've created."

"Shut up," Strauss squawked, then shoved him aside. "I'm not leaving until I've checked every one."

He fired at three more caskets, shredding the oak panels and spraying wine everywhere. Strauss stood there, confounded. He knew Tom and Sarah were here; he could feel their presence.

Reloading his weapon, Strauss walked toward the east corner. He perused the remaining caskets, raised his weapon, and unloaded the entire magazine. One by one the caskets burst open and wine spilled out, all except one.

19
A REVELATION

Strauss rushed over to the empty casket, reloaded his weapon, and fired ten more shots directly into the middle. In a fiery rage, he smashed open the front—it was empty.

"What? Impossible," he shrieked, his body shaking with rage.

"Not every casket is filled with wine," Brother Michael said, relieved no one was inside. "May we clean up this disaster now? You've set us back an entire season."

Strauss was livid. In a confused daze, he stepped away and marched toward the stairs.

"They have to be here," he shouted. "Scour the entire abbey."

* * * * *

Now safely in a tunnel reinforced with brick and makeshift beams, Gabriel, Alistair, Tom, Sarah, Fontaine, and the Resistance men scurried along the damp ground. One Resistance man led the way with a flashlight, and the other covered the rear. The barrel-vaulted ceiling was scarcely five feet overhead, requiring everyone to slouch.

"Another minute, and I don't think we would have made it," Alistair confessed, slightly hobbling.

"That was close, wasn't it?" Gabriel commented, seemingly unfazed by the danger.

"Any idea how far it is?" Sarah asked, still tense after seeing Strauss again.

"About ten miles," Gabriel informed them. "It's a long walk."

"That's a lot of digging," Tom speculated, impressed by their resourcefulness.

"We enjoy our work," Gabriel reflected happily. "Aside from gardening, making wine, and copying manuscripts, we dig."

"Still?" Tom questioned, surprised.

"Not as often, but with the changing times and the rise of evil, I'm sure we'll be called on again."

"Alistair, you're wounded," Fontaine remarked, all of a sudden noticing his limp and the trail of blood behind him.

"It's nothing," Alistair said dismissingly. "One of the bullets caught me."

"Hold up, let me see," Fontaine insisted.

"I'll be fine, Inspector."

"Please, Alistair."

Everyone stopped for a moment and Fontaine knelt by his side to examine the wound. A bullet had penetrated his hip and lower abdomen. She noticed the pain on his face.

"This looks bad," Fontaine reported, worried. "Did the bullet go through?"

"I don't think so."

"Does your team have a medical kit?"

"Yes, Inspector," one of the Resistance men answered, handing her a container marked First Aid. "We're always prepared."

Fontaine opened the lid and removed what she needed.

"This is going to hurt," she warned him, holding a surgical vise-grip in one hand and a shiny probe in the other.

"Do whatever it takes," Alistair said bravely.

Fontaine sprayed the wound with disinfectant and probed for the bullet. Tom and Sarah quickly glanced away, feeling rather nauseated.

After a moment, Fontaine located the slug and gently removed it. "I'm going to stitch you up," she said, preparing him for more discomfort.

Alistair nodded, clasping his hands in pain, his forehead covered with beads of sweat. Fontaine delicately stitched the wound together. When she finished, she gave Alistair a shot of penicillin to prevent infection and bandaged the area.

"It's only temporary, but it should help," Fontaine said reassuringly.

"Thank you, Inspector," Alistair acknowledged.

"Can you move?"

"Of course," he answered. "We have a long walk ahead, so let's get to it."

* * * * *

In Paris, Henry and Oliver met with Marquis Devonport, who was one of Henry's most trusted friends. Devonport had been working with the Resistance for years. Henry briefed Marquis on all that had transpired and what they needed: secure passage to England, a safe house in England, and a team of trained men and women to help arrest the prime minister. Knowing the risks of confronting his brother and going public with what he knew, Henry wasn't taking any chances.

In the game of cloak and dagger, where shadow governments ruled the world, Henry required assistance. Thankfully, his list of trustworthy contacts and fellow patriots was impressive. Plenty of men and women were willing to risk everything for the right cause.

After receiving instructions, Henry and Oliver hurried to the French coast. Mackenzie and his men continued on the journey, offering protection.

By now, most of the Resistance groups throughout Europe had gone active, with every member on high alert. The news that the lost Britfield prince had been found and the story of Tom's heroic journey spread like wildfire, inspiring a whole new level of loyalty and dedication. The Resistance was also aware of what had transpired in Bordeaux. The Committee's unquenchable desire for power and world domination had reached a tipping point. What had continued for years as a covert game of hide-and-seek was out in the open. The Committee was now more brazen, no longer concealing its activities in the darkness or behind closed doors.

Using its media empires, the Committee had for years promoted its nefarious agendas through films, television, and false news reports. They twisted the truth, attacked human rights, undermined family values, and subjugated humanity in order to establish more oppressive laws and regulations. There was a war brewing, an all-out battle of good versus evil and a crusade for the truth.

Under the cover of fog in the early morning hours,

Henry and Oliver took a small fishing boat from the Normandy coast to Brighton, England. They were met by a British Resistance team, who were equipped and ready to assist. Oliver was nervous, not sure how to approach his father.

Henry had shielded Oliver for years, but it was time for his nephew to know the truth. During the boat ride, Henry shared more details. Although it was difficult to hear, Oliver had matured during this ordeal. He had gone from a carefree college student to an adopted member of the Resistance, proving his courage. Oliver had risked his life, been shot at, and had begun to understand how the real world worked. He had gained a lifetime of knowledge in less than a week. Henry was proud of him.

Knowing that his father spent the weekends at his mansion in Liss in East Hampshire, Oliver, Henry, Mackenzie, and their team approached the property. The security would be tight, but Oliver had a few tricks of his own. Having grown up here, he had an intimate knowledge of every square inch of the estate.

* * * * *

In the predawn hours, everyone emerged from the tunnel by an abandoned farmhouse, close to the French-Swiss border. There was a small village situated among the hilly countryside and a medieval castle, weathered by centuries of exposure. The moon was still visible, peeking out from behind a veil of clouds.

Exhausted, they collapsed on the grass.

"What's the safest route?" Fontaine asked Alistair, scouting the area.

He turned on his phone and checked the coordinates. "It's northeast, although we'll still need to hike out of the valley and over the hills."

"Can someone meet us?"

"Of course. I'll make the call and have a team pick us up in the next town," Alistair replied in a faint murmur, his face feverish. "We have a safe house close to Genève, Switzerland. Once we're there, we can rest and prepare for our journey to northern Italy."

"I don't think you're going to make it much farther," Fontaine confessed, her voice sympathetic. "You'll need that wound attended to."

"I'm not leaving Sir Thomas," Alistair vowed stubbornly.

"Alistair, please," Tom interjected, watching this brave man rapidly deteriorate. "You've done an amazing job protecting us, but Inspector Fontaine is right."

"Let me look after you, my friend," Brother Gabriel offered, his words soothing. "I'll make sure you get the proper attention. There's an abbey nearby that is safe."

"You're not coming with us?" Sarah asked, dismayed.

"My mission ends here," Gabriel responded stoically. "I've completed what I was called to do, and there are many others who need my help. I have faith that you'll safely arrive at your destination."

Alistair tried to stand but was too weak. Not wanting to leave Tom, he struggled. This was his duty and responsibility. However, he was injured and could endanger the mission.

"Alistair, please go with Brother Gabriel," Tom insisted, concerned for his friend. "Inspector Fontaine will look after us, and your men will make sure we're protected."

"As you wish, Sir Thomas," Alistair yielded, exhaling with a deep sigh. "Once I'm well, I'll rejoin you immediately."

"I know you will." Tom smiled.

"Make sure you find the Britfields," Alistair stressed. "Right now every hour counts. They won't be in Northern Italy for long, especially with everything that's happening."

Fontaine stood, brushing herself off and helping Tom and Sarah to their feet.

"Thank you, Alistair," Tom said as they firmly shook hands. "You're the reason I can find my parents. I will never forget our friendship."

"It's been an honor, Sir Thomas," Alistair stated fervently, his deep blue eyes filled with wonderment. "You've brought us a hope I could never put into words. Your presence and the information Detective Gowerstone has gathered will be the spark that ignites a revolution."

Sarah leaned down and gave Alistair a tender embrace, a strong connection between them.

"Your leadership has been extraordinary," she said with reverence. "I feel like we're kindred spirits."

"We are, lass." Alistair nodded. "It's comforting to know that Scottish blood is watching over Sir Thomas."

Removing a pencil and paper from his pocket, Alistair wrote down an address with coordinates. "This is the Britfields' last known location," Alistair revealed, handing the information to Fontaine. "Memorize it and then destroy it."

Fontaine reviewed the address and shredded the paper.

"I'll watch over Tom and Sarah and make sure they remain safe," she promised. "It's been a privilege knowing you, Alistair."

"You've handled yourself magnificently, Inspector," Alistair conveyed with admiration. "I have great confidence in you."

It was an odd moment. Two exceptional men from different parts of the world had played such a profound role in Tom's and Sarah's lives. One was a hardened Scot and the other a kind, elderly monk. Knitted together by an unbreakable bond, they had become part of Tom's and Sarah's extended family.

As they prepared to leave, Gabriel approached Tom.

"I have some good news to tell you," he began, bursting with enthusiasm. "I received word earlier this morning, but I wanted to wait until we were out of the tunnel."

Sarah's face brightened. "Please share."

"Professor Hainsworth is alive."

"What? Are you serious?" Tom blurted out, a heavy burden lifted from his heart.

"Yes, he's resting at a seaside village on the western coast," Gabriel divulged with a smile.

"Does he know we're okay?" Sarah inquired.

"The archbishop has shared everything with the professor."

"What happened to him?" Tom asked excitedly. "Where has he been?"

"All I know is that after he was rescued from the ocean, he has been terribly ill, but he's now recovering."

"What a blessing," Sarah said, walking over to Tom.

They both hugged, rejoicing that Hainsworth was safe. This monumental news was an answer to many unspoken prayers.

"I knew he was alive," Tom exclaimed, exhilarated.

"So did I," Sarah added. "I knew he was still with us, out there somewhere."

"Can we see him?" Tom asked eagerly.

"Now's not the best time," Gabriel advised. "Your parents are awaiting your arrival. Once Professor Hainsworth recovers, I'll notify send word, and I will also update the archbishop with the latest details."

"Okay," Tom acknowledged.

"Before you go, there's one more thing I need to tell you," Gabriel shared, an animated look in his eyes. "It's a revelation the Archbishop of Canterbury entrusted me with."

* * * * *

Henry, Oliver, Mackenzie, and a group of trained Resistance men and women stood outside the prime minister's enormous Tudor mansion.

The house was a masterpiece of sixteenth-century architecture: brick and stone masonry, half-timber framing on the upper floors, curvilinear gables with rectangular moldings, arches over the doors and alcoves, and patterned brick chimneys topped with ornamental features. The building was surrounded by immaculate gardens, enclosed courtyards, and classical fountains.

With the help of Oliver's knowledge of the grounds, they made their way over the wall and through the estate, avoiding security cameras and motion detectors. Oliver had snuck through the property many times in his youth.

Considering his position, the prime minister's protection detail seemed light, indicating the Committee was planning to remove him soon. As the Resistance men and women spread out, they used tranquilizer darts to neutralize the security. Guards were struck in the arm or chest and instantly fell.

Oliver escorted Henry and Mackenzie through the stables to a concealed door that led to the basement. This entry was often used by the PM for clandestine meetings with corrupt individuals. Oliver had used it before to sneak out when he was younger.

Dashing through the darkened basement, all three made their way up a stairwell and into the main hallway. As guards approached from both sides, Mackenzie rapidly fired, hitting the men with darts. They crumpled to the floor.

It was Mackenzie's first glimpse of the opulent interior: twelve-foot high ceilings, exposed beams, gilded moldings, antiques, and priceless oil paintings throughout.

"Which way do we go?" Mackenzie whispered.

"He's probably in the library," Oliver guessed, feeling awkward about approaching his father.

They eased their way over the oak flooring and stopped in front of an eight-foot-high paneled door that stood ajar. Oliver entered first, and the others followed.

The prime minister stood in front of a fieldstone

fireplace, sipping from a tumbler of scotch. Staring into the flames, he did not realize he was no longer alone. Oliver's father turned, shocked to see Oliver, his expression revealing everything: hurt, betrayal, and sadness. The prime minister glanced at Mackenzie and then Henry, their eyes locking. Instantly, the prime minister knew his time was over.

"I take it my guards have been disposed," he presumed, unnerved by the confrontation but determined not to show his fear.

"They're out but not dead," Mackenzie clarified, revealing the tranquilizer gun.

Oliver stared at his father, struggling to muster his confidence and strength. "Why did you do it?" Oliver asked unsteadily, not sure where to begin.

"It's complicated, son," he sighed, walking away from the fireplace and sitting heavily in a chair. "I'm sorry you had to find out this way."

"I need to know," Oliver persisted, heartbroken.

The prime minister poured more scotch from a decanter on the table next to him and took a long drink, collecting his thoughts.

"It started simply enough," he began. "When I was younger, I was approached by some prominent men who saw something in me. They offered access to the best schools and top positions if I went along with their agenda. Suddenly I was given amazing opportunities and was rapidly promoted, passing more qualified people. At first it seemed straightforward, but everything came at a price. I was asked to do things I didn't believe in. I had to lie and support policies I knew were bad, but I was already so far in. As time went by, the activities became more despicable."

The prime minister leaned forward, burying his head in his hands. He exhaled deeply, realizing for the first time the magnitude of what he had done.

"The compromises continued, and the sacrifices got harder," he went on, his voice grave. "When I realized who these people were, what they really wanted, it was too late. They had devastating information on me—photos of me taking bribes, false documents I had signed, and countless lies I had perpetrated. There was no way out. I had fallen down a rabbit hole I couldn't escape from."

"Did you ever kill anyone?" Oliver asked timidly, appalled by what he was hearing.

"Not directly, but the people I work for do it all the time," his father explained, ashamed. "Anyone who disagreed or caused trouble was eliminated."

"Why didn't you tell me?"

"I couldn't," the prime minister contended, defensive. "It was too dangerous for you to know."

"Then my whole life with you was just a lie."

"No, not us," he stated truthfully. "You're the best thing that ever happened to me. I'm so proud of the man you've become."

Horrified by everything else he had heard, Oliver was still relieved to know that his father loved him. In spite of what had happened, it was important for Oliver to know that his father hadn't completely abandoned him.

Henry stepped forward, ready to arrest his brother.

"I suppose I'm finished," the prime minister gathered, knowing the end was near.

"Completely," Henry confirmed.

Mackenzie raised his weapon.

"That won't be necessary," the prime minister assured him. "I'm ready to confess what I know. It's been eating me up for years."

"I shouldn't have waited so long to stop you," Henry admitted.

"These people you want to expose, they're killers," he warned. "I won't make it past the front gate. Neither will you."

"We have our own teams, our own surveillance, and our own army of loyal people," Mackenzie asserted, grabbing the prime minister's arm and escorting him toward the doorway. "We'll get you to the proper authorities, and you'll pay for the crimes you've committed."

"I'm sorry, son," the prime minister confessed, broken. "I'm so sorry."

Unable to control his emotions, Oliver hugged his father.

"So am I, Dad," Oliver whispered into his father's ear. "But I still love you."

* * * * *

Later that morning, Gowerstone reached the seaport town of Ipswich, in northeast England. He had driven for hours, determined to finish what he had started. He had called Kate Watson when he had reached the British shore, and she eagerly awaited his arrival.

They met at a secluded cottage on the outskirts of town, next to the windswept cliffs of the North Sea. A storm raged as Gowerstone approached the back door. Kate answered, her eyes beaming. She was ecstatic to receive his call, knowing the catastrophic effect his information would have on the enemy.

For years Kate had risked her life by publishing the truth. Now she had the story of the century—countless stories, in fact. This was the kind of moment she lived for, the reason she risked so much: access to information that could topple dishonest politicians, destroy corrupt corporations, and expose those behind the curtain who pulled so many strings. Living in a shadowy web of lies, the Committee feared exposure more than anything else. Making this information public could change the course of history.

Kate's cottage was sparse except for numerous hard drives, a labyrinth of wiring, and a wall covered with computer screens. Gowerstone stood dripping in Kate's living room, holding a large waterproof backpack. He unzipped it and removed the documents.

"Here's a copy of the Britfield Codex," he told her in a temperate voice. "I hid the original in a safe place."

"Excellent," Kate said enthusiastically. "I never dreamed all of this existed."

"Here's a flash drive with thirty years of data, along with files I've collected over the last six months. Like an octopus, it starts at the top and works its way down through hundreds of corporations and global organizations."

Kate flipped through the files, then inserted the flash drive into her computer. She stared in astonishment at the screen. Never had she seen such a wealth of detailed evidence: documents, photos, and recordings.

"This is way more than I expected," Kate admitted, her eyes bulging.

"You can get all this information out?"

"Absolutely," she guaranteed. "I have a network of bloggers across the world. They'll send this out through their own contacts, and it will grow from there."

"It needs to go global."

"Trust me, Detective, it will," Kate assured him, smiling.

Kate continued reading as she downloaded the files. "Once I post this, I'm leaving Britain," Kate confided, her tone solemn. "There's no way I'm staying here after this."

"That's a good idea," Gowerstone approved. "I would have insisted on it."

"What about you?"

"I have some unfinished business," Gowerstone replied, his thoughts on the prime minister. "Once that's completed, I have friends I need to catch up with."

After another hour of downloading and organizing the information, Kate turned to Gowerstone. "Are you sure about this?"

"I've never been more certain."

"Then you better get ready for things to change."

"All we're doing is stirring the hornet's nest," Gowerstone stated prophetically. "The real war is just beginning."

Kate pushed the send button. The files flew into the ether and off to every continent in the world.

*****

Everyone waited to hear what Brother Gabriel had to say. His tender eyes showed a mixture of excitement and hesitation, confidence, and uncertainty.

"I wasn't sure if you were ready, Tom. Or if you needed to know," Gabriel confessed. "But I believe the time is right."

"Tell us," Sarah exclaimed, leaning forward with anticipation.

Brother Gabriel paused as he gathered his words. "There's another Britfield heir, a younger one."

"What?" Alistair gasped, sitting upright.

"I-I have a brother?" Tom questioned, overwhelmed with joy.

"Or a sister. I don't know which," Gabriel replied candidly.

"But how?" Tom wondered, his mind racing with thoughts.

"Your family, the Britfields, kept it a secret from everyone, even their closest contacts," Gabriel explained. "After you were kidnapped, their other child was immediately hidden with a prominent family up north."

"Northern England?"

"No, Scotland."

Tom chuckled to himself as the revelation settled in. He eased his eyes over to Sarah and cocked his head to one side. She shook her head and began to laugh.

"Dream on, Tom," Sarah jested. "There's no way we're related, so don't even think about it."

"You never know, Sarah." Tom laughed, marveling at the idea.

"Only the Britfields will know who the other heir is," Gabriel continued. "For now, your mission is to find your parents."

Alistair was stunned. "There are two Britfield heirs," he mumbled with a sense of awe. "God be blessed."

"God be blessed indeed," Brother Gabriel added majestically.

* * * * *

After Alistair and Gabriel left, Tom, Sarah, Fontaine, and the remaining men crossed the Swiss border and made it to a Resistance safe house, a quaint cabin nestled in the Alps.

They sat by a warm fire, sipping tea, sharing a meal, and discussing everything that had happened. It had been an amazing journey from Mont-Saint-Michele to Paris, through the heart of France, and finally on their way to northeast Italy.

So many people had helped them. Countless unsung heroes had sacrificed their lives. These selfless acts were woven together into something that served a greater purpose: hope in an orphaned boy, a prince who was destined to become a king and an extraordinary leader.

Tom was not only on his way to see the Britfields, he was going to see his parents. He was one of them, a royal prince confirmed by blood. However, Tom's family was much bigger than a name. His family included everyone who became a part of his life along his journey. He was excited about what the future held, what it would be like to meet his parents. But after all was said and done, through all the risks and trials, challenges and sacrifices, he was most excited to have Sarah by his side. She was his best friend.

* * * * *

The next morning computer screens, blog posts, and online mailboxes were flooded with proof of the corruption that ran through government, big business, and high society. Videos and photos of secret trade agreements; files of black ops budgets; underground labs conducting unspeakable experiments; documents showing money laundering; photographs of presidents, prime ministers, and prominent people engaged in illegal activities.

There was a document that showed a pyramid chart of all the secret groups, each member and all their wicked endeavors. The truth was finally revealed. The public was outraged, patriots took a stand, and arrest warrants were issued. Dirty officials were indicted, fraudulent bankers were arrested, and corrupt corporations were bankrupted. Parts of the Britfield Codex were also released, showing irrefutable proof of the Britfields' rightful claim to the British throne. Europe erupted in controversy, but scholars provided research to support the claims, and lawyers began to investigate centuries of lies.

This was a brutal and devastating strike against the Committee and its web of nefarious organizations. The days of the shadow government, this secretive cabal that had been running the world, were numbered. The Revolution had begun.

*****

Hainsworth sat at a table, his beloved Anna nearby, as he read the news on his laptop. He smiled through the tears in his eyes. Hainsworth knew that Tom and Sarah were safe, and that the truth was finally coming out. Like the son and daughter he never had, they had changed his life, and he was eternally grateful.

LA FIN

As for Tom and Sarah, their adventure continues in
BRITFIELD & THE RETURN OF THE PRINCE, BOOK III.

One year later, the Committee has struck back with a vengeance, crippling the Resistance now scattered throughout Europe. When Devonbury Academy in Switzerland is attacked, Tom and Sarah's only hope is to make it to a safe house in northern Italy by relying on their own experience, covert training, and martial arts. Overpowered and outnumbered, Tom and Sarah are ruthlessly hunted throughout Italy by the Black Nobility and a merciless team of killers. Henry and Oliver discover a devastating truth, Detective Gowerstone is confronted by a dark secret from his past, and Inspector Fontaine is pushed to her limits. Will Tom and Sarah ever find the Britfields? Relationships will be challenged, new friendships forged, and an unparalleled finale of sacrifice, romance, revenge, and loss.

Born in Newport Beach, California, **Chad Robert Stewart** is an international award-winning, bestselling author, global strategist, and creativity educator with over 25 years of experience in writing fiction, non-fiction, and screenplays. Chad founded the prestigious Britfield Institute, dedicated to creativity and advanced learning; and Devonfield, a media empire committed to the highest quality in education, publishing, and film productions. He received a Bachelor of Arts in British literature and European history from Brown University; earned an MBA from Boston College; and is pursuing a Master of Science in Advanced Management and a PhD in Strategic Innovation at Claremont Graduate University. Now based in San Diego, he is a strong supporter of education and the Arts; an adjunct professor at Fermanian School of Business, PLNU; and past board president of the San Diego Ballet. Chad enjoys world travel, reading, riding, swimming, sailing, tennis, and the arts.

We'd love to hear what you thought of **BRITFIELD & THE RISE OF THE LION, BOOK II**. Please feel free to email us at Britfield@DevonfieldPublishing.com

1) What was your impression of ***Britfield & the Rise of the Lion***?

2) What was your favorite scene and why?

3) Who was your favorite character?

4) Any other comments about ***Britfield & the Rise of the Lion***?

Make sure to experience
The World of Britfield
Britfield.com